HIST

PEREGREN:

A LOOK BACK, THE

PEACEMAKER

The Right to Bear Arms
and Mete Justice
Book III

J. M. Berlingieri

PublishAmerica
Baltimore

Hardcover 978-1-4560-9093-7
Softcover 978-1-4560-9092-0
PUBLISHED BY PUBLISHAMERICA, LLLP
www.publishamerica.com
Baltimore

Printed in the United States of America

Brandyn returns to Rothaynen to secure shelter and food supplies for the exiled Leemites in Wendover. Since April was rescued by a neighbor Brandyn believes that it is hopeless to pursue April anymore.

King Graedon and Princess Elayne realize that they are prisoners in their own castle. Brandyn's sister Meaghan is being forced to marry the cruel Morden against her will. Vanessa and Lucio use this wedding to devise a scheme to lure Duke Barton and Duke Welledon into a fatal trap at Braemar Castle.

Nodunn, the Huynsten king of kings, sent his forces to collect taxes in Xemaya and punish Kirman rebels. Nodunn is now poised to take Beracka to eliminate trade competition. Following that conquest he will move on Leems.

The marriage of Mara to Haaron in St. Steffan's Church was supposed to strengthen Leemite and Karpretian relations. However a Saracen caught up in the festivities got inebriated at the reception and killed a young Christian knight. The delicate union is put to the test.

To help against Huynsten aggression, Leems needs an alliance with Beracka and Craigroyston. In Beracka Stoldar's affection for Mara is rekindled by Naveed Al Bhutan and the evil Petrofar. In Craigroyston Queen Enyja is led to believe that Haaron took the throne away from Mattic's heirs. Not only must Leems stand alone but they may be attacked by those who should be their allies.

Beware the peacemaker. Not all men are their brother's keeper.

JMB

Never the Same

On his return to Wendover, Brandyn did not receive the warmest of welcomes. He was a knight, and the Wendover community had quite enough of 'noble' knights and their rule of late. Brandyn noted the new sign hanging from the Wendover Tavern. ''Winslow Inn', it read. The sign inferred that the tavern was under new ownership. Brandyn rode by the tavern slowly and went to see Pyotr, the farrier instead. There he inquired of his mother and sister but all that Pyotr told them was that they were no longer there.

"Andrea and Meaghan left the tavern with Morden and his knights. They went to Braemar Castle," Pyotr told him.

"Has there been any word about my father?" Brandyn asked him.

"There has still been no word about Malcolm," he answered softly.

Pyotr had known Malcolm since he started his apprenticeship with Walter, who was the former Farrier of Wendover. Everyone assumed that Malcolm perished the night of the raid. It was assumed, but no one would affirm the fact or question what happened.

The people seemed to be indifferent toward each another. There was suspicion present among all the people of Wendover. In Brandyn's mind, it was certain that one of the king's own knights killed Malcolm to prevent him from speaking the truth about the 'raid'. He could imagine the night of the raid. His father learned of the treachery and approached a knight of the king's to report his findings. Then Malcolm was killed for what he discovered. His body was likely tossed into the sea.

The operating of the Wendover Tavern now fell to Winslow and Tamyra. They previously worked another farmer's land and had a family of their own. Brandyn calculated in his mind that there was no way that they could purchase anything with savings of their own. Through some arrangement though, Winslow and Tamyra were now the new proprietors of the tavern. When word got out that Brandyn had returned, the new owners of the tavern got worried. They immediately fetched their papers of legitimate ownership. They had a silent partner that took care of the finances. They assumed that there would be some explaining to do, so they got out the proof. They made themselves busy tending to their patrons while they waited for Brandyn to enter the inn.

After learning about the sale of his father's tavern Brandyn thanked Pyotr and left Vento in his care. Brandyn then went to the church to see Pastor Mattews. He passed by the tavern without as much as looking at the building. Winslow and Tamyra looked out the window and were surprised to see him pass by. Brandyn did not want to rush in with questions and accusations. He wanted to learn all that he could before taking any action. If Brandyn was to barge into the tavern, they would no doubt be prepared and his emotions would run over. They could draw him into an argument and ambush him. Witnesses would put the blame on him. With the sour feeling that the Wendover community had for knights they might beat him senseless. He could not rush in and exact vengeance, such an act would not set him apart from the other knights who ruled by their desires. Some knights took what they wanted when they wanted. There was a due process to follow that was proper. Besides, he remembered what Woodcroft once said. 'If you want a bird to sing, you do not put it in a cage'. For now, he would bide his time and learn all that he could.

After greeting and talking to some of the people that he knew, Brandyn still had not learned much. The family friends were fully aware that the tavern was sold, but they were not sure of the reason. There was speculation, but no one knew exactly why Andrea sold the tavern and left with Meaghan for Braemar Castle. They did not even say good-byes before leaving. Brandyn guessed at an idea. Perhaps his mother thought that Malcolm and he were dead and she could not keep the tavern. With Morden representing the law, it was certain that there was some foul play with the sale and ownership of the tavern.

Brandyn immediately assumed that Morden gained a fee with the sale of the tavern. Brandyn did not realize just how much Morden gained. In his mind at least, Brandyn took comfort in knowing that

10

Andrea and Meaghan were alive. He also had the added responsibility of the new Leemite settlers. When he entered Plenitude Church he was greeted by Paolo, one of the Bendire Brothers. Brandyn learned that Pastor Mattews had disappeared the night of the raid without a word as his father had. Now he had to focus on the task at hand. With the help of the Bendire Brothers he would have to accommodate the displaced Leemites. Although Paolo and Carluce were ready to cooperate, Brandyn realized that there was much work to be done at Wendover.

Greens and Grains for the Green Knight

The Leemite settlement in north Wendover was practically raising itself with the determination of the inspired Leemite newcomers. A dozen men actually stayed the night, while a handful made the trip back to Wendover, for supplies daily. It would soon be winter and these shelters would be needed. The challenge of providing adequate shelter would be met. The competitive spirit of Leemites and the volunteers from Wendover made it a noble task. The building task became a friendly competition to display their skills and craftsmanship. Their pride in craftsmanship made work on the new settlement move along smoothly. The proximity and availability of timber were a big help too. Officially it was assumed to be the King's Forest where they were cutting down trees. In all fairness however, it was under the direction of one of his knights. The area had formerly been wilderness as the howling of wolves could be heard in their vicinity at night.

There were no wasting supplies. Any scrap wood, was used to build fires to keep warm and to heat the houses that they built. It would not be an easy winter. Even the firewood that was readily available did not have time to dry properly. The race was on against nature. The traditional first snowfall had not yet come but the shortest day of the year had. It was then that Brandyn received good news, and not just news. Brandyn had been waiting for a reply from Welledon. He had requested grain to feed the Leemite outlanders. What was even better than the reply was that he received the actual grain and potatoes as well as collards and turnips. Welledon sent the aid from his own granaries directly with some of his men along with the reply. The grains were delivered to Plenitude Church and awaited direction as to their distribution by Brandyn. Martov also told Brandyn that the old duke requested that he come to see him at the earliest possible moment. To Brandyn, it was like being called home.

Welledon could not be more proud of Brandyn whom he gave the ring intended for his sons, the ring with the seal of Galles. Not only had Brandyn represented Rothaynen with wisdom, honor and courage across the sea at Leems, but he had proven himself worthy and responsible for the lives of the exiled Leemites. Martov was fully aware that Welledon was supportive of Brandyn and anxious to see him. When Martov arrived at Galles with the message, he had observed a firm countenance on Welledon. Martov then recounted the actions that Brandyn took while he was in Leems and Welledon smiled and could not help being proud. Welledon told Martov a few stories about Brandyn when he was a squire for Woodcroft. It was certain that Brandyn had a home here with Welledon.

Now that Martov arrived with the grain, he assured Brandyn that he and Cambryn could manage the completion of the building project and the distribution of the grains. With their reputation for fairness, Paolo and Carluce could assist with the distribution of the grain to the people. Some of the grain would have to be supplementing Wendover farmers for their losses during Morden's occupation with the army. Brandyn remembered the look that he got when he assured Mitchell that he would be compensated for feeding the Leemites. Brandyn immediately summoned some Leemites to take two sacks of grain back to Mitchell's farm that they had passed on their way to Wendover. Cambryn was asked to accompany them and turn the grain over to Mitchell with a note of thanks. It would certainly surprise them to be paid back so soon, thought Brandyn. With the grain that came, it took pressure off feeding the needy Wendover community and the aspiring Leemite one. Work on the new community could continue with confidence. Brandyn also authorized hunting for game in the king's forest. There were more mouths to feed, but there were more hunters too.

With the thick wooden beam roof structures up on the new houses, the work of the weavers was next. There was no time to quarry shale from Galles to construct the fine durable roofs. They would construct the traditional thick grass roof for the time being. The grasses in the wild grew thick and long. Despite the frost and dampness of the grass, which was cold on the weavers' hands, work on the roofing continued at a fast pace. When the roof was completed on the first few dwellings, the heat from the fire place made the dwelling cozy. The dampness of the grass and the homestead in general vanished within a half day. It was done, the provision of shelter, the second step in survival. The Leemite exiles had a home and community of their own. Thanks to Welledon who looked after the first step of survival. The grain that he sent would assure that these people would not go hungry at Christmas. After construction was done on the community hall, and a few farm houses, there were still furnishings to make. Tables and chairs and beds, they would require material and time to make, but now there was a place to stay that shielded the people from the elements of winter and those of nature. There would be plenty of time during the winter months to complete the furniture and get some hunting in. For Leems' exiles that were willing to work, it would be a busy winter. Since the community hall was complete, the naming of the new community was all that was left to do.

Brandyn thought that the Leemite people would appreciate naming the region New Leems. The new town however would be named Woodcroftston. It was a small accolade to remember a good knight who had dreams of justice and peace for all people. Brandyn knew that the gesture would please Welledon. Brandyn foresaw the building of a new church and using the common town hall for teaching young children to read and write just like Woodcroft had wanted to do. Woodcroft did not fear a learned man, he only feared the ignorant ones. Learning to read and write was a good idea, he thought. The help that Welledon sent provided a good start. With Welledon's influence with Graedon at the court in Braemar Castle, New Leems would get the opportunity that it was hoping for and deserved.

Brandyn also dreamed of the future of these new inhabitants. They could be called upon to build a castle stronghold at the Wendover Harbor with an enclosing wall. Brandyn himself realized that it was a very ambitious dream that would take at least 40 years to complete. Brandyn remembered how it was rumored that it took that long to build the wall alone around Petrinvincit on the west coast of Rothaynen. In his mind, it was a good plan and worth investing 40 years, well skilled labor and materials from the land. He reasoned that it had to start sometime and with the new hands it was now possible to start. The sooner they started the better. Brandyn had a plan; all he needed was an order of operations drafted by the masons to proceed logically and with common sense. There was no reason that the foundations could not be prepared and laid. Stone masons could start quarrying stone from the escarpment that spring after planting. There was nothing wrong with dreaming about great things. Great castles should be built high and majestic with prestige to stand the test of time. They should also be made to look beautiful so they could act as beacons of inspiration and hope for the generations that followed. All that was needed was the opportunity and will to start. Once you had put the foundations down, all you needed to do was keep building with pride. With the support of good government and enthusiastic labor, it would be easy.

Since the new community was rapidly approaching completion and the return of Martov, Brandyn was clear to report to Welledon. Brandyn told Cambryn and Martov about the naming of the region and town. Both knights were happy with the names that Brandyn chose for the community and they knew that the Leemite refugees would feel more at home. Brandyn was tempted with going to Braemar Castle to seek out his mother and sister before going to Galles. Not this time however, he would go directly to Galles via Mead. It was time to speak to Welledon whom he had not seen since he gave him the ring on tournament day. It was time to see what his silver hair had to say about matters. Brandyn felt bad about leaving Cambryn and Martov. He felt bad about leaving before he could celebrate and rejoice with the people who made the new community possible. Brandyn had a personal attachment to the work force and the structures that they built. He considered Cambryn and Martov to be colleagues. They had done battle together against overwhelming odds at Strachan. The equally dangerous, escape plan to spring Haaron out of prison was another bonding event. Martov told Brandyn that he should go to Galles. It was his duty to report to Welledon, the Duke of Galles. Martov had sensed that the old duke was like a father to Brandyn, and that he should go.

"Go. You need to thank this generous man. Thank him from all of us. Besides, there will be many more Christmases to spend with us," Cambryn reassured Brandyn.

These two comrades in arms were understanding and supportive of Brandyn. Brandyn did all that he could to assist the Leemite people during their plight. Now all he had to do was to get the permission to build New Leems and use the king's forest. Brandyn was reluctant. New Leems was under construction and the King's Forest already provided timber and food for the Leemite exiles.

"But the people here—are you sure?" Brandyn asked.

"Rest assured, we will see to the people's needs and after you return we can do some hunting deep in the forests around here," Martov replied.

And so it was time to go home for Christmas. Brandyn truly needed to visit with Welledon. Brandyn briefly stopped off at Plenitude Church to speak to the Bendire Brothers before he left for Galles. There Brandyn learned some good news from Carluce. The monk told him that the land that 'New Leems' was constructed on and the hunting was not the King's Forest. The land that they used to find a new home for the Leemites was granted to the church. Generations earlier the land east of Peregren and north of Thermanden Bay was chartered to Cardinal Wilkieson for the building of a religious monastery. Brandyn rejoiced as it was one less thing to worry about.

Going Home, For the First Time

Brandyn had been in Galles Castle before. He attended Woodcroft as his squire and dined at the same table with him and his father Welledon. He had never been at Welledon's castle of his own accord, but Welledon had requested his presence. Brandyn rode the west road to bring him closer to the lands of Galles. It was strange that he was leaving Wendover to spend family time away. He was still not happy with losing April and when he passed Mitchell's farm he rode by without stopping. As far as he was concerned, the account for feeding the Leemite exiles by Mitchell was settled. He knew that April was there, but he could not face her anymore. Brandyn had a heavy heart when he thought about April, but she was the reason that he returned from Leems.

Both he and Vento rode on through and stopped at Mead for a meal at the Brewers Inn. They had made good time in arriving at Mead. It was Brandyn's intention to ride onto Galles even though he would arrive late. After eating the meal and drinking some ale, the fatigue set in and he decided to stay. Perhaps it was the ale that relaxed him and made him want to sleep. The atmosphere in the warm, cozy inn lent itself to the lay mood he fell in to. Outside he was sure that it was cold and the wind could compound matters.

There was a young maiden who worked at the inn who was rather attractive. She was not the hostess who brought his food to him, but she was very pretty. Brandyn had looked at her repeatedly and she knew that he was looking at her. The girl came from a good family of local farmers in Mead. Brandyn thought about how beautiful her face was with skin that looked so soft. He wondered how she would look if she let down her brown hair that she had tied up behind her scarf. Brandyn thought that she was everything a girl should be; everything except that she was not April. Brandyn took his time with eating his dinner. It was no use to try and rush off to Galles as it would get dark soon and he did not want to arrive past midnight. With Vento boarded at the local stable, he thought that they could both use the rest. Brandyn decided to take a room for the night at the Brewers Inn and retired to it after his meal.

In the early morning, both Brandyn and Vento set out toward the lands of Galles. When they arrived at Galles, the Gallesian fields were poised to receive the first snowfall of the year. It was a pretty picture. The produce of the land had been gathered, the deciduous trees shed their leaves and the evergreens stood proudly in green contrast. There was an aroma of the evergreen trees that was crisp in the cold weather. The ground was covered with fallen leaves that the wind had collected in groups wherever there was a change in the contour of the land. The stubble in the field where wheat and grains were planted and harvested still laid testaments that the land provided for the farmer. The black dirt of the field revealed frozen foot prints embedded in it. They were made by the farmer who had gathered his potato crop. The grasses that were once green and growing so fast that they had to be cut back had lost their color and were frail and lifeless. There were a stillness and silence.

Soft snowflakes came down gently and broke the silence. Then it happened. It was the first snowfall of the year. It covered the field like a fleece blanket. It was hard not to feel happy. A smile came to Brandyn's face. The snow came just like it did the year before. It was not an angry snowfall governed by high winds and the cold that turned the soft snow into knives of ice. If you listened for it, you could hear it. The only other noise was the pounding of Vento's hooves. The steed's breath could be seen let alone heard in the chilly air. The smell of autumn would soon be masked. It would soon be Christmas and everyone in the kingdom had scurried about to make preparations to celebrate the holy day with a trip to the church and then a prompt return home to feast with family and friends. Despite any hardships that occurred through the year, it was the desire of everyone to celebrate Christmas with loved ones.

The Castle at The Foot Of The Mountain

When Brandyn got closer to Galles Castle, the first thing that he could see was the east gate tower. High above the castle tower a rod of iron was affixed at the highest point to reach higher into the sky. At the end of the iron rod the colors of Galles were affixed. The green dragon on a gold drape heralded proudly over the dominion of Galles. It felt like a true homecoming as the scenery and memories of past experiences at Galles were happy ones. How Brandyn yearned to call out for his father and mother, and the comforts it would bring to have someone answer that call. He had never called Welledon 'father'. He had although fantasized about Woodcroft being his older brother and he himself being an heir of Welledon. Woodcroft would have been his brother, actually his brother-in-law. If only he had lived to marry Meaghan, that fantasy would have come true for more than one person. He knew how much Meaghan loved Woodcroft and how taken he was with her. Then he realized that he was wearing the ring that Welledon gave him. In fact that part of the fantasy did come true. Brandyn was a knight of the realm. He basked in the thought for the moment. Brandyn's thoughts were interrupted when one of the guards at the castle gate began to shout something.

"He's here!" Ippolito yelled out.

Chardi, the other guard went to alert Welledon forthwith of the arrival. Welledon had requested that Brandyn come at the earliest convenience. With the loss of Welledon's brave sons, it could not be too soon.

There had been no word of Brandyn after the raid on Wendover. Christmas for Welledon began when the message arrived with word from Brandyn that grain and supplies were needed for the Leemites. Only then Welledon learned that Brandyn was alive. It was Christmas time and Christmas is for family. As mighty a man as Welledon was, he too depended on the key religious times when it meant that family would come together to break bread and share company. Even a firm

19

ruler in a position of great responsibility needed the love of a family. When Brandyn arrived at the castle gate, the veteran guards welcomed him home.

"Welcome home!" proclaimed Ippolito.

Ippolito was the Keeper of St. James' Gate, the main gate to the castle. Ippolito, who was long in the service of Welledon, had minded the main gate to the Glen Eryn Castle for Welledon's father Aldryn. The gate was named after St. James who was not much for words. The good saint practiced economy when he spoke but when he spoke and what he spoke were pearls of wisdom. Ippolito knew what the return of this particular young man meant to his liege.

For months Welledon had anticipated the worst when no word came of Brandyn after the raid on Wendover. He feared the worst since he lost two sons previously. The aging duke's spirit was low. After the raid he had dispatched riders to Wendover who made inquiries of Brandyn. Morden sent word back to him that unfortunately Brandyn probably perished in the raid. Welledon did not believe it. When Martov arrived at Galles with the dispatch from Brandyn, Welledon became excited as a child who finally got the wish that he yearned for. Welledon spoke to everyone about Brandyn's deeds. It was obvious to his councilors and castle staff that his spirits were uplifted when he had heard the news of Brandyn's deeds in Leems and his efforts in Wendover. The news traveled fast. He was gaining the reputation of a hero. Brandyn had studied under Woodcroft and was an apt pupil.

The people in the marketplace turned from their marketing and cares of the day to welcome this 'son of Galles'. Word had even gotten out to them about Brandyn's deeds across the sea at Leems and his efforts in Wendover.

"Well-done Sir Brandyn!" proclaimed a merchant.

"Welcome home!" cried out a woman.

"Well-done Sir Brandyn of Galles!" yelled another.

They all cheered at the arrival of the young knight that bore the ring with the seal of Galles. Everyone recognized the fashioned armor to be an heirloom of Welledon's family. He was one of their own and had done them proud. He had earned their respect. Brandyn received the friendly homecoming welcome with humility as well as pride. He remembered that it was the same welcome that Woodcroft and he received when they returned from crusades. Up from the windows that overlooked the court and marketplace stood Welledon. The duke looked out with happy eyes at the scene that played out before him. He took comfort that his good people would have a worthy heir some day. All his councilors and captains knew the duke's wishes about the matter and they respected those wishes. The young boy that came to them earlier had not only grown older, but wiser and had represented them abroad with honor. After providing shelter and putting food on the table, honor preceded even these.

Welledon watched as long as he could from the castle window until he could no longer see Brandyn who was entering the castle doors. Welledon turned and looked at his decorated hall to make sure that everything was fine. The great hall looked like it did when Welledon himself was a younger man. He could recall that his children played with their toy figurines on the heavy rug before the fireplace. He looked at the fire in the fireplace and reminded the servants to assure it was kept blazing so its heat could be enjoyed. Welledon was aware that the first damp cold of winter was worse than the latter cold of deep winter because people were not used to it. He was considerate of everyone.

"Get more wood, keep the fires going," encouraged Welledon.

Somehow it did not matter what temperature it was, Welledon had an inner glow that beamed out warmth. He was a happy man. Brandyn entered the hall straight away as he could not wait to see Welledon. Imagine the great Welledon responding so true heartedly to his request for grains to be sent to the Leemite exiles in Wendover. Welledon could have passed the request onto Graedon, which would have taken precious time being debated in court. Brandyn had made plans to solve a problem and he had been taken seriously. He was made to feel that his judgments meant something, and they certainly were worthy at that.

"My son," proclaimed Welledon.

Welledon uttered those words softly to himself. He must have been unsure as to how Brandyn would feel about him referring to him as his son. As Brandyn approached, Welledon could not help himself.

"My son!" Welledon affirmed.

The old man did not wait for Brandyn to cr0ss the floor entirely. Instead he walked down the stairs before his throne to greet Brandyn with a heartfelt embrace. Welledon was so happy that tears came to his eyes. Brandyn was so happy to be in Welledon's arms. Here was the only place he could let his guard down and feel safe. Welledon was the only semblance of a father that was left for him now with the fate of his own father and family looking grim and unsure.

"My father," Brandyn said.

Brandyn said it with all his heart. Their embrace was solid and long, heartfelt and reassuring.

Finest Pork Roast

It was not Christmas yet, but you would never know it with the feast that the cooks prepared in the kitchen. There was a fine pork roast, covered with apple sauce that was salted just right. In Galles, they knew every way that there was to cook and prepare potatoes. On this occasion the potatoes were boiled, allowed to cool, and then cut into strips. Sliced onions were added. Then the potatoes were salted and peppered, and then baked. That part acted like bread to accompany flesh at a fine meal. There was apple pie as well to bring the meal to a conclusion. Apple cider or Galles' own dark ale were the perfect drinks to wash down the feast.

There was a stark difference between the atmospheres in Welledon's court at Galles compared to Graedon's at Braemar. Perhaps the reason was that all of Rothaynen was represented at Braemar compared to only the nobles of Galles. With a greater number of regions to represent, the need for each region to assert itself lent itself to selfishness and bullying. Welledon managed to rule Galles with an even hand, but he was fortunate to have the noblemen that he had. A good leader keeps well informed about what he is responsible for. In Braemar you could hardly enjoy your meal when you sat for supper. There was pushing and pulling over the table scraps, and not necessarily for what was on the table. It seemed that you always had to be on guard at Braemar. At Welledon's table you were made to feel at home.

At Glen Eryn Castle that night, Brandyn was the center of attention with questions that the nobles and army staff of Welledon had for him. Brandyn had been familiar to Welledon's knights. They got to know him when he served Woodcroft. What was amazing was Brandyn's baptism by fire in warfare with his experiences at Leems. When Brandyn recounted his story, he was not boastful but humble and truthful. Despite the trials and the right to boast, he remained ever humble. Brandyn realized that he was fortunate to be alive and he told them so. Welledon's seasoned knights were impressed with addressing this sincere, humble young man who would one day be the duke in

Galles. The young squires were in awe of Brandyn's person. He set for them an excellent example of what a knight was expected to do and the attitude to take. There were genuine excitement and zeal in the court's enthusiasm toward Brandyn. There were sincerity and humility in the words that Brandyn spoke and Glen Eryn was the place to call home. Even a humble pork roast with 'patate e cippole' made an exquisitely fine meal for the light hearted.

Christmas Time at Galles

Welledon and Brandyn enjoyed a happy, peaceful Christmas time at Galles Castle with traditional customs of Galles. The minstrels made merry with music as the lords serenaded their ladies about the hall. The fire places were fed logs of dried wood to keep them happy to continue giving off their heat. The smell of the garland and the holly berries created an enchanted feeling of peace and love among the people gathered there. The Gallesian people knew how to celebrate the holy holiday in the spirit of family among the community.

Christmas this year would fall on a week day; a Thursday. Preparations for a fine meal at court were already made. Guests of Welledon would be treated to a splendid feast, and the music of minstrels. At St. James' Cathedral the angelic voices of the choir would accompany Bishop Michael's words in his observance of the holy holiday. It would soon be Christmas. The day after Christmas was more like a day of rest and thanksgiving for all the gifts bestowed on the hard-working people of the kingdom. The fuss and flurry over preparations for the celebration of the birth of the Christian Savior brought family and friends together over that bounty.

Welledon managed to distribute opportunity fairly to those in his kingdom. If a person was willing to work, they would have enough to eat. Rich or poor, high and low, everyone was satisfied with their portion of happiness administered by Glen Eryn Castle in Galles. Welledon and his nobles provided opportunity and justice. The people in Galles lived in confidence. After that opportunity it was up to the industry of each man to work their lot in life.

Fresh in their minds was the reminder of the year that blight rendered their agricultural efforts fruitless. It was the year that their potato crop failed. To be alive, in good health and not be in want of food was appreciated and not taken for granted by the subjects of Galles. On that occasion Welledon negotiated for what his dukedom desperately needed to survive. He might have used his army's might but it was not fair to other farmers who toiled to earn their living. In deciding to join his Galles to Rothaynen, Welledon gained the needed food to sustain his people through that rough winter. The people of Galles learned that Graedon was truly a great king in Rothaynen. Graedon did not take advantage of the plight of Galles by insisting on a terrible price for grains. Instead Graedon sold grains to Galles for same price that he charged any of the dukedoms in Rothaynen. Nobody had to go to war in order to survive.

Welledon had managed to keep Galles free of fighting and strife when he could. With the exception of aiding their allies fighting in a good cause with a planned timetable and, a definite goal for victory, Welledon governed his people with the wisdom granted to him by God. When people fight for the right cause, it is their duty to be victorious. It is their duty to be victorious as soon as possible and with as little sacrifice as possible. If good people do not stand up against tyranny, it will flourish like weeds choking the grasses on the open meadow. The secret was supposedly to recognize tyranny and stand up against it before it got a grapple hold on the throat of the people.

A Wedding Invitation

It came five days before Christmas via the king's post. It was a scroll secured by a thin leather ribbon that was wound around it. Inside the scroll was paper that was wound and sealed with wax. The wax bore the seal of Graedon on it. After Welledon broke the seal and unrolled the paper he learned that it was a wedding invitation. It was addressed to Welledon requesting his presence to attend the wedding of Sir Morden of Aangehart at Braemar Castle. The seal of Rothaynen was distinctly present on the head of the letter. In a fancy hand, the invitation read;

By Royal Command,
The honor of your presence is requested at
The marriage of Meaghan, daughter
Of Malcolm and Andrea of Wendover
To Sir Morden of Aangehart,
Son of Sir Borden of Aangehart late, and
Dame Mary of Aangehart.
The wedding to take place at nine o'clock morning,
The 27th of December in the year of our Lord 984,
In the Cathedral of St. Zorren at Braemar Castle.
A joust and games of skill will take place
At Braemar Courtyard in the afternoon.
The Wedding Feast will take place that evening
At the King's Court of Braemar Castle.

The traditional scroll was signed by Graedon's hand. As far as Welledon was concerned, it was Graedon's hand and nothing to be suspicious about.

The truth was that the idea of celebrating the wedding of Morden and Meaghan at Braemar was supported by Lucio and more so by Vanessa as it played well into their scheme. The wedding of this knight from the northern country was to be celebrated at Braemar, the king's castle. Aangehart Castle was even further away than Peregren Castle. There was no way anyone wanted to travel north to Aangehart that was deep

27

in snow by now to celebrate Morden's wedding. The smell of sulphur in the air at Aangehart was not very attractive. The pits of Peregren where iron ore was mined were on the way there. The topography of the rock and land looked ugly. However, Peregren was a paradise compared to the lonely, forsaken lands around Aangehart. Even what little forest there was at Aangehart looked thin and tired. The thicket choked everything in its path. Having the wedding at Braemar was a better idea that well served Vanessa and Lucio's purpose. They would have all the knights of Peregren, Aangehart and Sydor castles that were loyal to Lucio under the same kindred roof as Lord Barton, and Lord Welledon. Those loyal to Lucio would also have a plan and be prepared to execute it to the finish this time.

It was very easy for Lucio to get Graedon to approve of the use of the castle for such an event. Weddings were for the most part happy events. Although Graedon was informed and approved the wedding to take place at Braemar, his signature was forged by Lucio. It was faster and easier for Lucio to affix the royal signature himself rather than wait for Graedon to do so. With the king's failing health it was a nuisance to have to wait for him to sign anything. In the end it was a wedding. The occasion was a happy one. Everyone loved attending a wedding. One of their own faithful knights was getting married. Morden was to be wed to this charming, wholesome farm girl from Wendover.

It was a good idea to make a fuss over this prominent knight's wedding to a commoner from Wendover. Graedon was reminded that Morden had formerly served faithfully under Federics at Peregren and that it was a fine thing for this sworn bachelor to finally be marrying. The truth was that at Peregren Federics asserted no control over Morden and he did not trust him. Morden had not supported or served in good faith under Federics at all. Instead Morden followed Vanessa's orders and guarded Lucio's interests. Lucio told Graedon that this marriage would endear Wendover to Rothaynen. The idea pleased him.

"Imagine one of your knights marrying a farm girl. It would show that the interests of Wendover, the bread basket of the entire region is clearly important to you, my king," Lucio insisted.

Graedon could not disagree with what Lucio was saying but he became confused. The king realized that he had been deceived by Lucio before and that there was something more to this wedding.

In Vanessa's mind, Morden's aggression with Meaghan was the best thing that happened to advance the full union of Wendover to Rothaynen. It was also good for the advancement of Lucio. Lucio's next step, which was concocted by his scheming mother, would entail once and for all the elimination of Graedon's noble dukes. It pleased Vanessa that the wedding was slated for the 27th of December. It was a very important date to the worshipers of her cult. It was the start of an evil celebration that would end in the next month after the New Year. For the Furminatae, every 17th of January meant that some poor, unfortunate souls were sacrificed to her deity. Morden did not object to the plan as all official resistance to their cult would be put to death on his wedding day to make the 17th of January, the Sabbath of Janis, the most memorable ever. They would now be able to sacrifice lambs at will with no one to defend them. The lambs that Morden referred to in his mind were the God-fearing people who fastened their trust and hopes on a weak and absent God.

Vanessa planned to make a really generous sacrifice to her god Deimon. The celebration would be led by the lengthy torture of Pastor Mattews. The others who waited their turn to be tortured would see this valiant priest and former knight sacrificed first. Mattews would be made to worship and bow before Deimon before being put to death. Vanessa's disciples would partake in the drinking of the blood of their sacrificed victims in order to gain the strengths of their enemies. Vanessa on this day would celebrate the defeat of her god's enemies and the investment of her son Lucio as king in Rothaynen. Then, to her way of thinking, would there be freedom from the oppressive rule of that absentee landlord, God, and that failure of a son of his whom they killed. It even disgusted Vanessa that this Almighty God would allow the death of his Son at the hands of common people. In her way of thinking, that was no way for a god to act. If He were truly the all-powerful God, why did he not help his Son?

A true God would not have allowed his Son to be taken, humiliated, scourged and put to death like a rabid animal at the hands of a mob. After all that happened, God did not even punish the mob, why, because Vanessa believed that He could not.

Vanessa realized that to create stability they would need to gain the support of the mob of people whose popular opinion made a pleasant difference. When fleecing sheep it is easier if you have the consent of the sheep. The support of Cardinal Spehar was very valuable on two counts as he represented the church and he controlled a significant cache of gold. To add authenticity to their claim to the throne, Lucio would take the princess Elayne to be his wife. In a short time she would bear Lucio an heir. The birth of this bloodline heir would consolidate their power legally. Their claim to the throne would gain legitimacy 'in the eyes of God'. That is how they would promote their claim to the people. Vanessa planned to exploit the people's worship of God. Lucio and she would both refer to doing things in God's name. However in their mind they meant their own god, Deimon.

Vanessa noted that Spehar already worshipped Mammon the god of wealth. Church money that could have served the needy was denied to the so called 'lazy miscreants'. By now Spehar controlled no small fortune in gold that he would do anything to keep. Who would be better to impose on to exploit religion than Cardinal Spehar?

As head of the church, Spehar could influence Princess Elayne, and he came cheaply. Silver and gold were all that he worshipped and cared about. It was such a small price to pay for a man of the cloth.

Elayne was not only beautiful, but a clean, virgin girl. This was important to the Furminatae. They believed that a fallen girl was already on their side doing their bidding. On the other hand Elayne was kept clean by her morals and belief in the teachings of her God. It was of no consequence to Vanessa though, Elayne would be taught anew in the ways of the world. It would be safe to take and drink her blood.

She was a clean girl. Vanessa would waste no time extracting a pint of her blood after she and Lucio were wed. She counted the days. To Vanessa, drinking the blood of a young virgin was the secret of youth and life everlasting. Indeed Vanessa could not wait to drink the blood of this girl. She was young, clean, and a virgin. Elayne's lineage stemmed from anointed royal blood. Vanessa believed that her blood would wash away years of aging. The high priestess of the Furminatae was very discriminating, she preferred young, healthy virgins of high stature.

After providing an heir and securing Lucio as King of Rothaynen, Elayne would then be made to serve Vanessa. In public Vanessa would appear as the dutiful mother-in-law, but behind the scenes she would have control over matters. The young queen would be made to serve Vanessa in her cruel designs that would involve humiliation, pain and suffering for the innocent girl. Vanessa's heart would overflow with gladness if she could convert Elayne to be a willing disciple of hers. Elayne would be compelled to follow as her own offspring lay in the balance. Vanessa and Lucio were just beaming with how the turn of events was unfolding in their favor.

After the serious setbacks of the past in dealing with Graedon's ancestry, Vanessa's people could come out of the shadows and take what was denied them. Vanessa just counted the days until her appetites could be satisfied. Her dream of installing her son Lucio as king would finally come true. Then they could put their god in his proper place. Then they could persecute Christians as they had done to them by denying them their rights to worship. Vanessa's master already owned Nodunn so making an arrangement with King Nodunn would be a matter of paying tribute with the people's grain. Vanessa could see the day that all of Rothaynen would pay tribute to the Huynsten 'king of kings', follow the rule of King Lucio who spared them from annihilation, and bow before her god, Deimon in worship.

Objection

At Galles Castle, Brandyn was dumbfounded when Welledon showed him the invitation. As happy as he was to hear affirmation that Andrea and Meaghan were alive and well, he wondered if they had gone mad. How could his sister agree to marry such a vile, conceited and evil man?

If she had gone mad, how could his mother allow her to marry Morden?

Brandyn was objectionable to the idea of Morden and marriage. Brandyn thought that Morden was hard on everyone, but he should never be around women let alone be married to one. The biggest objection that Brandyn had was the fact that Morden was marrying his sister, Meaghan. Morden was a far cry different from Woodcroft who was Meaghan's true love. Had Meaghan forgotten Woodcroft?

Brandyn wondered how it had come to this. He had the same thoughts regarding the Wendover Tavern that was now under new management. It was inconceivable to believe.

The difference between Morden and Woodcroft was night and day. Brandyn was sure that his sister would be better off alone with the memory of Woodcroft over marrying the corrupt Morden. It had been noted by the elders that 'it was better to live alone than in bad company'. Now Brandyn wondered if his father was alive. The impression that Brandyn got from the invitation was confusing. It let him believe that his parents were with Meaghan, which was his hope for the matter. Malcolm, his father, was also mentioned in the invitation, but that may have been to avoid declaring that his father was dead. What explanation could there be for this?

What was Lucio up to now?

It bothered Brandyn that he knew that Lucio was up to something, but he could not yet figure it out.

Welledon waited patiently to see how Brandyn reacted to hearing about his sister marrying Sir Morden. Although Meaghan was Brandyn's sister, she was the young woman that his son Woodcroft had planned to marry. Morden could not be more different from Woodcroft in demeanor and in his beliefs. For his part Welledon could no longer present Woodcroft to Meaghan anymore. Despite that, Welledon did not want to see this young woman that his son loved, fall into the hands of some rogue knight. Besides, she was Brandyn's sister and Brandyn was now his son. Welledon waited to hear what he would say first. Brandyn felt more confident now with telling Welledon how he felt and what he thought.

"There is something quite wrong here. Meaghan would never agree to marrying Morden," Brandyn proclaimed, "she despised him."

Welledon continued to listen.

"I am sure that Meaghan is being forced into this. Morden is not the marrying kind. He has contempt for everyone but especially for women. Morden feels that everyone on this earth was put here for his general use. Once I heard him say, 'why buy a cow if you get milk for free'," Brandyn told Welledon, "that is not the attitude to take toward a woman."

"Perhaps, the man has had a change of heart," Welledon suggested.

Welledon himself did not believe what he was saying as he was biased against Morden as well. The old duke thought that it might be possible that the love of a woman could change a man. Welledon gathered that Meaghan was a good, sincere, God-fearing, hard-working girl. What man on earth would not be willing to improve himself for want of such a girl?

"Oh, it is possible, but highly improbable that my sister would want Morden. I am sure that she was forced to accept. My family's tavern was sold, so something is up," Brandyn summed up.

"I am sure that you are right. Judging by the last time we all met at Braemar; there are surely some dark figures in Graedon's court. What do you suggest that we do?" asked Welledon.

The old duke already had a plan but he wanted to hear how Brandyn approached the problem.

"I would inform Lord Barton of our suspicion. By now he has received an invitation as well. Next, I never thought that it would come to this, but we need to send spies to Braemar Castle to find out what is really happening," Brandyn said reluctantly.

He knew that Welledon was above board and would not support spying on anyone let alone his majesty the king. Spies were despised and to be caught meant torture and death. Before Welledon joined his dukedom to the Kingdom of Rothaynen, he trusted both Graedon and his cousin Barton. In the past, a man's word was his bond. If a man fell from trust, his reputation was ruined forever. The old saying applies: 'a fence does not protect the pasture, it is the fear of being caught and falling from honor that does'. Welledon thought on the idea. Sending spies was against every instinct in his body. A person had the right to his privacy and spying took that away. It was unethical to spy on people and in this case could be construed as treason. Welledon was raised on good Christian morals that forbade lying, spying and cheating people. These were woven into the same courtly virtues that bound kings, dukes, cardinals, bishops, knights and soldiers to duty.

"Were people in the past more vigilant and God-fearing?
Are people today more cynical?
Are people desperate to turn to unethical methods to achieve their goals?" Welledon wondered.

Welledon understood that by spying they were actually serving Graedon and Rothaynen by their efforts. He would inform Lord Barton of his idea. If matters were found to be normal then no harm would come of it. It was still a most difficult decision to make.

After some thought, Welledon stated, "Perhaps there is no harm in sending a scout ahead to learn what is going on at Braemar. However we must let Lord Barton know."

Welledon's decision pleased Brandyn as he felt that danger awaited them at Braemar Castle. The duke collected two trustworthy men, Tubb and Scrugg who were both clever and loyal to Welledon. He briefed them on their delicate mission. He then sent the men with two fine horses and a horse-drawn cart full of produce to bestow a gift for Braemar Hall's Christmas feast. The two fine horses they would secure in the forest before entering Braemar Castle. With the cart bearing produce, it was certain they would gain entry into the castle. Tubb and Scrugg were to ask for accommodations for the night. In place of staying they were to secretly find Graedon. They were instructed to introduce themselves as secret messengers from Welledon. If there was anything to worry about, Graedon would tell them. After learning what they could, they were to scale the castle wall by night, collect the horses in the nearby forest and leave that same night for Galles. Tubb and Scrugg were never heard from again.

The Tradition Continues

The fall Moon Harvest Games saw a handful of squires gain knighthood that frosty fall. Of the eight squires, six of them served knights aligned with Lucio. The other two, Kent of Cardiff in Langton and Osvald of Mead were welcomed to Lucio's alliance with all the camaraderie befitting a brotherhood. Lucio's faithful were to win them over so when the time came, they would not question any directive that Lucio gave. All day the two squires from Mead and Langton were treated with all the dignity befitting competing squires. Although the two squires were a little reluctant to follow, the fact that their host squires were friendly and loyal to Lucio seemed to justify getting along.

Osvald, who was the younger of the two, did not stray from the course of good for anything or anyone. His loyalty lay with Graedon the king. Kent noted how sneaky some of the other squires were and how they all reported to Ruitnik who, try as he did, could not feign friendly at all. Kent and Osvald built an immediate rapport and decided that they could trust each other.

"All the squires sing of the praises of this Lucio to the point of worship," Kent gathered, "has he ever led men into battle or does he just send them in?"

"If the man is worthy we shall learn soon enough," Osvald summed up, "as for me, my loyalty is with King Graedon."

Osvald was overheard speaking these words to Kent. The report made its way to Ruitnik and soon Lucio was made aware. Despite Lucio's attempts to appear modest, he seemed to bask in the forefront of all places of honor and activities. Lord Lucio as he was called now was King Graedon's chief advisor. That fact was clear among knights and lords and merchants. The people of the realm follow the leadership provided by these factions of society. Lucio was placed very high on the chain of command. In fact only one person was ahead of him and that was King Graedon.

On this occasion of the Moon Harvest Games, King Graedon was absent. It was the only time that Graedon did not attend since he himself was a young prince. To keep up appearances, Elayne sat next to her father's throne seat at the games. Graedon's throne seat sat empty as a sign of everyone's respect and devotion to their king. Lucio humbly stood behind the princess to illustrate his servitude. The announcement made to the subjects was that there was no cause for alarm over the absence of their monarch. The people were told that the king was merely overcoming fatigue related to the changes in the weather. Vanessa sat next to the princess in the company of all the ladies in waiting with all the colorful gowns that they wore for the event. Close by was Lucio feigning to be at her majesty Princess Elayne's beck and call.

On that day there was an incident that bore mention. One of the two squires, that were not owned by Lucio, the young man from Mead, was hurt in the joust. Osvald of Mead won the swords competition, won the silver arrow at archery and finished second at the axe throw, but the joust was a different matter. In his very first run, an unlikely hero named Monro made a pass with his lance that he could never repeat in a lifetime. Monro's lance thrust around his opponents shield and by chance struck him square on the seam of his right shoulder. Osvald dropped his lance instantly. He turned in pain and leaned forward on his horse. The horse returned to the starting post and stood still. In an effort to climb down, Osvald fell on the ground. As he lay motionless and in agony on the ground, he could sense that something was not right. All that he could say was, "No, God."

Oswald knew that something was ghastly wrong. As he regained his composure he made an effort to get up. In Osvald's effort to get up, he realized that he had lost control of his right arm. As he got to his feet, his right arm dragged down beside him. Monro, the challenger could not believe his good fortune as he had not done well when it came to the joust. Ruitnik looked at Lucio from the tournament field. Neither one expected as much from Monro. They could not be happier. Elayne turned her eyes away for a moment. She could not stand to see the young man ruined. Then she turned and ordered Joseph, the king's physician, to attend to the squire promptly. It was a command that Lucio did not like, but he nodded in approval.

The physician immediately went to the injured squire. Joseph followed the others who escorted Oswald to his tent. Cheers were heard from the crowd as Osvald was up on his feet. Osvald supported his arm as he bravely endured great pain while he made his way to his tent. Joseph noted that Osvald's arm was knocked out of its socket. The lance caught the young squire on his breast plate and was directed toward his arm. It was at the seam where the arm is attached to the torso. The chain link that prevented his arm from being pierced could not withstand the shock at impact. The arm could well have been cleaved from the body.

The force of the blow was great enough to push the bone in his arm well into its socket. The socket itself was fractured from the great pressure. The muscle and nerves took quite a crushing blow as well. The bone in his arm was crushed at the end from the impact with the socket. Osvald's arm then fell out when the socket bone that was fractured could no longer keep the bone in his arm in its place. It was a serious injury for a squire with a pure heart who put forth an outstanding effort. Sir Bryan of Mead was very proud of his protégé. It was Osvald's dream to be knighted and serve Graedon and Rothaynen. Now the boy was removed from the field and brought to a tent to be attended. Osvald did not notice in all the pain and confusion, but it was easy to see what was on the hearts of the squires loyal to Lucio. They were pleased with what happened to Osvald.

Joseph, the physician, assessed his patient. He would do his best to set and attach the arm. Given the serious nature of the injury, he knew that the boy might not ever have full use of his arm to pull on a shirt, let alone swinging a sword, pulling back a bow or jousting. Osvald was brave for the young man that he was. Apart from the grimace look on his face, he did not cry out. He was offered spirits to drink but he refused them. The pain was mounting. Joseph insisted that Osvald drink the spirit but he could not. Osvald tried to stay awake but he slipped in and out of consciousness until he passed out from exhaustion. It was easy for those around Osvald to learn what was in his heart as he spoke during unconsciousness. He kept repeating to himself.

"I love God, Graedon and the princess Elayne. I must stay strong to keep the princess safe, I must—keep her—safe," Osvald spoke deliriously, "I love Elayne. I love Eee—l—-"

Joseph was quite capable with his skills at practicing medicine and as an apothecary. He knew what had to be done. It would not be easy. He worked diligently to place the arm in its socket and then wrapped bandages around the arm and shoulder to prevent it from moving. It was the best that he could do. The rest would be up to God. Joseph had managed to put the arm back into its socket. The fracture was a major one, but not unlike smaller bone fractures that needed a few days to set and mend. Osvald's arm and shoulder were a larger consideration so more time would be required. The arm and shoulder would need to stay wrapped up tightly and kept immobile for at least a fortnight. That was the key, to keep the arm immobile.

In that time Joseph hoped that the bone would begin to heal itself. A cloth wrap bound the arm in front of him and kept it stable. For the pain Joseph prescribed spirits and wine to work their miracle, but so far Osvald refused them. Jeanne, the doctors assistant wiped the sweat off of Osvald's face. Despite the sweat, she noticed that Osvald was shivering. Jeanne put another blanket over the young squire. She thought of praying and did so. Elayne instructed Joseph that at the earliest possible moment Osvald should be moved into a guest chamber in the castle. There he could rest and recover in comfort.

Now Joseph only hoped that Osvald's arm would repair and heal properly. Even if Osvald was lucky, it would take some time for him to move the arm about like before. In fact he might not ever be able to move the arm about like before. Osvald's future was not certain and it did not look good. In fact the incident cast an omen over the entire day. In the history of Rothaynen, no squire had ever been seriously hurt in a tournament. There was an allowance made for being thrown off a horse and the odd scrape at the swords competition. There was consideration for the other person but an accident could happen. Cuts and bruises were expected, but never had there been such a serious accident. This was an accident yet it signified so much more. Consideration of others had fallen by the wayside.

The joust continued until there was a winner because everyone likes a winner. Eventually Ruitnik of Sydor from the northern part of the kingdom won the joust. Even some spectators relished the shock that probably crippled a young man's arm. The only way to describe it was to state that there was a movement toward violence. More and more the people enjoyed it.

At the end of the contest the princess was very regal when she awarded the tournament champion and knighted the squires. This year the tournament champion was Ruitnik of Sydor and he was awarded a gold bar with the seal of Rothaynen stamped on it. Elayne took it from a purple pillow with gold fringe and turned toward Ruitnik. The unpolished Ruitnik almost grabbed it from Elayne's hands as he raised it in his own and turned toward the crowd. In his turning, he dwarfed Elayne. Elayne looked at Lucio who observed the whole matter. The crowd cheered and looked on the gold bar. It was the first time a gold bar was the tournament prize.

"Ruitnik will now crown his choice of fair lady for 'lady of honor for the tournament'. Our fine knight and his lady fair will have the honor of the first dance at the castle tonight," declared Elayne.

The crowd cheered as Elayne handed him a wreath. Names of the maidens were being called. Ruitnik however knew exactly who to bestow the honor upon. The gruff knight took the wreath firmly in his hand and marched across the grand stand. The planks he walked on bowed as he made his way to the section with the most beautifully dressed maidens.

"Ashleigh!" he called.

Ruitnik looked on no other girl but went directly to Ashleigh who accepted the wreath that was placed on her head. The crowd cheered. Then Ruitnik grabbed up Ashleigh who by contrast to him was rather slim and dainty. He then kissed her gruffly. The gesture was not courtly by any means. The crowd cheered even louder. It was yet another first for tournament day at Braemar Castle.

In the fashion of her father, Elayne prepared to bestow the oath of knighthood to the eager young squires at the tournament. Between Ruitnik's enthusiasm and the presence of most of the squires that stood before her, it made the princess uncomfortable. Elayne could hear their heavy breathing as they stared and watched her every move. Lucio intervened with a surprise for the princess. He declared that these brave knights would be formed into a special order to pay homage to the Princess Elayne herself.

"Good subjects of Rothaynen! Good subjects of Rothaynen! There is a special notice today. These new knights will take a special oath to protect the honor of the princess. They will wear her colors in battle. I give you the 'Order of the Princess' Knights'!" exclaimed Lucio.

There were cheers from the crowd. Elayne did not know what to say. Apart from one of the candidates, the rest of them were boisterous. They had mannerisms and instincts that made them the people that Elayne felt that she should avoid. Elayne merely proceeded to knight them with the traditional accolade. Elayne bad the knights to kneel and when they had done so, she raised her father's sword.

"In the name of God, St. Michael and St. Zorren, I declare you to be knights to protect all the people. You are charged to vanquish Ignorance, Oppression and Selfishness," declared Elayne.

Elayne then walked toward the first candidate. Lucio told Elayne his name and where he was from. She tapped him on the shoulder and addressed him Sir Monro of Darvell. The next knight was introduced as Kent of Fanlay. Fanlay was northwest of Marmora. Kent gave the impression that he was gentle. Princess Elayne followed through until all the squires were knighted by her. During her duty in the ceremony, Elayne thought about Osvald and how he deserved to be knighted as well.

That evening there was a celebration that followed at the castle. A good meal was prepared. There were minstrels that entertained and provided the music for dance. The ladies of the court looked their best in the colorful gowns with their lovely faces, figures, hands and free-flowing, long hair done up with combs. Some of the younger knights had too much ale and were behaving rather rudely. They seemed to blend in with the older knights who had schemed to get them drunk. The phrase rings true that 'in vino veritas', or truth in wine. Upon consuming wine, ale or spirits, it was easier to speak the truth or at least, what was on the mind.

The next day these squires would be baptized in the Dargell Stream. For now, they would carry powerful headaches and uneasy stomachs. Elayne managed to post pone dancing with Lucio. She was certain that he would ask her. Lucio was certain that he would dance with her since there were no other eligible partners and his knights knew of his wishes. Once the opening ceremonies got under way, Lucio would casually ask Elayne to dance. Princess Elayne however was nowhere to be found. Lucio inquired of the servants and one suggested that she retired for a brief moment, but that she would return.

After the celebration got started, Elayne summoned Sean and Ornelda and stated to them that she wanted to check up on the ailing squire. She instructed to Sean to collect her father's sword and bring it to Osvald's chamber. That task was not difficult for Sean as he was Graedon's page and was privy to his master's possessions. Ornelda was sent to fetch Cardinal Spehar's assistant Pastor Andrei with specific instructions. Ornelda had no difficulty getting Pastor Andrei to leave the drinking fest in the Great Hall of Braemar. Upon being informed of the princess' wishes, the good priest left the festivities with Ornelda. He was told where to meet the princess and sent word with Ornelda that he would be there. Pastor Andrei went to St. Zorren's Church and collected his chrism oils and a holy book before going to see Osvald.

After the treatment administered by Joseph earlier that day, the princess spoke to the physician and Jeanne who suggested keeping the patient warm. Jeanne also told Elayne of the words that Osvald spoke while he was delirious. The young squire spoke of his love for the princess along with his loyalty to her father. While she saw him competing it was obvious to Elayne that Osvald would make a worthy knight. He was so modest yet bold. Osvald did not allow himself to be swayed by the knights and squires loyal to Lucio. Osvald reminded Elayne of another squire who competed at Braemar who had not returned. After Joseph's treatment, Osvald was moved into a guest chamber within the castle at princess Elayne's command. In his unconscious state, he could not remember being carried there. Sean saw to it that the fire place was kept blazing to keep the room warm and the damp castle walls dry.

The princess was announced at Osvald's chamber within the castle. Elayne met Sir Bryan of Mead, Osvald's sponsor who promptly welcomed her in. There she spoke to the young man whose dreams had been dashed. Elayne listened to the young man talk for quite some time. He appeared to be boastful and bragging at first but in his eyes Elayne could see the sincerity and gentleness behind the bull-necked facade. By all rights he would have won the tournament. Osvald was angry with his predicament and scared. He sounded more like a frightened little boy would sound in the same predicament. The young squire did not know how this accident would turn out, neither did the doctor. Osvald was a humble servant of her father's who fell short of his dream and needed to tell his story. Osvald did not talk too much as a matter of habit, but Sir Bryan let him speak on. It had been Osvald's dream to be a knight and serve the king, he repeated over and over. And now, he was in the presence of the princess whom he adored.

In Mead, King Graedon was considered their true and noble king. Graedon's noble knights and army kept raiders from the sea at bay. Fair prices were paid in trade between Mead and Braemar so no one could ask for more. Lord Welledon of Galles even joined his realm to Rothaynen due to Graedon's reputation for justice and fair rule. Osvald had worked and trained hard under the stewardship of Sir Bryan who was loyal to Graedon and very proud of his squire. Osvald had won many events and stood a very good chance of winning the joust as well. The odds of making the impact that injured Osvald bordered on impossible, but in fact the odds had crossed that border. The squire Monro was clumsy but managed to raise the lance at the precise moment. His hit on Osvald was clean at impact. Monro's luck did not hold out as he was eliminated in his next challenge, but he managed to eliminate a major contender. That pleased Lucio very much. It seemed that winning the joust was not meant to be for Osvald. With his prior wins, he would have been tournament champion hands down. He was certainly the favorite with the common spectators of the games.

Osvald had said everything that he could think of saying in the presence of the princess. It was as if he would never see her again and he wanted to cram in an entire lifetime of conversation. Sir Bryan reminded Osvald that he was a humble squire after he finished speaking. Elayne smiled. Still it was hard to keep humble after doing as well as he did and yet falling short. Osvald believed that there was no justice in what had occurred to him. There was a silence as Elayne continued to sit by his side. Elayne was reminded of the sailor from Irminia. Jeremy had not returned for the joust that year. The princess enjoyed making his acquaintance when he attended the year before with his uncle.

Sir Bryan was impressed with Princess Elayne's empathy for Osvald. She had been most kind in sending the king's physician and accommodating Osvald with the guest chamber in the castle. Her majesty had taken time to visit with a true crusader for justice. Sir Bryan could attest to the hard work and dedication and discipline that it took to bring Osvald to this point. Perhaps that is what heightened the sense of waste. Would Osvald ever retain the use of his arm?

Pastor Andrei entered the chamber and introduced himself to Sir Bryan and Osvald. He knew everyone else so he wasted no time. He got out and set up his oils and opened up his book. Sir Bryan guessed at what was going to happen. The good pastor wasted no time and was direct with Osvald.

"Do you believe in God, his Son Jesus Christ and the Holy Ghost?" asked Andrei.

"Certainly I do," replied Osvald.

"Then you better be good and upright, and defend those who seek justice: young or old, rich or poor, healthy or sickly," concluded Andrei.

"Certainly, I will," answered Osvald.

Andrei poured water over Osvald's head to baptize him again. He also administered chrism oil and bestowed blessings upon him to help heal the worthy boy.

"Remember my son to trust in the Great Physician. The Lord God Almighty can do the impossible," Andrei assured, "if you will only believe on Him."

Then Andrei sat in the corner and began praying silently. After some time, Elayne rose from her seat and asked Sean for her father's sword. Osvald was a little surprised. He tried to rise out of bed quickly, but found the pain disabling.

"As it is more practical for me to rise," Elayne started, "you may not get up as it will bring you discomfort."

"Oh your majesty, I must get up," said Osvald.

The patient struggled with pain as he attempted to get up from that bed. Since his right arm was well wrapped he could not use it to balance himself as he arose from the bed. The grimace on Osvald's face was telling everyone who saw him that he was in pain. It was painful but he got onto his feet without disturbing his arm. He guarded that arm jealously. The arm and shoulder were so well bandaged that he could not move them. Joseph had done a fine job. Osvald favored his right arm in the sling. Now he tried to kneel. Elayne waited patiently and with consideration. She did not want to forbid him from doing what he thought that he had to do. Osvald managed to kneel, but it was difficult without the aid of his right arm and shoulder. He still supported it tenderly. Osvald's head began to spin so he shut his eyes and stood still.

"You have proven yourself worthy on the tournament grounds. It is easy to read your character and sincerity. You are a welcome subject and have brought honor upon Sir Bryan and Mead, from whence you came.

"When you have healed yourself, you shall return to Braemar a knight in the service of my father King Graedon.

"Now, in the name of God, St. Michael and St. Zorren, I give you the right to bear arms and mete justice. It is your duty to vanquish ignorance, oppression and selfishness. Arise, Sir Osvald of Mead," Elayne spoke the accolade.

The princess tapped Osvald carefully on his right shoulder then the left and the right again with the sword. Elayne was very careful.

"Oh, your majesty," Osvald said.

The young man was so moved that tears came to his eyes.

"I swear your majesty I will serve God, King Graedon and you with my entire mind, all my heart and all my soul. What you have bestowed upon me is an honor that I will earn your majesty," replied Osvald, "I swear it."

"You already have earned it," Elayne judged.

Elayne smiled at him before she left. If some demon had descended upon the youth on the field that day and tried to destroy him with injury and misery to accompany the misfortune, Elayne made the misery disappear. There was a renewed hope in him. Osvald felt that he had to get better, could get better, despite the dismal circumstances and the pain and discomfort that he was in. He looked directly into Elayne's eyes.

"I love you, your majesty. I have loved you from the moment I saw you at Mead. Meeting you in person only confirms my affection for you. You are the most beautiful and caring person that I have ever met aside from my mother. I love you and I will love no other maiden or lady fair so long as I live," declared Osvald.

Elayne realized that his declaration of love was more personal than that of a subject for his monarch,

"We just met. You do not even know me," replied Elayne.

"I met you when you visited Mead with the king and queen. I was given the task of taking care of your fine horse, Butler," Osvald told her, "I knew that I loved you when I first saw you outside the Brewer's Inn at Mead."

Elayne remembered a chubby little boy with a cute face that the farrier handed the reins of her horse to. Osvald stopped himself from saying more now that he was dizzy. In the predicament that he was in he was only too happy to lie down again. With his eyes shut he made a vow. A tear collected at the corner of his eye.

"Princess, one day I will show you that I can do everything that I could do before, so help me God," Osvald said.

Elayne was quite taken by the sound of Osvald's voice, his words and his sincerity. It was like the pledge of a child made earnestly. Ornelda smiled but before she could say anything, Sir Bryan interrupted her.

"A knight of Mead never lies, nor does he exaggerate," Sir Bryan declared proudly.

"Thank you, Sir Bryan. I am certain of Sir Osvald's sincerity," Elayne said, "I heard it in his voice. Now I must not neglect my other guests.

As Elayne arose, Sir Bryan walked over and personally opened the chamber door.

"We are grateful for your visit your majesty," Sir Bryan said, "Your presence has done more than you know to bring hope and comfort to my boy."

"Sir Bryan," Elayne acknowledged.

Elayne left the chamber followed by Ornelda.

The Sprain

On the return to the Great Hall in Braemar Castle Elayne turned to Ornelda. She anticipated being asked to dance by Lucio. Elayne was not really in the mood to dance at all this night.

"What shall I do to avoid Lucio?" she asked.

"Why if your majesty suddenly had a sprained ankle, it would be an excuse not to dance," Ornelda told her, "but then you will not be able to dance with any other fine boys in the hall."

"I am really not in the mood for dancing at all but I am not about to feign a sprained ankle," Elayne replied proudly, "What do you think about Osvald?"

"I think he loves you, your majesty," replied Ornelda cleverly, "I heard him declare so."

When Elayne and Ornelda arrived back at the king's hall, Lucio was the first to ask Elayne to dance. Elayne could not refuse. As Lucio took her hand and led her to the dance floor, she tugged at his hand as though she was catching her balance and let out and 'auow!'

"Your majesty, are you alright?" asked Lucio

"My ankle," Elayne said with a long face, "I fear that I have sprained it. Thanks to you though Lucio, you saved me from falling."

The court attendants arrived, but Ornelda pushed forward and came to Elayne's rescue. She supported the princess and would escort her to her chambers.

"You will need to keep your ankle elevated, your majesty," assessed Ornelda, "send for the doctor! Get some compresses and cold water."

"Lucio," Elayne called.

"Yes, your majesty. Is there anything that I can do?" replied Lucio.

"Would you see to the comfort of my guests?" she asked.

"Naturally, your majesty," replied Lucio.

Although he was in command of the party, Lucio was disappointed. He held the princess by the hand and was escorting her to the hall dance floor. What a run of bad luck he noted. Lucio had no luck when it came to courting the princess.

The Knighting Ceremony

On the next day before the church service, the people gathered to see seven monks of the Bendire Monastery dunking the new squires in the Dargell Stream before the red-vested Cardinal Spehar. After the ceremony of baptism in the Dargell Stream, the candidates dried off the water and walked to St. Zorren's Church. The continued absence of King Graedon was understood as it was explained the day before. The fact was troubling to Elayne. She had never seen her father miss the tournament games nor the accolade and the swearing of oaths at church. After the mass and communion, Elayne knighted the seven young men anew before the altar of the Lord God with Lucio looking on. Lucio could not have been standing any closer to the princess during the entire ceremony.

Elayne's Plan

Graedon's condition was not improving. Elayne got daring enough to ask Ornelda to take a message to Lord Barton at Petrinvincit. Elayne was afraid to be left alone with the servants in the new face of government at Braemar. There was treachery looming everywhere. With the help of Graedon's page, Sean, whose father worked in the royal stables, they managed to get a horse for Ornelda to set out with a note from Elayne. The dependable Ornelda knew how to take care of herself for the journey to Petrinvincit. She would be traveling at night on the king's road but there were several towns that she could find shelter in.

Elayne figured that if Ornelda could leave the castle without being missed, the trip through Marmora would be among gentle farm people along the way. These farm people would not hesitate to assist a traveler, especially a woman traveling with purpose to get to Petrinvincit. Elayne gained confidence with the thought that when Lord Barton received her note, wrapped in a leather pouch with the royal seal, he would know that it came from Elayne. Then with Barton made aware, he would know what to do and how to do it.

Elayne remembered that Lord Barton said something about fishing the last time he was at Braemar. It was on the day of that incident with Lucio and Barton, and of course the flying plate that saved his life courtesy of Brandyn. Elayne smiled as she thought of Brandyn and imagined the whole flying plate scene. Elayne wondered what happened to Brandyn, he seemed so determined to get back to Wendover. She wondered if Brandyn reached the girl of his dreams. Elayne thought that he was a handsome, considerate young knight with a ruddy complexion when she met him. He was pretty calm for someone that Lucio was trying to kill. Perhaps that explained the ruddy complexion.

Elayne's thoughts turned to Barton's remark about fishing. She did not remember when her father ever got excited about fishing. Even in the 'Smelt Run' in early spring when the fresh smelts made their trip from their inland tributaries to Thermanden Bay, Graedon was not overly enthusiastic about fishing. Graedon had done battle and seen men drawn and quartered; bone and marrow, blood, muscle and tissue all hacked beyond recognition. Those sights did not bother him but with regards to fish that was another matter. One thing Graedon could not stand was the sight of fish organs and their smell. In Graedon's mind, the best part of the 'Smelt Run' was the freshly baked bread cakes that the monks at the Bendire Monastery made to accompany the cooked fish for the occasion.

Regardless of the remark about fishing, Elayne made her own plan and Ornelda was going to carry it out. While Ornelda was sent away, Elayne thought that she might investigate the south tower. Elayne was not aware that Ornelda was betrayed and taken to Vanessa's personal chamber of horrors in the same south tower. Unfortunately for Ornelda, she could not communicate that she had been captured. Elayne would try to find this secret route out of the castle without being discovered herself. She was sure that there was a means to escape from the castle via the south tower canal. Of course, Elayne realized, when fresh fish were brought to the castle, they did not come from the market but directly to the castle from the bay. Fishermen would bring their catch to the south tower on their boats, by water. The south tower gate to the castle was not visible from the south side of the bay. The castle tower was circular and the gate to the canal faced north.

Elayne figured out what Barton meant when he suggested fishing. She knew that her father did not like fishing. Elayne went to Graedon and asked him about what Barton had said. Graedon then informed her about the secret route of escape. Apparently there was a means to get in and out of the castle via the south tower. There used to be a waterway in the castle that led right to Thermanden Bay. No one could see the barred gate because it lay on the inside of the circular tower facing the castle wall. A person looking at the castle from the outside could not see it. In Elayne's memory she had never seen it being used before. Graedon told her that the passage was barred by a wrought iron grate. The grate allowed water through, but not a boat. A person however could swim under it but in this cold weather would freeze to death in the cold water. They might need help with the barred gate as naturally it would be heavy as well as locked. She did not inform Graedon of her plans. She knew that her father would worry about her. Elayne ventured out herself to explore the south tower foundations.

With the help of Melanie, a young servant girl that worked in the kitchen, Sean managed to get work clothes for Elayne. Sean brought the work clothes with him when attending on Graedon. Since Elayne's every move was watched, she was careful not to be seen. Despite it being her home, what little others knew about her plan could make the difference between the success and failure of her plan. If she could discover this passage, then Graedon and she could try to escape via a small fishing boat. She would have to learn how practical this route was. Elayne took Sean, her father's page into confidence. She reasoned that he could easily learn of her plans anyway and besides she needed his help. Sean agreed to help and excused himself to acquire the key to the locked door that lead to the south tower dungeon.

Upon his return, Sean carefully led Elayne in her disguise through the castle. They stopped in on the kitchen to collect a mop and bucket with dirty water. When they got to the south tower they found a locked door. Sean unfastened the lock and pulled open the door. He told Elayne that he must leave the door locked. They agreed that he would check the door every twenty minutes with a soft knock if it was possible. If guards appeared, Elayne would have to wait until she heard him knock. If Elayne got back before he returned, again Elayne was to hide and wait quietly on the other side until he gave the knock. Elayne agreed and entered through the doorway as she heard Sean close and lock the door behind her. On the other side of the door there was a set of stone stairs that descended downward. It was damper here as she could feel the heavier air. The lack of light made it hard to see where they landed. Elayne surmised that the stairs would take her to the foundation of the south tower so she started to descend them.

Disguised as a servant, Elayne carried a bucket of soap water and a mop with her. So far there was no one around. Despite that, she was careful and approached humbly. She did not look up so as to look at anyone directly. She might be recognized. Looking directly at people would quickly give her away as servants did not look into the faces of the nobles. Elayne managed to get to the bottom of the south tower stairs. The guard saw her enter the foyer to the staircase that led down and observed her. When she descended down the stairs, she did not know what to expect. She had heard that Vanessa had a work room of some sort down there. She did not want to disturb that sanctuary. Elayne certainly did not want to run into Vanessa at all. If the rumors were correct though, Vanessa would at this time be up in her castle chambers, asleep for her beauty rest in the daytime.

Elayne's disguise was convincing enough to gain her access to the lowest level of the castle. To keep in character, she actually started mopping the floor. On that very first day that she gained access to the dungeon she overheard a conversation between some prisoners and Lucio on the level below the waterway. It was Lucio's voice and he seemed to be upset. Before she could hear anymore Elayne was abruptly asked to leave by the jailor on that level. She bowed her head and did so agreeably. She did not utter a word. A few days later Elayne tried again. This time she managed to elude the jailor that dismissed her days earlier. It seemed that the jailor was on an extended lunch. Still Elayne would have to be careful if she was to avoid him. He could return at any moment but she thought that she had the perfect cover. Elayne certainly acted the part.

Again Elayne began to mop the stone floor. In no time at all the soap water was a dark grey. As she mopped her way down the hall, she came to an open arch in the stone but it was guarded by an iron bar fence. The tall gate was padlocked and without the key no one was going anywhere. There it was however, the canal. A small boat could easily slip out of the castle. Hopefully the cold water that was not yet frozen would stay that way or it would be a short boat trip. The stone floor stretched across to the bank of the canal but she could not see around the corner. She could not see if a boat was there. Suddenly Elayne was interrupted.

"Hey! You there! What are you doing?"

It was the jailor.

"What are you doing here?" he asked.

"Oh, sir, I was sent to clean this ungodly sight. To 'clean it immaculately', are my instructions. You will not complain about me, will you? It is not easy to get all the dirt. Some dirt has been ground in. I would dread to learn what my next punishment is," Elayne told him convincingly as she demonstrated by scrubbing a small area vigorously.

"So, you are being punished, are you?" the jailor grinned.

In his mind it would have to be punishment to unlock the door and send a young girl to clean in this place.

"This place is dingy and grimy. Just look at my water," Elayne directed innocently.

She diverted his attention to her bucket. He could not have cared less but it did prove that she had been cleaning and that was her only concern. The jailor's suspicion was satisfied.

"How long do you propose to be here?" the jailor asked gruffly.

"Not any longer than I have to," Elayne replied humbly.

The look on Elayne's countenance demonstrated the displeasure for this chore. It seemed that she did not want to be there any longer than she had to.

Elayne continued, "If only I could change this gritty water without having to climb up and down those stairs, I am sure I could finish much quicker."

The jailor thought for a moment. In his resourcefulness, he made a self-satisfying suggestion.

"If you dump the dirty water in the canal and draw clean water, it will save you the trip up the stairs. You can finish in no time," the jailor said smugly.

Elayne looked at him as though he was the most enlightened man that she had ever met.

"Yes, that would do it. It would be a big help," agreed Elayne.

The jailor then he reached for his keys with pride as if he had solved the riddle of the ages.

"Hurry it up then," the jailor said abruptly.

He witnessed the young girl pick up her bucket. In turn he walked to the closed gate with his keys. He opened the padlock on the gate to allow Elayne to enter the canal area. Elayne did not feel comfortable in the presence of the jailor.

"I will be back shortly. Be quick about it!" he reminded.

"Oh, yes! Thank you, sir. Ever so much, thank you!" Elayne told him.

Now that Elayne had access to the canal she promptly went to the waterway and dumped her bucket of dirty water. Elayne reached in and drew a cleaner bucket of water for cleaning, but all the while she was looking around. She did see two boats, small boats. They were turned over. With the dust and spider webs in the surroundings it did not look as if either had been used in a long time. Apparently by the odor in the air, a coat of linseed oil mixed with animal fat was applied to one of the boat's hulls and was drying. It seemed that the boat was being readied for next spring. A little further down the canal, there was light coming from outside the castle tower walls. Elayne looked down and sure enough there was an iron grate blocking the entrance to the tower. She thought to herself, 'how was anyone to escape from this place?'

Since Elayne saw all that she could see today, she thought that she should leave before the jailor got suspicious. She rinsed her mop once more and dumped the water in her bucket into the canal. Not too far away in a lower level cell an observant prisoner asked his roommate what the name of the princess was at Rothaynen. He was informed that it was Elayne. As she was about to rush out of the lower south tower foundations, she heard a voice call her name.

"Elayne. Elayne," whispered Calogerus.

She stopped in her tracks and wondered who it was that was calling her. What is more, why would anyone suspect her of being Elayne? What would Elayne be doing there, and she was in disguise too?

"Elayne!" Calogerus called boldly.

"Quiet," she replied, "do you want everyone to know who I am?"

Calogerus knew that she was alone for the moment. Mattews was astonished. In the cell he looked closely at Calogerus. Elayne climbed down the stairs to the lower level and discovered locked cell doors.

"How did you know that Elayne was down here in the south tower foundation?" Mattews asked him.

"I did not know that Elayne was here. I just knew that the princess was here. It was you that furnished me with her name," Calogerus explained.

Calogerus had cleared the matter up quickly. Mattews was amazed and made note of the incident. He thought to himself, 'how could he have known?'

Elayne managed to find their cell door. It was the same place that Lucio stood in days earlier when she heard him there. She found Calogerus and Mattews sharing a jail cell. Neither was familiar to her as she had never seen them before. It was unusual for Elayne to hear her name called from such as dismal place. She was supposed to be in disguise too. Apparently, the jailor paired up these two prisoners for some sport. He was not given specific orders to keep these two apart, so he jailed them together and planned on giving a smaller portion of food to them. He wanted to see the old man get pummeled by the young one so they would fight to the death namely over scraps of food. Then the survivor would be executed for murder. Instead, the devious plan failed. The two men shared the smaller portions of food equally and respectfully. The jailor thought that it was a matter of time before they would fight.

"Princess Elayne, you do not know who I am but it is very important that I speak to King Graedon," Calogerus told her.

Elayne approached the cell door and listened. She thought to test the captives.

"I suppose you are innocent and wish the king's audience so justice may be done," Elayne said.

"I was sent by King Jonquis and Queen Ellen of Craigroyston on a diplomatic mission," started Calogerus.

At that moment Calogerus had a premonition. It was when he mentioned Jonquis and Enyja. Something was amiss at Norsendan Castle. Calogerus sensed that something serious happened and an eerie feeling came over him. He wanted to return home to his king and queen. He did not enjoy being jailed and the uncertainty that came with it. With the trip he took to get to Braemar and his present accommodations, Calogerus reasoned that the strange feeling must be the result of the added stress that he was under. He concentrated deeply and sensed that there were still two monarchs in Craigroyston. One was from the house of Roysford, the other from Craigton. At least that fact was a relief.

At that instant the sound of the jailor returning scared Elayne. She thought that there was no way that she could explain being in the lower level of the jail. Elayne quietly rushed down the corridor to a dark unlit part and hid inside a door well with her back up to the door. She listened as the guard or jailor walked about and then sat down at his post. After a good quarter sandglass she heard him snoring and she carefully returned to the jail cell.

"If you are a diplomat, then what are you doing in jail then?" Elayne whispered nervously.

She was concerned about the jailor awakening. Calogerus regained his composure and answered.

"It was Vanessa and Lucio who put me here, in fact, they put your good Pastor Mattews here too," Calogerus claimed.

"Pastor Mattews?" Elayne repeated.

She had heard that name before. Of course Elayne remembered, he once used to serve as the Cardinal's assistant at St. Zorren's Church.

"And your name, sir?" asked Elayne.

"Calogerus," he replied.

"What did you do to get yourself arrested? I thought by virtue of your being a diplomat you had special rights in the absence of treason of course," questioned Elayne.

Elayne was well aware of protocol when it came to matters of state. She was welcomed and encouraged in this area by her father King Graedon.

"Believe me, it does not take much to get arrested," interrupted Mattews, "I came to warn Graedon of the treachery at Wendover."

"Wendover!" Elayne said with concern, "what has happened there?"

Elayne remembered that Brandyn, the new knight whom she had helped escape from Lucio's wrath was returning to Wendover. Elayne could relate to the plight of these two prisoners given who was running matters at Braemar Castle. Naturally, she reasoned, the good people would be silenced and jailed. The world was being turned upside down. Lucio recruited the cut throats and emptied the jails of them so they could serve him as spies and assassins and do his bidding.

"I fear for the king's subjects at Wendover. Chadryn and the king's soldiers tried to kill me. There were soldiers scurrying about everywhere. I do not know what else has taken place," informed Mattews.

"Dear Princess, we need to speak to your father," Calogerus reaffirmed.

"I am afraid that my father may not be able to help. By the way Calogerus, my father would never mistreat anyone let alone the envoy of a friendly neighbor. I could inform King Graedon, but there is little that he could do at this time. I fear his health is in jeopardy let alone his kingdom. Even if he was over his ailment, I fear that my good father is no longer with the favor of the nobles and the army," Elayne confessed.

"What ailment?" asked Calogerus "tell me more of the king's affliction?"

The jailor stirred and Elayne believed that she should go now that he was still asleep.

"I will return," she assured them both.

Elayne got away from the cell door and climbed to the jailor's level. She then climbed the large stone stairway that led to the locked door. She hid in the shadows and waited for the signal from Sean as planned. It was quite some time before the faint knock came to the door. As Elayne made her way back to her chamber, she thought that she must know more about Mattews and Calogerus and what had happened at Wendover.

A Dark Veil

The matters at Braemar Castle were not improving for Graedon and Elayne. Ornelda was sent with a message for Barton but she was caught. Elayne did not know about Ornelda's capture and that she was held in Vanessa's chambers in the lower extremities of the castle. Apparently she was betrayed by Sean, the king's page in the castle staff. However, Sean did not betray her directly. As soon as Sean made arrangements, at Elayne's request, for a horse for Ornelda to ride, word got out at the black smith's shop. Ornelda was given her horse. Word was given to open the main gate of Braemar to allow her to leave. She was allowed to leave the castle as anyone watching could witness. However, shortly after getting onto the north shore road, Ornelda was stopped by two men that were sent riding ahead to intercept her in the brush. One of the men had a cart situated in the middle of the road. He feigned that he was having trouble. Ornelda was forced to stop her horse and inquire about what was amiss. Out of the trees another man grabbed her horse. Ornelda made a valiant effort to defend herself as her horse bucked. The blow to her head however, rendered her unconscious and she was quietly returned in the wagon to Braemar Castle via the north gate.

At that time in the cold winter night, there was little chance that anyone would be watching. If some0ne happened to be watching, the two men sent to apprehend Ornelda had draped a tarp over her and tied her horse to the wagon. They rode to the north gate in no hurry. They looked like two merchants returning late, bringing their wares. After they entered the castle, Ornelda was taken to the dungeon. The deed was cloaked under the dark of night. Lucio did not let Elayne know that Ornelda had been taken prisoner or that he knew of their plan to alert Barton. Elayne was not informed so she would continue to feel at ease. In fact Elayne still believed that Ornelda was well on her way to Petrinvincit Castle to summon Lord Barton to their cause.

Ornelda was taken to a lower hall in the castle that Vanessa occupied as a private chamber. It was a large dungeon cell that Vanessa kept locked and only she had the key. Ornelda was exclusively at the mercy of Vanessa herself. There were chains bolted to the wall of the dungeon.

Vanessa had Ornelda shackled with her hands above her head and gagged her mouth. When Ornelda revived from the blow to her head, she was beaten unconsciously with a whip. Then she was unshackled and brought down onto a cross. Her arms and legs were tied to the cross and she was raised upright when the cross was anchored into a hole in the stone floor.

Vanessa knew that Ornelda had not liked her from the moment she made her appearance at Braemar Castle. Ornelda's influence with the princess and the ladies at court was moral and it was strong. Ornelda had a manner of blending humor into her wise quips that informally educated those who were in higher lot than she. For this, Vanessa wanted to make her as uncomfortable as possible. Ornelda sensed that Vanessa was no good before. She did not need proof. Now she had the proof. Somehow Ornelda could sense the evil in Vanessa from the moment she arrived at Braemar Castle. Unfortunately, now she was trapped and at her mercy.

Vanessa had surmised that Elayne was suspicious of her and Lucio, but the letter intended for Lord Barton left no doubt about how clever she was. Vanessa learned that there were servants so faithful to Graedon and his daughter in the castle that they could not be bought. They were willing and ready to help the 'poor princess'. Vanessa wondered how loyal they would be at the end of a hot iron. Vanessa became even more suspicious of anyone that was not sworn to her or Lucio. In the terrible ordeal, Ornelda bravely insulted her captor because she was sure that Vanessa would kill her in the end. It was her hope that she die before she could be humiliated senselessly. Ornelda mustered all her energy to tell Vanessa how she felt about her. She had never used profane language before.

"You whore! You filthy, blood-sucking whore!" Ornelda said with hate.

Vanessa kept calm. To keep Ornelda from speaking her sharp wit, Vanessa had an idea. She arose from her veiled seat of judgment and walked toward a nearby table. She took an apple from a plate of fruit on the table in the room and went to her.

"You must be hungry," Vanessa acknowledged.

Ornelda had not eaten or drank at all since the supper before she was captured. She was tired and her head was sore. Ornelda was kept with her hands tied above her head on that thick wooden beam.

Vanessa shoved the apple in her mouth. Juice sprayed out and ran down her face. It was most uncomfortable for Ornelda. The apple held her jaw open. As hungry and thirsty as she was, she could not shut her mouth. She tried to draw back some of the juice but could not. She could not even lift her head to acquire some of the juice of that fruit. She would have devoured the apple before anyone took it from her if she could, but could not. Then Vanessa tied a kerchief around her mouth to keep it firmly in place. The apple was lodged so deep in Ornelda's mouth that the kerchief was an unnecessary formality. Vanessa called her a pig to notes of laughter coming from her servants. Ornelda's saliva ran out of her open mouth onto her chin and dripped on her clothes. With being tied up and gagged with her mouth opened, Ornelda became thirstier and more anxious as well. Vanessa gained vengeance over Ornelda but she was not through with her yet.

Vanessa introduced Chelle and two other local girls who were gathered from the countryside. They were under Vanessa's influence and did her bidding. These girls had been cast out from their respective families and communities. They lived as cast down undesirables and were denied work. They were put down and labeled the undesirable. No one would have their company. Like everyone else though, they needed food, clothing, a place to stay and acceptance, so Vanessa took them in. She took them in but then schooled them in the art of pleasure and service to mankind. Concocted elixirs were introduced to these girls that brought about unimaginable pleasure, but then at the end of their potency brought about unspeakable pain and horror. The girls became dependent on the elixir. They were enslaved by the elixir. But alas Vanessa would have the next batch of the concoction ready for them so they could continue their work.

When pestilence found its way to the young girls and inflicted itself upon them, it was not notable immediately. The infected girls could spread the infliction without taking note themselves. They would come into contact with many men until they were no longer desirable. It seemed that the day that they would no longer be young and desirable was far away, but one moment at a time that day came. In the meantime the pestilence would spread to unsuspecting lives and bring unsolicited suffering. When the girls' own beauty finally faded, and nothing remained since their self esteem was long cast aside, they were on their own. Those, who could not scratch out a living, turned to the mercy of the church for meals and cast off clothing. For the girls that suffered from the pestilence, only death would free them. It was Vanessa's way and it was so easy to dispose of these girls long thought dead to their own kin with no one to claim them for their own.

Vanessa offered them a chance to take revenge on a society that had discarded them like a basin of dirty water. The girls gathered quite a following especially among the ranks of the army. There was no need for the soldiers to court and marry. The soldiers could find comfort with any of these girls whenever they desired very cheaply. They could have their pick and could change girls too, whatever their salary or savings afforded. Deep in the heart of each girl kindled wrath and contempt for the men that they served and manipulated. There was no love behind their ways, but plenty of love making. The fallen girls became each of them unto the other like sisters and disciples of Vanessa. The girls were turned away from family, the ways of the church and God. There was a new god now. There seemed to be a competition for who could please Vanessa the most. The girls conformed and competed to please Vanessa and make her happy. Those who failed or fell ill were looked down on and passed over. Those who were in the way were not missed when they were found absent.

It was late that evening so the girls awoke from their rest and anticipated the work of the night. Chelle, who was Vanessa's most apt pupil, was indifferent and merely smiled when Vanessa told her that Keveyn was dead. Chelle did not respond despite her former attachment to the prominent young knight. Her only desire was the elixir that she depended on. Chelle appeared and led two other girls into the chamber. Mandy and Ashleigh were scantily dressed. Chelle came across to where Ornelda was tied and looked at her condescendingly. Here was a prim and proper dame of the court. The fallen girl put her arms around Ornelda and took her face in her hands. Chelle raised her head upright and supported it. It was very tiring to be tied up and confined in that uncomfortable position. Who could remember how long that apple was lodged in her jaw?

She reached around her head and untied the kerchief that gagged her. Chelle then carefully pulled out the apple from her mouth and let it drop to the stone floor.

Ornelda was grateful for the relief to her jaw. Her jaw was very sore and she could not readily close it. She could not rub her jaw to favor and bring relief to it. Chelle took her slender fingers and rubbed the apple juice that ran down from her mouth all over Ornelda's face. It felt good that the muscle and nerves in her jaw were being favored, but then Chelle licked her face sensually. Chelle then abruptly put her lips on Ornelda's and kissed her. Ornelda immediately spit at her and shook her head away. She did not appreciate being kissed.

Chelle stepped back and looked at her. Then she took the back of her hand and swung it at Ornelda's face. Her hand caught Ornelda's face square on and it turned her head aside. She quickly slapped her again and then again. Chelle then grabbed her head and kissed her again. Ornelda resisted the best that she could. Chelle did not like her victim's lack of compliance. She punched her in the stomach to make sure that she was more submissive. Ornelda bent her head over in pain. Mandy on the other hand, appeared to take pity and came to Ornelda's aid.

"Maybe we should get her down. What do you say, Mandy?" said Ashleigh.

'Get her down', she heard. Ornelda thought that this was her chance to escape. Once they got her down off that cross, she would leash out against her captors with all the remaining strength that she could muster. She would subdue them and run for the door. If she failed she thought that at least she would force them to kill her. Ornelda believed that there were things far worse than death. There were tools close by on a table. There were leather whips of different sizes. These instruments were used to scourge victims. These instruments were in plain sight. Ornelda thought that she could grab the large whip and turn it on their scantily dressed backs. She planned to scream if she could. Surely someone would hear her. Now was her chance she thought. She would not have a better one.

What Chelle meant by getting Ornelda down however was not off the cross but lifting the cross out and laying it down. When she realized that she would not have the opportunity to do what she planned, she fell into despair. The cross was set into the stone a good foot and a half. With the help of Mandy and Ashleigh, they lifted the cross up and out of its base, and let it fall to the ground. Face down the victim fell with the heavy cross on her back. At this point Ornelda could not even scream. Ornelda merely relived in her mind the steps that brought her to this point.

The Bride to Be

What young maiden does not appreciate and look forward to her wedding day?

The notion conjures up many wonderful thoughts such as a commitment of true love. It makes the assumption that an anticipating bride and groom would profess their love for one another before God and family and friends. The ladies of the court continued their ritual of meeting to exchange harmless gossip. Since the advent of Vanessa however the gossip became more and more personal and meaner. Now all that malleable information was channeled to Vanessa's ears. There was cruel intent with some of the gossip that came out. Some of the ladies that were once respectful toward Princess Elayne now scoffed at her and showed indifference. They seemed to sense that the royal family was no longer in charge anymore. It is in these times and such occasions that one learns who is truly worthy. By this time however it is too late. The allegiance of some people is like a reed in the wind. The problem at Braemar was that it was the wrong wind.

All the niceties at court amount to nothing if sincerity and looking after others well being is not behind them. It was obvious to many that King Graedon was absent and no longer in charge of his kingdom. The king's painful ailment left his mind clouded and left him incapable of ruling. The man could not get out of bed. Some of the ladies at court were ready to snap at Elayne to prove their new resolve. They acted like enraged hens fighting for the last grain of corn in the mud. Vanessa preferred matters this way. It made for easy management of the ladies when each was competing for the same table scrap. With the return of Morden and his cohorts to Braemar, there were some new faces in the group. Apparently the rumor was that Morden was to be wed. His betrothed and her mother had joined the court at Braemar Castle.

From the start Elayne noted that for a bride to be, Meaghan was not overwhelmingly happy. In fact she was not happy at all. Elayne noted that Meaghan was a good, gentle person and yet there was something that was troubling her. Elayne had been familiar with her name. She had heard her name spoken before. Then when Meaghan and her mother, Andrea, were introduced as coming from Wendover, Elayne remembered Brandyn. It might just be his sister and mother that were in her midst. Andrea and Meaghan were overwhelmed with all the questions that the ladies of the court asked. With all those questions being asked it felt more like an interrogation to Andrea and Meaghan. With each question, the ladies tone and demeanor grew more and more condescending. Despite Sir Morden being the intended groom, the ladies of the court seemed to have little respect for the country cousin and her mother that came from Wendover. The manner in which they dressed spoke volumes of their lot. Elayne for her part remained quiet and observant.

That evening, Elayne left her chamber after hours to go to Andrea and Meaghan's chamber. She waited for the guards outside her door to do their rounds. There would be just enough time to slip out unnoticed. It got late because Elayne waited for her chamber guards to fall asleep before she left. The guest wing of the castle was on the floor below the princess' chamber. Elayne merely walked down her hall to the set of stairs that led her to the guest chambers. Elayne stood a moment to listen at the door. On the other side of the door Meaghan was still awake. Although she was fatigued, she could not sleep. Her mother, Andrea, was fast asleep and tired under the weight of their whole ordeal.

Andrea sold her tavern and left her home at Wendover. Then there was the dilemma that her daughter was in. Andrea had prayed to God for wisdom and guidance on how to handle this ordeal that she was in. So far all that she could do was done. Meaghan was frustrated. She positively hated Morden and yet she was pregnant with his child. Meaghan's thoughts were about her Woodcroft. She felt ashamed of her condition. It was Woodcroft, her true love that she had yearned for. To have been in his arms was the only thing that she wanted. Not even his death kept thoughts of him away from her.

There came a knock on the door. It was a gentle knock. It was nothing like the firm knocks that came to call them for their meals. The knocking startled Meaghan. Although the chamber was more than adequate compared to a jail or dungeon, Meaghan felt captive in this room. She learned that a person did not have to be in irons or confined to a cell to feel trapped. The knocking came again. She asked herself, what would anyone want at this late hour?

Meaghan collected herself and climbed down from her bed and pulled her tunic across her chest. She went to the door and listened. The knock came again. Elayne did not risk knocking harder to avoid alerting the guards that made their rounds in the castle corridors.

"Who's there?" asked Meaghan softly.

"It is Elayne. I have come to speak to you," whispered Elayne.

Meaghan took the key ring hanging on the wall. It was strange to pick up the key. The locked door was supposed to protect the inhabitants of the chamber and allow them to come and go as they pleased. It seemed like Andrea and Meaghan were at liberty to come and go. However, when and where could they go?

It would not have been different if they did not have a key at all. Their movements in the castle would be monitored relentlessly. Meaghan put the key into the lock. She turned the key and unlocked the mechanism. Meaghan hesitated a little because she was not sure that Elayne was alone. Then she pulled back the heavy oak door a little and was relieved to see that indeed it was the princess and that she was alone.

"Come in your majesty," Meaghan greeted.

Elayne entered the room quickly. She shut and locked the door behind her quickly and quietly.

"We need to talk," Elayne pressed urgently.

"If I am not mistaken, you and your mother are related to the new, young knight, Brandyn," started Elayne.

"He is my brother," replied Meaghan, "and there asleep is our mother Andrea."

"Do not disturb your mother. I came because I could not speak freely to you at supper in the king's hall. You will have to excuse my rudeness, but court is not the same since my father took ill.

"I do not trust everyone, so I cannot trust anyone for fear someone will betray my trust for small favors. I knew that you were Brandyn's sister, I met your brother when I helped him escape from Braemar Castle to return to Wendover," Elayne told her.

"Brandyn spoke very kindly of you, your majesty. He was grateful for your help escaping from Lucio," confided Meaghan.

"Then he did make it safely back to Wendover?" questioned Elayne.

"Yes, your majesty, but then he set out to see his girl and we never heard from him again. April and her mother came to the town the next morning and said that Brandyn never got there," Meaghan told her.

Elayne was saddened to hear this and she paused to collect her thoughts. Brandyn, the new knight, she thought was probably killed at Wendover. Elayne was truly saddened by the thought.

"I am afraid that Lucio and his mother have undermined my father's kingdom. There are a lot of strange things going on in Braemar Castle and no doubt Wendover.

"In our own castle, there are tapping noises, howls heard in the wind and shadows that appear and disappear. It is as though a dark veil has shrouded the castle," Elayne told her trustingly.

"Who is this Lucio? Why does he have so much influence on things?" Meaghan asked.

"If I may answer that question with a question, why are you marrying Morden?" Elayne asked directly.

With that question she answered Meaghan's question. Meaghan looked away with shame and hopelessness. She was pregnant, out of wedlock due to that savage animal. Morden did not love her. It was only his desire to take her for his pleasure that was responsible for her situation. Meaghan felt guilty as though she was to blame for her condition. With the change in Meaghan's demeanor and the look on her face, Elayne guessed the worst.

"You are with his child," Elayne said.

"It was not my will or fault," Meaghan said with agitation, "I did not want anything to do with that—"

Meaghan could not speak the word that she wanted. Elayne reached across to Meaghan and embraced her like a sister.

"I know that you would never want anything to do with that cold, heartless animal," affirmed Elayne.

Meaghan broke into tears.

"I was in love. I was in love with Woodcroft. He was a knight from Galles. He loved me too. He told me. He respected me and I yearned to be his wife so that I would bear him children. Look at me now. I am with a child: Morden's child," confessed Meaghan.

Meaghan spoke in short sentences, sobbing in between. Elayne knew Woodcroft and was happy for him when he had found his true love in Meaghan, the very girl she spoke to.

"You could not report the attack on you to the authority because Morden was the authority. How could any woman in those circumstances attain justice?" Elayne summed.

Meaghan found comfort knowing that Elayne understood and empathized with her. Elayne understood all right. She realized that it was the same fate that Lucio planned for her. After he married her as a matter of the public record, the usurping of power was bonafide legally. Elayne understood that once Lucio was married to her and she bore him an heir, her own life would be of no consequence anymore. Elayne's usefulness would wane and she too could be poisoned like her father or worse. At least Elayne made a friend of Meaghan and she knew that she could trust her. Elayne fully realized the implications of her own captivity. Although it seemed hopeless, she just had to escape this fate. Elayne pinned her hope on Ornelda delivering her message to Lord Barton. Ornelda, she thought, would be back within a matter of days with help.

Petrinvincit Welcomes a Friend

Far off the coast from the fortress of Petrinvincit, the lookouts spied on the horizon out at sea. A warship was spotted approaching the shores of Teresforte. Coming from the north, the lookouts could not see any markings on the sail. The watchman blew a horn and word was immediately sent to Lord Barton. When he arrived and saw the ship he recognized the sail. He was certain that it was from Craigroyston, but he kept the garrison on alert. Within the quarter sandglass when it was ascertained that the lone ship was indeed from Craigroyston, Barton ordered a welcoming party to the docks. He intended to greet the ally when he arrived. To Lord Barton's delight, it was Selwyck who captained the ship. He was greeted cheerfully by Lord Barton.

"It seems that repairs were made to the Courage," remarked Barton, "she appears to look anew."

"Greetings, Lord Barton! Sturdy she is at that. She would have to be for travel this late in the season," replied Selwyck.

"Is there some matter of urgency, something pressing that brings you here to us so late in the sailing season?" asked Barton.

"Calogerus, our high councilor was sent to Braemar on matters from my lieges. I am merely here to collect him and return him home for Christmas festivities," Selwyck informed.

"Then you and your mariners will be my guests at Petrinvincit until you meet with him for your journey home. Come, it is still early enough for breakfast," invited Barton.

"We have already eaten our breakfast ration, but sailing in those cold gales worked up quite an appetite. My men will be happy to join your table after the ship is properly attended," accepted Selwyck.

Despite the mooring chore that awaited them, the look on Selwyck's men was rather a happy one as they anticipated a more complete hot meal sitting at a table in a warm hall.

The accommodations were most generous as Barton welcomed this friend and hero who saved Graedon's forces and Wendover from falling into Huynsten hands. Selwyck's bravery that day bordered on madness, but Barton believed the Huynstens would have secured a beachhead that day if it were not for him. In fact the Huynstens would have secured more than a beachhead that day. This dutiful young sea captain had saved Wendover from falling under Huynsten influence. Before winter, Graedon's castle would have been overrun with the juggernaut enemy and Christmas would have a new connotation for Rothaynen.

At Barton's table, the fried pork, eggs and bread cakes were a favorite among his sailors. Selwyck started to wonder why it was taking so long to hear from Calogerus. At this point Selwyck thought that Calogerus should have well been finished his meeting with King Graedon, set out for Galles to speak to Welledon and made his way to Petrinvincit to complete his diplomacy with Barton. He thought that perhaps it took Calogerus longer than he thought to cover the distance from Roysford to Braemar. It would not hurt to wait a few more days, but the seas were getting more treacherous and the temperature was dropping too. Selwyck knew that King Jonquis and Queen Enyja were expecting Calogerus back home to their court for Christmas. If the coastal waters iced, Selwyck's entire crew would be stranded in Teresforte indefinitely.

A Letter from Welledon

It was then that Lord Barton received a sealed letter from Welledon of Galles. The message referred to the wedding invitation that he had received earlier. It was a wedding at Braemar Castle at the King's request for the 27th of December. Lord Barton was planning on visiting his cousin for Christmas anyway. Now he would have to stay on for this wedding. Weddings were happy times and Barton had looked forward to attending a knight's wedding in particular. It was a knight of Rothaynen that was getting married. It was an honor to attend due to the honorable services that a knight performed. It was a stately time of celebration. Barton was somewhat surprised when he realized that Morden was the knight that was getting married. It seemed out of character for him, but then Barton surmised that Cupid was a carefree archer. The arrow of chance had struck Morden in the same fashion as other confirmed bachelors. Perhaps, he thought, that love had conquered him too.

Then there arrived the message from Welledon of Galles. The message from Welledon alarmed Barton. Welledon had confided to Barton the suspicions of Brandyn the young knight. Barton was fully aware of who Brandyn was. You do not forget a brave, dutiful, young knight who saved your life. Since it was the sister of Brandyn that was to be married to Morden, who else would know if there should be something objectionable?

Welledon mentioned in his letter that he was concerned over this wedding feast. Once again an occasion would collect all the nobles and knights from the kingdom of Rothaynen under the roof of the Great Hall at Braemar. It was to be a joyous event to follow Christmas festivities. 'There was a good chance that the merry making would be disarming' the letter read. Welledon did not explain his thoughts with any depth, but Barton surmised what the faithful duke was alluding to.

The last time that the knights from the northern part of the kingdom were present, they unconditionally supported Lucio in every way to the point of fanaticism. These knights were not willing to listen to reason or deliberate over matters. These knights did not have anything to say.

They were simply present and ready to serve Lucio and do his bidding. It was obvious that they supported Lucio. As Barton read on Welledon proposed for Barton to march his army to Marmora and situate it nearby Braemar Castle. Barton thought that this would create suspicion if they were discovered, but he agreed. Barton sent a message back to Welledon suggesting that he increase of the number of his bodyguards when he enters the castle. He also suggested waiting until they met up so they could enter Braemar Castle at the same time. They would cue their bodyguards ahead of time to be alert, stay sober and look out for them both, without arousing suspicion. In the meanwhile both Barton and Welledon's armies would camp a few miles from the castle in case that they were needed. Welledon noted that the December march in the crispy, cold climate would keep the men poised and alert. It was not a popular directive. The soldiers were also looking forward to feasting and celebrating a gentle family time of their own.

It was during the supper that evening that Barton and Selwyck talked over matters. Lord Barton trusted Selwyck implicitly despite serving the Kingdom of Craigroyston. Selwyck's concern over Calogerus was well founded. He knew that Calogerus was not one to procrastinate when something had to be done. There was more than enough time for Calogerus to have achieved his goal. Selwyck now wondered whether Calogerus made it safely to his destination at all. Selwyck confided his concern to Barton. Barton was not surprised with the loyalty and caring that Selwyck had for his monarchs and his friend.

Selwyck told Barton that the message that Calogerus was going to relay to Graedon was that Craigroyston would aid Rothaynen with establishing a navy of its own. Then as a matter of principle and respect, Calogerus was to inform Lord Welledon and Lord Barton. Selwcyk told Barton this: 'there was nothing else that would make Calogerus linger or that required more time'. It was a simple message that required Graedon to arrange and send a party of negotiators to Craigroyston. There negotiations to coordinate the building of a new navy would take place. Selwyck believed that Calogerus was confident with his method of travel and no one was more skilled in the wild as he. So where was he?

With the message that Welledon had sent and the plan that Selwyck revealed, there was all of a sudden a reason to be concerned over Calogerus' whereabouts. Selwyck invited Barton to come with him and proposed to sail the Courage up the River Brae as far as he safely could. In that way if Calogerus was there, he could board the Courage and they would be home bound sooner. If things were as Welledon and Barton feared, then a warship in the vicinity could lend support and would give Lucio's forces something else to think about. A warship could discharge fiery catapults to counter those from the castle. Selwyck suggested that supplies that were normally brought on horseback could be loaded on the Courage for quick transport. In this way the burden on horseback would be saved in the deep snow. The courage could not only be used as a depot but a more comfortable command post for Barton and Welledon. Something told Selwyck that he and his crew would not be back in Craigroyston in time for Christmas. Lord Barton had the same feeling as the army was put on alert and half of his force would accompany him to set up camp in Marmora within the sights of Braemar Castle.

In the east of Marmora by the River Brae was the ideal place to position the army. There were rolling hills and patches of forest and fruit trees that could provide some cover. The cover would have been better realized in summer when the leaves provided more complete cover, but in mid December that advantage was not realized. Although there was safety among the rolling hills, their presence did not escape the keen eyes of the scouts at Braemar Castle. However Barton's army had access to water, supplies were easily accessible on the Courage and Barton could communicate from the comfort of the ship. Unfortunately, the size of his army was easily spotted from Braemar Castle. That was one reason that the king's castle was strategically located in its place. If Lucio should become suspicious and asked about the army camp before Braemar Castle, Barton planned to explain that a relief effort was taking place in Marmora. It was highly unlikely that Marmora required relief, but Lucio would have to call Barton a liar. For appearances sake Lucio could not risk calling Barton a liar again, not before the wedding anyway.

Since Selwyck invited Barton to sail along with him in the Courage, the army of Petrinvincit in the field was left with Dosco. Dosco was an efficient, worthy knight who cared very little about appearances. Dosco's armor might have looked dull, but his mind was not. He was a virtuous, dutiful man who held the safety of his soldiers in high regard. All that was left to do was alert Welledon with the new development in plans. Barton then called for Marius. He elected to send Marius, who was the fine, young knight from Marmora. Lucio had planned to win Marius to himself, but regardless of the lure of authority and popularity he could not be made to serve an unscrupulous master. Marius could not serve Lucio as he discovered at the tournament.

Marius rode out and informed Welledon of Barton's movement. The message was that 'upon receiving his message, Welledon should set out for Braemar Castle'. Barton instructed that they would meet before Braemar Castle on the Eve of Christmas. It was an ambitious time table as Welledon would have to hurry, but as long as he and his body guards arrived on Christmas Eve, the greater part of his army could follow shortly thereafter. With any luck they would all arrive at Braemar on time. Together they stood a better chance in case there was a problem.

A Royal Visit

Elayne could not get away to visit the prisoners. It was three days since Mattews and Calogerus saw her last. Elayne was rather worried about Ornelda whom she sent with the message for Lord Barton. Elayne lost hope for the plan to get her father in a boat and sail into Thermanden Bay. Despite the threat of the cold water in open view, Graedon was too frail to go anywhere. Elayne doubted that she could get Graedon to the lower level of the south tower without someone informing Lucio. Elayne did not mention to her father that he had a visitor from Craigroyston. She felt that her father would confront Lucio about it. In the end it would be too much for him to worry about in his frail condition. Elayne thought that if she could help Mattews and Calogerus, they might be able to help her and her father.

When Elayne came to their cell door, Calogerus went up to it. Elayne explained how she could not return earlier. She told Calogerus and Mattews that she did not inform her father of their presence. Calogerus understood that the matter in Graedon's castle was serious. Mattews also understood matters full well. Graedon was not responsible for what happened at Wendover. Mattews considered what the princess was up against and had an idea of his own. Mattews thought that if Elayne could send word to Brother Michael at the Bendire Monastery, he could quietly send some brothers in a boat to the south tower docks. All they had to do was set a time. Once the monks got in, they could overpower the jailor and his guards. Then it dawned on Mattews, it would be known who rescued them and the brother's at the monastery would be blamed. If Graedon was found in the monastery, they would take him back. Then who knew what actions Lucio would take against the brothers in the monastery?

It was not a good plan.

Calogerus asked Elayne if she could get a blacksmith's hammer. He realized full well the danger that Elayne would be in if she got caught, and so did she. Elayne thought that she could trust her father's page. Sean was the same person that she trusted to help Ornelda get on her way. Sean had made the arrangements for getting Ornelda a horse from the blacksmith shop within the castle walls. Although Sean was trustworthy, the blacksmith's assistant was not. It was Ted, the large blacksmith that sent word to Lucio about the sudden need for a horse at that late hour. With the capture of Ornelda and Elayne's letter to Lord Barton, Lucio of course rewarded Ted handsomely. Ted continued to keep his eyes and ears in the service of Lucio. He also kept his mouth shut.

To save time Elayne would go out to the blacksmith shop by herself. She found Sean and asked him to come with her. She told Sean that she wished to take a horse ride in the country. When they got to the blacksmith, Sean asked for two horses to be ready for a ride in the country. It was cold out and the snow had collected considerably. The snow now blanketed the entire ground and the tree branches. The scenery around Braemar Castle was breathtaking. While Sean was communicating Elayne's wishes, she was busy looking for a hammer that she could hide in her robes. Ted the blacksmith sent his assistant away and in no time Lucio himself appeared. He had been informed of the Princess Elayne's wish and came to investigate.

"Is there anything that we can do for you, your majesty?" Lucio asked.

He was still rather disappointed at the princess's sprained ankle but not discouraged.

"Lucio, it is my wish to get out on horseback and ride around the castle for some fresh air," Elayne told him.

"Your majesty, you had a recent sprain. I must insist against this idea. It is very dangerous to be riding out today. The weather is extremely cold, and there are hungry wolves ever on the prowl for food. You need a proper escort of men," Lucio insisted.

"It would not be very far. I just wanted to get out for a short ride," Elayne replied, "perhaps you might be willing to escort me for a short ride, if you are not too burdened with matters of state?"

Lucio was beside himself. Here was Elayne now asking him to escort her on a ride. It was the second occurrence in as many days.

"Well, your majesty, I may be able to get away for a short ride," Lucio accepted.

Lucio thought that this might be the opportunity of winning Elayne over to himself if they were alone on a quiet winter's day. It was cold, but the wind was calm and the sun shone. It was a good idea to be alone with Elayne for a while, he thought.

"Good, then summon an escort to be ready promptly. It is cold out and I shall need a heavier blanket," Elayne said, "come along Sean."

Lucio was not happy that Elayne expected an escort to be arranged. It was Lucio though, who said that there were wolves out there. Elayne knew that he was one of them. Elayne then turned and abruptly left the blacksmith shop. Her mission was accomplished. She managed to locate and steal a small hammer. Elayne fixed the hammer to hang on her belt under her shawl. She discovered the hammer well away from the blacksmith's immediate work area. Elayne took it while the blacksmith sent his assistant away. She thought that he might not miss it, if he did not realize that it was gone in the first place. Elayne led Sean toward the castle kitchen door and they both entered. Lucio approved of the preparation of the horses and went to give instructions to the escort riders. After entering the kitchen, Elayne changed her clothes to those of a servant. She quickly went to the dungeon with the hammer placed inside a bucket with a wash rag, soapy water and vinegar. She also took a mop and a broom with her.

In the dungeon her expectations were not working as she anticipated. John, the jailor, confronted her with her return.

"What is there to clean today?" he asked abruptly, "you cleaned the floor just the other day."

"Yes, but I was told to sweep the walls and wash the doors as well," Elayne said humbly.

"Should you not have swept the walls and washed the doors before washing the floor then?" asked John.

"I had not thought of that, but then they never told me," replied Elayne.

"No wonder they give you the worst jobs. Look at dust and the spider webs up there on the beams. When you clean them, they will mess up walls and the ground again. Do you call that cleaning?" asked John.

Elayne feigned looking humble and sorry. She did not say another word. Elayne even thought about crying a tear. John was out of sorts this day, but when he saw the young maiden pouting, he relented.

"Now, now, fine then, he paused, "you can do your cleaning."

With that Elayne wiped her eyes as if she had drawn tears. Then she wrung out the wash rag in the bucket. The soap suds hid the hammer that lay on the bottom of the bucket. She then proceeded to wash the heavy oak doors. John had been suspicious about the maidens cleaning detail, but now he could see for himself. Elayne added vinegar to the soapy water that was plain to sense with the nose. Cleaning with a little vinegar was a common tradition among people that took their cleaning seriously.

After Elayne washed down the doors she asked John if he could unlock the doors so she could wash the other side of them. Since Elayne was convincing in her cleaning role, John obliged her with the empty cell doors, but instructed her to leave the doors of occupied cells. After he unlocked the empty cells, he remembered something and left on another errand. After he was gone, Elayne immediately went to the cell where Calogerus and Mattews occupied and opened the bolt to the small door used to bring food and drink to the prisoners. She was in a hurry as she did not know when John would return.

"Here, quick," Elayne whispered.

Calogerus was aware that she was there. He quickly received the small hammer that Elayne pulled out of the soapy water.

"Well done. Now get away," Calogerus instructed her.

Elayne closed and bolted the small door. Then she swiftly wiped up the spilled water with her mop and spread it out on the ground to dry. She then took the bucket with dirty water and ran up the stairs. Sean waited nervously at the door at the top of the stairs. Lucio he thought might send someone. Sean was happy to hear the knock. Elayne then rushed to the kitchen and removed her cleaning apparel and ran up the stairs to her room.

Worth Waiting For

In the time it took for Elayne to get the hammer to Calogerus and Mattews, the horses had been made ready and Lucio and his cohorts waited. Apparently Lucio was not a patient man. Lucio had sent his cohort Tim to call on Elayne. Elayne had changed out of her servant's attire and raced up the stairs. She went up the stairs to the corridor that led to her room. When Elayne got to the top of the stairs, she walked hurriedly to her room. The guards stationed outside her door opened her chamber door for her. It was not a moment too soon as someone was coming up the stairs at the other end of the corridor. Elayne peaked out and saw that it was Lucio's cohort coming to call her. She quickly closed the chamber door and went to her mirror to look at her hair. Then the knock came to the door. She picked up her brush but noted that her hair was fine so she placed the brush down and went to the door. When she opened the door she saw that Sean and Tim were waiting for her.

"Lord Lucio sent me along to escort you to him, your majesty," Tim said, "He was worried that your majesty had changed her mind."

"Changed my mind on such a beautiful, bright, crisp, winter day? Nonsense, I was merely making myself more presentable. We should stop wasting time though, let us proceed," Elayne declared.

Tim noticed that Elayne looked very much the same as she did when she left the blacksmith's shop earlier.

When they arrived in the courtyard the horses and riders were ready. Lucio noted that Elayne did not change into warmer apparel. In fact she was dressed in the very same apparel as before. He also noted that the sleeves and other parts of her garment were wet. Lucio reasoned that she probably washed her hands and face to freshen up. Then he noted that her hands had smudges of dirt on them and that they looked like she had been working. It was puzzling to Lucio, but then Elayne was a young girl and prone to doing things that did not make sense. Lucio was upset that he had accomplished nothing after his breakfast that morning. He had agreed to the horse ride but he imagined that Elayne and he would be alone. All this time he waited in the courtyard sitting on his horse. In his experience, Lucio was told that a good woman was worth waiting for. He had often imagined this and believed it too, but you could not tell from the look on his face.

A Plan of Their Own

Calogerus could no longer wait and depend on others to rescue him. His motto was: 'to depend on others was good, but not having to depend on others at all was even better'. Elayne managed to get him a blacksmith's hammer. He did not like leaving things that he could do, for others to do. Other than being missed for Christmas at Craigroyston, no one would know of his true circumstances. By that time it might be too late. Calogerus correctly surmised that no one would be calling for Mattews either. Their escape from the dungeon of Braemar Castle would depend on them. Princess Elayne had graciously helped them enough. Calogerus did not want to involve her anymore. If she got caught she would lose what little freedom she had. She was already under observation and watched closely. Things could certainly get worse for Elayne if Lucio learned that she had helped prisoners in the dungeon.

Calogerus figured that Mattews was a skilled fighter. Despite the accommodations Mattews had somewhat recovered from the attack he incurred at his church. The rest did wonders for his fatigue. After the ordeal at Wendover, the trip he made to Braemar was not easy nor was being jailed in his king's castle. The cold and damp of the dungeon were not helping either man. Calogerus realized that except for the small hammer, not only were they both unarmed, but they were outnumbered as well. There was a frost forming where the water had leaked into the tower foundation. It gave Calogerus an idea. He simply did not like seeing things destroyed but this would be in a good cause, namely his freedom and Mattews. The very next time that the jailor came to the door, he would request a walking stick. He would tell the jailor that it was needed to help him to move about as the dampness in the dungeon cell was making his back and legs stiff. Calogerus would appeal to the jailor's ability to empathize with an old man.

In the mean time Calogerus thought about what facts he did know. Braemar Castle was built on the bank of the bay, where it met the river. Calogerus could tell this from his walk from Bendire Monastery to

Braemar Castle. He could sense that this dungeon cell was below the level of the water. Calogerus was not sure which tower, but this was one of the south towers. Whether it was the east or west tower he could not tell for sure, but the north towers were built along the road that he had taken. It was certain that the cell that they occupied was below the level of the water, but just how low Calogerus was not so certain. He had a plan in case the water level rose above their heads in the cell. In fact he counted on the water level rising high.

Mattews was certain that Calogerus had something on his mind and it was about how to get out. As the time passed, they were interrupted by a sound outside their cell. It sounded like the jailor was coming with their supper. It had to be supper because the last meal was breakfast. There was no dinner at midday when you were in jail. You were at the mercy of those who were responsible for running the jail. If they were late, who could you complain to?

What was to stop them tampering with your fo0d if they pleased? If you were mistreated who cared?

"Tell me good man, would it be possible for you to give an old man a walking stick to help me get about?" asked Calogerus.

The jailor was opening the small door to deliver their meal and broke into laughter.

"Get about! Where? You do not have far to go in that small rat hole!" the jailor snarled.

"It would also allow me to defend myself," Calogerus added in a low voice.

Mattews heard what he had said but merely looked at him. He said nothing. What was his cell mate up to, he thought?

Calogerus continued his appeal for the walking stick by adding to the list of wants. He sounded very childish in his requests and reasoning.

"A walking stick is not that much of a request. And a blanket," added Calogerus, "it is so cold and damp in here, and pumpkin pie. I did not get my piece last time."

The jailor thought that the old man had gone mad but a stick could be used to start the scuffle that he intended to happen. Mattews started to wonder. The jailor replied with sarcasm.

"Pumpkin pie, now? I shall pass your request onto the kitchen." said the jailor.

The men's meals were slid through the small door across the stone floor into their cell. The small door was promptly shut and the latch was bolted. They could hear in the cell, the sound of the jailor's laugh as he walked away with his keys clanking.

"Perhaps you should have asked him for the key to the cell outright so you would not have to bother him in case you wished to take a stroll," Mattews kidded.

"I asked for three things: two practical, one totally unnecessary in his mind. I bet you I get my walking stick," Calogerus said, "now shall we eat?"

Mattews looked over to his companion in prison and it seemed to cheer him up. There was nothing to do for now but eat their meal. With the portion they were given it would not take too long. Calogerus knew that Mattews was a good man who had his hopes and dreams rattled. Calogerus needed to find a way to get him to believe in good and get him involved again.

Prisoner in Her Own Home

Elayne was quite aware of the new order of things at Braemar Castle. The thought of the Christmas season only made things worse as she had enjoyed wonderful times with her mother and father in that castle.

Elayne realized that she could continue her role as the princess so long as she did not interfere with the plans of Lucio. Everywhere she went, she was closely watched. She visited her father often and spent much of her time in his company. Apparently this was satisfactory with those who guarded her father as they knew where she was. When Elayne moved about the castle, it made Lucio's spies nervous as they were responsible to learn of Elayne's every move. It would not do to displease Lucio. When Elayne wanted to contact Calogerus and Mattews, she went to her father's chambers. There she dressed up as a servant and left with Sean when he came to attend the king. Elayne even became fearful of making those visits.

Graedon's condition was getting worse. Graedon was concerned for his daughter's safety. He did not want to see his daughter, the princess, married off against her will. Elayne's happiness meant everything to him. He counseled her to escape and go to Lord Barton's castle at Teresforte. Graedon believed that Elayne would be safe there. He then also realized that Elayne would be equally safe with Welledon in Galles. Both routes posed challenges and were equally perilous but Graedon weighed the danger. Although going to Teresforte was a more direct route with a well traveled road, Elayne would have to cross Marmora. The people of Marmora were gracious but the region was under the jurisdiction of Peregren knights since before King Graedon's time. On the other hand to go toward Galles, Elayne would have to cross the bridge. Either route depended on her first getting out of the Braemar Castle unnoticed. Either route was watched like a hawk.

Despite his delirious state brought on by the toxicant tea, Graedon kept turning ideas in his mind. Barton mentioned going fishing, which he did not particularly enjoy. He thought that he had spoken to Elayne about it but he was not sure. He recalled that there was a means to cross Thermanden Bay without using the bridge at the front. A small boat in the dark could make its way westward over the damned waters toward Marmora. In Marmora Graedon thought that Elayne might find good people who would recognize her and give her assistance in getting to Teresforte. Then Graedon had an even better idea. Elayne could go to the Bendire Monastery and hide there. If the water was totally frozen, then Elayne could actually walk on it. She could slip out and walk around the castle and escape by night. Given that ice had formed along the banks of the river but not yet frozen over, Graedon thought that Elayne should not risk swimming. She could freeze to death in the cold water if her lungs gave out. Graedon was not sure what he had discussed with Elayne and what he did not. Graedon's mind kept wandering from thought to thought. Graedon's mind rambled.

Graedon actually had told Elayne of the escape path in the castle cellar. At one point the circular castle towers faced the outer castle wall. There was an iron grate covering the opening. The grate went down about two good feet below the level of the water. It was possible to bob your body under the grate, and swim outside the castle walls. In that temperature though, you would need to get dry in a hurry. Perhaps heading for the Bendire Monastery was the best idea. Then from there Elayne could travel to Teresforte in disguise or at night. Sometimes you have to go east to go west, he remembered his saying.

The grate was barely noticeable to the eyes when looking upon Braemar castle from across Thermanden Bay. Its presence had been forgotten because it was not used. Apart from the smelt run in early spring there was not as much fishing taking place. The trout stocks were depleted in Thermanden Bay. Stocks of dry salted cod fish were traded by Irminian boatmen at Petrinvincit. From there, about half of that stock was taken by cart to Braemar Castle and provided a source of food for winter months. Even those who knew about the water way, did not know that you could swim under it. There had never been a cause to do so. All that was needed was a trusty boat waiting on the other side and the chances of escape were as good as they could be. Graedon labored with the thought, 'if only there was some way to get word to Brother Michael at the monastery for help'.

In the mean time, Princess Elayne courageously ventured into the lower extremes of the castle to communicate with the jailed diplomat and pastor. Elayne had all but given up on the means of escape that her father told her about. It was too risky and if Lucio discovered the escape attempt that would be the end of King Graedon and Princess

Elayne. With her disguise and Sean's help, Elayne made her way down to the castle cellar to further investigate the canal and grate. The gate leading to the canal was locked. Instead she went down the set of stairs to the lower jail level. It was noticeably damper and cooler in this part. At the bottom of those stairs was the hallway that led to the jail cell occupied by Calogerus and Mattews.

Earlier Elayne had overheard their conversation with Lucio as their voices carried easily into the empty spaces of the dungeon. After Elayne met and spoke with them she knew that they were not outlaws. By virtue of her own plight Elayne realized that these two did not belong in jail. Given that Lucio had usurped power, it was understood that those in jail were there for resisting his will. Anyone who deserved to be in jail was probably recruited in the service of Lucio. Elayne went to the cell door and opened the small door at eye level and looked into the cell.

"I beg your pardon," Elayne began, "we could not talk very long last time. It has been very hard to get away as I am now carefully watched. You were conversing with Lucio. Please tell me more about who you are and why you are here? Do you know Lucio?"

"Well, we know Lucio, but we are no friends of his," remarked Mattews.

Elayne could ascertain that fact. They were in jail.

"You were here at Braemar before. I remember that you had white hair for a man so young. You said that your name was Pastor Mattews of Wendover," Elayne stated.

"Yes, Princess, I was attacked by the king's soldiers at Plenitude Church. I slew Chadryn, a 'Carte Blanche' knight and his soldiers that were sent to kill me," started Mattews.

"Why would they want to kill you, a man of the cloth? I thought the order of 'Carte Blanche' was strictly prohibited in our realm?" inquired Elayne.

"'Carte Blanche' is a dark order and answers to no king of the aerde. The only thing 'blanche' about it is the paper that their names appear on. These fraternity members draw their own blood to affix their name to an ancient manuscript and order. The identity of their leader could not be ascertained, but I have an idea now," reflected Mattews.

"How did you come across these, this 'Carte Blanche' order, and why did they come after you?" asked Elayne.

"I was knighted from the northern kingdom to serve the young King Graedon. Times were changing. Terrible things happened to the good and upright knights in the northern part of the country. Any knight who did not fall into the 'Carte Blanche' order met an untimely death. Ambushes, assassinations and poisonings were not uncommon.

"The unjust slaying of these knights that were just and true forced me into hiding. My friend was ambushed. I was supposed to go with him that day. He reassured me that he would be fine. Being lazy I let him go on alone. They murdered him. After his murder, frightened, I turned to the church for protection. I was taken in at Bendire Monastery.

"My studies began as a seminarian under Brother Michael. He was impressed with my ability to apply bible teachings to everyday life. When Cardinal Spehar called for another assistant, I was sent to him. Cardinal Spehar was not pleased with me so I was sent back to the monastery.

"Brother Michael convinced the cardinal that I was ready to preach so I was sent to Wendover. Nobody wanted to leave the comfort of Braemar Castle to go to Wendover but the people needed a pastor. I was sent. With the help of the people of Wendover we built Plenitude Church. So to the people of Wendover, I am Pastor Mattews," he stated.

"And Calogerus is from Craigroyston?" questioned Elayne.

"Can you believe it?" interrupted Mattews, "Lucio jailed a diplomat from Craigroyston."

"Tell me princess, how is your father?" inquired Calogerus.

"My father is ill," conveyed Elayne, "he seems to be getting worse."

"I will bet that sorcery is to blame," concluded Mattews, "Graedon was always fit as a falcon."

Calogerus mused over Mattews conviction as he knew that Vanessa was capable of anything. He turned to Elayne.

"Tell me, has your father consumed some unusual food or drink?" asked Calogerus.

Elayne looked at Calogerus eye to eye.

"No, he has not," Elayne reflected, "of course, there is this tea, but my father enjoys it. In fact it is all that he requests as it is the only thing that brings him comfort. It seems that he cannot do without it."

"Tea," Calogerus paused, "do you know the name of this tea?"

"Autumn tea, but it cannot be this tea. I have seen Vanessa drink it herself," replied Elayne.

"It is possible that Vanessa adds something to the tea that she gives Graedon." added Mattews.

"Are you sure it was not Lotumna tea?" asked Calogerus.

Elayne looked at Calogerus.

"Yes," confirmed Elayne, "that is the name, Lotumna tea."

Calogerus collected these facts and stood a moment in thought. He put them together: the king's ailing stomach, dependence on this tea and Vanessa. In his experience, there were extracts and elixirs brewed from grasses and roots that were harmless unless taken in an unwise combination or with prolonged use over a period of time.

"He must discontinue taking the Lotumna tea! Before they apprehended me, I was told that Graedon suffered from stomach discomfort. That was when they lured me to Graedon's chamber and there I was seized. If the tea is Lotumna, then he must stop taking it.

"He will probably crave more tea, but you must not give it to him. Your father has developed a dependence on the tea. Instead, give him warm water to help flush out what poisons remain in his digestion.

"If he positively must have the tea, give it to him watered down. As for the effects of prolonged use of the substance, your father will have to bear the consequences. It will be most painful but he must break himself of its poison and his dependence on it," Calogerus urged.

"Poison?" Elayne questioned, "Bear the consequences, what consequences? He did not choose to drink this tea with disabling powers. Will my father recover from it?"

"If he continues to use the tea, he will die. If you make him aware that he has become dependent on it, he may gain the will to fight it. He must stop taking the tea. Give him herbal teas preferably Chamaemelum nobilis, that is chamomile tea. The rest of us will all pray to God for his deliverance," Calogerus encouraged.

Calogerus tried to comfort Elayne, but she understood that Graedon was in serious trouble. Mattews was surprised with what Calogerus said. For a practical man who had worked only with knowledge and solid facts, Calogerus had also recommended praying to God.

"It is imperative that I get my father out of this castle. Teresforte or Galles would each be an ideal place to take him. My father told me that in this tower there is a channel that was built to allow the water from the bay to enter within these walls. Attached to the wall is an iron grate that does not extend far below the level of the water. I have found this room," Elayne told them.

Calogerus now knew that their cell was well below the level of the water in the bay and now he had an idea just how much. Mattews resolve to duty returned to him with the knowledge that the king and his daughter were in trouble.

"You must trust us with your life and that of your father's, princess. When we escape we will come to your aid and that of your father's," pledged Mattews.

"For now princess do nothing but comfort your father and keep him drinking water," Calogerus advised.

She knew that they were supportive of her father, especially since one was a former knight and good priest, and the other a diplomat from the country that came to the aid of the Wendover Lowlands. Elayne was desperate to get her father out of Braemar Castle.

"There is something else, princess," said Calogerus.

"Please call me Elayne," replied the princess.

"Elayne it may be very dangerous, but is there anyone that you trust that you could send a message to Lord Barton at Teresforte?" asked Calogerus.

"A message that I dispatched with a faithful servant may well be in the hands of Lord Barton as we speak," replied Elayne.

Elayne was confident that when Barton learned of her father's fate, he would come to Braemar with his forces. Then Lucio would be brought to bear the consequences of committing Braemar's force to defend against Lord Barton's. It would be brother against brother. Elayne believed that her father's force at Braemar would not attack Barton's force. She had pinned her hopes on Barton intervening after receiving her dispatch. It was then that Calogerus had a bad feeling about the fate of Elayne's faithful servant.

The Quiet Escape

Calogerus' advice with regards to the tea proved to be right. At first there was more agitation and discomfort with the effects of not taking it. It seemed to drive the gentle Graedon to madness. With the watering down of Vanessa's tea and the introduction of chamomile tea though, Graedon's condition improved slightly. With great pain and restraint, Graedon was making gains against his dependence on the tea. It would not be easy to break the habit. His mind and body had taken a beating. The addiction did not come on overnight and it would not go away overnight. For Graedon, who had to go through the withdrawal, it was an eternity. At one point Graedon got up enough strength to stand up briefly. Graedon's improvement was kept a secret. With every meal that came to Graedon's chamber a large mug of chamomile tea accompanied them in the place of the Lotumna tea. Seeing Graedon's improvement, Elayne got encouraged. She was anxious to escape and made her plan.

Graedon's mind was not as cloudy as it had been. The bed ridden monarch lost a lot of muscle strength however. The drug that clouded his mind prevented him from moving about and using his body as he normally would. Now his legs would not respond in the fashion that he as accustomed to. With the blessing of her father, who was just as anxious to get his daughter away from Braemar, Elayne decided that there escape would be now or never. They decided to escape to the Bendire Monastery and get horses from Brother Michael. From there they would ride like the wind for Teresforte. By the time anyone realized Graedon and Elayne's absence, they would be well on their way across Marmora.

The plan was already under way. Graedon and Elayne had gone to St. Zorren's Church to pray late in the evening. Elayne was questioned as to why they went to chapel so late. She merely told the nosy guards that her father's condition did not keep regular hours. In the chapel they prayed and waited for night to fall. All the while Graedon rested up. Upon their return to the castle, they went through the kitchen. If anyone was still awake, they could claim that they were hungry. There was no one in the kitchen. With the hopes that everyone had fallen

99

asleep, Graedon and Elayne traveled down the hall to the door that leads to the south tower. They had informed Sean, their lookout, to be there with the key. Sean opened the locked door for them. He handed his liege the lit torch, but Elayne took it instead.

"Good luck your majesties," Sean bid them.

Quickly they entered the passage and began descending the stairs. Graedon could not move very fast, but it was the early morning hour and no one should suspect their escape. As Graedon paused to rest, he reached into his vestments and produced a master key that would open pretty much any lock in Braemar. Being king did have some privileges. Elayne thought that with Calogerus and Mattews their escape would be complete. Graedon told Elayne to run ahead and open the iron barred gate that lead to the canal. He felt that he could manage the stairs slowly.

"Run ahead and open the gate," Graedon commanded.

Elayne did not know if she could trust her father to manage the stairs himself. She did like the idea of recruiting Calogerus and Mattews to their escape.

"Go on my dear, time is everything now, and I will be fine," assured Graedon.

Graedon sounded more like himself. With hearing her father speak confidently, Elayne knew that he would make it. She descended the stairs alone. The torch lit only a section at a time. Finally when she reached the foot of the stairs she could see that there was something in the dark. She paused to ascertain what was there as her father continued to descend the stone stairway by himself. Both Graedon and Elayne saw a familiar silhouette appear. Lucio was standing, waiting there with a company of guards in the pitch dark. Some of the guards, who carried torches, lit them.

"And where would we be venturing out to on such a chilly night, your majesties?" inquired Lucio.

Graedon had mustered up all his resolve to fighting his dependency on the Lotumna tea. He finally gave up his diplomacy in dealing with Lucio. The king realized without doubt that it was Lucio who was more than ambitious. He was the treacherous villain who would lead the king's people into war against each other to secure comfort and power for himself. It was Lucio and Vanessa who undermined his authority. With all that Graedon had done for the mistreated, orphan boy and his widowed mother, this was his reward.

"I know that you were mistreated as a child, but were you not delivered from that tyranny? Federics loved both you and your mother," Graedon appealed, "Now you would see others mistreated measure for measure with the misery that you once had to bear."

"There is only one way to rise above treachery and that is to be in charge. With nobody above you and everyone doing things your way is the only way. I will have what my heart desires. My will shall be their command. And of course, I now have the power of life and death over people," Lucio replied.

"What about my good people, all they need is opportunity and good leadersh—," Graedon started.

"People do need leadership! They need to be told what to do. Of course it is a good idea to have a council to hear ideas. It is always good to know how people are thinking and who is thinking what.

"It is always good to know who the trouble-makers are. But in the end, a select few who know what they are talking about are all that is needed. Ultimately the right choice can only be made by one man.

"One man, who knows what is best and does not waste time on the weak and helpless. Opportunity is missed when waiting for people to come to agreement. People want and need leadership, leadership that rules with a firm hand." Lucio professed.

At this point Graedon fell silent. He had been betrayed and now his people would pay. He felt like a fool. All the kindness that he had showed the orphaned boy and his supposed widowed mother were all for naught. Graedon was hurt because his misplaced trust now threatened his people and the one person whom he loved the most, his daughter Elayne. Graedon did not appreciate the tone and attitude with which Lucio spoke.

"Would you mind escorting their majesties back to their chambers," Lucio gestured, "their chambers are certainly more comfortable than a dungeon cell."

"I dispatched Ornelda with a message to Lord Barton," Elayne declared, "his forces might surely be on their way even now!"

Lucio produced a scroll with a broken wax seal that looked just like the one that Elayne gave to Ornelda to deliver to Lord Barton.

"Was this the message?" Lucio asked.

There was an ache in Elayne's heart. There was the look of disbelief and sadness on her face. It was the look that a child gave when an object of desire was unjustly denied. Elayne was concerned for Ornelda. If Lucio had the scroll, where was Ornelda?
What had he done with Ornelda?

"What have you done with her?" asked Elayne firmly.

Lucio did not answer. He gave the guards a look and they started to escort the king and princess. Graedon saw the anguish in his daughter as she worried over a faithful servant. He turned to look back at Lucio once more with a renewed determination. The king stood up straight and tall.

"No harm had better have come to Ornelda!" exclaimed Graedon.

"Or what?" Lucio scowled.

Lucio stared right back at the king. The guards were expedient at following Lucio's orders. The guards raised their spears to indicate that the conversation was over. They guided the ailing king and his daughter away as they started up the stairs. In that instance Calogerus who had been listening from his cell called to Lucio.

"Lucio! Lucio, a word!" shouted Calogerus.

"Oh, yes our distinguished prisoner from Jonquis' Court," Lucio stated.

Graedon heard what Lucio said. Graedon was not informed that a diplomat from Craigroyston arrived at Braemar let alone his being imprisoned in the dungeon cell. Jailing a diplomat, a messenger from another ruler, was utterly disgraceful and shameful. A messenger was just a messenger and was not to be mistreated.

"If it were not for the intervention of Craigroyston's navy, we would be fighting for our very survival. Their emissary is neither an enemy nor a spy," declared Graedon.

"No, just a nuisance," declared Lucio, "my mother had made arrangements for the ruling of the entire kingdom for a measly tribute."

Graedon then remembered that Lucio had arranged the force for Wendover but did not go himself. Lord Barton asked for more men and supplies as he could not ascertain the enemy's numbers. Lucio was confident that enough soldiers were sent. Graedon's anger grew into rage.

"Treachery! Treachery! Treachery! We are in the midst of a Traitor!!!" Graedon yelled with all his might.

Graedon's strength poured out of him through his words. Elayne helped her father up the stairs but could not speak. The king realized that Lucio was fully aware of the Huynsten invasion. It did not matter anymore, his humiliation was complete. The imprisonment of Craigroyston's emissary was without his knowledge and there was nothing that he could do. It was another stark reminder to Graedon that he had lost control of his kingdom.

On the way back to his royal chamber Graedon thought back to the manner in which he managed his kingdom. In an effort to avoid all the fighting that his forefathers did, he wanted to employ reason and be progressive. He thought that if he appeased some of his ambitious lords, they would get into the spirit of how things should be. With prosperity came wealth and a satisfied people. However, over the years, the more that Graedon appeased them, the more ground they gained. The more wealth that was attained, the more they wanted. It was hard to take back what was given to them. Graedon realized that he was wrong to appease the aggressive lords and knights. He remembered the council meeting that nearly resulted in the murder of Barton. On that night he should have supported Lord Barton who spoke with truth, honor and justice. If that would have resulted in the crumbling of the northern kingdom so be it. At least he could fight them. Now he was confined to his bed chambers. The enemy had a grapple hold on Graedon's throat in his own home.

Graedon remembered one triumph that he was proud of though. It was when Welledon joined Galles to Rothaynen. Graedon thought that the example that was set by Welledon would carry a message of brotherhood for all his dukes to appreciate. All Rothaynen would strive to work together for a common prosperity, free of spilling blood to achieve the means. Together with his dukes, they could have eliminated want in Rothaynen and provided hope, opportunity and justice for all. The opportunity for Graedon to accomplish that goal was lost. His very life lay in the balance now as he pitied himself. The guards escorted Graedon and Elayne back up the stairs to their chambers. They were already under arrest but now it was official. Graedon was bed ridden. Elayne knew that she was confined to her chamber and feared that she had a certain future. She wondered, what had become of Ornelda?

Calogerus was aware that Lucio was nearby and called after him for an audience to speak to him. It was for sport that Lucio descended the stairs and went to Calogerus' cell before leaving the dungeon.

"What can I do for you, Calogerus?" asked Lucio.

"Now you get my name right. Will you not open this door so that we may speak eye to eye?" Calogerus inquired.

"No, I am quite familiar with your sort; black magic types. You may deceive me and escape. Worse yet, you may talk me into friendship," Lucio said.

It was ironic how Calogerus was referred to as a black magic type.

"You, Lucio, are a victim of black magic! I do not deal in black magic, petty potions and manipulation such as your mother. She is a true witch who has used all her knowledge and all her power to feed her vanity.

"At any cost, she has served her purpose of surviving and staying young. She has manipulated men with her sexual allure; promising indescribable pleasure and then betraying them to their doom," Calogerus summed up.

"Then I am very fortunate, being her son. I know that she has done it all for me. She has not denied me anything and has done everything to advance my position in life," replied Lucio.

"She has done everything to alienate you from the people around you. She had cut you off from consideration of others and mutual respect. She has promoted you at the expense of others. She has led you to ruin by driving a wedge between you and humanity.

"The only people that you can associate with are those who fear you. You keep company with cut-throats and murderers ready to act on your whim. Your mother has clouded your vision and ability to reason.

"The evil spirit of your mother has seduced you too. Good people avoid you. Surely you know that you cannot fool all the dukes in this kingdom. And, how loyal will these self-serving miscreants be?" Calogerus proposed.

"I already have enough dukes and nobles, knights and oh yes, the army. And, by the way, do not call my mother a witch," Lucio demanded.

As Lucio turned to walk away Calogerus posed a question. It was a question that had not dawned on Lucio before.

"Do you know how old she is?" asked Calogerus.

Lucio stopped in his steps and lifted his head slightly.

"From the time that I knew her, she has not aged a day. How many times has she played her hand since leaving me and how many times before me?

"Like a true witch, she uses her charms to feign affection; to lure men to their own demise. She has done everything to ensure her survival regardless of the cost to others. Her time to fall will come too. However, it is not too late to turn from your ways," advised Calogerus.

"Oh, but you see it is. And, I would not turn away anyhow. Why be a servant to Graedon when I can have it all myself?" Lucio replied.

"Boy, I am your father," Calogerus told Lucio.

Calogerus had hoped to invoke some kind of compassion or at least some consideration in Lucio. Lucio did not reply. There was an awkward pause in the conversation but Calogerus appealed to him again.

"I did not get the opportunity to see you grow; speak to you; teach you; get to know you. You were taken away from me when you were a child. On that day I felt my heart fall from my chest, the very life in my body departed.

"I had great dreams and plans for my wife and I, and my son. I was going to teach you to read; everything that I learned, you would know and more. It is never too late.

"Release me and return to Graedon what is rightfully his. He is a good man and will understand. He will show mercy. He will let us leave. I will take you home, to my home in Roysford," Calogerus pleaded.

"Your home," Lucio teased, "a hovel in the forest or some dark cave, where do you wizards live these days?"

"It is no use to try, friend," Mattews told Calogerus, "he has committed his soul to the works of self-serving and self-destructive plans. He has committed his soul to the evil one."

"So, you make friends easy. It is of no consequence, you will be confined to this dungeon cell so long as these walls stand, and, it is a well-built castle," laughed Lucio.

"They are your words," confirmed Calogerus.

Lucio's laughter turned to fury as he had wanted the last word. In a childish manner he searched for something hurtful to say.

"You cannot imagine my disappointment in learning that you should be my father. No wonder my mother left you," Lucio concluded.

Then it dawned on Lucio that both Mattews and Calogerus shared the same cell.

"Jailor! Jailor!," Lucio called, " What are these two doing in the same cell?!"

John the jailor appeared worried and he did not dare speak to explain why the two prisoners were in the same cell.

"Get them separated before I have you separated!" Lucio commanded.

With the guards present there, John fumbled with his keys to open the cell. John unlocked the cell door, but Lucio looked into the eyes of Calogerus. For some reason he changed his mind. He did not want to open the cell door. In his rage Lucio changed his mind.

"Oh, never mind!" Lucio said abruptly, "Quick! Lock it back up."

Calogerus' power is no match for my mother's power, he thought vainly.

Then John locked the heavy door of the cell anew. Lucio had lashed out at this man who claimed to be his father. He figured that he was like another Federics who acted like a door knob. Where was the substance in him to take what he wanted?

Lucio had done without a father for so long that it did not matter what the circumstances were. He quickly turned and walked away from the cell door before another word could be said. His firm footsteps could be heard on the stone floor of the poorly lit corridor. Lucio meant to hurt Calogerus and he achieved that goal. Calogerus was ever hopeful of reaching Lucio, however now he knew where he stood with regards to his son. Lucio had made his choice. Calogerus saw that he could not be moved to show mercy so there was no good left in him.

The Wizard and the Man with the Collar

The exchange of words with Lucio hurt Calogerus. It was as if he aged during that barrage of hateful intentions directed at him. Calogerus was hated by the one being that he had suffered over not knowing his fate. Earlier in Calogerus' life, it was a blow that nearly finished his ability to think and his will to go on. Mattews realized that his cell mate was shaken. He was thinking on how he could get him to talk about the matter. As a pastor, he knew that if he could get a troubled person to state what the problem was, it was half the battle to solving the problem. Sometimes all that anybody needed was for someone to listen to them.

"So, that was your son," acknowledged Mattews.

Calogerus was slow to answer, "Yes, he is a part of me."

"We must have seen his mother's side of him," Mattews jested.

At this time Mattews did not know that Vanessa was his mother. After all the heartache, Calogerus looked at Mattews and smiled nervously at that comment.

"Where do you suppose his mother is?" asked Mattews.

"She is within these very walls. It was she that surprised and captured me. Vanessa looked the same as she did many, many years ago," Calogerus said, "She caught me looking."

"Do you mean Vanessa from Peregren," asked Mattews.

"I suppose you would know her as Vanessa from Peregren," said Calogerus.

"I remember Vanessa from when I was first knighted at Peregren. She was a young maiden. She was the mistress of the mighty Sadar. He was not a gentle man. He could not bring himself to marry any mistress let alone Vanessa and yet, he could not be departed from her.

"Despite feigning submission to him, it was Vanessa that influenced Sadar's actions at Peregren. There were rumors that she attacked his manhood whenever she wanted something. Sadar would roar in protest. He even struck her and slapped her about, but in the end her will was done. When Sadar went against Graedon's father Orendyn, it brought needless bloodshed and nearly became a catastrophe. On that day, it was Vanessa who influenced Sadar to rebel and in the end Lucio who killed him.

"I was present once when Sadar slapped Vanessa in court. She was bruised black and blue, and attracted sympathy from the entire court. Somehow though, the bruise did not last into the next day. Beaten and bruised, it never took long for her to regain her complexion.

"I have not seen Vanessa for many years, since I joined the brothers of the Bendire Monastery," Mattews reported.

"She still looks like a young maiden. You told Elayne why you left your knighthood and lands and took refuge with the monks, but why did you stay at the monastery?" Calogerus asked.

Calogerus was in pain over the exchange with Lucio and only time could set it straight. He was of course genuinely curious about this priest who was once a knight.

"The world was not a safe place for an upright man. I thought that by entering the priesthood, I would promote unity, common purpose and find some measure of peace," paused Mattews, "there is as much corruption in the church as anywhere else that depends on the hearts and deeds of men."

"Did you know that a fish rots from its head? Corruption is linked to the character of those who take the places of honor," Calogerus confirmed, "One cannot just put the blame on the corrupt. Everyone must be diligent. You cannot leave the making of decisions to the few who should make the right decisions but choose to serve themselves."

"Due diligence! I agree, you must be diligent at all times. There is no rest from evil. It is ready to strike out at any time and at any place. Just when you think you have defeated it, something small and petty bursts into flames. It is as if Evil knows when and where you are weak," added Mattews.

"Perhaps you were tired?" suggested Calogerus.

"Perhaps I was scared," Mattews admitted, "a dear friend was killed over defending the just owner of property. A greedy knight acquired the property by might. In court he used his family name, a forged document and paid a bribe to witnesses to cheat the true owner.

"The only evidence in the poor man's favor came from Winn, a true and upright knight. Winn's testimony left the conspirators speechless, but the case was lost. After the dubious decision in court, the rightful owner was run off the property with his family. Winn was not heard from again.

"I was supposed to set out with him to hear a plaintiff in another land dispute. Earlier that week I had bruised my ribs in a scuffle with brigands that Winn and I subdued. He told me that he would go and be back in three days. He did not return. Later I saw one of the brigands wearing his gloves. The truth is that I could have gone, I was healed well enough."

"You do not think that your story is unique do you?" questioned Calogerus.

Mattews sighed, "No, I guess it is not unique. But why must we accept it and live in fear? I think that I have hidden behind these robes far too long. It is time for me to transfer to the fighting saints division."

"Injustice flourishes because the single common man does not stand up against it," Calogerus declared, "your courage and leadership is needed again.

Mattews realized that his goal to get Calogerus talking and taking his mind off the pain of his loss had turned around and seemed to be benefitting him. Mattews was clear and confident with what had to be done now.

Mattews looked at Calogerus and told him what was on his mind. It was a rather personal observation. Mattews decided to ask him, after all, what did he have to lose?

"Do you know what good work you could do if you were vested as a Cardinal?" asked Mattews.

"A Cardinal! Am I to start at the top?" Calogerus replied.

Mattews gathered the sarcasm in his voice.

"I would say you have already put in your time in at the bottom. With your knowledge of the elements, the earth, water, metals, plants; human nature and even inhuman nature, everything that you acquired all your life, I would say that you have already done your apprenticeship.
"The laws of nature are not strange to you, but if you include them with the teachings of the 'good book', you could do the almighty God a great service. And, I will bet that you are already familiar with His laws."

Calogerus smiled and looked over in deep thought at Mattews. He appreciated the complement because it was sincere. Calogerus thought that the service he provided his monarchs was along the same measure. He took Christian principles into account. He thought that there was nothing wrong with Christian principles, if only Christians put them into practice. It was strange but at that moment Calogerus remembered when he was happy just to be in his mother and father's company. At no other time in his life was he ever as carefree yea though it did not last long.

"Presently, we should endeavor to leave this place," Calogerus reminded.

As Mattews excused himself and prayed for a solution, Calogerus began to blush like a child. Never had anyone come to know him so well so quickly. Never did a stranger suggest such a prestigious and honorable position for him. It was a great responsibility to provide a conscience steeped in wisdom for the people. For starters you had to be solely dedicated to the church doctrine. Calogerus was upset that his son, whom he never had the opportunity to know or raise, was so heartless toward others. Lucio was destroying himself, slowly. He was not shown the path of the righteous, rather only to take what he could and fend for himself. Lucio's soul was his no more.

"Keep what I said in mind," Mattews told him, "but remember sometimes it is hard to see the forest because there are trees in the way."

Calogerus put the compliment behind him and focused on the task of gaining escape for Mattews and himself. He did not look toward the door. It was the only plausible opening to freedom, but the hinges were on the other side. The window in the wall of the tower was too far up and only wide enough to stick an arm out. Instead, Calogerus looked toward the wall.

"I believe we should wait until the guard is alone and comes to open our door. You could surprise him with that small hammer," Mattews said plainly.

His cohort continued to examine the wall.

"That is a good idea," agreed Calogerus, "but there are others out there who have been well fed. We will need some sort of diversion."

"One of us can be sick or act dead," said Mattews.

"No," replied Calogerus, "they will see that coming."

Calogerus had the blacksmith's hammer in hand and looked at the foundation. He obviously had another idea in mind.

Rebellion at the Church

The disgruntled peasants had reached a fever pitch against the arrogance of Cardinal Spehar. Through the years their support of the man as spiritual leader waned. The spiritual community that started supporting him without question met with disappointment. It came to the point that some people just came to church to keep in touch with their neighbors. It happened over the story of the moneychangers in the church. According to the Cardinal, the son of God was upset with his people being cheated in His Father's Name. The poor brought forth their sacrificial lamb and upon inspection, it was deemed not clean, but for some more money, they could exchange it for a lamb that was clean in the pen. It was more of an exchange program with the religious leaders and merchants in league with each other. It was not too long before the lambs in the unclean pen were moved to the clean pen.

On top of that the greedy merchants were selling their lambs, doves and artifacts expensively to people who did not have their own lamb to sacrifice. The religious leaders and merchants were taking advantage of the people and to the farmers the irony struck close to home. Cardinal Spehar encouraged the purchasing of pardons. In that way the church coffers were sure to be full. The rich could purchase a pardon for their sins. The poor and weak bore the shame of their transgressions. The result of the manner in which things were set up was that you could deliberately do wrong and then buy your way out if you were rich. It was clearly not in the spirit of good faith. The wealthy seemed to have the advantage here and Cardinal Spehar would not have it any other way.

Walter was a strong, hard-working peasant farmer who was God-fearing. He was God-fearing in the sense that he realized how easily it is to get ensnared in evil and he feared that this would keep him from his God. He was insistent on all his children and his spouse living by the good book. They attended church religiously every week regardless of the weather or what did not get done on their farm. Throughout the year though, he became increasingly upset with Spehar's homilies. To Walter, a devout Christian who looked for leadership for his young family, Spehar's homilies were judgmental, condescending and insulting. He remembered the homily on the prodigal son where, according to Spehar, the younger brother was at fault for foolishly squandering his inheritance on wine and women and now returned for a cut of his brother's inheritance. In Spehar's reasoning, there was nothing wrong with the elder brother who resented his younger brother's return. To the cardinal it was natural that he should be worried about his inheritance.

Maybe it was months earlier when in late September Spehar announced the generous contribution of a certain merchant of the pastoral flock. Walter was not an educated man, but he was not stupid either. He calculated that what he and his fellow peasant farmers gave to the church; his tithe or tenth of his earnings, was more than the wealthy merchant whom they were all supposed to revere. It was not easy for a family to give up a tithe of their wages, and they were God-fearing and honest enough to give their share. Spehar made such a fuss over this 'pious, generous, servant of God'. The Cardinal set him over the people as an example to follow. In reality this Miller character was dishonest. He was not dishonest with people who were wise or like Walter who were able to defend themselves. No, Miller took advantage of the lesser peasants who were not as bright and could not defend themselves. He robbed widows and orphans of their true earnings only to turn around and be generous toward them with his own handout for some personal gain. Some of the peasants would like to have seen Miller ground under his own millstone.

Spehar passed judgment over everybody. It may have been that he was aging, but then he was already acting old when he was young. He often upset the children who were casting stones at a nearby tree in a contest of accuracy. Spehar was able to weave in the biblical story of 'casting the first stone' to the matter at hand. It was so inappropriately tied in that it confused the children. The children did not like him very much except that they were told that he was the cardinal and that meant that you showed him respect. In the bible there was a story about 'suffering the little children to come unto their teacher', but that was not the case here. The children avoided him entirely. Spehar walked about with an air of holiness and importance that was clearly not Christian. To avoid the common man, that was his goal, and he was good at it. He delegated all of the duties of service to the community onto the associate pastors and brothers from the Bendire Monastery.

That day on the 'prodigal son' sermon, he followed through with his black and white judgment. The prodigal son was bad and the son who stayed in his father's service was good. To the working man with all the repetitious chores day in and out, you gain a certain rhythm when getting your work done. It allows one to think deeper, to ponder ideas and relive significant moments so as to better analyze them. With the physical labor of farming came the time for the mind to rest and entertain thought. For people without the ability to read, they could certainly ascertain what was right and what was wrong. To hear Cardinal Spehar's version left the church goers in want.

As the story goes, the prodigal son asked for his share of the inheritance and left the farm. Cardinal Spehar stressed that he associated himself with rough company and squandered his wealth on women and wine. After the money was spent, the young man who went out in the world found himself alone. He found a job and did not like it so he returned to his father. Walter thought that, if the prodigal son truly was evil, would he not follow the ways of his newly made friends and turn to stealing and taking after those who took advantage of him?

Would he not join them to look for new victims?

In Walter's mind, the prodigal son wanted to go home, but the shame of his losses prevented him from facing his father. He had spent his entire inheritance which his father had intended for him to make a life with. Instead the young man remembered his instruction and upbringing that he learned under his father's stewardship. He turned to finding honest work, the work that he was used to and capable of. He relied on the honest skills that he had learned from his father. He was taught well and had learned well so he could earn his keep. He let his services out to a farmer and he gave of his labor to the best of his ability. He considered himself fortunate and gave thanks to God.

In working for his new master, he received enlightenment from the Lord for his prayers. Although he was grateful for the opportunity to work and support himself, he did some thinking. He was able to assess that even the servants that worked for his father were paid better and ate better. He came to his senses and confessed to God that he had done wrong by his father. He had earlier assumed that he could stand on his own two feet independent of his father's guidance. He had reasoned that with all that money that was his inheritance, how could he fail?

He realized that he went astray. Now he was able to face his father though with a heavy heart and confess his failure. It took a lot of courage to finally realize and admit that he was wrong. Now he could admit it to the man that fed him and clothed him and wished on him only good things. The prodigal son was not rude to his present master despite the wages. After thanking his master for the opportunity, he decided that he would go home. He left on good terms with the master for he was not certain whether his father would accept him.

Walter imagined that the journey home got harder and harder for the prodigal son as he got closer and closer. He realized that he was returning a failure without any of the purse that he left with. In his heart he could not blame his father if he was asked to leave. He was frightened and only prayer strengthened him in his resolve to return home. As he neared his father's land, his person was noticed. It was his own father that he saw walking the ploughed fields amidst the laborers. The father noticed the stranger approaching his lands, but this was no stranger. Upon his boy's return, the father was overcome with joy. Nobody recognized the prodigal son in the dirty, well-worn clothes that he wore, none but the father. A sense of joy came over the father. When he saw his son returning, the father could not wait to see him. The father was overcome with joy. He did not wait for the son to come to him. The father ran out to greet him.

"My son, my son!" he cried, "you have come home!"

The entire farm was alarmed with what was going on. His own brother went to see what the matter was.

118

When the older brother learned that his younger brother had returned, he was not too happy to see him. In his mind, he thought about his own inheritance. With his father being so generous and forgiving, his own inheritance would be less if his father decided to give his brother any more money. You can imagine the disdain when his father called for the slaughter of the fattened calf to celebrate the homecoming. The brother charged at his father with contempt. Walter imagined the conversation.

"You kill the fattened calf for 'him'. He took your money; his inheritance and squandered it, and now you greet him with all favor?"

"My son," replied the father, "all that you have worked for is yours. But, your brother was thought to be dead, but has returned to us. Is that not a cause to rejoice?"

Walter thought that the Cardinal did not see that the story had a deeper meaning. In one way or another, Walter thought that each and every one of us is like one brother or the other. We have either gone on the wrong path and need to come home, or have been dutiful but fear that the brother who went astray and returns will get what is ours. Walter could see this because he had worked hard to govern his family and farm. He would be the first to admit that his wife Heidi worked even longer and harder than he did. Not only did she assist him with the chores, but she also raised their children in the straight and narrow path of the Lord. It was mind boggling what his wife did to raise their children and come to his aid. Walter was very wise never to complain go her about what had to be done.

When Walter heard Spehar's rendition of the turning out of the money changers being attributed to merchants' lack of giving value, he lost his temper.

"No! It was not that. It was literally kicking out the grubby money changers from making the place of worship a market. The Lord said,

'Let my people come to me without the burden of money looming over their head and tripping them at their feet'," Walter interjected.

What Walter said was not exactly in the bible but the people applauded what he said. He could not read, but that was not the point. God's people went to church to hear His guiding word and were compelled to give or spend their money on some scheme. Cardinal Spehar was furious with him. Walter said all that he said before he realized that he had. Cardinal Spehar looked at him with sullen eyes, as if to say 'who is this man who speaks out in my church?'

Spehar knew full well who Walter was. He had an opinion about this brawny man with no education who dared to speak out. He was an informal leader among the peasants. The farmers respected and liked Walter. He organized the farming community into a team that looked after its members. Together, many barns were erected that could not have been done solely by one man. Many harvests were gathered as a team community.

After an awkward pause Spehar said, "Who is this man who speaks out in my church?"

"You collect tithes from the people, you have a poor box, you sell artifacts, and all the labor on church projects and maintenance is a gift from the people. Yet, you despise people. The poor are condemned, jailed and often trampled down in the market so they stay away. They are forced to find work in the country. Often they work for food, and are grateful to get that. So tell me," Walter asked, "what is done with all the money that is collected for the poor? Where does it go?"

The Cardinal did not answer but his face looked more like his ruby, red robe.

"We have a heretic in the church," Spehar started firmly, "repent you blasphemer! How dare you question the church of God?"

"I do not question the church of God, I question your ability to deliver God's word let alone to abide by it," replied Walter.

He then stood up and left his place on the fifth pew on the right side from the back of the church when you face the altar. His family, who was a fixture in that pew for all the time that the congregation could remember, followed. Surprisingly to Spehar, so did others. His anger was kindled. Some soldiers that were attending the service stood up, but were stopped.

"God does not need these heretic, rebels. Blasphemers! Get out of my church! Let them go!" yelled Spehar.

Spehar turned it around and made it appear that it had been 'his' idea to drive them out of the church. Outside St. Zorren's Church a few peasant families and others who left the service collected for a talk. Walter regretted what he did because he should have shown more restraint, but Spehar was impossible with his airs and poor interpretations of scripture. When he praised the nobles for their contributions, it was more than he could bear. His friends seemed to think so too.

"You should not have followed me out, that stubborn donkey will have me excommunicated," Walter told them, "and you too."

"For what, telling the truth?" a neighbor replied.

"I can imagine that there are those who do not understand my dissatisfaction with our Cardinal. I fear that we will be divided. So, I will wait here and apologize to him," Walter said.

Some people had stopped coming to the church because of their poverty, others confessed that there was no God in Heaven. To them the only damnation was the repetitious work that they did day in and day out to pay the king's taxes, the church's portion and to scratch out a living. Many hard-working peasants observed their children in want. Perhaps all the toil of work and responsibility had left them weary. Walter knew that it was not the work that discouraged the people. It was the hopelessness of empty promises and taxes that never returned. Walter figured that if tax money was spent wisely, it would serve the very person who paid it. How could the people continue to have faith in their God when His priests were thieves and hypocrites?

Not all priests did the work of the Lord, nor were all the farmers hardworking, nor did all knights follow the courtly virtues.

Walter and the others waited for the service to be over so they could talk to Cardinal Spehar and explain the matter. The church service would be over soon, but before that, soldiers from the church came out and marched over to the crowd.

"Which one of you is the man they call Walter?" asked a guard.

They knew full well who Walter was, but they could not pass up the sense of creating an air of grandness and suspense.

"I am he," replied Walter.

"In the name of Cardinal Spehar, you are hereby placed under arrest for disturbing the peace in God's holy church."

Walter made no reply. He looked to Heidi and gestured with his eyes for her to leave with their children. The soldiers took Walter into custody. Cardinal Spehar had no consideration for what would happen to Walter or his family now that winter had arrived. He was Cardinal Spehar, the voice of God on earth, so he thought.

Jail Mate

Walter was taken to jail to await a court hearing to try him on the charge of heresy and disrupting the mass. It was certain that the hearing would not take place until after Christmas. In fact Walter was just the man that Vanessa needed for her plans to celebrate the Sabbath of Janis. While Walter was taken to his cell, the commotion was overheard by Mattews and Calogerus.

"What has happened out there!" yelled Calogerus.

"No talking among prisoners!" interjected the jailor.

The jailor took his keys and opened a cell door next to Calogerus and Mattews. With the aid of his guard he unshackled Walter's arms and legs. He was then shoved into his cell and the door was shut tight and locked. You could hear the lock mechanism as the jailor turned the key. The prisoners waited for the jailor and the guard to leave before getting the new prisoners attention.

"What happened, why are you here?" yelled Mattews.

The prisoners could not even see each other and had to raise their voices and listen carefully to talk to each other.

"It was the Cardinal! Who does he think he is?
He looks down on us with disdain just because he can read. He may be able to read the holy book to the letter, but he does not know what it means. He presents himself as holier, more superior, better, but he stinks!" Walter affirmed.

"Speak not out in anger gentle person!" Mattews replied, "The man whom you describe is not a priest to begin with. There are many like him that preach and feign righteousness. You need not follow them!"

"How are we to know which priest to follow and which one not to?" asked Walter.

"Do as I say and do as I do," Mattews summed up, "if any priest, yea anybody can speak words that come from the good book and practice them, then they are surely setting an example worth following."

"Trust no one," Calogerus advised, "not every teacher is a teacher, not every physician is a physician, not every lady is a lady, and not every man is a man."

Mattews was surprised with Calogerus' comment. Although he was not the church going man, he was not against the church and its teachings. Perhaps, he thought, Calogerus had a bad experience like Walter.

"You do realize that a priest is only a man. He can serve good or he can serve evil. It is very much like fruit trees. Many are planted, but not all produce. After a well-laden tree produces a good yield, it needs a rest so it may not be as productive in the next year so it is given a chance to produce again in the following year.

"However, if a tree is pruned and fertilized watered and cared for, and it does not produce this year or the next, or the following year, then it is of no use. The farmer cuts that tree down to use for firewood to cook his food and warm his house. You do understand the principles of the good book," asked Mattews.

"I have read it," confessed Calogerus, "it truly is a brilliant history steeped in wisdom. It is a plan on how to live life, for those who confide, trust, and live by it. Most people cannot read it and those who do, ironically treat others condescendingly."

"Why then do you not openly support the church? Could you imagine how many people would follow you? How many people would be influenced in turning to God's church for counsel?" Mattews asked boldly.

"I am not against the church but I have seen elements in God's church that do not follow what they teach and seek to destroy what they do not understand.

"My mother was a victim because she had the knowledge of how to save warriors destined for death. She saved them from death with her powers of observation and applying the herbal knowledge and physical knowledge that she gained from treating wounds since she was a little girl.

"There was no shortage of hacked up men and the dying to practice on, so she acquired much experience. And, after she learned and applied her knowledge and experience for the good of her fellow men, what gratitude did she receive?

Certain members of the church stepped up and labeled her a witch. The fact that she herself caught disease and became disfigured did not excuse her from persecution. The people were eager to believe the misinformed church members who labeled her. Her skin condition actually lent credibility to their claim. They said that her appearance was proof that she served evil," Calogerus recounted.

"It was unfortunate that she was not appreciated," Mattews asked, "What happened to her?"

"What happened? Despite my father's influence, reputation and dying in the king's service, we were treated as outcasts until the day she died," Calogerus recounted.

Mattews had reached out to Calogerus on this sensitive point. He wanted to know why Calogerus thought the way that he did. It would be up to Calogerus to decide whether he would talk about it.

"What happened? Truly I can tell you that there are witches. There are women who use their sex to lead men astray, but my mother was not one of them. We were fortunate to be protected by our king who gave us shelter in his castle.

"None of the other children spoke to me. They talked about me behind my back, even in front of me. The king's son, Prince Cardem, was a friend. He was my only friend. Today I serve Cardem's daughter and her husband in Craigroyston.

"The people merely tolerated us. We were handy to look down upon. My mother sure came in handy when they needed someone to put down or a scapegoat.

"People looked upon us with disdain, but if one of their loved ones, a husband or father or son came back from battle in a dire state, they were certain to call on my mother for her help," reflected Calogerus.

"It is just like some people who do not understand matters to turn to fear and silly superstition. Even people in high places and places of honor like the king and the church who have great responsibility can make errors," Mattews confessed.

"A true person of honor learns from his errors and prevents others from making the same mistakes. They try to make things right. The more common practice though, is that people in high places who have influence seek only to justify their acts so they do not appear to have erred," Calogerus added.

Mattews had struck a very sensitive chord with Calogerus. He had wanted to ask him more about his mother and especially about Vanessa. He decided that it was not a good idea for the moment. Calogerus had spoken a lot. Mattews respected him, but now he had a deeper understanding of the man.

"Ask yourself this. If a prostitute attended church, what reception would she receive? Would she be made welcome or would she learn never to come back to that place again?" Calogerus asked.

A Sunday to Remember

On the castle grounds, the merchants had long finished selling their wares and produce and anticipated the day of rest. The odd leaf of lettuce and produce refuse was trampled into the ground. The aroma of the produce that filled the air in the early morning had all but dissipated. All the merchants vacated the castle but would return the next day to observe Sunday Mass in the church of St. Zorren. On the next morning the castle grounds had grown thick with the peasants and their families who were there for the church service. The day started out innocently enough with the fourth Sunday of Advent but an unusual occurrence would take place in the church. It took place during Cardinal Spehar's homily. It would have been better to forgive the slight of conduct of the peasant farmer, but for the man in authority. Needless to say the robes of power should be worn lightly, but some choose to weigh them down further than they have to in order to make their point. Cardinal Spehar left no doubt as to how far he would go to defend his honor.

The peasant farmers had paid their taxes and tithed to the church based on their portion. It was easier for the wealthier nobles, merchants and farmers with larger plots of land to give because they had more to begin with. The irony of course lay in the fact that the more fortune that a person acquired, the less they paid in taxes and the less tithing they did as well. On a point of thanks, the subject was brought forward in Cardinal Spehar's homily. The Cardinal did not learn anything from the incident in church a week earlier with Walter. Again he wanted to thank especially the generosity of one of the nobles who this year had given more than the others in his class and was worthy of note. It had inspired the others to give more.

To Erdman, a young farmer who together with his wife and young children worked a small farm, it did not make sense. Erdman was going to prove that what he tithed was greater portion of his earnings than these nobles. The nobles took the place of honor at banquets, took their portion, took the peasant sons for the army, took their daughters for servants, and took whatever else pleased them. It was perhaps ill

127

advised, but Cardinal Spehar should have been more sensitive about who he praised about tithing.

Spehar merely wanted to recognize the generosity of Bourke a nobleman who oversaw the eastern part of Marmora. Apparently the spirit of the season had caught up with Bourke and he decided to increase the portion that he allotted for the church. It was the hope of Cardinal Spehar that the other nobles and merchants would take note and perhaps increase their donations. The cardinal would be sure to mention their generosity during church masses that followed. As he spoke the entire congregation listened from high to low, rich to poor, it was another reminder of the increasing taxes that they had paid since Lucio's investment to Braemar Castle as its seneschal. After deducting the tithe for the church, finances were lean in making-ends-meet with winter at the doorstep.

Erdman waited for the cardinal to finish his compliments to the wealthy. Then he merely pointed out that relatively speaking, the poorest farmer actually gave more. In his words the message came out loud and clear.

"If you measure the portion that we farmers give up by the sum total of everything that we produce, we give more than our nobles do," Erdman claimed.

There was a silence that you could hear in the church. Cardinal Spehar looked out and noted the look on the faces of the nobles and merchants. They were offended. The knights sitting by their ladies fair, kept their composure. Being a major church celebration, Lucio was in attendance sitting next to Princess Elayne whom he escorted to the service. Elayne understood what the peasant farmer was saying but in the absence of her father, the king, she did not say anything. Lucio did not say anything either, but the look that he gave to the Cardinal communicated clearly his displeasure as well. The Cardinal collected his thoughts and spoke out.

"We forget to pray, we forget to give thanks and we forget who provides the opportunity for all of us to earn their daily bread. If not for God, the king and his humble councilors and army, the land would perish. There would be no order and we would not be in such good estate," professed Spehar.

The nobles and merchants felt vindicated by these comments. In their minds, if the king, his council, his knights and army did not maintain order, who would protect these farmer peasants?

Erdman interjected, "Without the peasant farmer, who rises early in the morning and toils on the land from before the sun rises to the time it sets, there would be no—

"That will be enough!" interrupted Spehar.

This had been the second such uprising in his church. It was intolerable. Spehar was frustrated by these peasants who did not know their place.

Erdman continued, "The farmer, yea though a peasant, contributes—

Spehar interrupted, "Do you profess to teach us? Be silenced lest your vanity impugn—

"My vanity?" replied Erdman.

"Remove yourself from our presence until you regain your composure!" The cardinal directed at Erdman.

Lucio looked over to the side where there were guards who escorted his party to church. Two of the guards decided that they would escort the man out.

"The man is obviously possessed. He comes to disturb our peace," remarked Spehar.

The cardinal had the full support of the gentry. In the presence of Erdman's wife and children, the guards who approached gestured that he should come with them. After a word to his wife Cate, he proceeded to make his way out of the pew. Erdman's young children sat there next to their mother befuddled as to what was going on. The last comment that Cardinal Spehar made offended the upright man. As Erdman reached the end of the church pew a guard took his shoulder, and he shrugged away from the hold. Both guards then grabbed Erdman as he struggled to be free.

Now Erdman was a big, strong man. He had been tall and slim as a youth but hard work gave him a formidable figure. There was chatter among the people of the church. The peasant farmers knew Erdman the young farmer. They who sat at the back of the church did not like to see him apprehended in that manner. The farmers spoke out to the guards to protest what they observed. Cate was afraid and collected her two children by her side.

Two more guards arrived and struck a blow to his head that would down a regular man. Erdman kept his balance on his feet but the strength and resolve to fight off the guards left him. While he was in this weakened state, he was taken down to his knees. Erdman's hands were bound behind his back with a leather lash that one of the guards had. To escort him out, a wooden pole was placed under his shoulders and behind his back to secure him. Then he was taken away to prison as the senior guard professed.

The church service continued the only people who went up for communion were the gentry. Princess Elayne was the first to receive communion with Christ. She had hoped to gain strength during this trying ordeal. Even Lucio who had never been baptized decided to set an example and go for communion. Communion however did not mean a thing to him. It was a surprise even for Cardinal Spehars to see him at communion. The peasant farmers were in shock over the ordeal with Erdman. They protested by remaining in their pews. Some close friends of Erdman and Cate of course were going to appeal for his release from prison. They had to be careful. The farmers waited patiently and silently at the back of the church. They planned to appeal to their princess directly as she left the church.

With the singing of the recessional advent hymn, the service was over. Cardinal Spehar left the altar and entered the vestibule adjacent to the altar. The gentry prepared to file out by rank down the aisle. Princess Elayne left her pew after the recessional hymn was sung and walked down the center aisle followed by Lucio. As they passed the peasant crowd, an appeal came from Cate. She had her arms around her children.

"Your Majesty, could you please release my husband? He is not the rabble that he may have appeared to be. He truly means well. He works hard and we need him. He should not have spoken out. He knows that now. Please your majesty!" appealed Cate.

The peasant farmers waited to hear what their princess would say as her procession followed her down the aisle. Elayne was still the princess and these were her people. If she gave a command before this assembly of people it would have to be carried out or the people would know that she was in trouble.

"Do not be concerned with this matter," counseled Lucio, "the rabble will be dealt with."

"What will become of him?" asked Elayne.

"No doubt a flogging will be administered to remind the peasant of his place and to keep his tongue firmly behind his teeth," replied Lucio.

Lucio planned to keep Erdman as Vanessa would require him for the Sabbath of Janis Festival. Elayne looked into the eyes of Cate and saw fear for the well being of her husband. She also noted that she had two young children who days before Christmas Eve needed their father at home, healthy and sound.

"Your children's names are?" asked Elayne.

The princess had suddenly remembered herself. Duty came first.

"Mac and Sara," replied Cate.

"They are lovely children. Do you not think so Lucio?" Elayne asked.

Lucio was surprised by Elayne turning to him and looking into his eyes when she asked that question. It was not often that Lucio was bedazzled. Perhaps, he thought that Elayne was recognizing her place as she realized it was futile to oppose Lucio. He thought, could it be true that Elayne, who was suspicious and despised him was now looking at him and speaking about children?

"They certainly are your majesty," replied Lucio.

"It would be a shame to keep their father from them, so close to the Christmas," suggested Elayne.

"It would be, your majesty," replied Lucio.

"How would you feel about being away from your children on such a holy holiday?" asked Elayne.

Lucio did not know what to say. He noted that Elayne was actually speaking to him and not in one word sentences. She was looking into his eyes when he addressed her. She spoke of children and holidays. It was in the presence of the king's subjects. Lucio simply could not lose this opportunity to gain Elayne's favor in front of the commoners.

"Perhaps we could keep him until he remembers his manners and then release him to his family," Elayne professed.

The crowd of farmers and peasants were supportive of this idea as they leant their cheers of approval.

Elayne's suggestion was a smart solution. It relied on Erdman 'remembering his manners' casting the blame on him. It did not imply that Cardinal Spehar was wrong. It was a compromise that could achieve the goal of releasing the honest farmer without the authorities losing face. Lucio did not know what to say. Actually he did know what he wanted to say. It was no! Vanessa was counting on prisoners for the celebration of her holiday. In his mind punishment should be forthcoming and it did not matter in the least that this subject would miss Christmas with his family. Although he was perturbed, Lucio feigned collective and calm.

"It would seem that in the spirit of the season, we should restore this man to his family. Ah, when he remembers his manners, as you said your majesty," spoke Lucio.

The crowd of people cheered the decision.

"There was another man who was jailed a week ago," stated Elayne firmly.

"Yes, your majesty. Do you see what he aroused among your people? It is the second incident in church in as many weeks," noted Lucio.

"We should release him to his family as well. In the spirit of the season," Elayne smiled and turned to address her people, "we will have no more disrespectful outbursts in the house of God. My good people need to remember who they are and where they are!"

The people cheered louder in support of their Princess Elayne's mercy, tolerance and generosity.

While Lucio relished her smile, Elayne had communicated rather regally to her people. Lucio was compelled to follow through with her mercy. After all she was the princess in the absence of her father the true ruler of Rothaynen. He had to follow through on Elayne's edict or the people would know that something was wrong. Lucio turned to a guard and summoned him to wait until the noise died down in the crowd of people.

"When all these people have remembered themselves, then we shall release the peasant farmers," Lucio reiterated.

He knew that releasing these good men would not please Vanessa, but he had no choice. Besides, she did not know about them yet. There was plenty of time to round up others quietly, he thought. Lucio was certain that he had made advancement with Elayne's favor.

Incident at the Jail

While the church service continued after the interruption, Erdman was led to the south tower dungeon. Across the castle grounds he was dragged. Despite his strength and coordination, his hands were tied behind his back. A spear was used as a binding pole that bolstered his shoulders squarely back. He fell on the ground face first and scraped his knee as his pant leg got torn. In the castle he had to wait against the wall. The guard with the key to the dungeon stairs was away. After quite some time he returned. The large door was unlocked and opened. Erdman was led down to the lower level where the cells were. With his hands bound and his shoulders squarely back, the guards marched him to the jail. One of the guards that escorted him from church decided that he would take sport with him.

"You look strong, are you?" taunted the guard.

Erdman did not answer but expected that he would receive some kind of abuse since he was a prisoner.

"Seriously now, how strong are you?" the guard repeated.

Still Erdman did not answer. So the guard thought he might impress his other colleagues who escorted the man from church by teasing him. The others merely watched. Not every soldier in Rothaynen pressed his advantage against the king's subjects. Since Vanessa and Lucio came to Braemar Castle, the moral character of the king's court and army deteriorated. Acts of pettiness by the king's soldiers were not challenged and did not meet with consequences. It was easier for a person in a position of power or who was stronger to press their advantage. There were no consequences. In fact when a complaint was made against a member of the king's army, the offender actually benefitted from it. The soldiers who pressed their advantage, yea though they were in the wrong were looking for promotions from Lucio's captains. Regardless

135

of these ill-spirited promotions, there were still knights and soldiers who conducted themselves as though God was their witness.

"I would not tease this man," said one guard.

"He sure showed up Spehar," chuckled another guard.

Those two guards represented the difference between the ones who served and the ones who desired service.

"Strong enough to protect that pretty wife of yours?" he waited,
"After bearing children, some women, how shall I put it, lose their appeal, but I got a look at your wife. Your wife looks soft and —-

The jail guard stopped in mid sentence as he was interrupted by the snapping of the wooden pole behind Erdman's back. Everyone there took note of what happened. Erdman had flexed his shoulders forward and broken the binding pole. The spearhead fell to the ground but the longer piece remained under his arm pit against his back. He did not rush out against his captors as his hands were still bound and he was outnumbered. The look in his eyes though was feral and he would have killed the fool if his hands were free. Erdman did accomplish his goal.

"Hey, he broke the binding pole," lamented a guard.

"Now that is the kind of man we need in our army," remarked another guard.

"Maybe he needs a lesson in manners," said yet another guard.

"Here let him share a cell with his farmer friend," said John the jailor.
The threat was made while Erdman's hands were bound. There was a rift of disharmony between the guards and soldiers. They were not accountable in their duties. As John unlocked the cell door, they were interrupted by the authority of the messenger that Lucio sent from

church. Robert, the messenger was in church for more than just the escort he provided to Princess Elayne. He was one of Graedon's castle guards, loyal and God-fearing. He arrived just in time with his authority to instruct them to release Erdman before anything else happened.

"Release the farmer they call Walter as well. These are Lucio's orders," Robert told them.

The messenger stood before them with a sense of authority. By the uniform he wore, they were sure that he got his orders directly from Lucio. Robert watched as they untied the peasant's hands which released the longer part of the broken spear that fell to the ground. Erdman looked at Robert with gratitude. Despite Erdman's strength and resolve, with his hands tied behind him, he expected a beating. He realized that he could now go home to his family. He was spared the humiliation that he would have received at the hands of other less worthy men. Erdman truly was grateful and happy to be leaving the men who would intimidate a man with his hands tied behind him. With the cell door open, Walter came out and joined Erdman. They looked at each other and then looked into the messenger's eyes.

"Thank you," Erdman said.

Walter said nothing but the look of gratitude in his eyes was obvious.

"Best church service I attended," Robert said silently, "now let us get out of here. Come on you two get out, quick!"

Walter did not need an invitation and Erdman did not say another word. Both men followed the messenger's lead up the stairs, through the heavy door to a corridor in the castle. Down that corridor was a door that exited into the side courtyard. The door at the side led to the courtyard next to the church. There Cate patiently waited for her husband with some of their friends who wanted to see if they would really release the prisoners. Erdman's children were sent along home with other friends.

Despite the help from Princess Elayne to free Erdman, Cate was afraid. She thought that they would beat him regardless. When she saw her husband Cate noted that Erdman had torn pants and a bloodied pant leg. She ran toward him. For Cate being in her husband's arms was a miracle and no one believed that more than Erdman. Walter was allowed no visitors in the week that he was there awaiting trial. Fortunately for Walter, he was not whipped during that time due to a Furminatae rite. The sacrificial offerings had to be without blemish. Walter did not realize any of this but he was grateful to be out in time to join his wife and children for Christmas.

The Jailors' Jest

Back in the dungeon the jailor on guard, who witnessed the release of Erdman and Walter, was coming around to collect the prisoner's breakfast dishes that morning. Calogerus and Mattews listened to what had transpired, when they took Erdman there to be jailed. A wooden pole had been broken in two. Calogerus knew that the true character of a person came out when there was no one there to witness what they did. He surmised that not all these guards were cruel. There were those however, who for lack of something to do, would have beaten Erdman unconscious. After the beating, they would release him to go home as a cripple. They would have made Erdman an example of how those who disturb the law are dealt with. Not everyone in the kingdom was of the same spirit as Lucio and Vanessa. Calogerus knew that. He was insistent at calling the guard.

"Have you managed to find a blanket? You said that you would look. Did you, John?" Calogerus asked.

Calogerus overheard the jailor's name when they were there to release prisoners the night before.

"Look, for what?" replied John.

"You remember. You said that you would look for a blanket for me," Calogerus added in a lower voice, "and a stick to beat off this thief. He steals my food."

The jailor had made no such promise, but he was amused that the prisoner considered him a friend. John could not care less about these prisoners. To him everybody was innocent and he had heard it all before.

Calogerus was annoying the guard with questions and whining like a child. He merely persisted to talk. Finally his complaints came to fruition. John looked around and saw the broken wooden binding pole. John picked up the longer portion and noted that the one end was splintered and rather sharp. The jailor could not hand it to him in this condition as it could be used as a weapon that could be turned on him. He stepped on the end and pulled the shaft up breaking off the sharp end. He rubbed the broken end on the uneven stone ground and rounded it. John then went to the cell door and shoved the stick through the small door at the bottom of the door at Calogerus' feet. Calogerus stopped talking.

"There! Your walking stick," said John, "now beat your brains out!"

Mattews smiled.

Calogerus was certain that their escape could only be affected by a diversion of some sort. The diversion that he thought of was to affect a water leak in the tower wall. The ground level of their cell was damp and smelled musty. The level of water outside the wall was enough to entirely flood their cell block. The fact that the water would be near freezing would be secondary on the list of problems. Calogerus stood in thought. Simply put, if the dungeon level was flooded, they would have to move them out. Perhaps in the confusion, both he and Mattews could escape. Calogerus was sure he could disappear. As for Mattews he knew that he was a knight and could take care of himself. The idea was creating a diversion to affect getting out of that dead end dungeon. Springing a leak would provide that diversion and a little excitement too.

Before starting anything, Calogerus always thought out all that was possible so as to minimize the unforeseen. 'Taking the 'un' out of the unknown' was a favorite expression of Calogerus that he used when learning about plants, minerals and animals. He used it when planning and advising Jonquis and Enyja. Planning was a good idea and cut down on frustrations. It let the planner know where he stood, define what was to be done, what resources he had, what was needed and to foresee what problems might arise. It allowed the planner to examine different means of solving a problem and visualizing them as realistically as possible. Planning began by taking stock of what was already known.

Calogerus was aware that both the walls of Braemar Castle's south tower foundations were built upon the bedrock of the Thermanden Bay. The water from Thermanden Bay flowed over dolomite bedrock into the River Brae. The fall was a good ten feet, maybe a little more. There were times when the water level was lower but a steady fall of water from the bay fed the River Brae. In some places the limestone under the dolomite was washed away and harder dolomite blocks fell into the river. After the castle was built, the blocks of dolomite were replaced by stone masons to raise the level of water around the castle. During the low level of water, the stone masons leveled off the rock to make a base for the castle in the northwest corner of the bay. With the base leveled, it was prepared to lay their fashioned stone blocks on. On these stone blocks meticulously fit together, the castle was built. Then after the stone set, the water level was allowed to rise to its former height.

Calogerus noted that there was some seepage of water at the base of the floor in the cell. All that had to be done was to affect some form of crack in the bed stone that would allow the water to enter their cell with more volume. Calogerus foresaw the scene as water rushed into their cell in great volume. He would complain and scream like a madman until the guard opened the cell door. At that time he and Mattews would make their break. He told his plan to Mattews who was not too optimistic that the plan would work. He did have respect for Calogerus though.

"It will take some time to cut through the stone scratching with that pole and small blacksmith's hammer," said Mattews.

"Every great journey begins with a single and first step," Calogerus declared.

Calogerus got Mattews to listen for sounds by the cell door. He started pounding the rock with the hammer to remove loose rock. A new strange sound was added to the repertoire of sounds at Braemar

Castle. Calogerus managed to chip away and form a groove. Then he took the thinner broken end of the wooden pole and held it in the crack. He struck the other end of the wooden pole in an effort to wedge the pole into the crack. He kept pounding, applying more and more force on it until after a short while, the wooden pole got in deeper. He kept hitting the pole but it split into two pieces. Calogerus had put so much force on the pole that it broke into two sharp splintering pieces. He nearly impaled himself in the effort as he fell into it and against the wall. Mattews turned to see if Calogerus was hurt.

"Now I have a walking-stick too," Mattews remarked, "are you hurt?"

"Just disappointed that I did not see," Calogerus answered, "I should have shortened the pole in the first place. At least now I can wedge a second piece into the incision in the rock."

Calogerus always looked on the bright side of things no matter what the circumstances. Errors were welcome so long as you learned from them. So Calogerus worked on as Mattews started to take interest. The cold temperature of the rock made it more brittle to an opposing force. Calogerus pounded away. After some time hitting the crack with the hammer, the stone started to chip. Water started to seep through the small crack. The flow of water from the crack began to increase noticeably. Calogerus asked Mattews to tear the bed sheets into strips. To illustrate his intentions, Calogerus began to tear his bed sheet into strips. What little hay that there was in the mattress could also be used to shove between the cracks of the door. He then got Mattews to affix the mattress stuffing in the cracks between the large oak cell door and the floor.

"Here," said Calogerus as he handed Mattews some cloth, "secure all the cracks between the door and the wall."

Mattews took the bed sheet and followed Calogerus lead. Calogerus never looked more confident, but then Mattews realized that they had not known each other very long. The big oak door had a lip around it so the hinges on the outside could not be tampered with from a prisoner inside the cell.

"I am sure you will tell me what we hope to accomplish," Mattews inquired.

"An element of surprise is our goal. We do not want the water to leak out, just yet," said Calogerus.

"We don't?" replied Mattews.

Mattews now understood what Calogerus was doing. He thought that the entire idea was ingenious and clever, but there was one problem. If Calogerus' plan to flood their cell was to work, it was dependent on the jailor opening the door. If the jailer so desired, he could leave them in there. Mattews remembered that he did not do well in deep water.

The entire weight of the wall rested on the bedrock that had soaked in water for quite some time. If the bedrock stone was struck, it would have to bear the reverberations of that force as well as the weight of the wall on it. It might just be enough to widen the crack and allow more seepage of water. Once the crack was expanded Calogerus thought, the miracle that is water would do its work. Calogerus knew that water expanded whether it was heated or frozen. He observed that even the solid bedrock of the mountains was breached by the roots of the plant vegetation that grew on it with the help of water. The root canal left a path for water to enter. When the temperature dropped and the water froze, it expanded with great force. The force was so great that it was able to crack and displace the dolomite stone on those very surroundings. Of course even in nature the process took water and time and patience. Calogerus was hoping for a miracle.

Calogerus made an allowance that the idea might not work immediately. He realized that it would take time for this plan to work, but there was nothing wrong with assisting nature. The existing crack was already there for some time. The circumstances might be ripe for their plan. He now explained the idea fully to Mattews who started to have faith in it. The only drawback was that it would take time and not the time they had in mind. They would appreciate immediate results, but time is nobody's slave. Neither Mattews nor Calogerus realized Vanessa's plans for them on the 17th of January. They had about a month, their bare hands, a hammer and two sticks to work with.

"Well at least we can take comfort that we are doing something," Calogerus summed up.

If nothing else, Calogerus' attempt to break out of their cell had a good influence on Mattews state of mind. It gave him something to do while he hoped and prayed. To Calogerus, hope was a sea that you could drown in if you did not take action. Calogerus also knew that sometimes hope can be all that you have.

The small drip of water soon began to flow into a trickle. Soon water came into the cell and collected. It began to rise. The job that Mattews did on filling the cracks on the cell door was also complete and done well. The bed cloth stuck between the floor and the door absorbed water. It acted as a stopper. In effect the water level was rising in their cell. The two cell mates looked at each other. It was a small trickle, but the water was cold and it was damp enough in the cell to begin with. At that rate however it would take days for the cell to get flooded. Mattews wondered why he should be so happy. The water level would eventually fill their entire cell well above their heads. They had created a death trap; a dungeon of water. If their plan failed, they will have carried out Vanessa's plans for them. They would die a treacherous death suffocating on cold water as their lungs collapsed.

Calogerus asked Mattews to lift his bed against the height of the wall like a ladder. He demonstrated by taking his own bed, lying it length ward against the wall and then climbing up to sit on the head board. There was no sense getting wet and cold before they had to.

The guard would not be back until morning and by then the water level would reach a good foot or so. It would be significant enough to act as an element of surprise on the jailor and any guards that were with him. It was then that Calogerus and Mattews would have to storm out of the cell. It was a plan, and the way things looked, what else did they have to lose?

The element of surprise is truly surprising. The water trickled in at a low rate, steady and sure, for some time. Mattews had even gotten used to the rising water. Then the force of the water loosed and washed away the wooden stakes that were hammered in to expand the crack. The water flow increased. The weight and force of the water outside the tower pushed against the stone wall. The years of seepage on the foundation wall caused the entire tower to sway. The rate of the water flow increased. The water entered the cell faster and the water level rose faster and faster. The water in the cell was a good three feet and rising. Mattews was quick to point this fact out to his mate.

"The water is rising faster. The wall is shaking!" Mattews professed.

Calogerus had planned the diversion for morning but now it might be sooner. It was supposed to be a small diversion of three feet of water to throw the guards off balance. It looked like they would get more than three feet.

"It is fine. When the water reaches chest level, we will call out for help," Calogerus assured.

"Chest level?" Mattews repeated.

"Chest level," Calogerus reassured.

Mattews was reassured with his words and confidence. Although Calogerus too seemed surprised, his calm nature was reassuring. Then Calogerus looked at the door and began to look concerned.

Calogerus uttered, "Oh ,oh."

"What? You did not plan for something?" asked Mattews.

"It is the small door at the bottom," Calogerus noted, "if they open the small door, it will defeat our purpose. The water will flow out the bottom. They will be surprised but they will not open the cell door. At that point the plan will fail. They will leave us in here to drown in the cold water."

"We could jamb the small door at the bottom?" asked Mattews.

"Not likely," said Calogerus, "it opens up from the outside."

"Then we will have to pray that they do not think about the small door and open the large cell door," concluded Mattews.

"We will wait until the water level is about as high as the cell door. Then we will have to feign a fight. We will make them believe we are fighting. It is dark out there and they have nothing but torch light. Our yelling at each other will divert their attention from any water that trickles out the cell door and divert their attention from the small door," said Calogerus.

"But that will make more guards come," Mattews reasoned.

"Yes, more guards will come, but then the jailor will be sure to open the cell door. Once the door is open, the flow of water will sweep them away and give us a fair opportunity to escape," concluded Calogerus.

Well, it sounded good. The two prisoners waited as the level of the cold water rose and occupied more and more of their cell. The tower wall noticeably swayed back and forth as the water rapidly entered their cell. As the water began to rise inside of the cell, the swaying tower stabilized as Calogerus imagined it would. The wall stopped swaying.

"Oh, oh!" Calogerus uttered.

"What? Is there something else that you did not think about?" asked Mattews.

"Well, when the cell door is opened the flow of water will rush out and sweep the guards away," started Calogerus.

"Yes, that is the plan," confirmed Mattews.

"As the water races out of our cell, there is a good chance that the tower wall will begin to sway again. This time it could come crashing down on us," added Calogerus, "we will have to leave the cell quickly to avoid being crushed under the weight of the stone blocks."

"I will not be slow about it," confirmed Mattews.

Calogerus was right in his assumption. If the cell door was opened the water would rush out of the cell into the hall and fill the open area. Since the volume of water outside the castle walls was greater than inside the cell, the entire south tower would sway again. This time the water entering into the cell would cause the wall to crumble into the cell. If the two cell mates were not quick enough to get out of the cell. The falling wall of the south tower would crush them. The current of the water could easily carry them against a stone wall as well. As clever as Calogerus and Mattews were, would they be lucky enough to escape their jail cell?

Unjustly Labeled

The bravery of the young girl from Eisenholm would have been considered epic if not for the fact that she was a girl. Inge pressed on to climb the mountain and descend the other side. A party of hunters in Osterwald discovered the distressed girl and came to her aid. They had completed their hunt rather successfully and were about to leave for Suerda with their fresh game. Since they were on their way to trade at Suerda, they decided to bring Inge to Brento's court. Inge had survived a massacre, a brutal rape and managed to travel over the mountains to the people of Skarsgard. They were akin to what was left of her people at Hammarsgard, namely her.

It took great strength and courage to do what Inge did. Unfortunately to understand this fully, one would have to be the victim. Inge did not ask or expect this fate. Her family, her Bjorn, and her people were annihilated. She did not ask for her home to be burned. She did not ask to be raped, nor did she deserve this destiny. However from that point on she knew instinctively that what happened to her on that regretful day would affect every aspect of her life forever.

The cavalier attitude of some of people in the community of Skarsgard would not empathize at all with Inge. After all it was not their tribe that was attacked. The people of Hammarsgard went their own way years ago. What was their plight was their plight. Some warrior sailors at Suerda remembered when they had conflicts with their cousins from Hammarsgard on the open sea. Even berry picking created a conflict among those from both sides of the mountain. Most of the Arsgardians from Skarsgard failed to see that this massacre was their problem. Besides, it was not as if they at Skarsgard were attacked. Inge sensed this attitude in the people that looked at her. They seemed to look at her empathetically but passed judgment on her swift and sure.

Brento was a wise ruler and he did not agree with the general attitude of his people toward what happened at Eisenholm. It could have easily been them. Despite turbulent waters, Brento immediately dispatched two ships. The ships and sailors were sent foremost to scout their waters for enemy ships and for the purpose of confirming the story. Brento also resolved to send scouts to return to Osterwald and cross over to Eisenholm. If reports came back that Eisenholm had been occupied, he would waste no time in attacking the invaders regardless of the Evergreenfest. Brento would attack before the enemy had the opportunity to establish its position in Eisenholm. Brento was aware that if the enemy gained knowledge of the mountain path, it would put Suerda in a perilous position by land and sea if enemy ships entered the fjord where Suerda was situated. It was not hard to foresee the danger. Brento vowed that he and his warriors would avenge their cousins in Eisenholm.

The party of hunters who brought Inge from the eastern wilds to Suerda was there to trade the hides and flesh of their game. It would take a few days at most for them to trade their goods. In good times he learned never to accept the first offer. In the mean time Brento had ample time to prepare a band of warriors to send over the mountains. For sure Brento thought that this appalling outrage would stir all the Arsgardian people up. The seas were more treacherous to sail at this time, and the ships and sailors that he sent would be challenged. However, their safety and survival made it important for the ships to set out. By land the warriors that he was sending could easily cross over the mountain. The hunters from Osterwald thought that a good fifty to one hundred warriors would accompany them back. Then, the thirty-five or so other hunters from the Osterwald region would join them and cross over to examine Eisenholm. There they would either attack the foe or build a lookout and hold it in defiance. The hunters were ready to join the fight against whatever threat there was at Eisenholm. With the fear of war looming, the hunters of Ostervald sold their goods promptly to eager buyers. Brento sent out the land force without delay.

Inge remained at Brento's court. Though Inge was of great beauty, she had been raped by barbaric savages, and she might even be with a child. For some Inge became an object to possess, trifle with and leave. Those whose advances she denied labeled her a tramp for denying them. The truth was that those particular men were no different than the very label they gave to the barbaric savages. It was not enough that she was cruelly violated Inge would now have to bear the consequences of the lack of compassion, indifference and even the hate of some people.

Some girls hated this new comer to their tribe and did not hesitate to let her know her place. In their mind Inge's place was below them. Even young woman who unwisely chose to throw away their virtue were happy that now there was someone they could consider less than themselves. The nightmare only began with the massacre at Eisenholm. Inge would be reminded about her plight whenever it became convenient for anyone who needed to put someone down to feel better. After a few days in Brento's court the fact that she could not integrate left her desperate. Inge carried some food in a cloth wrap and ran away toward Osterwald.

Not everyone was ignorant and self absorbed. Marta, a middle aged woman from the Osterwald region met Inge on her return. Marta took Inge to her father's house that was close by. There her mother took pity on this young woman and welcomed her into her home. Marta, like her mother, was a practical woman who was not quick to judge. Marta lived with her husband Beni. There were other fine men and women with families that lived in Osterwald. Their community was east of Suerda and high up in the mountains.

In Osterwald they lived closer to the forest where they made their living. They were hunters and their women were used to living alone for blocks of time. Most of the clothing that the people of Skarsgard wore was once an elk, deer, wolf or bear that these hunters killed. The other women that lived in Osterwald were, hard working and very independent. It was here that the healing process began for Inge. Take note that the healing process began. Not all the scars that remain from a wound are visible.

Marta, Zuzan, Elbe, Elke, Basia and Naya were sisters. There were other women that resided in Osterwald with their husbands and families. What was unique about these girls was that the old, wise Ignaz and his wife Anghar had seven daughters. One of their daughters died. The fact that there were so many girls and no boy was a point of humor in the village. Ignaz was a mighty hunter and a ferocious warrior. He had red hair and was even taller than Brento. If you saw both Ignaz and Brento together you would think that they were brothers. Somewhere in the family tree they were related maternally but that was long ago. Ignaz was the only hunter in Osterwald that did not have a son. He would not agree with the notion that he did not need any. Ignaz' daughters were as feral as they were beautiful. When it came to getting things done as far as the workload was concerned, Ignaz' homestead was never in want.

Anghar was a wise old woman who had been through many births. Her suspicion of pregnancy was confirmed by Inge. Inge was afraid to confide and tell anyone. She did not know who to trust or what to expect. Inge desperately needed to tell someone. When she was sure about her company she admitted to Anghar that she was pregnant. The first emotion that was felt by Anghar was that of hatred for the invaders. Now their seed was growing in a fine Arsgardian girl. Anghar realized that it was not just that she should take out that anger on Inge. She could not account for how other people would feel?

Anghar comforted Inge. She told her to keep the news to herself for the time being and not to worry about what anyone thought. Anghar would tell Ignaz himself when he returned from accompanying Brento's warriors to Eisenholm. Anghar would tell Ignaz preferably before setting out on another hunt. In that way Ignaz would have time to think the matter through before making an impulsive decision. Once a decision was made, an Arsgardian man never backed down or changed his mind. Changing your mind was a sign of a weak man. Anghar thought that in Ignaz' fury, he would also be sure to return with a lot of game.

Anghar took Inge into her arms like one of her own daughters. She and Ignaz had lost their last child. The child was late in coming and Anghar had been ill during the birthing. The child's birth went well. Nusia the elder woman of their village told everyone that although Naya, their previous baby, was the most beautiful baby that she ever saw, this baby surpassed even her beauty. All of Anghar's daughters were beauty incarnate. It was not even six months that passed before the baby's skin got red blotches on it. The blotches were painful and the child could not stop crying from the pain. Nourishing the child was impossible as it dispelled more vomit and acid than the milk it ingested. Many cures were employed to help the baby overcome the rosy complexion that the tempest brought. Anghar herself had named the child Inge. After six daughters, Ignaz was tired of naming another daughter. Nusia was quite skilled in birthing. Every known cure that might help the baby was tried including hope. The baby stopped crying one day, forever. Anghar thought that Odin was punishing Ignaz for his ungrateful attitude toward his daughters. For Anghar, Inge's arrival was like the return of her own child who would have been about the same age by now.

Pregnancy is not something that you can hide forever. In the case of Inge it would not be too long before she started showing let alone experiencing the challenges of the experience. In the mean time several of the younger boys in the community of Osterwald had noted the beauty of Inge as a recent addition to Ignaz' other daughters who were not married. There was no jealousy among the daughters either. In their innocent way the young boys fantasized about winning the love of one of these fair maidens. They were very kind to Inge. She was better suited for one of their older brothers, but they had the same regard for her as any of Ignaz' daughters. They were considerate and kind until the day that a self-righteous mother instructed her son to keep away from Inge. This woman ascertained that she was with child and thought it her motherly duty to warn her son against Inge. The boy was too young anyway but some people have to assert themselves even when it does not concern them. The word got out and so did the attitude.

Soon everyone who saw Inge stopped what they were doing and looked at her. No one spoke to her or accused her of anything. Their treatment of Inge was like that of an outcast. The welcome feeling of community was lost now that everyone learned that Inge was with a child, the enemy's child. There were several older boys that took a liking to Inge as if she were one of the girl's from Osterwald. They had plans to win her dessert at the Springbokfest in Suerda. Things changed when they learned the news.

In anticipation of Springbokfest, Inge prepared by baking a fruit pastry with berries as did all the other eligible young girls. Anghar was impressed with the care that Inge put into her baking. The smell that came from the wild apple pastry would attract any man or woman for that matter. Inge had picked the apples herself in the clearing just before the forest wall. Often Inge had company when she decided to walk into the wild forest. A group of the younger boys would escort her. They accompanied Inge, to protect her of course, from any wild beasts that she might encounter. Of all the boys that liked Inge, Hansen was by far the nicest boy and truest for her. Hansen was rather stout and strong, and simple. He was a few years older than her and he had fallen in love with Inge. Hansen loved Inge but his concern was about what the others were saying about her and what they would think. In truth, Hansen was just the person that Inge needed to love her and, for his part, he would never regret it. Inge was an honorable, committed, dutiful girl who liked the gentle qualities of Hansen. They would have made a fine couple, but Hansen was still not fully mature.

Springbokfest fever came and Osterwald sent competitors to Suerda to face the finest contenders in games of skill from all over the country. All the eligible young men would compete in feats of strength, skill and cunning. It was their goal to win not only the competitions but the girl of their choice to eat dessert with. All the eligible young women competed for the young men's stomachs with baked pastries. There were a few instances over the years when the pastry was not that fine but that did not matter. If the girl was beautiful, the baking was delicious.

There was one year when looks did not win out. A young man named Bron, the village ox, won the dessert of one Brunhilde. She was thought to be the most beautiful girl ever. After eating her pastry Bron looked disappointed and went home, alone. Bron was not up to asking for any other girl without doing some thinking. It was the only time in Brunhilde's life that she was walked out on. She found it hard to believe. Brunhilde did not like Bron anyway and got to go with her true love, but she was offended just the same. There were many boys and girls that came from settlements all over Skarsgard. It was a great way for the youth to meet and compete and more importantly, choose a mate. The warlords and elders found it an excellent place to recruit the future warriors to sail their ships and find a worthy son-in-law.

Culture of Necessity

The elders favorite game was the axe throw. In the axe throw a young Arsgardian could demonstrate his usefulness if a raiding party planned to storm a castle. A series of felled logs were permanently fastened to the ground a good three feet like a fence. It was the competitor's task to throw five axes and then use the axes to climb over to the other side. In a raid, a castle drawbridge could be scaled and a few courageous, dependable men would enter. After overpowering the gate keepers, they would let loose the drawbridge for the raiders to enter. The logs were not only stripped of their bark but had long lost their moisture and were more like stone. Many of the younger boys could not get their axes to stick into the wood. Some axes did not penetrate deeply enough into the logs. The competitor only realized that when he went to scale the wall in the second part of the competition. If the axe did not hold his weight he would fall to the ground. It was not fun falling but then in a real battle it would cost him his life. Even betting took place as the elders bet a horn of ale as to whose axes would hold out.

Another favorite game of the elders was the tug of war. From old Arsgardian custom, a team of five men would challenge another team of five men. A long, thick rope was required. It was strung over burning coals. According to tradition the two teams would assemble on either side of the burning coals and take up the rope. On the word of Olaf, the standing champion, they began to pull. Olaf was the last member of the all time champion group. That group was never defeated in their lifetime. The other members were lost to battle, old age, and Borg fell off his ship in the fog and drown one night. Since Olaf was responsible for providing the rope, he expected it to be cared for. If the rope caught fire he would chase and drag back each team member and throw them butt first onto the burning coals. The result was that the losing team was swift to get the rope off of the coals. In the competition the winning team of course was the one that pulled the other team over the coals.

Another challenge came with the log role. Five thick logs were required for this event. The logs that were no more than 10 to 12 feet lay on the water fenced in by the docks. The competitors, two at a time, would climb onto the log and had to stay on despite the efforts of another challenger to knock him into the water. The competitors were allowed a staff and could use any means to cause the fall of their opponent. The log role was truly a game of skill. A competitor had to be quick on his feet. As the log turned he had to maintain balance while an unfriendly staff in the hands of his opponent could knock him off as well. If a challenger fell in, he was disqualified. In the end the competitor with the swiftest feet and balance that remained dry was declared the winner of all the logs in the water. To the spectators it looked simple and entertaining. Before starting though, you had to drink a horn of ale. When you added the ale that they drank to the rocking motion of the log on the water, and the skilled staff bearer on the other side of the log, it was tough. The older more experienced men who were used to ale were at an advantage in this event.

Every member of every ship challenged the other crews in the log role. Even the hunters were welcome to try their luck. The sailors did not take the hunters for granted. The hunters were very nimble and quick on their feet. With the added ale drinking, eventually most men fell into the water. Many fell in and received a cold bath in the waters that still remembered the past winter. It was all in food sport. Boys as young as 12 years of age were encouraged to compete. As these younger boys got more experienced with the passing years, some skipped their 'bath' by moving their feet and shifting their weight with purpose. They also learned to use the staff effectively. Practice truly does make perfect.

The competitors in broadswords made their own swords and shields. Hammers were allowed too and were quite a threat in the proper hands. In the past, quite a few swords were broken during this competition, but over the years the quality of swords improved. The art of sword-making was Bernun's specialty. Everyone desiring a sword consulted with Bernun or had him make the thing. There were others that experimented making swords for themselves as a matter of family pride. An award was given for the best looking shield, sword and hammer. The greatest award however was given to the shield, sword or hammer that belonged to the swiftest and strongest hands on the field. The art of competing with a war hammer counted too. The custom of swinging a hammer with a long handle in battle was a common weapon to the Arsgardian people. They believed that their god of thunder possessed both such a hammer and bolts of lightning.

Archery was an important skill as was battle with shields, swords and hammers. Archers made their own bows and arrows. Whether to use in hunting or battle, precision crafting was the key to possessing a fine bow and the arrows to discharge. The hunters of Osterwald had great success in the archery competition year after year. As a hunter your skill with a bow had to be flawless or you would know hunger. The warrior sailors were not to be outdone either with their raiding experiences and fighting on the rocking, high seas. A warring archer had to be accurate with his marks too. There were a great number of entries for archery at the beginning of the event, but it was a matter of time before the numbers shrunk to include only the most precise bowmen. The warrior sailors made their mark in this competition too.

Shipbuilding competition was encouraged as youths designed and fashioned their own small vessel and oars for about five hands. These smaller vessels would also be used to defend the fjord. They were set on fire and sent toward the enemy vessel in case it appeared on the water. Entries came from all the settlements of Skarsgard despite Suerda having the most skilled shipbuilders because of their vicinity to the water. Awards were given for the best looking ship. Hours of work on carvings were made by the boys. Then the true test came, the manner in which the ship handled on the water. In the race across the fjord, young men and old had to row to a small, rocky island toward the mouth of the fjord and back for the best time. The island was used as an early look out for enemies entering the fjord. The look outs were equipped with horns that warned if any foreign ship sailed toward Suerda. They also had the means to discharge burning arrows on an unwelcome intruder's sails. High on the mountains overlooking the fjord there were several other look out encampments. Early detection of the enemy was the key to survival. These small ships and the young boys that sailed them were also counted on to defend their home in case of attack. These would also take their place building and serving on the larger ships one day.

At an Arsgardian event there was fun and food and ale. It was traditional to drink ale in the horns of animals that they had hunted. Arsgardian tribes had learned to use as much of their natural environment including parts of animals to improve their lives. Ale and water were transported in both barrels and skins for travel on the ships or hunting. When the warrior and hunter were home, they preferred to drink in a more civilized manner from the horns of a ram or musk ox. A true skilled hunter would have amassed a complete set for his family and entertaining.

The staple food that they ate included dry cured flesh, roasted musk ox and of course the delicacy of smoked salmon. Raw carrots were washed and sliced with other greens to complement the meal. There were wild nuts of all sorts; walnuts, chestnuts, filberts and peanuts. Of course there were many grains that grew in the meadows. With the baked seven grain bread brought from the mountain tribes, the notion that bread and smoked salmon was all that you needed to live was a popular notion among the Arsgardian people.

An Added Attraction

Inge's return to the festival at Suerda only brought to mind the memory of her former community at Eisenholm. Then there were those who recognized Inge from Brento's court at Ragarsmut Rook. Some boys began to scheme about how to tease her. She would be an easy target. They approached her directly and treated her as if she was their property. Keemo, an informal leader among the boys, walked over to Inge and cut off her path. He rudely stuck his hand into Inge's wild apple pastry and broke off a chunk. Inge was sad as she could not enter the pastry now. Keemo ate it before her like the conquering warrior all the while looking at Inge with contempt. Hansen stepped in and punched Keemo in the mouth. Keemo fell onto his back. The dropped the pie as he went down, but it was not over. The entire community at Suerda was eager to be entertained. They prodded Keemo on with OOO's and Ahhh's. Keemo got up and favored a tooth. He stretched his jaw and spit out a tooth and smiled. The tooth he lost made his smile even more threatening.

Pound for pound Hansen was stronger and heavier than Keemo, but he also made a good target for swift moving fists. Keemo was carefree and fearless. He did not waste any time and struck Hansen with three unanswered blows. Two blows landed on Hansen's stomach the other across his face. They hurt, especially the one across the face, but Hansen remained standing. He braced himself, lined up his sight of Keemo and swung a blow at him. Keemo ducked it effortlessly and countered with another three blows. Hansen was hurt but he stood his ground.

"No! Stop this!" cried Inge.

Inge looked to see if she could see Ignaz, surely he could intervene and stop this.

Keemo decided to prolong the punishment of Hansen. He lined up his opponent and delivered a quick single blow, then another. Hansen weathered the blows and waited and waited. Keemo kept getting closer and closer to land his punches. Hansen kept weathering them as his aggressor got careless. Then with Keemo as close as he could be, Hansen launched the biggest and fastest blow that he could against Keemo. The blow set Keemo back as it was hard and heavy, but this only enraged him more. Keemo decided that he would keep away from those fists. He decided to deliver his beating slowly by striking fast from a safe distance. After numerous blows to the face of Hansen, Inge rushed out between the two. She turned and placed her hands on Hansen's face. Hansen was angry and pushed Inge out of the way. In pushing her away, he left himself open for another brutal blow to his face. The moment that Inge was shoved, Anghar rushed out to help her and called for the fight to stop.

"You brave young men! Pushing a girl!" Anghar protested as she comforted Inge.

"More like a whore with a bastard child!" replied Keemo.

There were gasps from the immediate crowd that heard what he said and waited for a reply. The rest of the crowd that watched did not hear it. Their merrymaking drowned out the comment effortlessly. Apart from the crackling fires, there was silence when Ignaz entered the scene. You could see Ignaz towering over the people who gathered to watch the spectacle. As Ignaz drew closer to the contest, Keemo stood his ground. He had nothing to lose. In the eyes of the spectators, Keemo had won. In his mind, the comment that he had made was nothing that was not true. He felt no guilt or remorse over beating Hansen, hurting a girl and making her cry. Keemo even tried to stare down Ignaz but that was going nowhere. Keemo turned away and was greeted by his friends. They handed him a horn of ale and patted him on the back and congratulated him with their laughter.

The noise came on again and celebrations resumed. Later Keemo's big mouth would be the reason for another fight among the young men who competed. This behavior was not out of place. The older warriors and elders encouraged this behavior. The men of Skarsgard were satisfied that it was healthy to keep their men alert and ready for battle. It was imperative to be ready for battle. None of the elders heard what was said by Keemo and some did not know the circumstances fully.

Words could not express the humiliation and loneliness that Inge felt. She was called a whore. Her child was labeled a bastard. The emptiness that she felt was in contrast to the infant growing in her womb. She felt empty and yet she was not. The agony made her cry in broken bursts. She could not speak. Her pain was so deep that her lungs were divided by breaths that supplied life to her body and breaths that pushed out the grief in her heart. It even hurt to breathe. At one point she seemed to stop breathing. Anghar did what she could by holding Inge in the fashion that a mother comforted her daughter in such a situation. With her one arm around her shoulders, Anghar took her free hand and patted Inge's head like you would to a little girl.

Inge's mind relived for her the harsh reality at the hands of the Huynsten soldiers and in the same instance, the present betrayal by her own people. In a slow pace she relived her rape, the intrusion of Keemo with the sticky apple filling and crumbs from her baking on his hands and mouth, the cruel fight between Keemo and Hansen, and then being pushed away by Hansen. The only positive item to place on the scale in an attempt to balance it was Inge being in Anghar's arms. All around her she saw faces of pity, or scorn. She heard the scorn of laughter. She felt that it was all directed toward her. Warriors, hunters, fishermen, women, and children: everyone else was enjoying the Springbokfest.

Inge saw Hansen favoring his wounds and retreating away as if he too was disgraced by his beating. Inge thought that Hansen felt disgraced and it was all because of her. Nothing she saw came across as positive to her. Inge was in a crowd and yet alone. Anghar called on her but her voice was distant in Inge's mind. Then it happened, she had an awful painful feeling. She began to lose the child. It was not immediately evident to those enthralled by the festivity around them. By the way that Inge grimaced, clenched her fists and grabbed her stomach, Anghar imagined it straight away. She would have to move fast and take Inge away from the commotion of all the people.

Anghar did not tell her suspicion to Ignaz, but protested about the commotion. Ignaz knew when his wife had enough and was anxious to leave. She told her husband that she had much work to do at home. Anghar told Ignaz that she would take Inge home to Osterwald with her. She was not expecting her husband to follow her. Anghar was not about to take Ignaz away from celebrating with his friends. Besides that, he still qualified for the next round in the archery challenge. Anghar collected Inge onto the cart pulled by their ox and left immediately.

On the way home Inge began crying but the discomfort had settled down somewhat. Then Inge had an uneasy pain. She let out a gasp and curled up in pain. During the pangs of pain she had to hold her breath. Anghar stopped the wagon and helped Inge climb down. Anghar accompanied Inge to a nearby stream but said nothing. The baby was lost. She realized that there were no words to speak that would bring comfort to the young girl. She would wait until Inge was ready to speak. Inge did not speak as she was exhausted physically and mentally, but she had many thoughts running through her mind. She was unjustly labeled and mistreated at the Springbokfest. She lost the child in her womb due to the hatred of her fellow men. The enemy forced the child on her, but her fellow men killed the child. It would be a matter of weeks before Inge uttered a word again.

After the regrettable day at Springbokfest in Suerda some time passed. In Osterwald, Hansen eventually came around to see Inge. He had taken time to think about what happened and regretted pushing Inge away. He truly cared for her but he had acted like a boy. He was sorry, but she paid him no mind. Inge had wanted to marry and raise a family of her own. It was her dream since she played as a little girl and her grandfather lavished her with puppets, dolls and ingenious little trinkets. They were wonderful gifts as she appreciated them. They were lost for all time now. As a young lady she learned about the difference between infatuation and love. Although he was not the most refined of sleek boy, she had saved herself for Bjorn. Inge saw Bjorn's face

161

in a dream. There he stood with that innocent, shy and sincere look. At one point she even wondered if he was he passing judgment on her too. She could see him in both faces.

When she awoke though, she realized that it had been a dream. The reality was that Bjorn was taken from her. He could no longer help her so she faced her present circumstances. Under the circumstances, Hansen was a sweet idea as she could have married him for love. Hansen's behavior at Springbokfest spoke the truth. Inge's past was too much for him to deal with. It was hard especially since these people were so cold, abrupt and uncaring. Inge now had another goal in mind. Although she had liked Hansen, she did not need him or any other man for that matter. She was going to train her body for combat. In her mind, Inge would never again depend on a man for anything.

Queen Enyja and Her In-Laws

As Ellen and her councilors left Leems and sailed toward Craigroyston, there was sad news. The kingdom of Craigroyston had the unhappy event of burying King Jonquis. Still a young man, the king succumbed to water in the lungs from a repeated chill that clung to him for dear life. Jonquis had been fighting that chill on and off since the end of summer. Before leaving on his mission to see King Graedon, Calogerus told his king outright to rest. The idea of getting rest was stressed and Jonquis assured his loyal friend that he would. The fact was that he did not change anything in his routine. In an effort to impress Enyja he almost pressed on with even more activity. In his sleep one night the king died. Jonquis received the proper burial fitting a king.

Although the power to rule Craigroyston remained in the capable hands of Queen Enyja, it was common knowledge that she and Jonquis had two daughters. There was uneasiness among the subjects of the kingdom. Someday the kingdom would have a new king, but who and from where?

It was a solemn occasion that Ellen's homecoming should be affected by the loss of her husband's kingdom and now to learn of the death of her brother. Ellen promptly paid respect for her brother's passing and gave her condolences to Enyja.

After the arrival of Ellen and her royal family to the safety of Craigroyston, it did not take long for her husband's ministers to start scheming. Haaron had insisted that Arno accompany Queen Ellen and her family. The good knight believed that the royal family would have good counsel if Arno accompanied them. With Arno present he could council Queen Ellen with matters of court. It was equally important to explain to monarchs of Craigroyston truthfully the circumstances surrounding the fall of Leems. The removal of Arno was the first thing to do on Ranton's list. On the third day of the voyage to Craigroyston Arno was lured into a conversation with Ranton, Rheymand and Danther on the deck at night. In the middle of a conversation, Rheymand struck Arno over the head with a belly club. As he fell Ranton and Danther caught him and threw him overboard while the clouds covered the moonlight.

At the Karley, the court in Norsendan, Ranton, Rheymand and Danther denounced Karnivron and feigned concern over the lost market for Craigroyston's cod stocks and agricultural products; namely lamb and wool from Roysford. The councilors and especially the merchants in Craigroyston were concerned over the lost market in Leems. The former Leemite councilors brought that point forward immediately. Ranton continued to bash Haaron for his failure to protect the kingdom from the barbarian Karnivron. Ranton, Rheymand and Danther got the attention of the Karley with their testimony about the events that brought King Mattic's Leems to its ruin. Of course they painted themselves in a good light. 'If only their counsel was adhered to', they told the councilors. They told the Karley that they did not blame King Mattic. The Leemite king was torn in different directions. On one hand Mattic was counseled to negotiate with the warlord. On the other hand he was encouraged to attack. The men of the army always want to attack, they claimed. Of course in this instance it was the exact opposite. In the absence of Arno, they lied. The councilors of the Karley listened to them.

It was common knowledge that Ellen was a princess of Craigroyston before she was Queen Ellen of Leems. Norsendan was her father's castle and childhood home. Since her brother had an untimely death, then the crown by all rights could fall back to her if necessity arose. It was especially favorable since Ellen had a male heir. What Ranton, Rheymand and Danther intentionally overlooked was that Enyja was the Queen in Craigroyston from a union between two former dukedoms. The Leemite counselors also overlooked the fact that Enyja gave birth to two heirs by her husband King Jonquis. The two young princesses Concetta and Julia were Jonquis and Enyja's daughters. Although they were not male heirs, they were heirs just the same. Then of course it did not pass Ranton's mind that should something awful happen to Enyja and her daughters, then Ellen by all rights would be the rightful heir.

The former councilors of Leems wanted to press the fact that Mattic and Ellen had a male heir. Henri and his sister Elyse were the children of Mattic and Ellen. Their grandfather was Betrand of Craigton, now Craigroyston. Coupled with the fact that Ellen was deposed from her husband's country by a barbarian horde, the people of Craigton welcomed their princess. Ranton hoped that these common facts might prove to be of interest concerning the good people of Craigroyston. What if perhaps the people of the realm were unhappy with their present lot in life under the reign of Enyja?

With the death of King Jonquis matters could get worse now that a woman was in charge.

Ranton counted upon human nature to complain in the best of times. In his experience he noted that in the search to make things easier, people have actually expended more energy than it would have taken to do the work in the first place. If you ask a tailor, there are some corners that cannot be cut. Having the right to complain does not mean that you need to. People forgot that in some places on the aerde, one could not complain though they needed to. Once a tyrant got the people by the throat and was established, he was awfully hard to depose. Tyrants rewarded the strong to subdue the masses to do their will. In his mind Ranton saw the Karley Council as easy to manipulate. Since there was a male heir from Betrand's line, it provided an option. Well at least it would prove interesting for the people of Craigton. The former councilors of Leems had nothing to lose even if they broke up Craigroyston into its two former dukedoms. So long as Ranton and his confreres could be in power and administrate over the people, who cared if the kingdom was split?

For the time being Ranton was satisfied with making connections in the Karley Council. He was happy to wait. In time Ranton believed that anything could happen and that anything was possible. If Ranton's life had a meaning, this was the meaning. Ranton also cultivated the merchants and appeared endearing to the people in the market. The very people that Ranton labeled as common, inferior and insignificant could be useful when it came to swinging a power struggle. Ranton knew that these people would be willing to listen if the right opportunity presented itself. Ranton, Rheymand and Danther used every opportunity to make friends from the greatest to the least in the Karley Court.

Ranton even cooperated with Arturus at the Admiralty informing him about the Karpretian numbers that took over Kilkenny Castle in Leems. Ranton claimed that the number of Karnivron's forces could not be counted. In his opinion though there was no further need to risk men and ships to retake the castle. Ranton thought that the only hope for Leems was for Karpretian disunity. The different tribes might occupy Kilkenny Castle for a while. As the supply of food dwindled though, they would return to their steppes. They will have tired of their conquest. When there was no enemy to unite these nomadic tribes they would return to fighting amongst themselves. It was Ranton's wish that somehow the disgruntled Karpretians would kill Haaron in the process.

As a matter of practice, Ranton and his cohorts learned who the sincere, dedicated, service oriented councilors of Craigroyston were and courted them. They also learned who had the most influence, who were hungry for more and who had the most influence. Some of these councilors, the considerate, were perceived as weak. Ranton and his cronies complemented them and engaged them in amiable discussions of principle that these councilors would no doubt be delighted to discuss. A lot of discussions about principles were brought forth and Ranton could be seen being most agreeable. Simple problems that were not of critical importance were posed to these fine Craigroyston councilors to gain their confidence. These councilors were only too happy to discuss and offer constructive advice. The councilors noted how Ranton, Rheymand and Danther were jovial souls and did a lot of listening.Ranton, Rheymand, and Danther, the chief rabble rousing councilors of Mattic's former court in Leems, praised the manner in which tax money was collected and allotted to strengthen the navy. To Arturus they stressed that the sooner that more warships were built, the safer everyone would be. They led the councilors that supported the navy to believe that too. Given what happened at Leems, taxes could never be too much for the purpose of defense, they encouraged. They added that the taxpaying people would just have to appreciate the matter. They agreed with every councilor of the Karley even though it was impossible to fund all their ambitious plans all at once.

The overall opinion of Enyja's councilors was that Ranton, Rheymand, Danther were fine individuals who had served King Mattic loyally. They were fine representatives of Mattic's former kingdom who had been routed from their homes. Enyja's councilors had consideration for the Leemite councilors that had lived through the terrible ordeal. Having been complimented and revered, Enyja's councilors grew bolder with their requests for more money for their respective areas of concern at the Karley. Their judgment was skewed. Ranton, Rheymand, Danther did the same with the nobles and merchants who paid taxes to the crown. With the opposite view, the nobles and merchants were made to question why so much money was being spent on the navy. They planted the seeds of malcontent amongst the satiated. The merchants questioned, 'how much tax is enough?

How many warships are enough?
Is there no end to the taxes?'

Ranton even gave them a reason for questioning the taxes. There was a supposed peace struck between the Arsgardian tribes and Craigroyston. Ranton learned about the agreement from discussions with the Craigroyston councilors and merchants. Ranton posed a series of questions to them that would lead them to question the increased naval spending. Ranton immediately added the point about peace with Skarsgard to their argument. There was peace, yet there were more warships being built. There could only be one explanation for that. They surmised that, for what reason were more ships being built, if not to go to war?

The loss of lives over the three ships that went to Wendover's aid was fresh in the minds of the people of Craigroyston. Although the ordeal was explained to them and they understood the long term value, they still sided with not getting involved. Nobody wished to sacrifice the flower of the land; their sons to face slaughter in order to keep others rich. Surely there were better things to do with the money, or perhaps better still the council should lower the taxes on goods traded or sold.

The people of Craigroyston forgot about the loss of two warships during the late summer. Those two ships should at least have been replaced. There were also other expenses associated with running a navy; the cost of maintenance and repair and sailors wages. The most important fact that was omitted from this argument was the sacrifice in human life if their neighbor's enemy had met with success. Given an option the navy of Craigroyston would sooner risk fighting an enemy on the high seas and foreign soil than on their own homeland. It would be a better option not to have to fight at all, but the people were no longer children. The cost of freedom sometimes called for and came at the price of bloodshed. Freedom did not come free at all and demanded the highest price. The desire to be free to live under God's laws required that men and women understood the call and contributed toward it to the best of their ability.

In only a short time the councilors from Craigroyston were across purposes and even began to question Enyja's rule. The people were made to wonder whether they were really doing well after the death of Jonquis. What would follow Enyja, a pair of princesses that were too young to realize their responsibility?

It was noted that Princess Concetta had an infatuation for Brento's son. Would an Arsgardian sit on the throne?

Would either princess marry the right man?

What, if any experience, would her husband have and where would his allegiance lie?

Could the kingdom afford to find out?

Ranton then cunningly suggested that Ellen could replace Enyja as queen should the need arise. After all this was Ellen's home long before Enyja came along. To top that, her male son, Henri was King Betrand's grandson. Danther made the comment to the Craigroyston Councilors that if Ellen were queen, she would be a much more reasonable monarch. He asked them to look at matters now. Could matters get worse with the stalemate that presented itself after much deliberation?

Rheymand proclaimed that Ellen would listen to their wise counsel. The councilors were told that since Ellen was not familiar with all the kingdom's affairs that she would rely on their guidance and expertise. She would need councilors such as them until her son could assume the throne again under their guidance. Some of Enyja's councilors had such a high opinion of themselves that they swallowed up the complement. Others saw an opportunity to press their issues. They thought themselves to be so wise, but the wool was pulled over their eyes.

The Eyre of Enyja

With the pushing and pulling that Ellen's councilors from Leems brought to Craigton, emotions ran high and erupted within the very castle walls at Norsendan. The growing sentiment that taxes were too high, caused a riot to break out at the market. Fortunately, those responsible were apprehended from among the many merchants and farmers alike. These people were jailed for instigating the revelry. Queen Enyja was very accommodating and sympathetic toward her sister-in-law, Ellen, but she needed to clear the air of misconception. Enyja considered that it must have been frightening for Ellen during the final days of Mattic's reign at Leems. Ellen lost her husband and their kingdom. She and her children fled for their lives. All the time surrounded by uncertainty. All that considered Enyja had a kingdom to rule too.

With the death of her own husband King Jonquis, the threat of the changing world around her and the absence of Calogerus it made the ruling of Craigroyston a challenge. These were trying times. The councilors had always brought their ideas freely to the court and in earnest discussed and argued to determine the best course of action for the kingdom to take. In the past, common sense prevailed in their decisions in the end. That was in the past. Enyja saw that all that it took was the rabble rousers from the former Leems to upset the balance and skew deliberation at the Karley. Mattic's former councilors had accomplished just that and it was by design.

To Enyja it was becoming more apparent who the influential voices at Mattic's White Brick Court were. Although she was kept well informed by those loyal to her, she had to take action. Enyja did not think Ellen was ill willed toward her or to have ambitions on her crown. In truth, Ellen had Haaron on her mind the entire voyage to Craigroyston and nothing else since. In the end Enyja believed that Ellen would not challenge her brother's wife. Enyja also believed that if the crown of Craigroyston were to fall on Ellen's head, she would not refuse it either. It was at this time that Enyja wished that Calogerus had returned from his mission to Rothaynen. Enyja knew what had to be done, but it helped when a trusted advisor that loved her like her father stood by her in support. Jonquis was not there anymore. It was time for Enyja to rule and rule alone.

Enyja visited Ellen in her chamber quarters and had a heartfelt chat with her sister-in-law. After talking about Henri and Elyse adjusting to life at Norsendan Castle, Enyja thought that Ellen should be made aware of her councilors plotting. Enyja needed to learn just how sincere Ellen was. She was not disappointed. After Enyja told her all about the scheme of Leems' former councilors, Ellen told Enyja about what happened in Leems. Contrary to Ranton's version, Ellen told Enyja how the loyal Haaron had advised Mattic to make peace with Karnivron. She told her how Haaron was imprisoned and about Mattic's ill advised attack on Karnivron.

Ellen was shocked with her councilor's shameless actions at Enyja's court. Despite being in the dark with their intentions, they were planning to invest her on the throne of Craigroyston. It was never her desire to interfere with Jonquis or Enyja despite the untimely death of her brother. In Leems Haaron was right about everything. If only Mattic had listened to his counsel all would be well. She never really doubted Haaron's loyalty but Ellen realized that she was blinded by Mara's presence. She realized that she was in love with Haaron. She realized that Mara was in love with Haaron as well.

"With all the kindness that your majesty has shown us, I apologize for the wickedness of my councilors. Has your majesty decided what to do with them?" asked Ellen.

Ellen was quite aware that the penalty for treason was death. If death is what Enyja had chosen for her councilors, Ellen would not dispute it.

"I have not as yet decided," Enyja replied, "but I will decide shortly. You must keep silent about what we have discussed. I will call the Karley to session this very evening. You will attend of course."

"Naturally, your majesty," agreed Ellen.

"I will leave you now," Enyja told her.

With having said that, Enyja left Ellen's chambers requited at least that while she was to be the sole monarch of Craigroyston, her sister-in-law had not plotted against her.

Not even Enyja's ministers were cued as to her intentions for calling court so abruptly on such short notice. Enyja would address them all in equal measure. The good, the wise and those who fell into the rabble rousers snare, all would hear what she had to say without them having time to prepare a response. There were also dignitaries that arrived from Skarsgard to pay homage for the passing of King Jonquis. The Arsgardian sailors planned to discuss trade routes and compare geographical cartes with Enyja's navy council at the Admiralty.

When the Karley was assembled, Enyja's entrance was announced and she took her place. The court was unusually silent as they all witnessed Ranton, Rheymand and Danther being escorted in irons to the place of judgment before the crown. The crown attorney presented the charges against the former Leemite councilors. The defendants were asked how they plead to the charge of conspiring to commit treason. They made no reply. Thad, the defendants' attorney, pleaded not guilty on behalf of his clients. Ranton looked away as he smiled. After listening to the witnesses statements as read aloud by their legal councilor, witnesses were cross examined. Even Ellen was called on to recount the painful tragedy at Leems. The Karley now heard to truth with regards to what happened at Leems. Then it was the defendants' opportunity to speak, but they declined. The councilors of the Karley, nobles and merchants alike were embarrassed to have been so easily ensnared by the ambitious Ranton and his cohorts. Ranton himself felt that there was nothing to say, but wait for the outcome. He was certain that they might be forgiven because they served Ellen and she was the queen's sister-in-law.

The crowd anticipated the worst for the prisoners. The crown prosecutor was satisfied that the evidence brought forward was ample to weigh against the defendants and bring down a verdict of guilty of treason. Treason against the crown and people of Craigroyston was punishable by death. The crowd anxiously waited for the words that Enyja would speak and the sentences that she would pronounce. Enyja began softly.

"Some need to be reminded that this is the kingdom of Craigroyston. My husband was its first king and I am its first Queen; equal rulers. Craigton did not get taken over, nor did Roysford. Both united; both to be ruled by Jonquis and I and what wisdom God bestowed upon us.

"We have been blessed and have given the kingdom two intelligent daughters as beautiful as any two young maidens anywhere. They are being schooled in every manner possible so that someday they may assume their responsibility to this kingdom. Julia and Concetta are the true heirs to the throne of Craigroyston," Enyja professed.

Enyja looked at Ellen. It was very clear where Enyja stood with regard to her sovereignty over Craigroyston. Ellen realized that her councilors had offended the queen with their social climbing and their thirst for power. Ellen knew that Ranton, Rheymand and Danther, who were now bound in chains, had been chiefly responsible for the rabble rousing that translated to a riot in the market. Ellen felt regret over it because she thought that they were doing it for her benefit. She thought of Haaron and how true he had been to her husband. She felt regret.

"Dear sister," paused Ellen, "your majesty—

"Sister was fine," interjected Enyja.

"Dear sister," Ellen continued, "I had no intention of disrupting your affairs here in Craigroyston. It would be wise to expel Ranton, Rheymand, Danther and any other Leemite that has offended you and interfered with you conducting your Karley and ruling your people."

Ellen was making a plea for their lives in an indirect manner.

Enyja understood Ellen's concern.

"Sound idea. I had a little more in mind for their disturbing the peace and stability of my kingdom," replied Enyja.

Enyja paused and turned to look directly at the convicted councilors. At this moment, the accused expected the worst. Ranton expected the worst but would not worry about it until it actually came. They thought that they would be sentenced to death or deported to Leems. At this point it was the same thing, thought Ranton.

"Your majesty, dear sister, it was on my behalf that Danther, Ranton and the others thought they should carry out their scheme. I wish to make an appeal on their behalf. Please do not put them to death," pleaded Ellen.

There was stillness and silence as the court awaited Enyja's verdict.

"You three are hereby banished from Craigton," proclaimed Enyja.

"Surely to be returned to Leems would be the equivalent of death," interceded Ellen.

"I said banished from Craigton," repeated Enyja, "the best place to send Ranton, Rheymand and Danther would be to my castle at Roysford. There they could try to speak out against me before my steward; the mean-spirited scoundrels. It is better than they deserve, the penalty for treason against the crown is death. My steward will find work for them. In this way perhaps they will learn how their daily bread is earned."

Ranton was fighting back a smile as he was so happy with the result. He tried to put a humble look on his outward face but he was failing. Ellen's interjection prevented Enyja from looking at Ranton.

"Dear sister this is more than they deserve, and I thank you for sparing their lives," Ellen said.

Ellen was grateful on behalf of her husband's former councilors. Enyja did not waste any time.

"You may take custody of the prisoners," Enyja proclaimed.

She called out to her palace guards. The guards approached the prisoners and waited for the word to escort them to their cells for the night. At daybreak, they would be taken to Roysford.

Everyone in the Karley remained silent as they waited for what Enyja would say next. Enyja looked at the other prisoners charged under the riot act with creating a disturbance, inciting a riot and damage to property. These were the fools who succumbed to the rabble rousers propaganda. They were in league with Ranton, Rheymand and Danther but who did not fully comprehend what they were doing. These were the merchants and farmers who would have washed away Enyja's authority and replaced it with a new self-serving brand. The new brand of authority would be the first to do away with them for starting the riot in the first place. It was the simple stupidity of the Karley councilors and her people that she was angry at.

"To you merchants and farmers of Craigroyston who considered yourselves worthy: your lives have been spared because what you did was as a result of utter stupidity. You were stupid and blind not to see how good your lot in life has been.

"What you did not appreciate was that in Craigroyston, I am queen. As queen my subjects have enjoyed their portion of happiness which was tied to your very own efforts. If you are not content, work more or work smarter." Enyja paused briefly, "to you former councilors of

Leems, know that it was your queen's intervention that saved you. If you should ever try to take part in any form of rebellion against my laws, or seek to seize power, you will meet your death swiftly. There will not be any need to go to trial."

Like a thief who is sorry only because he is caught, the scheming councilors looked to be grateful for escaping with their lives. Their heads were bowed. Ranton reasoned, that if you are alive you can still scheme another day. Again Ranton had to fight off smiling, he was so happy with the outcome. The three councilors fully understood that pastoral Roysford was Enyja's former home. What Enyja did not understand was that with showing mercy to these incorrigible, corrupt men, all that she did was pull a dandelion flower by the stem from the ground without the root. Everyone witnessed what happened to the flower, but deep in the ground of these evil men's hearts the capacity and desire to flourish was ever ardent to the disregard of anyone around them.

"Away with them!" Enyja blasted.

She was very angry and upset with the devious plan that upset her people and kingdom. She thought 'so this was the manner in which her hospitality to family was repaid?'

"As for the rest of you, how do you want to be treated!?" Enyja asked rhetorically.

Everyone was silent and came to attention when she boldly repeated, "How do you want to be treated!?"

The queen was visibly upset but very much in control of her emotions. She paused a moment. Enyja did not want to sentence the prisoners to death, yet she still did not trust them. She was sure that at some time, she would again hear from Ranton, Rheymand and Danther.

It was not easy to understand that such clever, educated men could be such self-centered wolves. Enyja addressed her people as a monarch.

"Do you want to cower before tyranny or would you rather be treated with the dignity that women and men everywhere only dream of?

"The freedom to speak still requires that you think before opening your mouth. And, if you should have nothing to say, say nothing. Say what you mean and mean what you say; speaking your truth plainly, simply and clearly.

"Greet every person with good morning or good afternoon or good evening or good night; as the time will dictate.

"And, if you should find yourself complaining, be grateful that you can. Before complaining though, make sure you have counted your blessings and have given thanks to God for your portion.

"Make sure that you have been considerate of and charitable to others less fortunate. Then ask yourself if you should complain.

"I am afraid that my people have forgotten themselves," Enyja scolded.

The entire court including the gallery was silent. They reflected on Enyja's words and everyone was indeed ashamed of their behavior whether they were in the market that day or not. They appreciated her as their queen and were ashamed of their inconsideration. She no doubt was still mourning the king's death. Then Enjya continued by suspending privileges.

"There will be no assemblies of any kind within the castle here at Craigroyston. Only ten people at one time can enter the castle market grounds to patronize the shop keepers and blacksmith that are established within.

"Until further notice, all trade and commerce that used to take place in the square is to be conducted outside the castle walls, and, under supervision of the army.

"If the cobble stone within our courtyard walls was too hard, perhaps the clay outside the castle walls will remind you to be more humble if not grateful," Enjya professed.

The merchants and farmers were not happy with having to conduct their business on the uneven field. They immediately imagined how muddy the field would be if it rained. The merchants and farmers were not happy but understood why their queen was punishing them. Having decreed the expulsion of the market inside the castle, Enyja turned and directed her attention to the diplomats from Skarsgard and apologized to them.

"Esteemed guests, if you will pardon me, please enjoy our every hospitality that is extended to you. We shall speak tomorrow, but this evening I am not in the condition to receive your fine company," Enyja told them.

Enyja abruptly arose and left her throne in the Karley and proceeded to the chamber at the back. It was customary for all present before royalty to stand and bow or curtsy at her entrance and departure, but Enyja did not wait for those who were seated to stand. They all bowed or curtsied to her back as she departed the court. She departed with conviction and purpose while everyone was scrambling to rise to their feet. All her subjects knew that Queen Enyja was not pleased with the riot that occurred within the castle walls at Norsendan. The riot was mere proof that her people had forgotten their blessings. The diplomats from Skarsgard might have been offended but understood that the queen had been disappointed and was unhappy.

During Enyja's reign with Jonquis, this sort of uprising had never happened. Enyja thought that this riot waited for now to happen after Jonquis' death. It was a young kingdom steeped in former tradition. The union of Roysford and Craigton was a mutual advantage for each dukedom. If only Jonquis had been by her side, she yearned. He was still so young and such a good father to his daughters. Enyja fell into the memory of Jonquis and despair came over her. Her only thought was 'why did Jonquis have to die so young and leave her alone with her daughters and a kingdom to run?'

Enyja would take some time to assess the matter again. She retired to be alone in her chamber. Her daughters were safely in bed and she dismissed her servants. Enyja started to cry. Tears rolled down her cheeks. It would take some time but after Enyja was finished getting over the hurt, she would emerge even stronger than before. It was this strength that Enyja needed to attend to her kingdom's affairs domestically and abroad. It was this strength that Calogerus had foreseen in her. She needed to call on this strength now.

Enyja's council had already proposed to open Craigroyston's markets to the people of Skarsgard. It was supposed to be a new market to expand in. With the loss of trade with Leems the proposal could not come at a better time. In her meeting with the naval captain sent by Brento, Enyja would announce her plans. For the time being that would solve the concerns of her merchants. A new dilemma however would present itself. Those whom Enyja banished to Roysford managed to fall into an opportunity to hatch a new scheme. The produce of Roysford would find a new market to the south in Rothaynen. Produce from Roysford was never sent to Rothaynen. They produced their own greens and grains. The northern lords of Rothaynen however would need a new source of food as their traditional venue at Marmora was cut off to them by Lord Barton. Even Enyja's loyal subjects in Roysford would support the scheme as it made good business sense.

The Search for Leif

Brento sent Eric, his reliable sea captain, to act as the envoy from Skarsgard. The news of the passing of Jonquis made its way to Suerda and Brento sent his condolences. Eric was accompanied by Sjostrom who was a skilled sailor and Laafe a fine map charter. Brento also sent them to Craigroyston to inform Queen Enyja of the Huynsten massacre at Eisenholm in Hammarsgard. It was a reminder of the constant threat that was looming over the heads of all people as the Huynsten navy went where and when they pleased and took what they wanted. Any time a report of Huynsten aggression made its way to the Karley, the people of Craigroyston grew more in support of Selwyck's action at Wendover. The people were happy that he did what he did. Selwyck stood up to the bully, that part was good but they did not like the risk. Some of his sailors did not return home. Unfortunately, you cannot have it both ways when it comes to freedom. The price of freedom sometimes demanded the ultimate sacrifice of human life.

There was another point of interest. Eric informed Enyja that Brento's son was reported to be seen alive on Tamerana the Great Continent. Sjostrom had sailed the high seas longer than he had walked on land and he was certain of two things. First he was sure that there was a water passage where there was not one before. Secondly he was certain that he saw Leif. Brento planned to sail out there at the earliest possible moment in the hopes of finding Leif. It would be at least springtime before the waters of the Alargentan Sea would allow Brento's ships to travel them without danger of being grounded by ice.

It was Brento's request that Queen Enyja send a larger Craigroyston warship to accompany his smaller ships through the Alargentan Sea to the south of Irminia. The large ship could carry food supplies without having to scavenge for them. Apparently there was a lot of piracy in the corridor between the Green Islands and Tamerana on the high seas. Brento wanted to assure that his ships on the sea stood a chance against the bigger, better armed Huynsten warships. When the councilors of the Karley heard that request, they immediately thought of the irony. Some of the merchants and councilors had past shipments raided by

Brento's ships. They did not speak out in court but it was easy to read their minds. Imagine, they thought, the Arsgardian tribes worried about piracy on the high seas. It was not so long ago that Arsgardian sails meant fighting to defend your life and property. The treaty between Craigroyston and Skarsgard was truly delicate.

Arturus, the high admiral was flattered that Brento, a long time enemy should ask for help. In keeping with Calogerus' diplomatic work, this was an opportunity that he could not let pass. Selwyck was expected to return from his latest patrolling in the Verdent Sea where he was to sail down to Petrinvincit to pick up and sail Calogerus home. Arturus suspected that Selwyck might enjoy the adventure of sailing south of Irminia into the Alargentan Sea. Selwyck was extremely knowledgeable with the seas east of Craigroyston, but other than the trip to Teresforte, he had never ventured further west or south. The search mission would certainly give the young captain a rest from certain sea battle in the Aggregian Sea. Sailing west would allow Selwyck to chart the new developments with the waters and land masses.

One of the claims that the visitors from Skarsgard made was in regards to the seashores of Tamerana the Great Continent. Apparently it was now possible to navigate further south along its western shore. It was reported that it was as if the land pulled apart. Arturus was curious to investigate that claim. Arsgardian sailors had pushed westward in an effort to find new lands that they could exploit. In doing so they charted out the far western reaches of the Alargentan Sea. Sjostrom was familiar with the western lands and Laafe brought maps that he made with him detailing islands and the eastern borders of Tamerana. Arturus called for Eric, Laafe and Sjostrom to join him in the naval council chamber at the Admiralty. Arturus also sent for Darren, captain of the warship Synden. In private they could compare maps and charts.

Darren returned almost a month late from his last mission. He was thought to be lost at sea but he and his crew denied it. Darren claimed that the Synden was not lost at sea but that there was more sea. The magnetic sunstone did not misguide them. With its noble indicator of true north, they were able to sail due south further than ever before.

At the time his claims were not taken seriously, but with the news that arrived from Skarsgard, the claim warranted investigation. Darren and his log book were called into the chamber.

In the naval council chamber they compared charts and maps. Arturus knew that to share information from maps was a danger to their defense, but he had to trust the new diplomats. Besides, the charts and maps that Laafe brought could be used against his people too. Upon immediate examination, the maps of the two neighbors were similar yet different when it came to the sizes of land masses. Their respective maps gave more detail where either party was most familiar. Together they could draw up a new, better detailed carte. Both Eric and Darren agreed on one item though. The land mass that was before them to the southwest on previous voyages, had given way to a water passage.

Arturus' naval staff along with Darren, Laafe and Sjostrom worked busily into the night to create a new tabula geographica of the new area. On the next day both Eric and Arturus would present their report and make a proposal to Queen Enyja. With the support of Enyja's naval admiral, the proposal was sure to be approved. As soon as Brento sailed his search party into Norsendan that spring, a warship of Craigroyston would escort them to the new waters. Brento could take command of the search mission and would be made welcome on the Craigroyston warship. The voyage truly promised to be exciting, especially if the changes to the land and sea were true. For Brento the chance that his son Leif was still alive was all that he hoped for. All that there remained to be done was for Selwyck to return and the icy seas to recede. Then Selwyck would be given the assignment for his men of the Courage.

Yuletide Wedding

According to Vanessa's wishes, preparations for Morden and Meaghan's yuletide wedding were occupying everyone. With Braemar Castle decorated for Christmas, it was hard not to feel happy with the colors, scents and the anticipation of the season. Everywhere there was fresh cut garland that smelled of pine, cedar and the outdoors. The sprigs of conifer breathed life into the stone castle in the gray skied winter. Vanessa had bided her time and expected Lord Barton and Lord Welledon to appear very soon. To her surprise their appearance was that very evening. The sun went down earlier and there were less hours of sunlight. With the amassing of Lord Barton's force on the plains of Lyndendor, it was obvious that he was not there to attend the wedding. A ship was also seen coming up the River Brae. The ship could not enter the River Brae without Barton allowing it to do so. To the south across the bridge on Thermanden Bay there was another force banding.

The news of the encroaching armies was reported to Lucio and he informed Vanessa. She had just awoken from her slumber to begin the work of the night. Braemar was mobilized for defense. The armed force that came from the south was a breach of agreement between Welledon and Graedon. The naval warship and the amassing of a force on Marmora's soil was also a breach of agreement perpetrated by his cousin Barton. Lucio was technically in the right to order hostility toward these armies. He did. There were soldiers on Braemar's castle walls who expected diplomacy to occur before any fighting should begin. The followers of Lucio though were well placed in rank to see that Lucio's orders were carried out without question. Reluctantly the soldiers of Braemar obeyed their orders.

Assault on Braemar

The hail of arrows from Braemar's castle walls was keeping the forces of Welledon at bay. The castle was well fortified and supplied with both food stuffs from Marmora and weapons from Peregren. Unfortunately there was the matter of travel time between Peregren and Braemar for new military supplies. The idea for building Braemar Castle was to center the king's castle geographically in Rothaynen. Strategically it was well situated with the bay for fresh water and quick support from Petrinvincit and Galles. From the point of view of prestige, Braemar was beautiful. From a military point of view however Peregren, the original king's castle, would have been a wiser choice. It was easier to defend strategically. The pits of Peregren were where the armaments were fashioned. The supply of iron and coal was abundant and the fires of their inferno were never ending. It was not pretty, but it was safe and smart.

With the forces of those loyal to Graedon, Lucio wondered how easy it would be to get supplies from Peregren if Braemar were put under siege. Even so, they had to wait and depend on others to supply them. Lucio gave thought that if he moved to Peregren, the old castle was definitely easier to defend against impending forces. If the supply of food was in question, then Peregren and the northern castles were not too far from Roysford. They had traded somewhat in the past with Roysford. Produce from Roysford was not in demand because of the abundant produce in Marmora. Prices were so low in Rothaynen that it was not worthwhile for Roysford to send their produce to Rothaynen for sale. However under the present circumstances the northern castles in Rothaynen would increase their trading with Roysford.

Lucio summoned Wyslav to go north to Peregren to rally his loyal forces there. Lucio was certain that Barton had sent word to Federics for support, but he believed that Peregren's army was loyal to him. Lucio would send Federics a dispatch of his own. In Graed0n's hand he signed a document ordering Federics to sweep down and come to his aid at Braemar. Lucio did not inform him of the truth. The dispatch read, 'Barton failed at Petrinvincit. An enemy force backed with a naval vessel was poised to attack Braemar. Come at once'. It was signed, "Graedon Rex'. If Barton did send a message to Federics it would be confusing. Lucio thought that when Federics finally arrived he would see a ship in the River Brae and that would lend credibility to his message.

With the forces of Barton in Marmora on the open plain in winter, they were sitting ducks for a rear surprise attack. Lucio wondered just how stupid Barton thought that he was. Lucio thought that Barton and Welledon had been wise to avoid their last party at Braemar. It was slated to be their very last. Lucio was aware that Barton and Welledon had come to Graedon's aid, but it was utter madness to think that they could put Braemar Castle under siege especially now. Lucio lingered on the thought. It was winter and the forces of Barton and Welledon were out in the open cold.

Lucio went to Vanessa with all that his thoughts. The mother and son had a discussion. Then Lucio sent for Wyslav to deliver another message to Kronar at Peregren Castle. Wyslav listened carefully as Lucio gave him every detail of his scheme to which Vanessa approved. Wyslav was to deliver one message to Federics in Peregren as if Graedon had summoned Federics presence. Then for assurance he was to deliver another message to Kronar, the Captain of the Guard. Wyslav informed Kronar, a disciple loyal to Lucio, to rally the knights and soldiers of Peregren and accompany Federics. Kronar was to be informed of the dispatches between Barton and Federics. He was also told to make sure that Federics did not arrive at Marmora. In fact when the force of Peregren arrived at Marmora, they were to immediately attack the unsuspecting force gathered on the plains in Marmora. The riders from Peregren were to be prepared to give a full charge to eliminate the unsuspecting force of Lord Barton once and for all.

The idea was that when the Peregren force arrived Barton would assume that it was Federics force. In fact to make assurances sure, Kronar suggested that Federics send a messenger ahead with a note. Federics did send a note. The note alerted Barton that Federics force was coming to join him by dusk. Then when the Peregren force arrived it would be totally as expected to Barton. Barton would take comfort in knowing that his kinsman arrived and that his flank was covered. After securing the note and nearly reaching their destination, there was no further need for Federics. Kronar murdered Federics with help from some of his own bodyguards. The bodies of those loyal to Federics lay on the blood stained snow beside him. If there was anyone else loyal to Federics among them, they did not speak up. The force from Peregren was clear about their objective. They would attack Barton's unsuspecting army that was stationed in Marmora from the rear. Kronar thought that if his force rested a little, it would be darker by the time they arrived at Marmora. He thought that the darkness would cloak their scheme. It would be better still.

Before Peregren's force arrived at Marmora, they prepared quietly to sweep into Barton's open encampment and attack. Kronar thought that Lord Barton was unsuspecting. Barton had been informed by Federics letter to expect the Peregren forces coming. There was no reason to question their advent to the lowlands that were covered with snow. When the force from Peregren was close enough, Kronar would give word to attack Barton's forces. The knights and soldiers from Peregren could then ambush the unsuspecting Barton and his men. After the attack, they could retreat to the safety of the Braemar Castle's north gate. The gates would be open to them alone.

Lucio insisted on the surprise attack. Even if only some loss was inflicted, the maneuver by the force from Peregren would demoralize Barton's soldiers. The betrayal of the Peregren force would weaken their resolve and the wounded army would feel the cold a little colder. In the cold winter weather, their losses would sting. They would be licking their wounds out in the cold. Lucio smiled as he pictured the whole scene in his mind. Barton would think that they were reinforcements with the loyal Federics in command. When they arrived at nightfall however, the force of Peregren would surprise Lord Barton's force from Teresforte.

Lucio was made aware that another light force had arrived and waited in the bush on the west road. They brought no heavy assault weapons. He thought that it just had to be Welledon's men. Lucio did not hesitate with what to do. Another mounted force from within Braemar Castle was given orders to assemble inside the front gate awaiting Lucio's orders. After a barrage of arrows from the castle walls, the mounted force would swiftly sneak out and ride over the bridge. There the riders from Braemar would surprise and cut down Welledon's army that was situated south of the castle.

The noble Welledon would not be able to assist Barton's force. His light force would be scrambling to maintain order in the ranks. In the darkness there would be confusion. In this way, the soldiers loyal to Graedon within Braemar could not identify the forces of Barton and Welledon as friendly. The soldiers would merely do as they were told. Lucio's enemies would destroy themselves. Then with the former dukes dead, there was only one person to turn to for order. The scheme was truly diabolical. By now it was not surprising how much Lucio was prepared to sacrifice in life, limb and bloodshed to achieve his goals. The scourge of battle was of no consequence to him.

Eyes Open Ears Stiff

When the messenger arrived from the Peregren force with his message from Federics, Barton had a return message. Barton sent urgent word for Federics to lead and situate his army north of Braemar and wait for the day. Further when Federics arrived he was to rendezvous with Barton in Marmora that evening. The messenger assured Barton that he would deliver the message but he knew that Federics was no longer in charge. He would report to Kronar that Lord Barton did not suspect anything.

Barton was no rank amateur at securing the safety of his army. To guard his position in the field of Marmora he sent scouts out. The best vantage point was the mountains that divided Marmora from Peregren. From there they observed the narrow corridor of flat land that the force from Peregren would have to pass by in their efforts to arrive at Marmora. The scouts observed that the army of Peregren stopped at one point and a skirmish took place. It seemed serious. After the army resumed riding, the scouts rode to down the mountain side to investigate. When the scouts arrived they found the dead bodies lying on the snow. They were frightened at the notion that it was Federics who lay dead. The scouts knew that this meant danger for their forces. They knew that they would have to ride like madmen to warn Barton. They also knew full well that the death of Federics would hurt Lord Barton. The delay that Kronar caused so his army could enter Marmora by night bought Barton's scouts the time they needed to ride back. When Barton's scouts returned they informed him that along the path that the Peregren army took, several men were killed and lay dead on the snow covered ground. The scout informed that when he rode out to discover the identity of the men, he recognized the leader. He was hesitant to speak the name Federics. It was the demeanor on the scout's face that told Barton who lied dead long before he spoke his name. Barton was heart-broken to hear that one of the dead men was Federics. Federics had served under Barton before and was granted the lordship of Peregren on his recommendation. Barton sent word and alerted Welledon of the development. It was with a heavy heart that Barton took the news of Federics murder. He was like a son to him, but there was no time to grieve right now. Barton knew full well what to anticipate now.

Barton instructed Welledon to ride away from Braemar due west along the River Brae. Lucio would not go south, if anything happened to force Lucio out of Braemar Castle, he would go north. Lucio's loyal lords were from the north. Selwyck was summoned by Barton to transport the bulk of Welledon's riders across the River Brae to the open ground at Marmora before Braemar Castle. Only a token force of Welledon's riders would be left in the forest south of Braemar. The bulk of Welledon's force would reinforce Barton's men on the plains of Lyndendor. This would have to be accomplished immediately. The reinforcements would be needed at Marmora as soon as possible. Barton's force in Marmora could battle the men from Peregren but if they were joined by the riders of Braemar Castle it would be hopeless. Lucio's forces could retreat to the castle but Barton's men were out in the cold.

Inside Braemar Castle it appeared as though Welledon's force was dwindling. Lucio was happy to hear that report. Welledon sent his riders through the wooded area to meet Selwyck's ship. They were not detected as they were transported on ship from the south to the north side of the river. On Barton's advice, Welledon stayed with his soldiers on the south side of the Thermanden Bay to provide a decoy. With their presence there, Lucio would have to mind them. Hiding in the forest, Welledon's archers were ready to cut down anyone crossing the bridge. Welledon also readied his men with long spears and shields to repel a cavalry attack should one occur. There he and his men waited. It was certain that Lucio would send out a force to attack them by night.

To the north of the River Brae, in Barton's camp, his force prepared to be attacked in a similar fashion. Archers were in place for a moment's notice. Shields and long spears were deployed to hold off an attack of riders. The archers from Braemar posed a problem though. Barton knew that they were spotted so he would merely move his army back out of the archers' range. All of Barton's riders were dispatched further west.

Barton had a plan. Barton's situated his infantry on the king's road. South of the king's road on the bank of the River Brae, Welledon's riders disembarked off of Selwyck's ship and joined Barton's riders. Barton felt that if his infantry's spears and shields could hold off the mounted attack, then the attackers would be engaged by the combined force of his riders joined by Welledon's riders coming in from the flank. For now Barton's men were out of the range of Braemar's archers, but if the Braemar archers decided to come out of the castle, they could be well within range in no time. They had to be ready. All they could do was look and listen with open eyes and stiff ears.

Finally it came, the sound of thundering hooves on the cold plain. Steady was the word that Barton spoke. Barton's force remained poised and steady. They knew that they had to make the riders from Peregren believe that they were caught by surprise. When the charging horses came within sight, then Barton's men moved into their defense formation. With their spears in hand and shields overlapped, it would leave the enemy no exposed target. With the many spears pointing at them, the Peregren riders would be like a wolf charging into a porcupine. Barton's infantry would have to weather the charge and then engage in bringing down what riders they could and finish them. At any time the onslaught of Barton and Welledon's riders would arrive and deliver their strokes against the enemy. It would be a surprise for the riders from Peregren that were loyal to Lucio.

It looked even more perilous to Barton when the front gates of Braemar Castle opened and a stream of archers ran out. If they attacked and assembled in their direction, it would be a costly battle. Instead the archers from Braemar assembled quickly and quietly but faced south. Barton saw that they wanted to pursue Welledon's force that had retreated to the safety of the forest. A band of riders collected behind them on the bridge before Braemar Castle. They were supposed to ride in after the bowman supposedly overwhelmed Welledon's men. Barton was concerned for Welledon as he knew that he was outnumbered. If Welledon's force had not drawn Lucio's interests south, on the plains of Lyndendor Barton's infantry that was assembled on the king's road would be a perfect target for the bowmen's arrows. Instead the Braemar archers moved in formation down the bridge to the south of the bay where Welledon's ground force was stationed. Barton was confident that Welledon could handle the matter in the forest. The Braemar archers engaged Welledon and his men who were well hidden and prepared. Not long after the riders from Braemar followed. Barton admitted to himself that he and his forces had been lucky.

The riders of Welledon and Barton led by Brandyn and Marius rode onto the battle ground. If they had been a moment earlier or would have been detected, who knows what strategy Lucio would have taken?

The archers from Braemar would have turned and attacked Barton's infantry as he feared. Their timing was perfect however. Peregren's mounted force turned to retreat after an unsuccessful charge. Barton and Welledon's riders were in pursuit of them and cut down what riders they could. Peregren's land force situated north of the castle was running toward the north gate of Braemar Castle. There as planned the north gate was opened for them and they entered into the safety of the outer yard inside the outer castle wall. Peregren's riders followed suit as swiftly as they could to avoid being cut down. They had but to enter the north courtyard of the castle to find safety.

Barton and Welledon's riders were still in pursuit of them. The force from Peregren were surprised themselves at the outcome of their attack. The noble leaders of Barton and Welledon's men noted that they were drawing nearer to the castle. The potential for archers from the castle wall to discharge arrows against them was too great, so one of the young knights who led the charge turned across the line of attack and called off the attack. It was Brandyn. One of Barton's knights followed suit by turning his horse and leading his men around. It was Marius. It was a very wise move. As they rode away, they looked back toward Braemar's north wall. A hail of arrows was making its way toward them like black snowflakes. At that point they noted despite the cloud cover that it was a full moon.

After the Peregren force's hasty retreat into Braemar Castle, the archers on the wall kept pulling their bows and letting fly with a piercing storm of arrows. Lucio engaged all his firepower. Fireballs were cast from catapults toward Barton's position to the west on the river. Selwyck was uncomfortable with the notion of fireballs being cast. He thought it wise to sail back well out of range. No sooner was the word given to hoist anchor when a fireball exploded on Courage's deck. All hands were called on deck to put out the burning oil. Selwyck controlled his emotions despite the shock and conducted the ship safely away while some of the crew fought the fire. The cold water of the River Brae was collected in buckets. Rope was tied to each bucket and dropped into the river. The fire was put out but the main sail was damaged. Other fireballs were directed at them but missed their mark fortunately. As Courage was moved out of danger's path, Selwyck wondered how he would explain this occurrence to the Admiralty. The instability in Rothaynen would not lend itself to the notion that they should have a navy of their own. He thought about Calogerus and what he might have to say.

The archers' arrows from Braemar Castle fell onto the frozen ground. Brandyn and Marius had read the situation correctly and had their men well out of range. They retired back to Barton's camp to regroup and report to him. Brandyn decided to keep Welledon's riders with those of Barton. The fastest way to Welledon's camp was across the bridge, but with the accuracy of the archers it was not safe. The night attack by Lucio's archers against Welledon on the south shore failed. Although they were just a token force, Lucio thought that Welledon's entire force was there and had retreated to safety. With the small force ready and waiting in the dark forest, it did not take long for the Braemar soldiers to call a retreat. The ruse worked as Welledon's riders were moved across the river to reinforce and assist Barton's force. Originally it was thought that the south road should be cut off to prevent escape. It was highly unlikely that Lucio would escape south, but both Barton and Welledon wanted to make sure of it.

Selwyck's ship incurred damage. In all the commotion, Selwyck did not fire upon Braemar Castle despite catching a fireball on his deck. For one thing, it was the castle of an ally. He would have to sail closer and turn his ship broadside, making it an easier target for other fireballs to land their mark. It was easier for Selwyck to cut his loss by not engaging. Finally, Lord Barton did not request him to fire on Braemar. Barton was still an ally of Craigroyston and Selwyck trusted him. One thing was evident to them all. In their rush to come to Graedon's aid, Barton and Welledon were outside the castle walls. Despite their success that late night, Lucio was still inside the walls of Braemar Castle and could attack them at will.

"I think we can rule out the element of surprise," said Brandyn.

"No towers, no catapult and no hope. We are trapped here. In our haste we did not even prepare ample food for the men. It seems that Lucio is laying siege on us," stated Barton.

"At this point we have nowhere to go but to the comfort of home. It would take a miracle to gain entrance to Braemar," affirmed Marius.

"When they realize that Lord Barton and Lord Welledon are out here, the men loyal to Graedon will turn," declared Brandyn.

"Then we really need a miracle. The reinforcements from Peregren are loyal to Lucio and will hold the men of Braemar to defending it against anyone, even us," Barton summed up.

"It has come to this and all that we can do is humble ourselves and pray," concluded Welledon.

The Braemar Stronghold

Since the south tower and south castle walls were built on the water, it made the entire south and east side of the castle inaccessible by land. To attack them, it would take a series of catapults and a greater resolve than those inside the castle. A navy warship could attack if it was on the sure waters of Thermanden Bay. The bay was practically landlocked. The rapids at the west side of the bay would not allow a small ship to pass, let alone a larger warship. These sides of the castle defended themselves as no sure footing could be gained against them. To approach the castle by small boat was self-annihilation for anyone who tried to do so in an offensive attempt. Archers could easily pick off anyone within their range. Selwyck's ship could not sail up the rapids. The Courage needed to get closer and turn sideways to discharge its volleys, but that too would put the ship in peril.

The bridge across the mouth of Thermanden Bay was built a good forty yards from the castle's west wall. In fact the only castle entrance accessible by land was at the northeast side. There were two walls on the north shore side that an enemy would have to breach let alone the northeast gate. There was the tall outer castle wall and an inner wall with a courtyard between them. If there was any danger of an enemy breaching the gate on the outer wall, there was a second wall and gate waiting on the inside. There would be skilled archers waiting for them anew on the inner wall. The castle forces could literally trap an enemy attack from the north side between the two walls. As an enemy entered they would be funneled into the courtyard through the gate. The confidence that an enemy obtained with taking the outer wall would be short lived.

Unexpected Surprise

Inside the castle dungeon, Calogerus and Mattews had affected the leak to increase in volume. The cell was now rapidly filling with water that bubbled up. The two captives had used the strips of cloth from their bed sheets, blankets and the straw inside the mattress to stuff the cracks in the door of their cell. There was not a single crack that did not get stuffed with cloth or straw. The precision with which the door was fashioned and fitted to its opening made stuffing the cracks an easy chore. Calogerus and Mattews could only wait now as the cold water flowed into their cell. As the water climbed to their knees they learned just how cold it was. They began to shiver as their skin got cold. It was cold enough to stop a human heart if a person were immersed in it too long. As confident as Calogerus was with the plan, he was a little nervous too. He looked over at Mattews and signaled for him to lift up his bed. Calogerus stood his bed frame up against the wall like a ladder and climbed up out of the water. Mattews followed his lead.

The tower walls began to show signs of cracking. In one instant a crack appeared along the mortar. They wondered if the walls would hold until they could escape from the cell. It was scary. As the water level rose though, the wall seemed to stabilize again. When the water level rose to five feet, they would climb up to the head boards of their beds and start screaming at each other. There was no judging exactly how long it would take the guard or jail keeper to hear them and come. One thing was for sure; the water level in the cell was rising according to plan.

Hopeless and Wasteful

All the while the archers within the walls of Braemar kept up their offensive strokes. Braemar's defenders followed their orders though there were those who realized the force outside the wall was Barton and Welledon. The emblems on the soldiers' tunics appeared. If that was not enough, the silhouette of Lord Barton with his head gear made things pretty clear. There was confusion in their minds as they questioned why they should be attacked by the king's cousin and a loyal duke. Welledon's force to the south was kept at bay by Braemar's archers. All that Welledon's men could do was weather the arrows by standing firm behind their shields. They watched the attack on Barton's force and the counter attack that ensued after. The offensive from the soldiers of Peregren supported by the archers of Braemar did not achieve its goal. They believed that they could surprise and slay the forces of Welledon and Barton under the guise of darkness. The early morning came. Both Barton and Welledon were no greenhorns. Although they held their own, they were still outside the castle in the cold. They were a far cry away from their goal to take the castle and rescue King Graedon. There were a number of dead and wounded on both sides. Welledon thought about what Marius said. Truly this time it would take some miracle to help them.

Knowledge, Hope and Effort: a Miracle

When Braemar castle was built the plans called for the south foundation to be built on the water. Besides beauty it added a greater sense of security for the defense of the castle. As difficult a task as it was to build, it was one tower that you could use to assault from without being assaulted. The entire premise of Braemar Castle was that unlike its cousin Petrinvincit on the sea coast, it should never see a foreign invader. If it should see an invader the castle could well withstand any attack. With the castle granaries full, the castle could withstand an attack for any length of time. In the meantime as it was planned, the force from Teresforte, Peregren, Galles and the other surrounding dukedoms would come to Braemar's aid. Ironically Braemar was attacked from within and it was Teresforte and Galles that came against it.

Back In the Dungeon

Outside the cell door the jailor was interrupted from his sleep. Finally he realized, the two prisoners had finally squared off in battle. It was what he had planned all along, but not at night during slumber time. There was yelling and screaming coming from the cell where the diplomat and priest were held. Despite holding the burning torch there was not much illumination. As the jailor was escorted by two guards to the cell he fished for the key to turn the lock. Something was not right. There was a small puddle of water outside the cell. He realized that when he stepped in it. In that instance he remembered the dampness and the young lady that was cleaning and dismissed it as being strange. He was still half asleep and dumbfounded as he called into the prisoners.

"What is going on in there?" he yawned.

"Help! Help! He took my stick and is beating me with it!" cried Calogerus repeatedly.

"You stupid old man! Go to sleep! I'll teach you to strike me with that stupid stick!" Mattews screamed back.

As their screaming and yelling continued, the jailor had guessed as much. He chuckled at Lucio's fear of the old man. The jailor believed that this wizard, 'so-called', was in trouble himself from a priest. He decided that he had enough nonsense from this old man. What magic could an old, beat-up man conjure anyway?

The gesture that the jailor made gave the guards the impression that all was well. The guards were now at ease again and anxious for slumber. The jailor fumbled with putting the key in the lock.

"Hey! What is the meaning of this!?" John cried.

The jailor was sleepy and angry, but he knew that something was amiss. He managed to fix the key into the lock mechanism. The lock had been stuffed with cloth. He had to force the key in a little more. In his anger he pushed the key in with more force. The key was a little harder to turn but with his determination, he managed to turn it. All the while the guards were convinced that this nuisance would be over in a hurry. A good 'hit-on-the-head' to each man, and that would solve this problem, thought the jailor. The door stood shut while the latch was bolted, but there was pressure from inside the cell. He drew the bolt back but it resisted so he pushed against the door in an effort to free it. He got the bolt free. The pressure of the water flung the door open. In an instant he was pushed away. The cascade of the cold water flowing out of the cell washed him and the guards back off their feet. The jailor was washed away with the keys in hand against the stone wall across from the cell door. He bumped his head and was unconscious. The volume of water in the cell just poured out the cell door and washed away anything in its path. The guards were clearly awake now. Now they were overwhelmed by the cold water that cast them against the wet stone floor and the wall.

As the water level in the cell went down, Mattews jumped off the bed. Calogerus followed. Mattews overpowered a bedraggled, wet guard. He took his spear, but the guard reached into his scabbard to pull out his sword. The guard could not even rise to his feet when Mattews knocked the sword out of his hand. Meanwhile Calogerus checked the jailor. The jailor was overwhelmed by the water and the blow to his head rendered him unconscious. Mattews took away the guard's sword and then the other guard's sword that had collapsed on the ground. There was a blacksmith working in an adjacent room that appeared. Noting that the prisoners were escaping, the blacksmith attacked Mattews. After avoiding a few wild sword swipes, Mattews swung his spear behind the blacksmith's legs and pulled his feet from under him. The man crashed to the ground onto the wet stone floor and was not getting up too quickly. Instead the blacksmith favored his sore back and his hurt pride.

Just then as Calogerus predicted the foundation of the south tower of the castle began to shake. The stress on the stone caused some rock to crumble. The tower wall began to sway. Stone blocks from the wall fell into the cell with a heavy splash. The top of the tower twisted before more mortared stone fell in sequence. Mattews looked at Calogerus. Each was grateful for getting out of the tower cell before it collapsed. Everyone in Braemar Castle was shaken up by the noise. The current that passed by the castle was not swift, but the weight and volume of the water that made its way inside the dungeon cell had stabilized to hold the tower wall. When the cell door was opened the water flowed out and the water outside the tower pushed against that outer wall and the blocks as it flowed through the crack. Slowly the stone blocks that were fashioned at the base of the tower began to give way. The tower wall began to sway and the weight of the stone blocks above them pressed downward. With no support under them, the entire tower started to shake and portions of it crumbled into the water.

Calogerus and Mattews could not leave John the jailor and the two guards unconscious. The water level would soon rise and drown them. Mattews called to the blacksmith to give him hand picking up the jailor and carrying him up the stairs to the floor above the level of the bay. Calogerus grabbed one of the guards and helped him up the stairs. The blacksmith complied and helped as well. It was odd in the blacksmith's mind that convicted prisoners should care about their captors. The guards were young men who with the jailor were doing their duty. Apart from being impulsive and childish, John, the jailor, was not an evil man. The blacksmith complied despite his sore back.

The Spectacle

Calogerus and Mattews climbed the stairs out of the south tower to a landing unchallenged. There was a window opening that looked out over the courtyard outside the tower. With the archers and soldiers at their post, they realized that the castle was under attack. They assumed that word did get out to Lord Barton. No wonder that there were no more guards to worry about, every soldier was engaged on the walls. Calogerus and Mattews did not realize that Barton and Welledon's forces began their attack to take the castle. Their escape diversion would prove a decisive factor in the retaking of Braemar Castle. Elayne had told Calogerus that she attempted to get word to Barton, but failed. Calogerus felt sorry for her devoted servant that was tortured to death for trying to alert Lord Barton. They did not realize it, but the wedding invitation is what communicated that there was something wrong. Brandyn had returned from Leems and could not believe that his sister would agree to marry Morden. Of course he did not know any details, but if something does not seem right, it is not right.

Calogerus climbed to the next landing and could now see over the wall. He looked over the wall and saw that there was a ship flying Craigroyston's colors down river. The sight truly lifted his spirit more. At this point Calogerus realized that they would need to create another diversion. The fact that the tower walls had crumbled at the base and the tower came down in its entirety was not enough. The good forces of Barton and Welledon could not enter by the south tower. They needed more help to inspire them. Conversely another diversion would create anxiety for Lucio and Vanessa. Calogerus was sure about what to do next.

Calogerus climbed down and went back to the blacksmith's pit on the level that was above their cell. Mattews followed him. The lower cell level was flooded. The blacksmith whom he had subdued was a little confused but loyal to Graedon. He agreed to help in any way that he could. So Calogerus grabbed the handle of the bellows that fed his fire. He instructed that any chair, table, wood and anything else that could burn be thrown on the fire. There was some oil in a bucket and he poured some over the coals. Black smoke began to rise. Calogerus doused the wooden cell doors with oil and set them on fire. The smoke grew and grew and rose upward through the tower opening.

Lucio sensed the shaking of the castle earlier. He heard the crashing of the stone blocks in the water. He merely sent someone to investigate. He consulted with Vanessa who was concerned about her disciples of pleasure in the lower bowels of the castle. She left her lower chamber and oversaw the attack against Barton's forces from the castle walls. Vanessa was unhappy that the surprise attack that she intended to finish off her enemies in the cold did not go well. Both Barton and Welledon, and their forces, had survived the attack. When Barton's knights were in pursuit of the retreating force that attacked them, they were smart enough to disengage from the chase just before they came into the range of the archers on the castle walls. Now with the south tower breached, Vanessa believed that it would be to their advantage if they left Braemar Castle for Peregren.

The south tower had collapsed. If they stayed, they could withstand the siege of Braemar Castle, but spring would come. Although there were blacksmiths at Braemar, who forged weapons within the castle cellar, they could not provide the volume of spear heads, let alone arrow heads that they could provide at Peregren. Eventually they would run out of arrows and spears at Braemar, but not at Peregren. In the midst of the fallen tower, Lucio considered the notion. At Peregren, he noted, there was a never ending stream of arrows, spears, swords and knives. The granaries were full and profiteering put Peregren on solid ground financially. They would be safe and secure in Peregren. From Peregren they could launch assaults at will and take what they wanted by shear use of force. In Vanessa's mind, they needed to get back to Peregren.

The turn of events had spoiled her plans, but with the Princess Elayne as their prisoner, the symbolic Braemar Castle was but a mere symbol. Vanessa was only too happy to return to Peregren, to her original chamber of horror. At Peregren Vanessa and Lucio could withstand any land force. Barton would be forced to gather his forces and Welledon's and ride to Peregren to lay siege. In full confidence Vanessa gloated that

Barton was welcome to try. It was now a matter of convincing Lucio that Peregren was calling them home. Vanessa knew that her son had so wanted to wed Elayne in St. Zorren's Church at Braemar Castle. Not that Lucio was religious but he did like the aspect of ceremony.

If Lucio decided to stay at Braemar, Barton could intercept arms shipments. Peregren Castle might even fall into Barton's skilled hands. Here at Braemar, there was no telling who was loyal to Lucio or to Graedon. Vanessa insisted that they should leave at once. It was the smart move. At Peregren the supply of ample war resources was never ending. The castle granaries at Peregren had been filled in anticipation of winter. The water was spring fed to the castle from the mountain behind it. It was also an uphill climb to the front drawbridge of Peregren that lay across a murky marshland. Peregren Castle was easy to defend against any army that challenged her, especially in the dead of winter.

As Vanessa explained her plan, Lucio believed that they could just as easily stay at Braemar. He imagined Barton and Welledon getting frustrated as their forces could not breach Braemar Castle. The fallen tower was water locked. Any force trying to enter by the water would be cut down by the archers in the attempt. It was still closer to the beginning of winter. Cold, snow-filled days lay ahead for an army that pitched tents in the open cold. Lucio relished the fact that they could raid them on the plains at any time and inflict further losses. It would not take long to demoralize Barton and Welledon's men who would rather be home in front of a warm fire place with the ones they loved. Then another report came in for Lucio. The messenger barged in with urgency.

"My Lord Lucio, black smoke is rising out of the south tower!"

Lucio's eyes opened wider. There was concern among his knights. Lucio himself wondered how this could be. The smoke cast black soot all over the golden stone work of the surrounding stone walls. The wind blew the smoke into the main courtyard. The fire had worked its way along the thick support beams of wood. Since the beams were well dried, the fire caught and spread quickly. When flames shot out the windows and through the hole of the crumbled stone of the tower, it was a clear indicator that they should leave. A burning tower was a testament to uncertainty in the castle ranks.

Finally the tall tower that swayed due to the crumbling base now lost the thick beam supports to the fire. The weight of the structure lost its support and failed. The tower began to collapse, crumble and fall. The blue slate roof of the tower fell and crashed into Thermanden Bay. The smoke furled in circles as it spread over the castle and the bay. There was a sense of loss and heartache at the sight of the burning tower that collapsed. Braemar Castle represented truth and hope for all its subjects. One of its towers fell.

It was plain to everyone that there was some kind of disturbance within the castle. Calogerus and Mattews did not stop with the fire in the tower. Next they went to the stables and released all the horses into the courtyard. To Barton and Welledon a burning tower signified one thing. It was the miracle they had prayed for. They noticed confusion on the castle walls amidst the smoke. The archers seemed to withdraw so Barton was informed. He thought that this was an opportunity to storm the castle so he gave word for his men to prepare. Welledon observed the same withdrawal from the castle wall after the tower collapsed. He knew that something was going to happen. Welledon prepared to move his men from the forest and planned to cross the bridge to the castle. A few men could try to enter via the fallen tower now that no archers were on the wall.

Inside the castle, the knights and riders that were loyal to Lucio withdrew from their posts and awaited their master's direction. Lucio gave word that all those loyal to him should collect in the north courtyard. From there they would make their escape and ride to Peregren Castle. It had been a long day into the dawn. Lucio decided that when all the men that were loyal to him were gathered, he would evacuate his forces back to Peregren.

Vanessa had already packed and was waiting. Her devoted disciples rode with the dark knights. Lucio had thought of that as a means to ensure their safe conduct to Peregren. With the Princess Elayne, Meaghan and other ladies held hostage and in clear view, Lucio knew that they could easily ride away unchallenged. Upon noting that there were young girls riding with the escape party, Barton's force that that was situated outside the castle did not pursue them.

If Lucio stayed at Braemar Castle indeed he would need shipments of armaments from Peregren. These shipments could be halted and confiscated by the siege laid by Lord Barton. As Vanessa suggested, Lucio decided to move his loyal force to Peregren and take the castle as his own. Braemar Castle had a burning tower. Federics was conveniently murdered and would pose no opposition. Peregren was much better suited for defense. An enemy could not easily move assault towers uphill against Peregren. An added feature in Lucio's mind was that since the water that supplied Peregren Castle was spring-fed, it could be cut off from the enemy. There was just an impassable stone shield at its back, tall stone walls at its front, the marshland before it and a long uphill grade that was easier to defend than to attack. Lucio hated to leave Braemar Castle in its entire splendor, but it did have a damaged tower.

In no time those loyal to Lucio were on horseback and ready to race to Peregren. Soldiers loyal to Graedon did not join them at the north courtyard but went to the front gate to open it. It was their goal to allow Lord Barton and Welledon's forces to enter Braemar Castle. Those gathered in the north courtyard got the word from Lucio. When the north gate opened, the dark knights led the way each of them carrying a female rider with them. They were followed by Lucio with Princess Elayne on his steed. Vanessa and her close confidantes followed in the royal carriage drawn by a team of six horses. Lucio's army followed with full fury leaving Braemar Castle behind them.

Barton figured that at least Braemar Castle was taken back and Graedon might still be alive. Lord Barton called off the chase and established his men inside Braemar to secure the castle. Welledon and his riders entered the main gate of Braemar as well. Both Barton and Welledon were recognized and their authority was respected. There was a sense of urgency to find King Graedon. Already there was a rumor that the princess was taken away by Lucio. There was nothing that Lucio would not do to attain power. His ambition knew no bounds. With the princess in his hands, who knew what to expect?

Barton and Welledon feared the worst. If Elayne was forced to marry Lucio and she had a child by him, civil war would ensue. Lucio's claim to the throne as regent would be legitimate. The people would accept this arrangement to avoid needless fighting and endless wars. It was truly a cold day in winter.

Lucio was forced to retreat. The loyalty of the army to King Graedon, the tower falling and then burning made him take note. Lucio was forced to leave Braemar Castle. He was reminded that he did not know who he could trust either. The armaments were limited and the confusion in the south tower wisely prompted Lucio to escape. His core of followers, hostages and of course Vanessa rode with haste to Peregren Castle. In Peregren, the supply of armaments was unending and they could hold out indefinitely. The problem of food would be a challenge. Lucio was concerned about the future supply of food. He rode to Vanessa's carriage to put Elayne on it. Lucio told his concern to his mother. He learned that she was not worried at all. Vanessa had an idea about what t0 do about that.

"Leave that problem to me," she said with confidence.

Vanessa was happy to be going home.

Peasant Revolt

There were local peasants that were locked inside the castle when Braemar was closed to Barton and Welledon. They chose to take refuge in the church. When Cardinal Spehar protested their presence, they rebelled against him. He was seen to be engaged not with enlightening his people but telling them to be well-behaved sheep for their master's shears. More people gathered and entered St. Zorren's Church. They were bent on revenge against those who promised rewards for their good behavior and support of the king and the church. It was obvious that they had just cause for grievance, but that did not give them the right to break in and steal from the church. Cardinal Spehar did not make his planned rendezvous with Lucio's band. He was trapped in his lodgings which were within the church. Spehar was removing his many treasures. These weighed him down. In the end they prevented his escape. The peasant uprising questioned why a Cardinal would want to run from the church in the king's castle.

"Why would you fear the uprising, oh cardinal? Is the church not supposed to remain neutral in the dealings of state?" questioned a farmer.

The man was armed with a war club. Spehar was a learned man and not unable to defend himself. On this occasion he was neither effective at using his intellect nor was he strong enough to stand against the disgruntled peasants. The mob looted and grabbed the large wooden chest that was so dear to Spehar. Spehar tried to hold on. He was struck on the face and pushed around. He was beaten to death before Mattews and Calogerus who made their escape, entered the church to address the commotion. Mattews understood why their escape from the dungeon was so easy. The castle was under attack, but from whom?

Mattews entered Spehar's home and Calogerus was not too far behind him.

"What have you done?" directed Mattews to the peasant farmers.

The revelry of the peasants scrambling to break open the chest and get their share of the silver and gold coins erupted into another fight between the mighty and the mightier. The peasants were now thirsty for the wealth within Spehar's wooden chest and the valuable jewels and adornments in the church. The peasants had forgotten their purp0se in the fight. It was as though they had license to sack and loot the church.

"This so called man of God, leader of the flock was running off with quite a treasure," professed Jack.

Jack was the informal leader namely due to his size. Jack was a big, brawny man. He believed that by standing up to Mattews, he could scare him into keeping his distance. It was not the case. Mattews marched straight to him. As Mattews approached, Jack uttered threats.

"Keep away! You had better stop!" Jack yelled out.

The big man was surprised to see Mattews approach him dauntless as if madness had struck him. Mattews did not reply.

"You had better stop!" Jack repeated.

This time Jack raised his club to threaten Mattews. Mattews did not want to hurt the man but he would not back down in his duty to defend church property from being looted either. Calogerus entered the church. Guards loyal to Graedon returned his staff to him. Calogerus ran ahead of Mattews and placed himself between the two men. He raised his arms and his staff and yelled out with authority.

"Stop!"

Calogerus had spoken with an authoritative voice. Even the looters stopped what they were doing and looked up to see what would happen next.

"Good people, you must not take that money from the church. It is to provide for the needy. To take it would be like stealing from God," Calogerus told them.

"We are the needy," proclaimed Jack, "it was that man that stole from the church."

He pointed to the lifeless body of Cardinal Spehar.

"And now you steal in his stead," Calogerus replied, "you cannot conquer evil with evil."

There was silence. The mob was made up of common people who were good. Most of them felt ashamed of themselves.

"We have had little to show for our efforts, and look at this chest of coins. It could surely buy comfort for our families," said a man.

He was a good man who felt guilty at his actions, but was confronted with feeding his family in this cold winter.

"We would be buying our very own produce that we grew. We paid our taxes with it and now are charged ridiculous prices. Our money is gone, our hunger revisits," another man informed.

"We have children to feed?" cried out a mother.

"Your grievances are justified, but do not attack your church," Calogerus charged.

"It was the church that stole from us. Cardinal Spehar took the side of the nobles and merchants who take more than their fair portion and then watch us beg and starve in the winter.

"They had no consideration that it was we that produced their food and brought it to them in the first place. They like to watch us grovel.

"They take our sons and daughters to work for them in their fine manors. If anyone dared complain, Spehar reminded us how poor Christ was, and that we should be patient," asserted Jack.

"It was not the church that stole from you but some ill advised servant. Not everyone who wears the cloth of the church is doing God's will. I promise you, that from now on, not only will your grievances be heard at court but you shall all find relief from the very proceeds of this chest," Calogerus said with conviction.

Mattews was amazed at how the people were captivated by Calogerus. It took some time but all the money they had taken was promptly returned to the chest. These people were no mob, but they certainly acted like a mob. The killing of Cardinal Spehar was serious, but the conditions that brought about their plight were even more criminal.

"We should find King Graedon and inform him of this matter quickly," Mattews said.

"Perhaps we can entrust these men to buy food and distribute it among the people. They know who is needy," Calogerus suggested.

"Perhaps you should be in charge of the Church's funds until suitable arrangements to replace the Cardinal can be made," suggested Mattews.

"The people are always asked to trust their overlord. This time it will be the overlord who will trust the people," proclaimed Calogerus.

Calogerus had not anticipated taking over the affair of distribution of the church's funds for the poor but there was no one else to do it, let alone do it as unbiased as he could do it and efficiently. Without wasting time, Calogerus chose a committee from among the peasants of Braemar. The very people who were looting in the church became the committee. They were vested by the strict notion that they would distribute the wealth fairly. They were not to use personal grudges against a neighbor or cheat anyone. Calogerus chose the members for his committee rather quickly, but he knew that they would not let him down. He charged them with a special blessing.

Calogerus raised his arms above them.

"Turn to me good people. Before the presence of God in his church, remember that you have been chosen to administer in good conscience the coins in this box to purchase food and comfort, and firewood for the needy and see to its proper distribution.

"In God's name you will distribute the food with the same fairness that you would use for your own families or yourself. To abuse this sacred trust would kindle the wrath of God against you. Do you understand?" Calogerus spoke with conviction.

Moments earlier they were a mob. They understood clearly what it was that Calogerus was telling them. They were being charged with a responsibility and they would not fail in earnest.

"I do," they all eventually replied.

Mattews was impressed at how this crowd of rabbles just moments earlier was transformed into the useful and the good. He knew that Calogerus was a natural inspiration and would make a fine church leader.

Secure the King

After the fall of the south tower in Braemar Castle, the army and archers were in disarray. Those who had horses and were loyal to Lucio mounted them. They collected at the north gate. From there they made their flight to Peregren Castle. Their assurances were the element of surprise. Only they knew when the north gates would open. Then there were the hostages in the form of Elayne, Meaghan and her mother who were used as shields. Vanessa's disciples also lent to the illusion. The presence of the women in their escape guaranteed their success.

It was imperative that Mattews find King Graedon. He was certain that the king was in danger. Mattews left Calogerus with the people in the church and went back into the castle. He climbed the stairs two by two. He came across a guard at the top of the stairs who was confused.

"Where is Graedon!? Where is the king!?" Mattews declared.

"In his chambers," reported the guard.

Mattews grabbed the guard by the throat.

"If any harm has come to him, remember you are the king's guard. You are responsible for his safety," Mattews professed.

The guard made no attempt to defend himself.

"Graedon is in there alright. It is the princess that Lucio took with him," the guard added.

Mattews entered the chamber and he saw King Graedon in bed. Mattews rushed over to him to ascertain his health.

"Your Majesty, how are you?" Mattews asked.

"Elayne! They have taken Elayne. Get after them!" Graedon said.

The sovereign spoke to the best of his ability, but the horror of Elayne's abduction was too much for the ailing monarch. He lay in bed clinging to his breath. The prolonged dependence and use of the Lotumna Tassessiae tea had taken its toll.

Mattews gave word to the guard to stay with Graedon. He himself ran to the north east tower. To the north was the only escape for Lucio. Mattews thought, there might still be time to save the princess. As he arrived to the tower window he looked out. There, inside the north gate, the Peregren force and the men loyal to Lucio were ready to make a run for it. With them were Princess Elayne and several other women. Some were scantily clad for a winter journey. From the tower Mattews yelled out orders.

"There they are! Stop them! They have the princess with them! Mattews commanded them.

The soldiers that were with Lucio though, were loyal to him. Lucio had posted lookouts to determine when the best time to make a run for it would be. They were of no consequence now.

"We go now," directed Vanessa, "open the gate."

"Open the gate!" commanded Lucio.

"We have hostages! You would not want to hurt the princess would you!?" Lucio yelled back to inform Mattews.

"Only brave men would hide behind women!" Mattews yelled out sarcastically.

It was his hope that some of the soldiers would remember their oaths to King Graedon and create a tussle in the north courtyard. It did not happen. The gates were open and the riders took off like thunder in the trodden snow. The earlier skirmish between Peregren's force and those of Lord Barton and Lord Welledon had packed down the snow for easy passage. Mattews had collected the force in Braemar Castle that were loyal to Graedon and directed them. He dispatched the archers to take their position on the north wall of the castle. When the archers took the wall, they captured the archers that were lookouts for Lucio. It was clear to see though that Lucio's force did have hostages. They were female hostages and for sure Princess Elayne was one of them. It was not courtly to use a lady as a shield. In Lucio's mind however, he believed in doing whatever it took to win. Most of the girls who were carried off on the steeds by the dark knights were Vanessa's own disciples.

By the time that Mattews returned to Graedon's chamber, Lord Barton and Lord Welledon had entered the castle with their forces. They found no resistance. Up in his chambers, Graedon lay in bed weak and frustrated. He was humiliated and now heartbroken over Elayne's capture. Calogerus entered and was present but he did not say a word. He knew that there was nothing that he could do now.

"The bastard took my daughter. Elayne is in his hands," Graedon said.

In the corner of his eye Graedon saw Brandyn and Marius. In his eyes they were two fine, upstanding knights and he garnered a measure of hope.

"You will rescue my daughter, you——," Graedon charged.

"Cousin, we will get her back. I promise," replied Lord Barton.

"Yes, good Graedon, we will get her back," assured Lord Welledon.

"Will you be in time?" Graedon gasped.

It was the last thing that King Graedon said. The good king died yearning for his daughter to be free of tyranny. Brandyn and Marius had observed the death of their king. Graedon died in humiliation at the crumbling of his kingdom and heartbreak over the abduction of his daughter.

"Perhaps we can set out after them," said Brandyn.

"They are riding with hostages. It will slow them down," added Marius.

"It is still too risky for the lives of Elayne, Meaghan and your mother, Andrea. These are desperate men and human life means nothing to them," Welledon interjected, "we cannot pursue them the now."

Welledon realized that he too had failed to save Meaghan who was the girl that his son once loved. He knew how much her rescue meant to Brandyn too.

Lord Barton agreed with Welledon that all they could do was wait now. Peregren Castle was not only uphill but well prepared and capable in its ability to defend itself. A visitor could be seen approaching the castle from as far as the east fields of Marmora. If they waited, Peregren castle would use up its food supply and need more. Their present food supply would cover them until spring. For the present time, Barton and Welledon would cut Peregren off food supplies from Marmora and Galles. The two noble generals would send a messenger to negotiate with Lucio but so far they had to admit that Lucio had the upper hand.

Peregren, they thought, would be forced to negotiate the safe return of the hostages. In the mean time they could keep watch around Peregren and wait out the winter. It was not the answer Brandyn wanted to hear. What could happen to the captives in the mean time?

Brandyn's mother, sister and Elayne would be there for months. What could happen in that time was too cruel to imagine. Brandyn remembered that it was Elayne who helped him escape Braemar Castle when Lucio was in pursuit of him. He could not stand by idly and do nothing. Brandyn and Marius exchanged glances. Both of the young knights wanted to meet to discuss a strategy to get into Peregren Castle and get the hostages out. The fact that they had not spoken in a long time did not diminish their friendship.

Brandyn and Marius Plot

After Brandyn and Marius were dismissed by Barton, the two friends went out to the north courtyard to deliberate on the problem. The last time they spoke was at the ceremony for their own knighthood. Brandyn and Marius had a lot of stories to exchange. They still had an instant rapport. Brandyn's adventure in Leems was extraordinary to say the least. Marius informed Brandyn that Jeremy, one of the competitors in the tournament games, was killed during a raid in Irminia. Brandyn was sure to remember. Both Jeremy and Brandyn had competed in the sword competition. Brandyn was sorry to hear that news, he thought very highly of Jeremy. Jeremy had even managed to dance with the Princess Elayne at the castle ball. It was sad to hear of his passing. Brandyn was brief with his news. He reported that Karnivron the Great was truly great. The Leemite knight Haaron married his daughter and a balance was restored at Leems.

Now there was the problem before them. They both agreed that an all out attack on Peregren Castle was out of the question for the same reason that they could not engage Lucio as he escaped. In an effort to keep informed of the events within Peregren Castle, Brandyn felt that they must get into that castle and spy. Despite the cost, they positively had to get into Peregren Castle if they were going to help the princess, Meaghan, Andrea and the others who were abducted from Braemar Castle. Marius could not agree more.

Where Brandyn had never been to the pits of Peregren, Marius was somewhat familiar with the layout of Peregren Castle as he often escorted the transfer of food from Marmora to Peregren. Marius even entered the pits of Peregren once. It was merely happenstance. He learned that it was true that 'the forgers' fires never went out'. Marius was sent there to acquire arms for transfer to Petrinvincit Castle at Teresforte. Since he had arrived early, the order for Lord Barton was not yet ready.

A task master bent on shocking the young knight allowed him to enter the foundry. Marius asked him his name, but he did not answer.

Instead he was led down a hall toward the back of the castle. Then there were stairs. Down and down they went to an unlit cave. It got darker and darker. Alone Marius feared that he could be apprehended at will. The air began to get hotter and hotter. The sulphur smell was not uncommon for a blacksmith's works but it was blended with that of sweat. The stench was more offensive than the combination of all the molten metal and sulphur. It was a frightening place.

Bravely he followed the task master on into the darkness, but it was not dark for long. The cave led to an enormous vault cut into the rock. From their vantage point all could be seen. Natural columns of stone supported the high ceiling. Natural gases that seeped from the bowels of the earth were harnessed for use in the furnaces. The rising heat from the kettles channeled into open holes in the cave's ceiling. It was as if this place was designed by nature for the common purpose to forge and create weapons of destruction. It was an eerie feeling. From there Marius overlooked the works. The fires of the deep pit illuminated the work area.

There Marius witnessed a cacophony of motion. The people that pounded the iron, shoveled iron and coal, chopped wood and worked the bellows were all focused on their tasks as though to part from them would mean death. Sickly looking mules that frothed at the mouth pulled wagons that were full of iron ore mined inside the mountain. When the whip was cracked the tired beasts did not utter a sound. The wagon master kept two torches attached to the wagon in order to see his way. The route never changed in all the days of his life. He rode forward and back, forward and back with a fresh load of ore. These laborers were not accustomed to seeing unfamiliar people and resented the presence of strangers. They much preferred the comfort of their task masters whip than any new face that they did not know.

Marius would never forget the feeling he got when the forgers of the iron looked at him through their soot covered faces. The whites of their eyes were yellowed and framed dark pupils that communicated their thoughts without speaking. One wondered if they ever saw the light of day. One wondered to which race of humanity, if any, they belonged to. Those that worked with picks, hammers and shovels formed bent over and could not straighten up when they moved away from the iron pit. Even their hands had grown to take on the shape of being clenched around the handle of a shovel.

Apart from the soot, there was no color to their skin. Marius wondered if these workers ever got outside the foundry. He wondered where they ate and where they slept. Marius saw a load of weapons loaded onto a platform linked to a pulley. The workers pulled the platform to the upper level. For some reason Marius wondered if Federics was aware of this place. He casually mentioned his name. The fact was that the task masters and blacksmiths did not appreciate Federics. They were angered with the mere mention of his name. Somehow Federics was perceived as the insatiable, undesirable task master of them all. These workers only answered to one master. Marius asked who they answered to, but the task master did not reply.

Apparently other task masters and foremen did not appreciate Marius' presence and scolded the task master that brought him among themselves. They spoke in a strange tongue accompanied by unfriendly grunts. The task master then escorted Marius back through another fork in the cave and another set of stairs surrounded by laid stones. He must be back in the castle portion he thought. Somehow that route led to a door on the castle's west tower that led to the courtyard. In the courtyard Marius could see where the weapons were being loaded onto the wagons. He was never taken there again and was rather grateful for that. Marius told Brandyn about this strange place.

"I know that there is a way into Peregren Castle from the mountains at the back of the castle. There are caves there that have to be linked to the foundry. Nobody would suspect a mere two people sneaking in," Marius informed.

"Peregren is supposed to be impenetrable," Brandyn stated.

"It is just that. It would be costly to attack the castle. They are well prepared for any force. I cannot imagine the loss of life if we were to storm the castle.

"However there are caves in the mountain that allow the hot air that rises from the forges to escape. We just want to escape the other way," Marius explained.

"Once we are in, do you know where to go?" asked Brandyn.

"The idea sounds easy, but I do not honestly know what to expect," confessed Marius, "it sounds easy. Those caves might lead to ground level or might be fixed directly over the kettles of molten ore. I imagine that the escaping air would be quite hot. We would have to get awfully lucky and choose the correct path."

"We do not seem to have any other option. It may be our only chance and it is worth taking," Brandyn encouraged.

"For starters we cannot be spotted by anyone as we climb down the orange mountain wall of iron ore. We shall have to climb the mountain from Marmora. As we get closer to the castle we shall have to travel at night time. Although there is very little vegetation, no one should expect us traveling there. That should be easy enough. Once we are inside the mountain cave we have got to get to the ground level. If we can get to the ground level, I may have an idea where to go," replied Marius.

Not knowing how hot the tunnels got was bad enough but they must not be seen as well. If they were spotted, the mission would be over and so would they. What if they could not hold onto the rock walls due to the soot?

What if the soot made them slip directly into a kettle of molten ore?

Questions began to arise, but one thing was for certain, they would go. For one, it was their king's dying wish. At any cost they would go to rescue the captives. Brandyn was getting especially fond of Princess Elayne who had helped him and was a captive with his mother and sister. One thing that the plan had going for it was that Lucio would not suspect it. He knew that Barton or Welledon could do nothing at this time of the year. The bitter cold would prohibit even the plan that Marius and Brandyn were hatching. The plan was perilous, but Brandyn and Marius had to do it. Lucio could not be in a better position and Peregren was impregnable.

Marius and Brandyn decided to inform Barton and Welledon of their idea. They could not wait and immediately went back to see them. After telling them about their scheme, it seemed that both Barton and Welledon gave it thought despite their reservations. In lieu of the fact that nothing else could be done, it became the only thing that they could do. The plan was so daring, it just might work. Barton and Welledon changed one detail of the plan. They both agreed to send others in their place. It was ascertained that both Marius and Brandyn were too well recognizable. There was another delicate mission that they were needed for. Barton thought it wise to send both Brandyn and Marius to escort Calogerus back to Craigroyston. After what happened to Calogerus in Braemar's dungeon, Barton saw fit to send an escort of these two young knights to accompany him in good faith.

When Calogerus, Mattews and Selwyck joined the senior dukes of Rothaynen, Lord Barton apologized to Calogerus. It was the first order of business as a friendly diplomat was thrown into the dungeon. Calogerus understood despite the hardship and risk he endured during the escape effort. There was much to discuss but they had to prepare for another sad event. Before them, lay the body of their dead king. Arrangements for the burial were made. Mattews informed the party that Cardinal Spehar was dead but he did not divulge the details. At that time Mattews was asked to prepare for the religious ceremony. He in turn suggested Brother Michael from the monastery. Mattews declared his return to knighthood. He was not sure of his lands as they passed to other family members but he pledged his allegiance to Rothaynen and the Princess Elayne. It was a positive note because she was still alive and the rightful heir.

It was then that Lord Barton got briefed about what happened to Mattews in Wendover. Then Brandyn told them what had taken place in Leems. Brandyn did not leave out a single detail. Calogerus listened to Brandyn with great interest as he heard the story of Leems unfold. It was important for him to know the reasons why Queen Ellen was removed from the throne. He would need this information to inform Queen Enyja when he returned home. Selwyck had ordered the repair to the Courage. It would take two days at the earliest. Lord Barton gave word that the materials for the repair to the Courage including tarp for a new sail, be provided forthwith. With the food supplies that Barton provided them, they could disembark for Craigroyston very soon. No one was happier to be going home than Calogerus.

There was an eerie feeling when Calogerus thought about home, Jonquis and Enyja. Calogerus guessed that something had happened to his king. Calogerus asked Selwyck about Jonquis and Enyja. All that Selwyck could report was that they were well. When Selwyck embarked for Teresforte to rendezvous with Calogerus, all was well at the Karley. Regardless of Selwyck's report, Calogerus was anxious to go home. There was something amiss. He could sense heartache in Enyja. Calogerus did not confide his concerns to Selwyck as they were ill founded at this time. Calogerus thought that while the ship was being repaired, they could attend Graedon's last rites. After the funeral and once they disembarked for Craigroyston, then Calogerus would confide his concerns to Selwyck.

Homeward Bound

There was much to be done after King Graedon's funeral rite. He would be interred under the church of St. Zorren with his forefathers. The greatest concern was the safety of their princess. Marius and Brandyn had introduced a plan to rescue Princess Elayne. Barton and Welledon received Marius and Brandyn's plan very well. They decided to act on it and sent three spies to Peregren. Marius appealed that he and Brandyn be sent due to his prior knowledge. The prior knowledge was not extensive though, as Marius admitted, so Marius and Brandyn would not be among them.

Instead both Marius and Brandyn were chosen to accompany Calogerus back to Craigroyston to explain to Jonquis and Enyja what happened in Rothaynen. Calogerus wanted Brandyn to accompany him to Craigroyston anyway. It seemed that the details of what happened at Leems were of great interest to Calogerus. Calogerus sensed that the Leemite councilors who failed Mattic at Leems would take advantage of Jonquis and Enyja's hospitality at Craigroyston. Calogerus was very anxious to get back. Marius and Brandyn were disappointed. They wanted to go to Peregren to rescue the Princess Elayne, Meaghan, Andrea and other ladies of the court who happened to be abducted. At Barton's bidding, the Courage was generously supplied with food for the trip home. Selwyck needed only for Calogerus and his guests to board and a little good fortune on the high seas.

Picking up the Pieces

Lucio immediately sent word to the northern castles about their plight and the notice to ration food stuffs went out early. Lucio had not yet begun to fight. With the northern castle's support, it would be a divided kingdom. If they could hold out in Peregren and survive the winter, Lucio felt that things would go his way. There was no more King Graedon and the princess was in his keep. He would take Princess Elayne for his wife. In turn Elayne would bear him a child of his own and that would lend authenticity to his claim on the crown of Rothaynen. Barton and Welledon could do nothing to stop his plan now and they would have to settle to keep the peace. In time Lord Barton and Lord Welledon would die and the kingdom would be truly united again, only this time he, Lucio, would be king.

A Squire for Mattews

It had been a long day. It was longer for Calogerus and Mattews who lived to tell of their enterprising method of escape. Calogerus decided to spend the night in Braemar Castle, only this time in a bed. He would leave with Selwyck early in the morning. Mattews suggested to Calogerus that he should join the religious order. He was the very man that was needed to profess the word of the Almighty God. People listened to what Calogerus had to say, and how he said it. As for Mattews, he decided to take up the sword. He again entered the order of knighthood as he had pledged his sword to Rothaynen. It was not easier now. There was someone after Mattews now bent on avenging the brother that he killed. He thought that there was work to be done for the forces of good and righteousness. Mattews was ready to take up the sword again. He was older, wiser and sure of God's purpose for him. Besides, there was no way now of escaping the wrath of Chadryn's brother, Khotryn, He knew that they would meet some day perhaps even at Peregren Castle. Mattews remembered the large man who was even stouter that Chadryn. He described both brothers to Calogerus.

"I will recognize the elder brother. They certainly bear the same family trait," Mattews quipped.

"Big ferocious men?" asked Calogerus.

"No, stupidity," Mattews replied.

Mattews thought about what he said about Khotryn. He regretted what he said as he was saying it. It made him look arrogant and boastful. He thought back that even though he had not done battle for years, he was able to subdue Chadryn, but that was with the help of God. There was no way that he could have subdued Chadryn on his own. Although Khotryn was an older warrior, why should he presume how he would fight?

He was afraid that he was being cocky. Within himself, Mattews turned to God and humbled himself. He prayed within, 'forgive me Lord for my arrogance. I presumed to claim your victory as my own. Do not forsake your servant though he was boastful. Instead keep every white hair on my head safe against the vendetta of this mighty Khotryn.'

"We must never presume to be invincible," Mattews relented.

With having said that, for the first night since arriving at Braemar Castle, both Calogerus and Mattews would sleep in comfortable beds.

There was a young page that joined the two walking down the corridor to their chambers. The boy came to bring water to their chambers. The young boy was impressionable, especially after all the excitement and change at Braemar. Mattews realized that the youth was enthusiastic about helping him. Not every page was that eager and chipper. With Mattews taking up arms again, he would need a squire. He thought that perhaps this young boy would agree to serving him in apprenticeship so that one day, he too would become a knight.

"What is your name?" asked Mattews.

"Harry," replied the boy.

"Who are your parents?" Mattews asked him.

"My mother Fann, works in the castle kitchen. She is the best cook," he replied with pride.

"And, where is your father?" Mattews inquired.

"He was killed in battle a few years ago," replied Harry.

Harry had a knot in his throat and his voice sank somewhat. Like every boy he missed his father. He continued to keep his cheery demeanor though. Mattews realized that this boy was a good boy. He was not mean spirited and very eager to serve. He wanted to ask him to be his squire, but not before asking his mother. Since his mother worked in the royal kitchen, Mattews would approach her about Harry becoming his squire. It seemed that Harry was a little too young yet, but what he could not do because of his size, he made up with heart and effort. Harry could not take his eyes off of Mattews. Mattews was a hero to him. Harry could not believe that such a young looking face would have hair so white like an old man.

"Why is your hair so white?" Harry asked.

Mattews did not know how to answer. If he explained that it was a family trait, it would take too long to explain and understand. He did not understand it himself, but he was grateful that he still had his hair. Often men would lose their locks as they grew older.

Calogerus interrupted, "The white in his hair is a measure of wisdom."
"Wisdom?" repeated Harry.

"Yes, it is a measure of wisdom. For some people, they must wait an entire lifetime before they gain wisdom enough for their hair to go white. By that time, they have lost their hair or have passed on. Others like the good Mattews here, well he gained his wisdom rather young," explained Calogerus.

Mattews smiled. The explanation was flattering coming from Calogerus. It was satisfactory enough for Harry. It did not matter what color Mattews hair was, Harry looked up to this particular man. Mattews was drawn to Harry like a son that he never had. He had dreams of marrying and having children of his own, but plans can get changed by circumstances in this aerde. Calogerus could see that Mattews work was not done. Since Calogerus was kind enough to speak what was on his mind, Mattews decided he too would do the same.

"You know Calogerus, you should enter the priesthood to shepherd God's people. You are a natural at this vocation," Mattews suggested.

"I believe that I am providing that very service in advising my king and queen. In that responsibility, my advice has always had common sense wisdom and values not unlike your Christian ones at its very heart," answered Calogerus, "you do not need a title or have to be a designated 'keeper of the faith', God needs the people who actually do the keeping of the faith too."

Calogerus was grateful for the complement and realized that in a relatively short time, he got to know Mattews very well. They smiled at each other. They parted company as each had his own chamber on this occasion. Lord Barton had persuaded Calogerus to stay the night before setting off in the Courage with Selwyck in the morning. Marius and Brandyn would accompany Calogerus to Norsendan Castle in Craigroyston. It would not be a long rest that night since the earlier excitement was still in their minds.

Return to Peregren

With the arrival of Vanessa, Lucio and their cohorts, Federics' servants were the only semblance of honor at Peregren. Their loyalty lay with Federics and King Graedon. When Lucio and Vanessa returned to Peregren with who they thought might be the princess and without Federics, they imagined the worse for their master. Lucio placed the girl and other ladies under a watchful guard in the guest chambers. Those chambers were set aside for dignitaries only, so the servants guessed that it must be the princess.

After being rejected by Vanessa, Federics was a broken man. The black magic that she weaved enslaved Federics. Clara was a young girl and one of his servants. She enjoyed working at the castle kitchen but in time she grew more than loyal to Federics. Clara fell in love with Federics and he too was interested in this lovely girl. Clara truly loved the lord of the manor and not for his position or wealth. After Vanessa intervened between them, Federics was too embarrassed and too hurt to pursue his true love. Clara loved Federics so much that to be in his presence was enough for her. She could wait forever for him. Clara hoped that someday her lord would forget his past mistake and notice her again. Federics was not above marrying the young servant girl who had saved herself for true love. Clara had never lost hope, but now she would have to awaken from her dream.

When they confirmed that Elayne was the princess, the staff that was loyal to Federics was at her service. They would do all that they could to make her feel comfortable. They were fully aware however that their actions should not offend Lucio and Vanessa. The two of them had resided at Peregren Castle before. Phyllis the cook who had a caring heart for Federics well being did not like how Vanessa treated the lord of the manner. She did not like her scheming ways. The good staff would have to learn what the princess and the others were doing at Peregren without the king and without Federics.

The Next Morning Came

The next morning came. It was a parting of paths for Calogerus and Mattews. Such a chance meeting in the castle dungeon as traitor and spy against the crown, it was unlikely that they should ever be free again. Mattews was grateful to have met this strange man. Calogerus was relieved to know that there were characters such as Mattews since he lost all hope of his own son turning from the playground of death and perdition.

"I will be joined by two young knights of Rothaynen, Marius and Brandyn. Selwyck and his men will give me a ride home to Craigroyston. I thank you for your company good Mattews," Calogerus told him, "May God keep you in the palm of his hands."

The two men embraced. Each was grateful to have made the acquaintance of the other. Each had served a purpose to each other. In their minds they knew that there was still much to do. It dawned on them. With all the events that took place, they forgot all about the time.

Christmas day had passed and the events of the day made the moment come and go almost unnoticed. The memories of all the past Christmases were a stark contrast to this dark one. The peasants celebrated their portion with their families. Unknown to them was that their king was dead and the princess was stolen away. Barton and Welledon's hearts were heavy and the sense of worry clung to them like their clothing. Brandyn and Marius could feel the sense of challenge for the future. How had it come to this?

Historical Peregren:
The Story of St. Zorren

In its early years, Peregren Castle was often put to the test. There were warring dukes and a band of knights loyal to Crendar the Horrible. Alliances were easily made and were easier to dissolve. Due to the vicinity of Peregren Castle to the mountainous Rockland, the Kingdom of Rothaynen was under the wrath of a winged serpent. The people feared this ugly beast with ferocious claws, forked tongue and glaring yellow eyes. From its mouth it could conjure and cast forth a fire and brimstone flame. The air around it smelled of sulphur and its stench bothered the eyes of those in its vicinity. Many a brave knight met their doom in battling this sinister beast with the reflexes of a lioness. The beast was quick to move out of harm's way and even quicker in attacking. Its scales were stronger than any manmade armor. Swords and spears that did land their mark reflected off like water on a duck's back. If that was not enough, the fire it spewed had roasted some brave knights within their own armor. They could not kill the beast.

In the nearby country by the Dargell River, there was a young boy who was raised by and old devout, God-fearing warrior named Tomett. This old man had outlived his wife and he had lost his beloved children to both sickness and wars. After these events he was miserable and he turned away carrying a personal hatred for God. Tomett held the Lord responsible for taking away the children that he loved. He had trained his sons well at the skill of warfare, so they could serve their king. One son was burned to death by engaging the serpent another was crushed and carried off in the beast's talons. The youngest boy was killed in battle by Crendar's guards as he bravely fought his way toward the old tyrant. Tomett's wife and daughters took ill and died slowly as the knight witnessed the color leave their faces and the desire to live leave their bodies. It took the coming of the young orphaned boy to make him realize that there was still work that needed to be done. The knight realized that the Lord did not take his children it was the evil that had seduced all mankind. Brother was pitted against brother for gain. The young boy who helped Tomett to realize this was named Zorren.

Apart from fair skin, Zorren had long, sandy hair, a strong build with large shoulders and a heart of gold. He was ever grateful and loving of Tomett, his adopted father. There was no one else that took care of Zorren like he needed to be taken care of. Tomett came about as Zorren became an adolescent. Tomett not only made sure that Zorren had food and clothing but guidance and a future. A good future was one opportunity that he would not get with his foster family. Zorren became a guest on his own land. Although Zorren was a gentle sort, he should not be mistaken for a fool. Then under the circumstances a lonely adolescent boy had to make allowances to ensure his survival. Principles are principles, but you have to be alive to take advantage of opportunity.

Upon the untimely death of Zorren's real parents during an earthquake their home was destroyed. He was left alone to live in a small hovel and fend for himself at 8 years of age. How could a boy of 8 years manage a farm?

The only remaining sows that Zorren had were stolen by his own hungry neighbors. It might have been nice to be invited to supper, but there was hunger in the land. The sheep and goats disappeared into the wilds at the edge of their land. Then a family that escaped the wrath of their landlord came upon the farm. They decided to stay. Zorren thought that this new family that came to live with him was the answer to his prayers.

The arrival of these people certainly solved the immediate problem of managing the farm and creating provisions of food, but his new foster father and mother were not planning to be stewards for him. If they were to do any labor on the farm, it would be for themselves. They passed themselves off as relatives and Zorren made no dispute. Without them he was alone. Zorren was treated considerately at the beginning, but as time passed it was clear to see that the guests were now the masters of the farm.

Zorren was no fool. He realized what was happening but what could he do?

Without these people he realized that he would have nothing anyway. He was losing his livestock and with little instruction, he was not a success at farming. At least Zorren felt that he was part of a family even though it was not his own. He had a sister figure in the person of Jill. She was the young daughter of Todd and Heather. Their son Angus, who was a little older than Zorren, was quite another thing. Angus took after his parents who were 'mano piglia' types, which refers to their being self-serving. Their young daughter Jill was anything but greedy or mean-spirited. Her parents saw Zorren as a safe keeper of their daughter. Zorren merely occupied her time so Todd and Heather could be free of her.

The Path to Destiny

As a young boy with limited means and lack of money, Zorren would often go on an excursion just inside the forest gate after his chores. Jill being young and relatively chore free would join him. The shade within the forest and fresh, crisp, clean air made the experience invigorating as well as inspiring to the senses. The most desirable thing that came from charting a new path in the forest was the sound that it made. The forest had a silence about it that sharpened the senses. Whatsoever chose to interrupt the stillness and silence in the forest was easy to discern. It was there that Zorren met Tomett the older knight. The knight kept an eye on this boy. They had often spoken and Zorren told him everything. At one point Tomett was going to punish Todd and Heather for their treatment of the boy, but he relented. The knight understood the boy's dilemma. These guardians, good or bad, were better than nothing. He also believed that Zorren was in love with their daughter, Jill.

Zorren had often ventured out on one of the king's roads where he met traveling people sometimes. Tomett, who grew fond of Zorren, was ever present to protect travelers from highwaymen. On one occasion Zorren was approached by two desperate men. These men meant to beat and rob him, but the old knight had a watchful eye. In his old age the knight discerned rogues from the law-abiding, and their need to be protected. Before the two men could bring harm to the boy, he appeared and questioned them. The two men made it appear that the young boy was with them, but the old knight knew better. After further conversation, the old knight told them to get out and fast. The two men may have been desperate with nothing to lose but they elected not to lose anything and left the boy alone.

Cliff Side Adventure

One day Zorren and Jill climbed the high cliff overlooking the meadow and spied an eagle's nest. Although it was sunny out, the light breeze made the air cool. The cliff was in a high inaccessible place but they were eager for the adventure. Zorren and Jill carefully managed to work their way up the steep cliff. When they climbed up to the rock ledge, they spied that the eagle's nest had three eggs in it. One egg was actually breaking up and a young eaglet was chirping out a cry of hunger. The other eggs did not stir yet, but soon they too would be punctured by the determined beaks of their occupants. The mother eagle was not there. She was not in the immediate vicinity either.

Zorren and Jill would never have been allowed to climb to the eagle's nesting ground if they had been present. The eagles would have perceived their presence as a danger to their nest. The mother eagle was probably out hunting for food. Her mate was probably chasing off some predator. For some reason, at least one of them was not at their post. Perhaps the mighty mountain walls were ample security that assured no trespassers. For Zorren and Jill, this was a miracle that they experienced. They felt joyful at the thought of watching the new eaglet work its way into the world. Its young feathers were wet and warm. The young eaglet could only see its immediate environment. The adventurers anticipated seeing the other eaglets break through. Their attention was completely focused on observing this joyous occasion as well.

The chirping of the young eaglet was a natural cry in its nature to alarm its keeper that it was hungry. Unfortunately it was also an indicator to its natural enemies of its presence and position. Out of the blue sky off in the distance, there was the mother coming back to the nest. As the flyer came closer to the high mountain wall, Jill pointed to it. It was not the mother, nor the father, nor an eagle at all. It was a flying serpent and it was drawn to the eagles' nest by the sound and now the smell of the young eaglet. The beast was a keen hunter and thought that it could easily swoop down and make a meal of the hatched eagle and carry off its siblings in its claws.

Zorren was not going to let that happen. He looked for a stone or loose rock to throw at the beast but on the cliff side all rock held firm. He would have to break a piece of rock off the striations in the stone face of the mountain. It would take time and he would have to work quickly. The winged serpent paused to assess the strange presence. Then it decided to approach the nest. Zorren did not have the desired stone free from the rock. Jill looked around as saw a clump of wild grass that was growing in the cliff side. She pulled it out with a considerable amount of dirt and handed it to Zorren. Zorren took the grass and dirt and flung it at the beast as it got closer. The weight of the dirt made the projectile easy to fling at the beast as it approached. Zorren hit the beast, but now it learned that there were two other beings that could not fly nestled in the cliff side in peril.

There were loose rock and stones in the immediate area that the clump of grass was taken from. Jill took a stone and threw it at the serpent. The winged serpent dodged the stone in mid air but was prevented from getting closer to the eagle's nest. The winged serpent was furious with the two defenders of the nest. It threatened the two by flying toward them and scratching at them with its claws. The beast then flapped its wings that made an uneasy sound. It let out a screech as it hung in the air. The beast then clinched its teeth and opened its mouth to send out a blast of fire. Lucky for Zorren and Jill, that it was a young serpent and the fire that spewed out at them was against the wind. Jill could still feel the heat on her leg that was stretched across the cliff wall to keep balance. In the mean time Zorren had acquired a larger rock and once more he flung it at the beast. The rock hit the beast on its stomach side and the beast relented by hovering back. The beast was now committed even more. It was not about to give up until it had its prize. Zorren and Jill kept hurling rock and patches of grass to keep the beast at bay.

At this instant the large mother eagle was returning with a mouthful of food for its young lings. She heard the screech and imagined the worst. The eagle's wings were spread out as it glided home carefree. It only shared the barren sky with the clouds. Upon noticing the danger to its young, the eagle, dropped the food and tucked in its large wings. It seemed to drop like a bolt toward the nest. The eagle closed in on the winged beast swiftly and crashed into it. The mother eagle opened its wing span and raised its talons at the last moment. The span was as wide as a man is tall. With her sharp talons, body weight and speed, the collision forced the winged serpent off its course and into a tailspin. It happened so fast that the serpent was stunned. About half way down the winged beast regained control and flew away. The mother eagle was ever grateful that no harm came to its young lings. It took notice of the assistance that Zorren and Jill provided. Normally humans were not welcome anymore. They had turned mean and cruel toward animals. There was a time when they were gentle and caring.

Upon landing on its nest and ascertaining that her young were in no peril, the eagle looked at the two young adventurers. The eagle was a majestic animal, fierce and proud. It was a look of gratitude, Zorren and Jill hoped. With its young ling chirping in hunger, the eagle was relieved that it was still there. Since the eagle dropped the food that it carried in its mouth in order to defend the nest, it still needed food. Zorren noted that there were worms under the clump of grass that Jill pulled up earlier and he gathered them and placed them on the top of a rock close to the nest. The gesture was accepted as the eagle went over to the rock and collected the worms and bugs to feed its young ling. Zorren and Jill had been very brave.

The eagles did not like their mountain-wall home disturbed by anyone. They constantly flew the skies in their area to defend against unwanted predators. Here was the male eagle come home at last. It was not happy to see the guests on its mountain walls, but the female eagle was not happy with his nest watching. It was understood by him that the guests were welcome at that. Zorren and Jill felt honored to be welcomed onto the eagles' mountain cliff. They stood very still to indicate that they meant no harm. In the end, they had befriended the warriors of the sky. Jill thought that they name their new friends so Zorren and she did so. They named the mother eagle, Mache and the father, Strom. They had difficulty choosing a name for the eaglet. They began to name names. Mache and Strom watched as the two adolescent humans chirped away amongst themselves.

Zorren and Jill were amerced in the task of choosing a suitable name for the new born eaglet. It was amusing to the eagles that their apprehensive guests were now so comfortable in their home. The two youths stopped talking as their name searching came to a lull. All that could be heard was the screeching of the eaglet in among the sound of the cold wind. At that height the temperature was cooler, but Zorren and Jill did not notice due to the adventure. It was the pure zeal of the two youths that kept them warm. Then at once Jill's eyes opened wide. She suggested they name the young ling 'Screech' because of the screeching it made. Mache and Strom were touched at the interest and kindness shown by Zorren and Jill. They understood full well that the sounds that the humans uttered referred to them. The mighty eagles felt as though they had been adopted. Zorren and Jill were also adopted. It was a memorable day.

Zorren and Jill would have liked to stay longer. They still anticipated the other two eaglets breaking through their shell. They might have stayed, but given the look on Strom, they decided that they did not want to over stay their welcome. Besides, they still had to descend the mountain, cut through the forest and pass the meadow before returning home. They would be late even if they started now and there would be some form of punishment in the form of a chore. In their minds though, it was worth having seen the birth of an eagle and making friends with its majestic parents.

Knighting By Fire

As time passed and Zorren got older and worked his body into a good shape, he was now ready to train as a squire. Sir Tomett, the knight, asked Zorren to be his squire and move into his castle with him. The old knight knew that he could depend on the boy's stewards to agree. For Todd and Heather, it was one less mouth to feed and the true owner of their plot of land was leaving probably to get himself killed. So, Zorren went with Tomett, to make his new home in the old knight's castle at Holmgren. There Zorren became the knight's squire and fulfilled the requirements of his training. Indeed when it became time to test Zorren for knighthood, Tomett was proud to escort Zorren to Peregren Castle for the Fall Harvest Tournament. The distinguished knight had been a proud sponsor of his boys and an ardent participant of the tournament. He was very close to the king. Those days were passed. Tomett was absent from Peregren Castle for many years. He had not spoken to his king in that entire period.

On the way to Peregren however, they heard a scream from the meadow that lay after the forest and before the mountain. A young maiden had ventured out too far to pick berries for her mother when she was surprised by a winged serpent. The serpent had her in its sights and cut off her path of escape. In fear and bewilderment, the girl fainted as she fell to the ground. Zorren heard the voice in distress and he knew that it was Jill. Both Zorren and Tomett raced their chargers toward the sound of the scream. Both raced to the meadow. Tomett was certain that it was Halitos, like Zorren was sure of Jill's voice. The dragon was an experienced, clever hunter.

When they got to the meadow they could see from a distance that the beast had trapped the maiden as she lay on the ground before a large rock. It closed in on her. The beast planned to grab her in his ferocious claw and carry her off. As fearful as the beast was, Zorren charged away at it with his lance in hand. In the instant, he did not wait for Tomett to give instruction. He was off before Tomett could open his mouth to speak. Tomett of course understood full well the reason. In Zorren's mind, Jill was in trouble and it did not matter that the beast consumed people at will. With the speed of horse and a well-directed lance, Zorren charged his lance toward the beast's back. The lance slid off the scales of the beast's back. With quick reflexes, Zorren lifted the lance, turned his horse around. Then using the lance as a spear, he directed it onto the end of its tail. The lance found its mark in the beast's tail. The lance pierced the shiny, scaly tail. The lance had found a vulnerable point and pinned the tail to the ground. With that the beast let out a cry of pain and anger that struck terror about. It then took in a deep breath, clenched its teeth, looked into the sky and let out a blast of fire.

The air around the beast became immediately foul. It flapped back its wings and caught Lento, Zorren's horse, squarely. With the force of the wings flapping against him, the rider and horse were pushed away violently. Zorren was thrown off Lento while the horse fell against the ground. Lento instinctively scrambled to get up and away. The beast fought the lance that pinned its tail to the ground. Zorren's lance was lucky to land in its mark. Tomett realized the danger his squire was in and advanced. He wanted to take advantage of the opportunity. In its anger the dragon discharged fire and brimstone from its breath to the surrounding area around it. It burned all the vegetation in its path from high tree branches to the lower bushes and brush on the ground. In its twisting and pulling the beast managed to break the lance from the ground. It swung its tail with the lance still through it, around to its mouth. It used its teeth to clench and pull the lance out. Then the beast flung the lance away.

The dragon was no longer pinned to the ground. As Tomett drew closer on his steed Gencro, the dragon's tail became free. With this freedom the dragon swung its tail at horse and rider squarely. The tail had sharp bones that protruded like fish scales, only thicker and sharper. Again the beast toppled both horse and rider to the ground with mighty resolve. Tomett had to follow through on his charge. He feared that with Zorren so close, he would surely perish under the dragon's tail. Now he lay on the ground unable to move.In the current distraction, Zorren tried to run toward Jill but the beast was fully aware of his intentions. It turned and ground its teeth at him. It discharged its fiery breath at him but for some reason it was a short blast. Its fire was limited in its range this time. The winged beast determined that it was time to go. The dragon turned and took Jill into its talons. It flapped its wings and started away for the high rock land west of the Peregren Castle region. Zorren ran toward Tomett to get his lance, but the beast was airborne. In the fall, Tomett had broken his back and was dying. Gencro was swept down like grains of wheat in a broom and thrown against rocky ground. The faithful steed was shaken and slow in getting up.

The old knight looked upon his squire for the last time, as he knew that he was dying. Tomett believed that Zorren would make a fine knight as he had proven to him. Zorren was impetuous for charging in at Halitos, but Tomett understood that his squire would have done anything to save Jill. Tomett believed that Zorren had the heart of a knight. Tomett had looked forward to returning to Peregren. He could see his friend the king and watch Zorren compete in the tournament. Tomett knew that Zorren would earn his knighthood with a splendid exhibition. The beast was now well away in its escape. Zorren turned and looked at Tomett with sorry eyes. He knew that he would not survive. Tomett turned his eyes to Zorren and looked into him deeply with pride. He suddenly remembered the words of his wise father before he set out to compete for knighthood.

"My son," gasped Tomett, "I tell you. Never be false. Never be cruel. Temper justice with mercy. If you can follow these rules, I shall always be proud of you."

These were the last words that Tomett spoke to Zorren. The old knight reached up to place his hands on Zorren's head. As Tomett mumbled something that was not distinguishable, his hands fell and he died. They were strange words from an antique time, but Tomett's actions spoke louder than his words. If not for Zorren, he would never have wanted to return to Peregren Castle. The memories of his own sons, that he loved and lost was unbearable and prevented his return. There he was at last, escorting Zorren to Peregren Castle to present before the king.

It was now clear to Zorren what had to be done. He must rescue Jill and slay the winged beast that killed his father. Zorren had always respected and considered Tomett as a father, but he had never called him that. He had imagined and dreamed and even hoped that Tomett would consider him as a son. More than ever Zorren wished that Tomett could hear him now.

"Father!" Zorren yelled.

The cry echoed into the mountains. He believed that if he yelled his loudest, Tomett might hear him and awake. Tears came forth from Zorren's eyes.

Tomett deserved a Christian burial but it might be too late if he did not immediately go after Jill. Zorren saw that Tomett's faithful steed, Gencro was still shaken so he removed the horse's saddle and armor. He took the blanket from Gencro. He carefully laid Tomett on his shield and took the sword from Tomett's scabbard. Zorren fixed the sword in Tomett's crossed hands. Then he covered the dead knight with the blanket. Zorren planned to come back to bury him properly, but that would depend on his return from vanquishing the beast. He knew full well that he might not be returning at all.

Zorren took a deep breath. He walked over and picked up Tomett's lance. Then he took the reins of Gencro and mounted Lento. He rode off in the direction of the winged serpent. The beast had long disappeared but he had to be somewhere over the mountains behind Peregren. On he rode through meadow and glen and forest. There was no road in the direction that the dragon took. It was hard to believe it was daytime as Zorren traveled under patches of forest cover.

He rode in the direction of the winged serpent until green vegetation ceased to exist. There was a foul odor in the air emitted by the bowels of the earth. It was the same foul odor that accompanied the beast's discharges of fire. It was the early evening. In his mind, Zorren did not know what happened to Jill. She may have already been consumed by the dragon for food. Zorren prayed for her safety, but at the same time doubted it given the ferocity and desperation of the beast. Then finally he pledged to God that 'if Jill was safe, it would be the last thing that he asked for'. He meant it too for he realized that he loved Jill with all his heart. Zorren realized that he loved Jill during his absence from the farm when he moved to Holmgren Castle. Tomett had known for quite some time.

As the sun went down, the evening darkened. He looked up at the mountain cliff and spied a rock face that could shelter any beast. When Zorren came to a stream, he got off his horse. It was a good time to water Lento and Gencro and eat something for himself. Both he and Tomett had packed food for the journey to the Peregren Fall Harvest Tournament Games. He would need it to keep his strength for the battle that he hoped would ensue between him and Halitos. The tournament games were over by now as it was the evening. Zorren missed his chance at the Peregren tournament. He did not compete and earn his knighthood before the people and King Lyndendor of Rothaynen. His knighthood however, did not matter to him so long as he got Jill back safely.

Zorren was so tired that he considered that place to make camp for the night and get rest. Suddenly there came a light out of a cave in the side of the mountain. It was unusual and if he had not been looking in that direction at that moment, he was sure to miss it. He did not miss it though. Zorren immediately collected his wares and Lento and Gencro. He walked his horses to the base of the mountain where the strange light came from. The way to the cave was rocky and uneven and upward all the way. Zorren kept his eyes focused on the goal of finding the cave. He was certain that it was the very one that he was looking for. He pressed on to get as close as he could before climbing the rock.

Zorren walked on guiding Lento and Gencro around the uneven rock ground. As he came closer to the cave that he had spied, he noted that the cliff up to it was steeper than it seemed off in the distance. Nevertheless Zorren was there. As he looked down, a small stream of water trickled down the rock almost silently and collected in the bottom of what appeared to be a large bowl. The water did not stir in this large bowl and it was green in color. He wondered, if he fell off the cliff into the bowl of water, whether it was deep enough to break his fall. He imagined that if it was shallow, he would smash his body in it. He would meet his end by drowning in pain. Zorren would have to be extremely careful in climbing the cliff alone. He could not bring Lento with him so he left them behind. He did not tie Lento and Gencro so they were free to move should some predator attack him. Zorren gathered his sword, shield and lance to himself.

Zorren carried the shield on his left arm, he held onto the lance in his right arm, and his sword, was sheathed in its scabbard. If he encountered the flying serpent that could swipe at him with wings, claws, a tail and breathe fire, he had better do it from a distance. The lance would keep him at a distance and the shield could protect him while he stood behind it. The climb upward was not easy and his armor got heavier. Tomett had provided the armor for Zorren from his own sons' storehouse. It was fashioned to him and painted anew by Stan, Tomett's servant. Despite the fashioning, it was still uncomfortable to climb up a mountain with. On a good note, the suit of armor kept him warm as the evening temperature cooled. Zorren had traveled far and was tired.

Zorren climbed up to the point where the cave was. He got a good footing on the ground that had some patches of dirt. It was cooler out as he felt on his hands, but his brow was dripping sweat. Zorren wanted to rest but he could not wait to find out if this cave was the one that lead to the dragon. The foul sulphur smell in the air was bothering his eyes. He thought that he heard the echo of a sheep baaing. There was a landing before the cave and he got onto it. He entered the cave with his shield and lance in hand. It was dark in the cave. Zorren was careful to make as little noise as possible, but his armor rubbed on the chain and link vest. The rubbing made a soft but repetitive sound. To the keen ears such as those of a beast the sound was loud and clear. Halitos detected that something was coming its way.

To prevent its victims such as sheep from leaving, Halitos placed its captives on a ledge overlooking a great crevice hole within the cave. There was no escape from that ledge that was governed by a few boulders that fenced in its prey. At some point in time that crevice hole was carved by the flow of magma that spewed up from the center of the aerde. If that was not enough, it was dark in the cave. The senses of smell and sound were now very useful as vision was limited. The dragon was alert and poised. Halitos' serpent tail swung around so it could turn and face the different paths that led to its den. It was concerned with only one entrance; the one with the noise. On Halitos turning around, the serpent took a mouthful of rubble and ground it into its back teeth.

As the beast left its lair, Zorren looked at what was behind it. There appeared a silhouette on the wall that came from across that ledge behind the rocks. There were some sheep and a girl. There was no mistaking the girl in the silhouette. As Zorren moved forward, he recognized that it was Jill. Though Jill did not see him, a sense of joy and warmth came over him. He did not call out to her for fear of alerting the beast. His realized that his prayer was answered though. No harm had come to Jill, apart from being frightened he supposed. 'Thank you, thank you, Lord God', he thought to himself. Now the rest was up to him. As he had asked, God saw to it that no harm came to Jill. Now it was up to him to be brave and face the foe. Halitos hunted its prey and stocked it away. With that ledge, he could keep his prey fresh until he needed it. Zorren's resolve was renewed in him, he did not worry that the dragon was large. He thought to himself, 'it is so big, how can I miss?'

Zorren thought that the beast was so big in this cramped cave that it was limited in its means to attack with all its weapons.

Suddenly and quite without warning, Zorren could see the dragon's eyes locked on him. The beast blocked the entrance to its den and roared at the intruder. Then it ground its teeth and breathed out the foul breath of its lungs that ignited into an inferno. Zorren was just able to get behind his shield. He held his breath. The entire pass was set ablaze as the hot air passed around Zorren's shield to escape out the cave opening behind him. The paint on Zorren's shield was scorched. Most of it peeled off and left the shield black. When Halitos was finished breathing, Zorren resumed breathing and he thought. If he ran back now, the dragon would pursue him out of the cave. Out in the open, Zorren knew that he stood no chance alone. The beast could use its tail and claws too. If he stood there, its fiery breath would cook him well. Jill began to scream at the spectacle of an enraged dragon. She feared that the dragon was angry and would turn that inferno on to her and the sheep in an effort to cook its meal. Jill was not yet aware that Zorren was the reason for the serpent's rage.

It took great courage not to run. Instead, Zorren waited for the dragon to expel all its fiery breath. Then he figured that the beast would need to breath in air at some point. When the dragon went to take a breath it also turned to acknowledge the screaming that came from Jill. The scream came from its hoard of food so it turned to look. With that distraction, Zorren acted quickly. He charged at the beast with all his might with the lance pointed at the beast's throat. The dragon saw the advance and was quick to act as it pulled back a little to increase the distance between it and Zorren's charge. It was ready to unleash its fiery breath again, but Zorren's lance managed to scrape its throat. The lance failed to pierce the throat. The scrape angered the dragon as it felt the poke to its throat. It swayed its head around to find comfort and catch its breath again. Zorren saw an opportunity in the instant and dropped his shield. He reasoned that if he was too close to his enemy, it would be harder for the dragon to inflict its rage on him. For a moment the dragon lost sight of Zorren as he scurried to get under the beast. Jill realized that the dragon was preoccupied with something. Perhaps a rival for the food stock, she thought pessimistically.

Zorren was swift with his feet and ran toward the dragon with both hands on his lance. He thrust the lance at the dragon's breast with all the might he could muster. The screeching scream that the beast let out was unlike the previous screams that invoked terror. In that screech there was the sound of pain that gave evidence that Zorren had struck true. The lance was lodged into the beast's breast but Zorren lost hold of it as the dragon squirmed away. While the dragon writhed in agony Zorren ran back to pick up his shield and drew his sword. Despite the wound, the dragon was not yet subdued and now more dangerous than ever.

As Zorren hid behind his shield he witnessed the mighty beast wrap its claw around the lance. The wounded serpent pulled out the lance and flung it aside. The dragon regained its composure and let out a blast of fire that bellowed out in curling waves of flame. Zorren quickly raised the shield to cover his head, but this time he did not crouch so his footwear caught fire. As the dragon replenished its breath, Zorren shuffled his feet in an attempt to put out the flame. The smoke and dust was suffocating him. He ran to the mouth of the cave to catch his breath. It was dark out. Except for the illumination provided when the dragon belched out fire, the night was black. Zorren dropped his shield to slap dirt at his lower legs to put out the fire on his leg socks. The dirt relieved the discomfort of the burn. All the while the dragon advanced steadily toward him through the smoke filled cave. Despite the darkness, Zorren could still see the glaze on the eyes of the dragon as they were focused on him.

Zorren was aware that he only had one bolt left. It was the trusty sword that Tomett gave him. It belonged to Tomett's son. It was a fine sword and would now be put to the test. Zorren realized that he could not fight the dragon up close. The fire from its breath, the swinging tail, a swipe from its claws could push him against the rocky terrain and smash his body. Zorren could also fall off the cliff and smash his body. There was only one hope and that would seal his future and Jill's as well. Zorren yearned in his soul as he mouthed, 'Come Holy Spirit'. With having focused all his thoughts on his sword, he visualized the point of his sword piercing the breast of the beast as the lance had done earlier. At that moment the dragon spewed forth a curling flame that was coming at him. As Zorren extended his shied arm out, he drew the sword back with his right hand. The dragon's fiery breath relented. With all his might he threw the sword from the handle like a battle axe. The screeching of the dragon testified that the sword hit its mark.

He had lost sight of the sword in the smoke and darkness. The strike to Halitos' breast stopped the dragon in its tracks. The fire stopped as the dragon fell back to favor its breast. There was a look of relief as Zorren noticed that the sword had penetrated the breast of the dragon considerably. It was not enough though. The dragon turned and made its way slowly to its feet. It managed to pull out the sword as it bled through the new wound. This time it flung the sword toward Zorren. The sword was thrown with so much force that it got lodged into a crevice in the stone nearby.

The beast started moving slowly and steadily toward its enemy. This time the dragon would not miss its mark. The cliff side was steep and the landing to the entrance to the cave was limited in space and uneven ground. Zorren knew all this too as he scurried back clenching his hot shield before him. The shield's handles were warm as the heat from the outside of the shield made its way to the leather straps and chain link from his arm. Now it was certain that the beast would deliver the final strike of the battle. All that Zorren could do was await it. He yelled out Jill's name so she would realize that he had tried to rescue her. The sound of his voice however blended in with the dragon's anger and lament.

The dragon mustered the deepest breath that it could manage. It ground its teeth to strike a spark and with the foul gases in its lungs sent forth an inferno. Other than any loose rocks that he could find, Zorren had no further weapon that he could use. He weathered the fiery blast and fumbled when he went to pick up a fair-sized rock. He could not loosen the rock from the ground, he settled for a smaller rock. Zorren threw the rock at the dragon just in time for it to prolong its expelling its breath. Although the dragon was wounded, it sent forth its fiery flame again. All that Zorren could do was to stay behind his shield.

Zorren's shield was quite hot now and the heat transfer from the shield to his chain link to his arm was becoming unbearable. In fact on the next wave of fire he might have to jump off the cliff to avoid being burned. He would have to take his chances in the large water hole at the bottom of that mountain cliff. Zorren could see that the dragon had grown wearier, but it did not stop in its resolve. Zorren knew that he was doomed in the minute and regretted sealing his doom and that of Jill. He wondered if that was all that he would see of Jill. 'Some knight I turned out to be', he chastised himself. The dragon was severely wounded but in its eyes was the desire to finish its foe. Halitos was aware of its fate. It found relief in knowing that it would have the satisfaction of doing away with its vanquisher. Halitos proceeded with all the strength and resolve that it had left.

At that instant a dark bolt fell from the skies. It was not seen by either combatant. It swooped down and pierced its talons on the dragon's face putting out an eye. The dragon screeched in horror as it experienced losing an eye. In fear and confusion, the dragon shifted its attention away from Zorren as it wriggled and twisted its body to find comfort. The eagle kept persisting with its talons as it hovered over the beast within safe means of escaping. The eagle was a skilled hunter. It attacked when it was safe to do so. The eagle never relented in its strikes.

Halitos fought back in its wounded, fearful state. The dragon spent all its remaining vigor protecting itself from the onslaught from above. The distraction was enough for Halitos to lose its footing. The tormented beast fell off the cliff. It struck a ridge that diverted its fall. It missed the large water hole and landed with a thud and a cloud of dust onto solid rock. The fall happened so fast and hitting the ridge spun the dragon around as it fell. Halitos had no time to use its wings to get airborne. As Zorren looked over the cliff, the dragon lay still as the cloud of dust arose around it. The fall shocked the beast and its blood spilled out of its eye and breast wounds. With the two previous wounds to its breast that Halitos incurred, it lied in pain and fell asleep. The beast breathed shallowly and did not stir at all.

From patrolling the skies it was one of the eagles that came forth from the nearby mountain walls. It was Strom, the male eagle that was suspicious of Zorren and Jill when they climbed onto his majestic mountain home. The eagle could see the look of gratitude on Zorren's face as it collected its wings back from its battle posture. The eagle walked over to the edge of the cliff and looked down to where the dragon fell. Halitos stopped breathing completely. Strom turned to Zorren and decided all that could be done was done so it jumped off the cliff. Zorren lost site of the eagle as it fell toward the ground. Then Strom flapped his wings and labored to gain some height. When Strom gained a desired height it spread its wings and caught a gust of wind. Strom stayed around and hovered over the area like he would do for his own offspring. The winged friend wanted to make certain that the young boy was safe.

Although he was saved from the dragon, Zorren still had to rescue Jill. He turned and rushed into the cave.

"Jill! Jill! Jill," he coughed in the sulphur air.

As Zorren entered the dark cave, there was still smoke and it smelled of sulphur. Jill who had been frightened called back to him. She heard Zorren's voice but did not believe that it could be him.

"Zorren? Zorren?! Zorren!" she cried back, "where is the dragon?"

When Zorren appeared, she could still not believe her eyes. Zorren rushed to greet her, but she cautioned him.

"No, wait!" Jill informed, "There is a large endless pit before me."

Surely enough Zorren slowed down to a stop and there before him was a pit. It was not certain how far down the pit went. Perhaps it had water in it like the one at the bottom of the cliff. He thought that it really was not worth finding out. He realized that it was about nine or ten feet across to the ledge where Jill was trapped. It was easy for Halitos to reach over. Zorren thought that he could easily run and jump over, but then they would both be stuck there. There was not enough room to gain running speed on the other side for the trip back over. He looked around but there was no timber that he could use to bridge the gap. Zorren had no rope, and the nearest timber was down the mountain and across back in the forest.

"I will have to go for help," Zorren said.

"Did you kill the dragon?" asked Jill.

"God works miracles. Remember the father eagle? The one that was not too happy with our presence. Strom swooped down and knocked the dragon off the cliff. The dragon is dead, I hope," answered Zorren.

Jill looked at Zorren with gratitude. Zorren looked at Jill with a yearning. It was as if he would never see her again. Jill had been just a friend but all he could think about at Holmgren Castle was she. Jill was only a short distance away from him, but still too far.

"Are you cold?" asked Zorren.

Before she could answer, he had removed his red cape, crumpled it up in his hands and threw it over to her.

"There are sheep over here, they have warm wool," blushed Jill.

She picked up Zorren's red cape and put it over her shoulders. She did not notice the burn marks on it. Zorren merely looked at her with his cape. She looked like a lady. He did not want to leave her alone, and yet he needed to get help. Who knew what other creatures inhabited that foul area, he wondered?

"You had best get started," Jill reminded, "I will be as quiet as possible until you return."

A sheep started baaing as she finished assuring Zorren. It was obvious that she would have to take her chances, as she could not control the sheep. The terror of Halitos presence must have scared the sheep to silence. Zorren finally pulled himself away from there and began descending the mountain side. In his zeal, he lost a shoe. His laces were damaged in the dragon's fire but the hard descend against the sharp and uneven rock stretched it off his foot. He focused on getting help and planning ahead. He needed to bring back food, rope and find an axe preferably. Then he recalled that his sword was stuck in a large rock outside the cave. It was easy to see when the dragon bellowed out the fire. It was too high a price for illumination. Zorren had forgotten the sword in the thrill of seeing Jill. He planned to cut a tree trunk about fifteen feet long. He could tie the log with rope and have Lento pull it to the foot of the mountainside. Getting it up the cliff side would be a challenge. Zorren assessed that he needed help. He needed a group of men from Peregren Castle to assist him with this rescue. Zorren's mind raced in every direction because he was eager to get back to Jill.

The Tournament Was Over

When Zorren reached the even ground at the foot of the mountain, he collected Lento and Gencro, the two horses. He rode away from that barren garden of rock that the serpent beast had led him too. It was late at night and he was tired, but there was the matter of rescuing Jill and seeing to a proper burial for Tomett. As he rode away from the mountain he realized that he had two options. Zorren could ride back to Holmgren Castle to return Tomett and return with the help he needed. The other option was to finish the original trip to Peregren Castle where they had planned to attend the tournament. He was sure to get help there. Besides Jill was still trapped in that dragon's den. The tournament at Peregren Castle was over by now. It saddened Zorren and naturally so. He had worked hard to compete and Tomett did not make it easy because he loved him like a son. Zorren had so looked forward to that opportunity, but he chose to rescue Jill. He thanked God that she was still alive. He recognized that she was not completely rescued yet. He thought that if there had been no dragon to engage, Jill would be safe and Tomett would be alive to witness him compete. None of that was going to happen. Zorren believed that it was the thinking of youth that occupied his mind. A person could wish their life away with what should have been, or deal with what is. Zorren had to focus on practical thoughts. The distance to Peregren was closer and since Jill was still in danger, he chose to ride to Peregren. He might even meet someone along the way.

Zorren approached Peregren from the north and there were no farms on that rocky barren terrain. The rich farmland of Marmora laid to the south of Peregren Castle. The castle had been built against the mountain for strategic reasons. Zorren retraced his route back to the main road and found Tomett as he had left him. He laid Tomett's body across the saddle of Gencro, attached his shield to the harness leather and collected his lord's sword. He climbed onto Lento and rode for Peregren Castle leading Gencro with the dead man draped across its saddle. The moments seemed an eternity as he rode on as fast as he could under the given circumstances. Zorren's thoughts were of Jill.

What if there was another serpent that had access to that ledge in the cave?

When Zorren entered the castle sights at Peregren is was if he had discovered the dividing line between night and day. On this side of the castle was a rock land under gray, clouded skies that the damp, foggy weather seemed to cling to. It was darker there, even in the daylight. On the other side of Peregren Castle shone the sun. Despite the patch of white clouds, the sky was blue. There was the green of the forest and the grasses magnified by the dew. There was the clear water in the stream that turned white and bubbled as it skipped over rocks in the brook. There were the voices of people conducting their affairs. As if out of nowhere you turned on the road and were met with trees, grasses, birds, people and all things living. At a distance you could see across the lowlands of Marmora's agricultural plain and see the blue water of Thermanden Bay.

The people saw Zorren approaching. It was the morning of Pentecost Sunday and the squires who competed in the tournament the day before were gathering for their baptism in the Dargell stream. The tournament was late this year after a long, cold winter. The good Cardinal Wilkieson who was getting on in years was late too. He had not yet arrived. The brothers of Bendire, who resided at the Bendire Church within the protective walls of Peregren Castle, were anxiously waiting to assist him with the baptisms. The advent of Zorren had stolen all the attention. They saw a fallen knight that was draped over his stead and a young boy in a sooty suit of armor and a bare foot. The young boy led that horse behind his own. Their coming made everyone take notice. The most compelling artifact though was the shield that was fastened to Zorren's stead. The shield looked like it was attacked by a blacksmith's fire and hammer. Zorren approached and climbed down from his horse. The people present noted that he looked as though he arose out of some pyre. All lay silent as they looked at him in the early morning.

King Lyndorn was on his way down to the Dargell Stream, the baptismal grounds of all the knights that served his realm. The ride from Peregren Castle was downhill and there was the tournament ground to pass. The king was especially proud this day because his eldest son Orendyn was to be knighted. Orendyn had distinguished himself the day before to his father and mother's pleasure. It might have been the same for Zorren and Tomett, but they could not attend. Zorren was pre-engaged with saving Jill and he had not yet achieved his goal. Jill was still in danger. Zorren's only focus was to get help for Jill and he had to hurry. Zorren was weary from having traveled to the dragon's den, fighting a battle and the return trip. He had not eaten food nor rested since he left Holmgren Castle early the day before.

"If you please, I need your help," uttered Zorren.

In his father's absence, Prince Orendyn came forward to learn what he could. He gave word for his father's guards to assist with the fallen knight.

"You have entered my father's kingdom. My name is Orendyn. You are tired. Tell us what happened, if you can?" Orendyn asked.

Orendyn was considerate and put the newly arrived stranger at ease. He accomplished this like a true prince. Orendyn was not familiar with the emblem on the shield of the fallen knight. He had never seen it before. Tomett had not returned to Peregren for many years.

"This was my lord, Tomett of Holmgren. We had set our path for Peregren and the tournament where I was to compete. On the way we heard the screams of a young maiden. As we rode closer, a serpent, beast with wings threatened to carry the maiden away.
"We both charged the beast and it swept us to the ground. My Lord Tomett broke his back in the fall. While I rushed to get a lance, the dragon flew off with the maiden in its claws.
"After trailing the beast I found its lair. The maiden was trapped. We did battle and an eagle dropped in and pushed the dragon off, but the maiden is still trapped in its lair," Zorren summed up.

"Halitos!" a knight interrupted, "you fought Halitos?"

"Halitos is dead?!" asked another.

After a pause, laughter broke out. It was hard to believe that anyone, let alone this boy, could have slain Halitos. When Zorren described being cast about, they believed it, but when he claimed that Halitos was dead, they did not believe it. Halitos hunted and raided at will. There was a knight discovered not two weeks earlier in north Peregren. He was roasted in his armor. The flesh had burnt away leaving the skeletal bones, charred skin and black armor. Orendyn however noted Zorren's charred armor and that the shield on his horse was scorched like it had been through a blacksmith's fire.

"Perhaps some of you did not notice the scorched shield and charred clothes of our guest," stated Orendyn.

Orendyn's words quelled the disbelievers to a whisper. Even the senior knights stayed silent to allow Orendyn to conduct the probing of Zorren. Even the boy's exposed foot was burned. Orendyn knew that the boy could not feign that.

"I beg you my lord, I must set out immediately to rescue a young maiden still trapped in its lair. If I could have a fresh horse, an axe, rope and a few men, I must be on my way back," appealed Zorren.
It was all that Zorren could say to inform his host of what happened and what needed to happen.

"Naturally, and I will come with you," Orendyn told him, "but should we not tend to that burn on your foot?"

"Oh no, my Lord, I will be fine. The dragon burnt the bindings on my shoe, and I lost it," Zorren replied, "please, your majesty, we must rescue Jill.

Orendyn could see the sense of urgency. The baptismal ceremony had not started and this was important too. Some of the elders were not going to prevent Orendyn from going. He was the prince who just earned his knighthood. Some wanted to see the new upstart in action. Some were anxious to see whether Orendyn might make his first blunder. They thought that the king and the cardinal would be furious with him if he left now. There were others who were truly concerned and respected his sense of duty.

"My lord," interrupted Carlen, "what about the baptism and knighting ceremony?"

Carlen had grown up with Orendyn and they were close friends. Carlen was a fellow squire who was to be baptized and knighted with Orendyn. Carlen had waited for this day and there was nothing going to prevent him from getting knighted. He made it clear that he would stay put where he was.

Orendyn did not have time to answer Carlen as he was anxious to set out on this rescue with Zorren. He understood the urgency that Zorren spoke of just by hearing the sincerity in his voice. Orendyn inquired about the need for an axe. After Zorren explained the predicament with the ledge and the pit, Orendyn made a proposal.

"Instead of cutting down a tree and dragging it up the cliff, we can take the floor planks from the tournament grounds. There are some that should be long enough. It will save time and they will not be needed until the next tournament," Orendyn suggested.

Zorren smiled. He looked at Orendyn and appreciated the constructive help he was getting. There was no way that Zorren would overrule a good idea just because it was not his. Here, he thought, was a fraternal spirit. Speaking of fraternal spirit, Orendyn's younger brother Arlenden came to their aid as well. Orendyn summoned the use of a wagon from a nearby peasant. Bill, whose wagon they commandeered, was a little reluctant but obliged his majesty, the prince. Arlenden gave

Zorren the use of Argen, his silver-gray horse. It was important that Zorren rode ahead to lead them. Arlenden rode along next to Bill in the wagon. They were quick to take action.

The first stop was to gather the planks that they needed. They rode to the tournament grounds that were in sight of the stream and meadow that they were situated on. The planks were about twelve foot lengths long, but some were bowed. They decided that two planks would be enough. The planks were long, thick and over twenty thumb widths wide. They certainly looked strong. Zorren was satisfied that they would do the job. They loaded four good planks instead of two, just in case they needed more. Orendyn noted that Zorren was tired, hungry and had been through quite an ordeal. There was the burn on Zorren's foot too. He knew that Zorren was fatigued, but understood that there was nothing going to keep him from rescuing the young lady that was trapped. Orendyn asked a servant to get some food and water and a pair of his suede boots for Zorren. He then summoned Maria, the nurse, to make a poultice doused in natural oils to apply to Zorren's foot. Orendyn had never worn the suede boots.

As the party set out there was some confusion between the people at the baptismal ceremony staying, or following after the rescue party. The event gathered many members of the community and the number of spectators began to grow. Gary a senior knight stepped in and directed matters and asked the squires to stay. With the news that Halitos was dead, you might imagine the excitement to ride out and see if it was true. The consensus among the crowd of people was that they did not believe it. The 'boy' was too young and here laid another knight, victim to Halitos. Gary, the prince's godfather was proud that Orendyn was able to make a decision and act upon it so fast. Gary acted fast too. He let the prince go, but he sent three other knights and accompaniment to ride after Orendyn and Arlenden. They would provide support, should any danger befall the young princes and their rescue party.

Gary was a loyal knight in the service of King Lyndorn and could have suggested sending others to investigate, but he let the brave Orendyn make the decision and see it through. Orendyn had distinguished himself the day before on the tournament field and won top honor in joust and sword. It was no surprise to Gary, because he had instructed Orendyn. Orendyn had the finest instructors and a full disciplined schedule to follow. It was always a big help when the student followed the teacher's lessons and worked hard to improve his skill. Orendyn was fully aware that he had advantages that others did not. He just took advantage of the opportunities and today was a day to bask in the glory.

Today however he postponed the baptismal ceremony to come to the aid of a subject. When King Lyndorn arrived, Gary reported the news to him. Not to his surprise Lyndorn was a happy man. He was proud of Orendyn and Arlenden who bravely followed his brother. At Cardinal Wilkieson's discretion, he thought that the rituals and formal service should be in abeyance until the return of their prince. Cardinal Wilkieson was overwhelmed with the news that morning. He had prayed for the deliverance of his flock from the claws, teeth, tail and the breathing fire and brimstone of that beast. Could it be true?

Wilkieson believed it. It just happened to be Pentecost Sunday and he believed that the Lord sent some fire of his own this day. Wilkieson also noted that the knight who lay dead was Tomett whom he had not seen for some time.

Cardinal Reflections

It was thought that the rescue party that left just after the break of daylight would return by the early afternoon. By noon those who waited were hungry and the meal that was to follow the ceremony would have to be consumed now. It was not certain when the rescue party would return, but it certainly was time to eat. Cardinal Wilkieson summed up for himself the fact that winter came late, spring was late, the knighting tournament slated for the week of Easter was late, and now the ceremony was going to be late. Perhaps they would have to postpone the ceremony to the next day. It did not matter to him provided the moral and physical health of his flock was good.

Cardinal Wilkieson had grown old and reflected that under God's grace, King Lyndorn had managed to increase the land holdings of Rothaynen and was joined by the warring dukes. The marriage of Lyndorn to Agate proved the decisive quelling of in-fighting disagreements whose origins were lost to present memory. Presently, their two princes guaranteed the succession and the king looked toward spreading his influence southward by building a splendid new castle on Thermanden Bay. Wilkieson had building plans of his own. He had planned a new home for the Brothers of Bendire with land that was secured for the church. From the new monastery, the Brothers of Bendire could develop the land around it and carry their religious service to the people who worked the land in Marmora and as far south as Mead.

Lyndorn granted the church a tract of land east of the Dargell Stream and north of Thermanden 'as far as the eastern escarpment'. There on that land, before the Cardinal died, he wanted to realize the building of a monastery for the Brothers of Bendire, and a new church in the new castle at the source of the River Brae. The land there looked much like the land around Peregren Castle without the foul smell of the iron ore and sulphur at its back in the mountains. The land around Peregren had some timber and meadows but was overrun with thorny thicket and marsh wetlands. The land given to the Brothers of Bendire left a lot to be desired as well however it was a good choice for building on. The land east of the Dargell stream was not as rich as the black soil of Marmora. Through careful, patient attention and work, the brothers would make the land flourish fruitfully. In fact the brothers made the land comparable to the fertile plains of Marmora. Marmora was considered the garden of Rothaynen. It was situated across from the lands of the Bendire Monastery.

One last item the Cardinal was pondering in his mind was who was going to succeed him. There were two candidates that had different qualities but could provide strong leadership for God's church. The generous and hard-working Bishop Walden was an inspiration. He led the people by example. His motto was, in all sincerity, 'do as I say and do as I do'. The motto was pure and simple like the man. The people trusted Walden and liked him. He was always among them and helping out in any way that he could. He was no stranger to labor and practiced what he preached. It was not uncommon for Walden to put in a full day of manual work and then return to his studies in the evening. Walden was popular with the children as well and always spoke encouraging words.

On the other hand there was Bishop Spehar. He did not have the work ethic of Bishop Walden but he was a clever man. He was sure to 'get the job done', but he had a mean streak in him. Spehar was not afraid to preach fire and brimstone. Spehar did not have the appeal that Walden had with the people and could be outright tough, but Wilkieson prayed for him. In fact he prayed for both as Walden's work ethic would without a doubt catch up to him at his pace. There were only so many hours in a day. Rich man, poor man: no matter who a person was, there were only so many hours in a day. The cardinal took comfort that when he passed on, there would be two good men ready to take his place.

Evidence of the Dragon

As the rescue party came onto the scene, they saw two eagles patrolling the skies over the caves mouth. They were Macha and Strom. With seeing the eagles, Zorren found new energy to speak. Zorren recounted to Orendyn the events leading to the killing of the beast that they called Halitos, giving full credit to his prayers with help from his friend Strom, the eagle. Zorren even explained the day that Jill and he witnessed the birth of the young eaglets. It was quite a story and Orendyn found it profound that these flying forces that governed the balance of nature from the skies, should befriend a human. Like a bolt Macha and Strom fell from the sky and set down before the cave. Together they had governed the sky to protect what they perceived was important to Zorren. The proud eagles waited for the rescuers to ascend to the cliff. Macha and Strom posed no threat to the visitors as they recognized Zorren. It was amazing to witness these powerful, majestic birds of the sky, in the role of support for a human being.

As the rescue party ascended the mountain side, they indeed saw the dead dragon. They looked at what was once the ferocious Halitos. The carcass of the beast lay lifeless, but daunting even in death. The people of Peregren would require proof of its death, and they would have it. It would be easy to cut off the head of the beast, now that it was dead. Orendyn realized that Zorren could not have defeated Halitos if he was not of a pure heart and good nature. In his mind, God had given this young boy the courage and bravery to seek out and do battle with the foe. Earlier, God had also allowed Zorren to befriend the two eagles who out of habit do not appreciate anything in the vicinity of their nesting. The eagles in turn came to Zorren's aid. If it was not willed by God for him to vanquish that terror of a beast, it would not have happened. Countless worthy others had perished from the wrath of Halitos. Orendyn kept this to himself as he assessed this sincere and worthy subject of Rothaynen.

Orendyn, Arlenden and Bill assisted Zorren with moving the planks up the steep cliff. When they arrived at the landing before the cave, Macha swept down to greet Zorren. Zorren smiled at them and thanked them as one would have a conversation with another individual.

"Strom, Macha, I cannot tell you how happy I am to see you again. If it were not for you my dear friend, I would have perished instead," Zorren deliberated, "You should have seen Strom do battle with the dragon."

The eagles seemed to understand him and quickly glanced at each other. Macha screeched at Strom who stood his ground proudly.

"Thank you ever so much for guarding the cave until our return. And now my dear friends it is time for you to check up on Screech and your other fine eaglets," Zorren reminded.

The two majestic birds glanced at one another again and cast themselves into the air. It looked as if they jumped off the cliff but in no time with spread wings they caught the current of air. The eagles climbed higher and higher and flew further and further away into the sun until they could be seen no more. The planks arrived on the landing. In consideration, Orendyn left it up to Zorren to carry the first plank inside the cave to rescue the beleaguered maiden and, as it turned out, some lost sheep. Arlenden and Bill assisted with the other planks. The planks were laid down across the pit that led to oblivion. Jill was so happy to see Zorren that she crossed the planks without a second thought. Jill gave him an embrace that she would have liked to last an eternity. Zorren wished the same. The rest of the livestock was hesitant and Bill went over to carry them across. Zorren caught sight of his sword. During the battle, Halitos had flung his own sword at him and it got lodged into the stone. It must have had some force behind it to get lodged so deep. Zorren walked over to it and grabbed it with both hands. After encountering resistance he pulled it out. He returned it to his scabbard where it belonged. Then he led Jill out of the cave.

After Zorren came out with Jill, they were followed by three sheep and a goat. Orendyn then entered the cave observing all that he could. Orendyn, Arlenden and Bill then retrieved the planks. Orendyn realized that Zorren had been through quite enough. The ordeal was none lighter for Jill either. On the landing before the cave, they decided to rest a moment. Jill put her arms around Zorren and could not let go. Zorren held Jill as though he might not ever see her again. Orendyn realized that the two were in love.

The knights that were sent to keep an eye on Orendyn and Arlenden arrived. They could not believe the sight of the slain beast. It was a good thing that they came. The knights assisted with cutting off the head of Halitos and loading it on Bill's wagon. They had to tie the sheep and goat to the wagon. Even dead, Halitos' head struck terror in them. Zorren requested that word be sent to Todd and Heather that Jill, their daughter, was alright. She had been missing since Halitos carried her off to his lair in that forsaken cave. He was certain that they would be concerned with her whereabouts. Orendyn sent word about Jill's safety with one of the knights in the escort. It was not until late afternoon that the rescue party returned with the young maiden Jill and the prize. Jill could certainly give her account of the story. Happily Halitos would not tell any more tales. There were lookouts awaiting the return of the rescue party. Before they arrived, King Lyndorn, Cardinal Wilkieson, the brothers of Bendire and the fiercest of supporters were poised for the baptismal ceremony. Orendyn himself felt hungry let alone Arlenden, the younger brother with a voracious appetite or 'hollow leg', so he could only imagine how Zorren felt. With all the dignitaries and the squires that awaited their baptismal rite into knighthood, there would be no more delay. Zorren was running on enthusiasm as he was just happy to have Jill safely by his side. Jill could not be happier than to be by Zorren's side.

Orendyn approached his father and briefly told him the events that occurred. The king was amazed when he heard that Halitos was vanquished. Now the proof arrived. There was cheering as the crowd scurried to get a look at the dragon's head in the wagon. Zorren climbed down off of Argen and reached up to help Jill down from her horse. There were those who recognized that Argen was Arlenden's horse. Arlenden stood up on the wagon and waved to his father and mother. He then climbed down and took Argen's reins from Zorren. At Orendyn's request, Arlenden handed Argen over to a bearer and collected Zorren's shield. Orendyn dismounted his horse, Aurem, and walked directly to his father. Arlenden followed in his footsteps with Zorren and Jill. Arlenden brought Zorren's shield with him and presented it to his father.

The shield spoke as evidence that Zorren slew the dragon. He quietly asked his father if Zorren might not be knighted with them that day. The king could see that Zorren's shield had weathered a very hot ordeal.

"It is true father, Zorren has slain Halitos. The dragon's body lies in the northwestern rock land and here before everyone to see is the beast's head. Halitos will terrorize your subjects no more. A fine boy like this was sure to do well in our tournament. Lord Tomett was bringing him to compete," said Orendyn.

"Lord Tomett was our loyal man whose castle at Holmgren guarded our north passage," Lyndorn addressed Zorren, "Zorren, my boy, I am saddened at the death of Tomett of Holmgren. If you only knew what he sacrificed for the good of our kingdom? No one could give more.

"In his absence I see that he was still thinking of strengthening our realm. I have made arrangements for his burial rites, tomorrow.

"This young damsel that stands beside you must be the reason for your inspiration," Lyndorn stated.

"Perhaps we could bury Sir Tomett tonight and resume with the knighting tomorrow," suggested Orendyn.

Lyndorn was proud of his son Orendyn. He was not self-serving and did not treat people condescendingly. In the king's mind, he was sure to pass on the kingdom of Rothaynen to a most capable monarch. Lyndorn wanted his son to rule in peace and prosperity. As a token to promote this, Lyndorn planned to build the most beautiful castle that would stand as a beacon for justice and opportunity. The castle would remind people that there was always something better to aspire to.

"It would be most unusual where tradition is concerned. Rain or shine we have always conducted our rites of knighthood with the church on a Sunday when most subjects would have the opportunity to attend. What would you do in my stead, if you were king?" asked Lyndorn.

Lyndorn was ready to honor his son's request. It was later in the day and only the devout followers of sport would attend church at this late hour. When the word got out that Halitos had been slain, it seemed that there would only be standing room in the church. Zorren interrupted by getting Orendyn's attention. Orendyn turned to Zorren who spoke quietly.

"Orendyn, if his majesty the king would allow the funeral to take place tomorrow, Jill and I would be able to mourn better rested," appealed Zorren.

Orendyn looked at Zorren and turned to his father.

"Given the gracious request of Zorren, he should like to bury Tomett in the new day. Let us honor his wish and continue with the plans of this day, father" Orendyn concluded.

The king was proud that his son was not afraid to propose an alternative plan, but then had the sense to re-evaluate. He was pleased and the feeling was shared by the queen.

"Agate my queen, if you could have your ladies in waiting see to the comfort of this young lady, Jill. As for Zorren, he is most welcome to join the brotherhood of knights," directed Lyndorn, "Cardinal Wilkieson, I believe we will be knighting one more today."

Orendyn was happy for Zorren who could not believe the king's decree. In all his time as Cardinal, Wilkieson had never spent an Easter Sunday in this fashion. The news of the demise of Halitos was worth the delay let alone the reality of the situation. Wilkieson sent word that another brother would be needed to aid with the baptisms, but Bishop Walden volunteered to assist. It had been quite some time since Walden had dunked a squire to baptize him for knighthood. Walden was always ready to assist with whatever needed to be done.

Orendyn turned to Zorren.

"Looks like you qualify, but that is only because I lied. I told the king that I saw you hop on your horse," Orendyn ribbed, "of course by now you feel so light that you could fly.

"It was indeed my goal to become a knight of Rothaynen. I wanted to earn my way with honor before the king and his subjects. I thank you, your majesty just the same" confessed Zorren.

"Thank you, for services already rendered. Zorren, you have earned this right. The honor is yours," Orendyn told him.

The cardinal left the king's canopy and slowly walked holding his shepherd's staff to the stone overlooking the stream. Cardinal Wilkieson was showing his years. The stream gleamed with many crystals as the late afternoon sun shone on it as it began its decline. The sky seemed to postpone the fall of evening, just to accommodate the ritual. All the squires had been assembled anew after the long wait. With the good news about the serpent beast's demise, everyone was as fresh with enthusiasm as they were that morning. The demise of Halitos was hard to believe.

The Bendire Brothers were in position to dunk the new knights of the realm. In fact Bishop Walden from Mead dutifully walked into the water with his ceremonial robes to bestow the honor of baptism onto Zorren. Other brothers were scurrying about handing out candles while Bishop Spehar from the northern kingdom stood by Cardinal Wilkieson. There were several priests from the region that walked about with larger candles that were lit. The people came to them to light the smaller candles that they held. The Cardinal was ready to start the service. The horns belted out a theme of pageantry that called everyone to attention. Cardinal Wilkieson stretched out his hands over the people.

"May the grace of our Lord Jesus Christ, the love of God and the fellowship of the Holy Spirit be with you all.

"We are gathered here today to bear witness to the oaths that these young men of noble heart, mind, body and soul as they profess to bear allegiance to God, king and country." said Wilkieson.

He turned toward the squires now standing in the water with a Bendire Brother at their side. He began with the questions of the baptismal rite.

"Do you believe in God, the Father Almighty, creator of Heaven and earth and the waters?"

"I do,"

"Do you believe in Jesus Christ, our Lord and Savior?"

"I do."

"Do you believe in the power of the holy spirit?"

"I do."

The ritual continued with all the pledges of baptism. They pledged to reject sin, Satin and his works and refused to be mastered by them. Of course this was a task easier said than done. The newly knighted boys swore out the knightly virtues. They swore an oath to provide safety to all men, women, children and those who could not fend for themselves. They swore to be generous, uphold the truth and bring justice. Cardinal Wilkieson reminded them that their oaths were a declaration of their duty which they would be held accountable for, even at the expense of their souls.

"Young knights, you think that with this late hour and the sun ducking behind the clouds that standing in the water is bringing chills to your spine.

"I assure you that it is the oath that you have taken that is bringing chills to your spine. These words are more than mere words.

"Would all of you come forth from the water and stand before me?"

Cardinal Wilkieson had watched almost every one of these boys grow into a man. He could not be more proud. He was being considerate about standing in the water for the remainder of the baptism. All the boys felt the chill, but Orendyn could only imagine the cold that Zorren felt along with his hunger. The monks wrapped a large blanket around each knight to provide comfort against the cool breeze.

The time had come to recite the Gloria. It was inspiring to hear nobles and a good number of farmers alike join in as they stood together with their lit candles. The experience made King Lyndorn and his Queen Agate feel humble and fortunate to govern a fine people with a good work ethic who appreciated the blessings of their God. Two years earlier, they were at war even over the Easter Season. They were especially grateful for peace and joined in the Gloria as well.

"Glory to God in the highest," began Wilkieson.

"And peace to His people on earth.
Lord God, heavenly King,
Almighty God and Father,
We worship You, we give You thanks.
We praise You for Your glory.
Lord Jesus Christ, only Son of the Father,
Lord God, Lamb of God,
You take away the sin of the world:
Have mercy on us;
You are seated at the right hand of the Father:
Receive our prayer.
For You alone are the Holy One.

You alone are the Lord,
You alone are the Most High,
Jesus Christ, with the Holy Spirit in the glory of God the Father.
Amen."

Before the service moved inside to the Bendire Church, the newly knighted defenders of the realm walked and stood before the cardinal who made the sign of the cross on their forehead with chrism oil. Then the boys were dismissed to dress into their full armor to continue the service inside the church. In the mass they would receive wine and bread in communion with Christ. Then the king would knight them anew.

The procession into the church was led by the Cardinal, who was accompanied by the king and the queen, the lords, the gentry and then the peasant farmers. Despite the late service, the church was full. When word got around that Halitos was slain, it was like a holiday. The knights dressed in their tents that were still up since the tournament day. Arlenden had suggested that his brother could lend Zorren a suit of armor. Arlenden meant well as he could see that Orendyn and Zorren might fit into the same suit of armor. Orendyn thought that the gesture might offend Zorren so instead they summoned servants to clean Zorren's armor. The noble servants managed to get the carbon and sulphur on Zorren's armor out and shined up as best they could. There were still streaks and scuff marks on the old suit though. The appearance of Zorren's armor did not bother him one bit.

The design of Zorren's suit of armor was quite plain. There had been newer designs and improvements made to the armor. Zorren's old suit of armor was as good as any and better than most, he thought. It was clear though that this suit of armor was a hand me down. Others might notice that the suit was old fashioned, but it was of no consequence to Zorren. It was one way to ascertain those who were over conscious of appearance. When the time came to enter the church, Zorren did not feel embarrassed to wear the suit of armor that served Tomett's son. Zorren had no illusion of having a new suit of shiny armor, his suit fit him and served him fine. Zorren still felt left out because he did not participate in the tournament let alone win his knighthood. He did not know any of the other boys that were being knighted, other than the prince.

Some of the other squires seemed resentful toward him as they put on a front of arrogance. Orendyn and Arlenden accepted him like an equal. Bishop Walden could see how Zorren thought and it was inspiring to see such a pure-hearted, modest boy. The bishop tried to set Zorren at ease. He believed all the boys would come around to accepting him in time. Although he was not fully sure that Zorren understood him, Walden professed, "Why worry about getting approval from a saint when you've got Jesus Christ with you?"

Walden was referring to the fact that Zorren had made friends and won over the two princes of Rothaynen, why worry about what the other squires were thinking?

The young knights were heralded into the church. There were seven of them and they marched in and sat across the front pews. They all looked regal although it was easy to notice the one with the well-worn suit of armor. When it came time for communion each of the knights were given a small portion of bread that was blessed and became the body of Christ. It was followed by a chalice with wine that was blessed and became the blood of Christ. Then the rest of the church body came up pew by pew to form a queue. The people received communion in the same form that the knights did. The bishops and priests and the Brothers of Bendire helped out with distributing the bread and wine. There were quite a few members of the church who received communion. These people had a clear conscience or had attended confession during the week. The resolve of Easter was still fresh in their mind and they depended on good growing conditions.

After communion, Cardinal Wilkieson called on King Lyndorn and then retired to his chair at the side of the altar. The king arose from his seat on the other side and came to the front of the altar. Lyndorn drew his sword and knighted each of the young squires by name. He did not knight his son first. He knighted Orendyn second last. Orendyn requested this of his royal father. The time came to knight Zorren.

The king raised his sword from Zorren's shoulder to shoulder and proclaimed,

"In the name of the Lord God and St. Michael the Archangel, I give you, Zorren, the right to bear arms and mete justice in the land. It is your duty to vanquish ignorance, oppression and selfishness,
"Arise, Sir Zorren of Holmgren!"

There were tears in Zorren's eyes. He had not heard lovelier words that committed his mind, body and soul to the service of his brothers and sisters. To have these words spoken to him by the king in the presence of God in the house of the Lord was the greatest honor for him.

"On behalf of Sir Tomett of Holmgren, the most selfless man I knew, I accept with honor this duty," Zorren said modestly.

The young boy turned and went to take his seat. He looked at Jill. The queen's ladies in waiting had given her a cast off dress. The dress was a light yellow pastel color in contrast to the sharper red, blue and greens. It did not matter because Jill made the dress look beautiful. It was certain that young lady could make rags look good. Zorren rejoined the other knights as he took his seat. He was relieved. The ceremony was over.

"There is something else. As you well know my son set quite an example on the field of honor yesterday and won the tournament sword which lies before the altar. Cardinal Wilkieson who is quite proud, as he should be, of the boys that he taught and disciplined through the years, has blessed the sword.
"I now call on my son Orendyn who, I am not ashamed to say, sets a worthy example for his own father who needs to be reminded of things from time to time. When we get older we tend to forget and need to be reminded of the splendor of youth.

"You know that Arlenden follows your every step. He is a loving and worthy brother, and he could not have a loving and worthier older brother. Here is my son. I give you Orendyn," Lyndorn said.

It was surprising that Lyndorn did not present the sword to Orendyn. To the church crowd, it would have looked more proper to present the sword to Orendyn rather than have him pick it up. Orendyn arrived before the altar.

"Cardinal Wilkieson we owe you our never dying gratitude for your leadership and instruction. Included are the lessons at the end of your staff," Orendyn said.

Orendyn was in earnest as the church crowd let out a chuckle at the humor. Apparently Cardinal Wilkieson did not spare the rod or staff for that matter.

"God save the king and queen of our realm. May they rule in happiness and glory, all of their days, and may they be many," Orendyn added.

Some in the church crowd yelled out, "Long live the king!"

Another subject added, "Long live the king and queen!"

"I have tried to follow the teachings of our church, the council of our good cardinal, and those of my father and mother. I do believe that it was their love and guidance that have led me to this point.

"The more that I pray and focus on their teachings and council, the more I see clear purpose in serving all of our good people.

"Sir Zorren of Holmgren come forward," declared Orendyn.

Zorren was embarrassed and shy. He thought the ceremony was over, now he would have to go up again. He remembered what Tomett told him. As a young boy, Zorren was often shy and passive. As Tomett got older he had less patience for childish folly. Tomett once told him that 'shyness to a certain age is the sign of a good upbringing, after a certain age, it is the sign of stupidity'. The adage advised from one extreme to the other. Those points contradicted themselves, but Tomett was not one to believe in false modesty. Zorren stood up and caught Jill in the corner of his eye. He looked back at her while he proceeded toward the altar. Jill smiled at him with pride. Anyone who witnessed this exchange of emotion could conclude only one thing.

Zorren walked over to Orendyn turned and stood beside him. He noted that all the newly knighted, the church crowd, the cardinal, the king and queen, and Orendyn had their eyes and ears on him. Although he was shy and humbled by the moment, he stood his ground like Tomett would have liked him to. Orendyn did not waste any time. Orendyn turned and picked up the sword that was placed on a small hammock before the altar. Cardinal Wilkieson had blessed the sword and sprinkled holy water on it. The sword was to be presented to the overall victor of the tournament games. Orendyn picked up the sword and supported it with both hands. He looked over to his teacher the cardinal. Wilkieson was proud of all his boys, but was especially happy that Orendyn would lead them in truth and justice. Orendyn turned to acknowledge his father and mother, who looked back at him with pride affectionately. At that point King Lyndorn did not dare say a word. If he dared open his mouth to speak, he would shed tears of pride from his eyes. Orendyn was about to give proof of his regal nature. Lyndorn knew exactly what his son was going to do.

"Sir Zorren of Holmgren," started Orendyn, "Zorren, I am honored to bestow upon you the sword of champion of the tournament."

There were some who were surprised by the gesture and stood there with their eyes and mouth wide open. The bulk of the people were caught up in the joy of the occasion. It was still hard to believe that Halitos was vanquished. As Orendyn walked toward Zorren with the sword in his hands to present it, there came an overwhelming cheer from the congregation. The people knew what their prince was going to do. To them the terror that was Halitos that struck fear in both man and beast was no more. Earlier that day, the people of Rothaynen did not believe that it could be so.

Not everyone joined in the pouring out of joy and gladness. Now that the dragon was dead, there were those who felt cheated. The opportunity to kill Halitos and become a hero was denied to them. They wished that they had slain the beast so they could be the hero. They did not understand that Zorren was meant to vanquish the beast. There were those who could not understand how the tournament sword should be awarded to someone who was not even there. A few of the new knights raised that question in their minds.

During the cheering, Orendyn handed Zorren the well crafted sword and summed up the events of the day. Zorren hesitated slightly but when Orendyn stood there, he humbly accepted the sword and took it in both hands. He made no gesture of the conquering warrior, but bowed his head in prayer instead. He knew that it was the work of the Lord that had saved him. How else could he have been delivered from that breathing inferno of a beast and sure death? Orendyn understood that Zorren was ordained to do what he did.

"Today we all got baptized by water, but Zorren was baptized by fire as well as water," proclaimed Orendyn.

The congregation gave a chuckle and cheer.

At the end of the service, before the closing rite, Cardinal Wilkieson reminded everyone about his homily on Pentecost and in particular, Orendyn's observation.

"Before we end our celebration today, I must remind you all that on this Pentecost Day, all the followers of Christ Jesus were baptized by tongues of fire. In those tongues of fire was passion and strength that nourished God's good people. Go out then and do his work. Treat one another as you would like to be treated yourself," Cardinal Wilkieson summed.

It was late, but Bishop Walden could not wait to race to the front of the church to acknowledge everyone who passed. He had removed his wet ceremonial attire after the baptism in the Dargell Stream and put on a modest, drier one. One of the Bendire monks lent him the simple habit of a Bendire Brother. Walden had a contagious smile and poured himself out for the people. Bishop Spehar would have been glad to call it the night and leave through the back of the church. He however reluctantly followed the enthusiastic Walden to do the same as no doubt the cardinal would take note.

The Funeral of Tomett

On the next day as was planned, the funeral of Tomett proceeded. To the new knights, other than Zorren of course, Tomett was an unknown. He had already served the king for many years before he grew old. In truth the old age did not catch up with Tomett. It was the heartache from the loss of his family to war and disease. It was like the case of Job in the biblical stories. In this case however when disaster came to Tomett, he blasphemed and spoke out against God. Tomett questioned God's motives for the senseless losses that mounted up. Tomett was aware of the dangers of combat. He trained his sons well and they died at their post with sword or lance in hand. The loss of his wife and young daughter though drove him to near madness. The blaspheming that Tomett did was a means to vent out his pain. In the end, Tomett did not turn and join the forces of evil. It did take the young boy that he adopted to make him remember who he was.

Cardinal Wilkieson was familiar with Tomett. The two went back to younger days in Rothaynen. Each man had an abiding respect for one another. There were words said in anger by Tomett against the cardinal when he tried to comfort him over the losses in his family. One loss followed after another though. Tomett grew weary. Wilkieson was empathetic despite the narrow view brought on by pain and loss. Tomett needed time away from the pain caused by the tragic memories. After years and no word, Wilkieson thought that Tomett was lost. Now Tomett was dead, but Cardinal Wilkieson knew that Tomett had made his peace with God. It was evident by his return to Peregren Castle with Zorren. Tomett was returning to join the realm and furnish Rothaynen with another fine, well-trained knight.

Tomett's body was cleaned and prepared for his burial. The king and queen would be on hand to attend the funeral mass. Then Zorren would take Jill to her parents and his father's body back to Holmgren. Arrangements were made with Bill to take Tomett back to Holmgren in his cart. Tomett would be laid to rest in Holmgren with his forefathers, his wife and children. Orendyn hired Bill, who let his cart for the rescue of Jill and the return of Halitos' head the previous day. Bill received a pouch with coins in it to bring Tomett's body back. The trip to Holmgren and back would keep Bill from his chores, but he was amply rewarded. Besides, Bill's sons were old enough to take up chores. They were to gather up the dead wood pruned off the fruit trees and start breaking up the soil. It was not quite ready to sow seeds just yet, but the soil could be prepared. It was not an unreasonable task to leave his boys with.

The funeral was a very dignified, solemn affair. When Cardinal Wilkieson made his homily, it was surprising to Zorren how much he did not know about Tomett. To Zorren it seemed that his foster father never left the confines of his castle. Instead Zorren learned how a band of renegade knights had once captured a maiden of high estate. The marriage of this young girl to a fine boy of the established house of Rothaynen was opposed by Malandrin, a dark duke. To prevent the marriage and union, and punish the good King Lyndendor, Malandrin planned to capture and sell the young girl into slavery. He knew that the bride to be chose Lyndendor so Malandrin would punish them both. For this chore Malandrin hired pirates so he could appear to be innocent. Wilkieson recounted how the girl was apprehended by Malandrin's men on the highway. Her entire escort was thought to be murdered. Then his men rode to the River Brae and handed her over to pirates who waited on their ship. From there the pirates would sail away with the girl who was never to be seen again.

The beautiful maiden was doomed except that the ship had to pass the great rock at the mouth of the River Brae at Teresforte. Tomett was on his way from Peregren Castle to meet the escort sent by Duke Rencert. Only one horseman was still alive to recount the ordeal as the others indeed were murdered. Tomett sent a rider with word to Peregren of her abduction. There was horror in the king's heart. Without delay, Tomett and his band of men rode ahead with great speed to the great rock at Teresforte and waited. Tomett also sent four men to merely follow the ship along the riverbank. The pirates took sport with them. While the young maiden was on board their boat, the pirates could not be safer. Throwing arrows and fireballs in an attack on their ship could ultimately kill the girl and ultimately make Malandrin's plan succeed.

Tomett had a plan though. He knew that Malandrin did not care about the pirates they could all perish for all he cared.

Tomett had a bold plan. As the ship proceeded to the mouth of the River Brae to escape to the vast broadness of the open sea, the pirates were confident. No one would dare attack them and soon on the open sea no one could attack them. Tomett knew that this would be their only chance. If the pirates were made to land and get off their ship, then it would be a fight on land. The odds of success would be better. Tomett ordered his men on the cliff to gather together many stones of a fair size that they could hurl. It was a plan in the absence of another plan. Tomett understood that being pirates though, if forced ashore, they might kill the maiden out of spite. The plan's success was going to depend on the young maiden too. She would have to put up a fight and survive; hopefully she could swim. It was very risky. If nothing was done though, Tomett knew that the girl was doomed. Lack of action would result in her being sailed away to whatever fate awaited her.

The pirates mocked the convoy of knights as they followed the ship down the bank of the river. The knights in arms and armor could do nothing but watch. The pirates were at ease until they looked up and saw the handful of men that were up ahead on the cliff. Their captain started to worry and gave word for them to focus and pick up the pace of their rowing. The quicker that their ship passed the narrow strait, the sooner they would be free on the open sea. The captain guessed that those stones would not put a hole in the ship's hull but they could be a nuisance. He believed that if their ship sped by it would have less exposure to the men hurling rocks at them.

As the ship drew nearer, Tomett lobbed the first stone over the cliff. The stone was about fifteen pounds. It caught the mast and deflected off it. The vibration was of no consequence to the vessel. Then the same stone landed on an oarsman below who was rowing. The upheaval began as some men stopped rowing to attend to the victim. Other men looked up to avoid having the same fate as other stones fell on their vessel. The uneven rowing strokes caused the vessel to turn sideways. The rocks did not put a hole in the ship. Instead the agitation caused the ship at its increased speed to veer toward the shallow rocks on the shore. An oar caught the river bed and was broken up. The vessel stopped abruptly and got beached on the rock. With that force the ship tipped and its mast fell to one side. The men on the cliff kept throwing stones at the ship to occupy the sailors with concern. Meanwhile the four men that followed the ship by shore were ready. The pirates were in disarray.

The young maiden who was prisoner in the cabin at the ship's bow was shaken by all the tumult. As the vessel turned on its side, there was a scramble for the pirates to get off and push their vessel free of the rock. The knights that followed the ship from the shore did not wait for them to land. Led by Gregyr, who was Tomett's son, the knights charged at the pirates. They rode their steeds and engaged them in the water. Gregyr was aware of the young maiden's danger. He removed his helmet and dismounted his horse into the water. He raced across the water in an effort to get on board the lodged ship. Gregyr wanted to rescue the young maiden before they killed her out of spite. The pirate captain kept his wits about him observing all that he could and directing his men's defense. He regretted the idea of sailing up river to take possession of the girl. It was Malandrin's idea, but that was beside the point now. The captain noticed how one knight had cast off his helmet and rode his horse toward the ship. It was obvious that he thought that he could rescue the girl.

The seasoned pirate captain that he was, he knew that he and his crew were in for a fight. If he and his men were going to die, he thought so would the girl. The captain cursed Malandrin as he turned to the loyal first mate that had the keys to the prisoner's cabin. He ordered the first mate to go kill her. As the first mate obliged to do his duty, the pirate captain noted that the knight had boarded his vessel and was fighting his way toward him. The manner in which the vessel was turned on its side made his embarking easy. The oars in the water kept the ship from falling completely on its side.

The first mate entered the lopsided cabin. The young girl had held onto a beam in the corner. The assassin did not immediately see her.

It was enough time for the girl to swoop down and use the strength in her legs and her feet to push the big man against the wall. The first mate hit the wall with a considerable thud. The young girl let go of the beam, jumped down and made her way to the cabin door. Outside on the lopsided deck, she saw that the pirate and the young knight exchanged swipes with their blades. Then she began to pull herself through the tilted doorway.

When the knight saw the young girl he yelled for her to jump off. She was about to jump, but the first mate whom she had startled reached toward the cabin door and grabbed the young girl abruptly by the ankle. The first mate continued to struggle with holding onto the young girl and getting out of the cabin. The young knight locked blades with the slim pirate captain. Gregyr pulled him toward him first, then he pushed him away using his free arm. The pirate captain fell back onto the pit where the oarsmen rowed. The first mate managed to get out of the cabin while holding onto the young maiden. As he climbed out of the cabin, he got a better hold on the girl. The young knight was free of the captain and turned to witness the young girl about to be stabbed. With great haste Gregyr threw his sword at the first mate and it lodged itself in his chest. It happened just as his deadly stroke against the girl was about to fall. Gregyr's sword stopped him in his tracks. The first mate let go of the girl and fell to his death in the water.

The knight was happy that he could save the young girl. She looked at him with gratitude. He was about to go to the young girl when he too was pierced with a sword. The pirate captain threw his sword at Gregyr's back in the same fashion that he done to his first mate. The young girl was horrified at the sight of the brave young man who came to save her. She saw the pirate captain make his way over the oars to get to her. In his mind there was still the matter of killing her. The young girl looked over at the knight. He was bleeding and looked up at her. He drew one last breath and yelled for her to 'jump!' She took one last look at the brave young knight, and jumped off the ship.

After the knights on shore stormed the vessel, Tomett rode down the cliff with his men to join the battle. He arrived in time to subdue the rest of the pirates and rescue the duke's daughter. Unfortunately, he lost his son. Gregyr was brave and showed commitment to duty and made his father proud. Gregyr saved countless years of fighting and bloodshed with his daring rescue. It was very important for the duke's daughter to be married to a Prince of Peregren in order to heal the land from the senseless skirmishes. Those skirmishes prevented the people from conducting themselves free of fear. Villages were plundered, harvests were raided and people got hurt or were killed during this dark time. If the fighting stopped, there would be enough food for everyone and the kingdom could grow.

The duke's daughter was named Agate in honor of her grandmother. She was truly beautiful and brave, and through the years you could add merciful and wise. Cardinal Wilkieson told them that the story was about their own Rothaynen. The perpetrator of the crime was known but it could not be proven. In a surprising change of heart, the dark duke offered his congratulations to the king's loyal knights and attended the wedding. The king overlooked the entire matter as the balance of peace was at hand. Cardinal Wilkieson accredited the peace and prosperity that was enjoyed to this day to the sacrifices of Tomett and his son Gregyr. The marriage of Lyndorn to Agate was the crucial beginning to unifying and healing a land torn apart by petty grievances, jealousy, avarice and greed.

Tomett lost another son, Germi, in a crucial battle just before the peace came. Another son, Anders, the impetuous young one, was lost to the dragon Fenryl. The story of Fenryl was an epic among all citizens in Rothaynen and the neighboring kingdoms. Tomett, the great knight who served his king with all his heart, all his might and those very dear to him, was wounded over the death of his sons. There was no comfort to be found. The added frustration with the loss of his daughter and wife were maddening. No comfort was found, no purpose or direction given to his life until Tomett found a young boy named Zorren. The cardinal turned to Zorren.

"Tomett must have thought the world about you," Wilkieson confided, "he loved his family so and their loss hurt him. For him to turn form his bitterness and take you under his roof, and govern you and train you, he must have loved you."

Zorren knew that. What Zorren did not know was the true greatness of the Tomett that he considered to be great. The cardinal brought comfort to the sorrow felt by Zorren at the loss of Tomett. It was reassuring to learn that your father was brave, respected and truly was considered a good fellow by his fellow men.

The Betrayal and Death of Zorren

It started innocently enough. Carlen considered himself close to the two princes; Orendyn and Arlenden. He was considered like family by the princes as well. Carlen was a year older than Orendyn and felt like he was the 'big brother'. Carlen often conversed with King Lyndorn and Queen Agate with the confidence as if they were his parents. From the moment that Zorren arrived at Peregren it was as if a stake was driven between the two princes and Carlen. Of course it was only his imagining but that is what he perceived. He resented that on the day of the knighting ceremony, the baptism was postponed from the morning to the evening. Everyone waited while Zorren, Prince Orendyn, Prince Arlenden and an assorted number went to collect a damsel in distress and a dragon's head. In Carlen's mind it was so story book.

While the entire assembly waited, Orendyn and Arlenden joined Zorren in actually rescuing a young, beautiful, fair maiden. Furthermore they returned with the head of Halitos. Zorren even got to ride Argen which Arlenden had not parted with since it was a colt. It was downright unbelievable when Arlenden actually made a gift of the horse to Zorren. On top of everything though, the sword that Orendyn had rightfully won at the tournament was given to Zorren. Carlen gave his best effort to getting along with Zorren. He tried to make room for him in the scheme of things, but it did not work out. Carlen should have known better. If you have to put an effort into liking someone, what are the odds of success?

There was something special about Zorren. Orendyn saw it. Arlenden saw it. The king and queen: Lyndorn and Agate saw it. Cardinal Wilkieson, who had tutored most of the young knights in Rothaynen, saw it. What was it?

Carlen felt more and more left out. He shrunk away from the company of Orendyn in the Peregren Castle. He was certain that he would be missed and when they realized, then, they would be sorry. Carlen was not the mirthful, witty soul that roamed the castle corridors with confidence. He was a sophisticated knight now. Suddenly he could not express joy anymore because he did not feel joy anymore.

The only thing that Carlen felt was resentment for Zorren. He would ask himself, 'why did Zorren have to appear?'

Personally, Carlen could not find anything wrong with Zorren. He had not offended him in anyway other than showing up at Peregren and becoming the center of attention. Now Zorren spent more time than ever at Peregren than he did tending to the affairs of Holmgren. Was there not something pressing that he had to do at Holmgren?

It was Carlen's observation and it was not right in his opinion.

Stories about the slaying of Halitos made their way about the kingdom and abroad. Zorren did not upgrade his armor or shield. He was used to using the humble, aged set that he was given. In Carlen's mind, Orendyn sure made a fuss over Zorren. Orendyn suggested that Zorren adopt a flame design of some sort to put on his shield. The flame would commemorate his slaying Halitos and being knighted on Pentecost. Since the shield needed more than a coat of paint Orendyn suggested a fair swap. The old shield and sword would go to Orendyn for new ones. Zorren already had a new sword so Orendyn had the company of royal artisans at Peregren guild the new shield design and paint it on the new metal.

It was very easy to identify Zorren on the battle field. The enemy was careful to avoid his shield and standard. In one battle however a reckless challenger took the chance. Zorren's faithful horse Marle was speared by lance. It brought both horse and rider down. Marle was writhing in pain and would not survive the hour. Zorren was angry and afraid, but he kept a level head. He fought on foot with smooth, decisive sword swipes. He fought like a killing machine. The consensus among the battle strategists was that he could not have fought his way out of that particular ambush if the Lord was not with him. Some enemy knights thought that Zorren was lucky, if indeed it was he that killed the dragon at all. After he proved himself on the field of honor, even the enemy thought that Zorren's accomplishments had nothing to do with luck. Zorren's reputation as the dragon slayer grew now that he proved himself in battle. All of Zorren's feats were credible.

Of course there was the incredible as well. A twelve year old knight was trying to prove his worth on the battlefield when he took a handful of soldiers and attacked Zorren's position from behind. Ted was the son of Hande, an irrational knight who could find fault with anything and anyone. Hande led the revolt against King Lyndorn's forces and was proud to see his son follow bravely in his footsteps. Ted was brave until Zorren knocked him off his horse. It seemed more like Zorren knocked the life out of his body. Ted's head gear was thrown clean off of his head. At the time all fighting ceased. From a distance, Hande witnessed Zorren climb down off his horse with sword in hand. The rebel duke anticipated the end for his son. Then he saw Zorren plant the sword before his son Ted, who lay lifeless. Zorren took Ted's hands and prayed. It was as though everyone could hear the prayer no matter what vantage point they were at that day. All hostility stopped.

"O Lord God Almighty, you can do the impossible. Let this young boy be spared from the darkness of Hades. Give him another chance in the light of Your goodness. I ask in Jesus' name." Zorren prayed.

All that were present looked and waited and expected a miracle. Hande was mounted on his horse, frozen to his saddle as though time was standing still.

It was not too long before Ted became conscious again. Zorren carried the boy in his arms across the battle field to his father. Combatants on both sides were overcome with amazement. Not even Hande himself could believe what was happening. The battle was over. All grievances were solved, without being heard. A loyal knight of Hande's returned with Ted's sword. Hande offered his son's sword to Zorren. Zorren promptly replied that the brave boy would be needing it himself in defense of God, king and country. Hande himself was converted that day in the light of so much goodness. He had come so close to losing his beloved boy forever. After that day Hande and his band of knights fell under the articles of Peregren with devotion.

Cardinal Wilkieson was amazed with the young knight's knowledge of scripture. Zorren explained to him that his mother was literate. She made sure that all her children were introduced to the stories in the bible. His mother would often start a bible story and then have her son finish reading it. The interest in the outcome of the bible story was so great that Zorren forced himself to learn how to read. Zorren believed these stories with the faith of a child. Somehow Zorren could understand how the sound of trumpets could reverberate and tear down stone walls. It was knowledge for the physical sciences and alchemists. Zorren's favorite story was the first story that his mother read about God's champion who slew a lion with his bare hands but was later himself the victim of a beautiful temptress. Indeed Zorren learned that love was sweeter than honey and more powerful than a lion. Later Zorren read and discussed biblical teachings with Sir Tomett, who was amazed and inspired with him.

Cardinal Wilkieson was happy to hear that Sir Tomett had picked up where Zorren's mother had left off. Wilkieson knew that Tomett had not turned from God despite his sorrow and anger at the loss of everyone that he loved. In fact after a long absence, Tomett was on his very way to Peregren Castle to enter his squire at the games. If Tomett had made it to the games, he was sure to address his king and queen, and he would have spoken to the cardinal. Wilkieson looked at Zorren as a Godsend who saved the soul of a great knight who was lost in pain. The boy had brought Tomett a measure of joy in his days up to his demise before Halitos. Zorren was much liked by the cardinal and like Orendyn he believed that he was sent for a greater good.

It was the manner in which Zorren spoke and conducted himself when he addressed manners of judgment. A knight would often have to make judgments but the good manners, respect and maturity illustrated by Zorren was years beyond a young man's comprehension. For Zorren it was easy to decide on how disputes should be settled. He had his father's land that was taken from him, but he realized there was no other way. He did not forget the basis for justice which was the whole truth. The people that Zorren served did not know of the plight that befell him when he was young and vulnerable. Through all that passed and he endured, the Lord had provided for Zorren. The Lord had taken an interest in this orphaned child, and it was plain to see. Otherwise shy and polite Zorren spoke with conviction when it came to preserving the law. Though a lion of the law, if a perpetrator was repentant, Zorren never spared showing mercy. Even his enemies respected him.

At court one of the captain's damsels who knew of Carlen's displeasure approached him. When she learned that Carlen would be a slave to her desires she decided to help him overcome this discomfort that Carlen had over Zorren. The damsel was young and her beauty was popular. In the absence of Sadar, the captain, Carlen was seen in the service of the lady Vanessa at court. To be seen in the company of such an influential beauty of the court was more than any knight could ask for. Vanessa was the lady of the king and queen's captain of the guard. In Sadar's absence, Carlen took his place at court. Lyndorn did not have any objection as he knew of Carlen's loyalty. Carlen had found another way that he could be important and what is more, sophisticated.

The new arrangement was prestigious for Carlen and he was satisfied. It replaced the status and the time that he had spent with Orendyn. As Zorren performed more 'miracles', as they were referred to, he posed a threat to the ambitions of Sadar. Slowly and craftily Vanessa went to work on Carlen. She was able to turn Carlen's resent of Zorren into hatred because it suited her plans. This hatred would result in one of two things: painting Zorren in a human light if he slew Carlen or bringing about his death.

These miracles that Zorren worked had to do with uniting people who had sworn off as bitter enemies. The warring overlords had grown weary of battle, the loss of fine men, and the misery that it brought everyone. Maybe it was because they had grown older. Perhaps they were sick at seeing the young perish or return with a portion of themselves hacked away. The lust for war took on a new flavor once it was sampled in all its reality. Like Tomett and Gregyr had saved Agate for her marriage to Lyndorn, so Zorren won over warlords to the side of Rothaynen. The sacrifices of these knights were shedding light on the darker years of struggle and the Kingdom of Rothaynen emerged as a beacon of hope for the people who toiled on the land to survive. There was no compromise when it came to the truth and justice. Everyone had it or none did. The people who thirsted for truth and justice agreed.

Not everyone was happy though. These brave and selfless acts of honor were stealing opportunity from Sadar. He had a plan too. Sadar had managed to survive many battles because of his shrewd negotiations and compromise. These negotiations took place well before the battle was fought. The agreements however did little to solve the problems. They merely preserved the preserved and had little to do with what was just. Conflict and battles kept occurring and recurring. With the advent of the brave and uncompromising Zorren to their side, it was ruining Sadar's politics. Sadar observed the army admiring Zorren without fear and doing what had to be done. Sadar used the lash, the yoke and the sword to command. He thought ironically that the army was like sheep to follow Zorren so blindly. Sadar confided his frustrations to his mistress, Vanessa. She knew how to help.

One evening she asked Carlen to her chambers. Carlen had been there before but there was always somebody else there. On this occasion Vanessa was alone. She had something to tell Carlen, but first she made him promise that he would not fly off and do anything rash. With his loyalty to Vanessa primed to a passion, she told him that Zorren had tried to take advantage of her. As Vanessa spoke to him her slender fingers grabbed the fabric on his arms. She tugged at his sleeves both pushing and pulling over and over until she situated her head on his chest. When she placed her head on his chest, her black hair cascaded perfume and her soft hands clenched his arms. It was easy for Carlen to imagine splendor with Vanessa. Even the 'whiter than white' Zorren could not be immune to the beauty and attraction of this young maiden.

One evening Sadar summoned a group of knights to the aid of Sydor Castle. They were told that a good number of knights were needed to support Sydor Castle from aggressors. The story seemed unlikely, but Zorren could always be counted on to volunteer, and he did. He volunteered with a pre-selected collection of knights that were loyal to Sadar. The only two that did not truly belong to that group were

Carlen and Zorren. It was Vanessa's wish that those two destroy each other. There was nothing like seeing your enemies fighting against each other; you could not lose on that account. The idea was to arrive at Sydor Castle and then single out Zorren from the pack. Carlen was supposed to take the lead at confronting Zorren about his alleged indecent advance toward Vanessa.

When the knights that were summoned to Sydor arrived just before reaching the castle, Carlen raised his hand to signal stopping. After stopping the knights broke formation and formed a circle around Zorren. No one spoke a word. Zorren realized that something was amuck. Zorren kept his eyes ahead of him as Argen instinctively turned about slowly. All the while there were mounted riders at his back no matter which direction he took.

"What did you do to Vanessa the other night?" questioned Carlen.

A look of astonishment was on Zorren's face. He gathered that it was no laughing matter. Zorren realized by the mannerism of the knights, that he had been convicted of something without a proper trial. The manner in which he was brought to the place affirmed that these knights had taken matters into their own hands. There would be no time for a proper trial so that he could defend himself. No matter what Zorren said, he faced a determined pack of fighting men bent on his demise. He drew his sword and raised it high with honor.

"This is treachery!" yelled Zorren.

The disgruntled riders with instructions from Sadar drew their swords and closed in on him. They looked to Carlen to lead them.

Carlen was lead to believe that he was in charge. Sadar himself had put him in command. The knights knew that Carlen could not disappoint them. Carlen advanced on the singled-out knight. There was something about the look on Zorren's face that told Carlen that he was innocent and this was a grave travesty. With Zorren's sword drawn, all the knavish knights threatened Zorren with advances on their steeds, but they did not strike out at him. Instead they waited for Carlen to be first to challenge Zorren's sword. The rogue knights encircled and closed in on Carlen's horse as well. They drove Carlen toward Zorren. Carlen's horse was forced toward Zorren. With his sword drawn like everyone else, he waited. As the moments passed Carlen knew that Zorren was innocent. Zorren knew that Carlen knew. Some knights moved forward toward Zorren. In the bustle of the horses and knights, Zorren turned. Carlen's sword struck against Zorren's sword quite unintentionally.

Since Carlen was acknowledged as the acting captain of the guard, it was what Sadar's knights waited for. They attacked and hacked at Zorren with their swords. They were merciless sword hacks fueled by hatred. When Zorren's faithful horse Argen was struck with one of the sword swipes in the ordeal, he let out a whinny and bucked Zorren off. Carlen did not intend for either Zorren or Argen to be hurt, but it was too late. Carlen realized that his jealousy of Zorren had gotten the best of him. He knew that he was not in command of this mob. He realized that his jealousy caused innocent blood to be spilled. Now even Argen would have to be destroyed due to its wounds.

In the mean time the other riders trod over Zorren. The worthy knight was crushed within his armor under the hooves of the horses. There was blood all over the legs of the horses that trod on the innocent knight. Even the rogue knights' faces and arms and hands were drenched with the innocent blood. The assassin knights noted the blood. It was not the same blood that they spilled in battles. This blood convicted them with the guilt of the ordeal. Some of the younger knights began to regret this murder. Smithorn, the elder knight of the group noted this regret. He thought it was ridiculous. Smithorn told the men that when they rode through the very next creek, the blood would be washed clean. On the other hand Carlen was sure that no washing could clean the innocent blood from their hands and faces and tunics.

Carlen saw that the result of the attack on Zorren yielded a crushed body drenched in its own blood. It was hardly a befitting end for a soul as noble as Zorren. Carlen read the ruse perfectly except that it was too late. Sadar had no intention of placing Carlen in command, he had been a puppet for his will. Carlen must now join the ranks of this dark fraternity of knights and sink into silence or be cut down himself. The sheer size of Khotryn and his younger brother Chadryn were enough to threaten him. Fear and shame forced Carlen into silence. Zorren's body was stripped of its armor and thrown in a gully. The wild animals would soon see to it that no evidence of Zorren's body was left behind. Zorren's armor was cast into the water of the Dargell River. A young knight named Morden proclaimed that justice had been done.

"This is the price of treachery among the brotherhood of knights. We wait for no court. If one of us, sworn to protect, is false, then a traitor's death he endures!" Morden professed.

Morden looked over to Carlen as though what had just happened was just and common behavior for the brotherhood of knights. Carlen knew differently though. He kept his mouth shut and his thoughts too as fear ran up his spine. Carlen was desperately trying to justify what happened. He was a knight. They were all knights. Knights did not go about killing without cause or a fair trial. Carlen was scared speechless. His eyes looked away from Morden. Morden smiled with satisfaction and looked over at Khotryn and Chadryn who were amused by frightened Carlen. The two giant knights waited patiently. Either knight was looking for a word or gesture from Carlen to give them cause to cut Carlen's throat.

For that day the deed was done. The party of knights returned to castle in the same manner that they left. Carlen fortunately was a good knight and his conscience would not stay silent even if he could. To speak out against that order of knights was death bonded. During his sleep Carlen dreamt that he was walking about in the forest wilds. He saw a boy in a white robe reaching into a river. The boy had discovered Zorren's armor. He pulled it out from under the water. Carlen was fearful that the story of Zorren's death would come forward. In his dream he was fearful of the discovery yet fighting his guilt. What would the king and queen who treated him as a son think?

How could he face Orendyn and Arlenden?

Why did he ring himself with those knights?

Carlen wanted to help the boy so he chose to go forward and help. The boy arose from the river shore and turned. It was Zorren. Carlen is stricken with shame and fear. Zorren bears no ill will against him, but Carlen holds himself in contempt for betraying innocent blood.

"Fear not. You did not know," the apparition continued, "you are in danger. Go, find Jill. Take her and run to Galles. Stay there, and take care of Jill."

The dream was strange. Zorren was not looking for revenge. He even wanted him to take Jill away. Galles was a neighboring dukedom to the southwest. It was separate from Peregren but Carlen could take Jill there quietly and find safety. At this point Carlen awoke in a hot sweat. He was drowning in a sea of self pity. 'God forgive me!' was his first thought. He realized that he had been seduced by a mob to betray innocent blood.

Carlen did not wait for morning. He sought out two people: Cardinal Wilkieson and Jill. He sought out Cardinal Wilkieson to confess his part in the treachery. Instead he was met by bishop Spehar who heard his full confession. Then Carlen set out for Holmgren to find Jill at Todd and Heather's farmstead. He planned to take Jill away with him to Galles. On the way there Carlen decided that he needed to visit the site of Zorren's murder. Carlen dismounted his horse and collected Zorren's armor out of the Dargell River. He went to the brush where the band of dark knights that he was with cast Zorren's body. Upon seeing the dead body though he began to weep. He went to Zorren's body and lifted it up at the shoulders. Carlen hugged him in a brotherly fashion and wept bitterly.

Meanwhile back at Peregren Castle, Bishop Spehar informed Sadar of the confession. Shortly after Carlen retrieved the armor the brotherhood of knights caught up with him. There was a pounding of horse hooves indicating that a good number of people were approaching. Carlen held Zorren in his arms and could not let go of him. Zorren's congealed blood was still red. The innocent blood smeared onto Carlen who did not fear it one bit anymore. Carlen faced the truth with regards to his part in the killing of Zorren. It was the very knights that he had been with the night of Zorren's murder that came upon him.

"You hated him that much?" Morden declared, "You spineless worm!"

Morden was disgusted with the murder of Zorren credited to the hands of Carlen. Sadar heard how Carlen had accomplished his task. All that Carlen could do was hold onto Zorren as if it meant being closer to forgiveness. He gave Zorren one kiss to his forehead and then he drew his sword. Carlen was no longer afraid of Morden, Khotryn nor any other knight.

"Let us find out how spineless I am, you vile vermin," challenged Carlen.

Morden stayed on his horse and looked at Carlen. Carlen did not appear scared at all. Morden did not know what to say, he had been challenged. Other horses were heard approaching. Morden looked over to one of his cohorts. It was a sign. An arrow was drawn from a bow at close range. The arrow pierced Carlen through his chest cutting into his heart. Blood could be seen spilling out of Carlen's mouth. Other arrows followed and pierced the repentant knight in the throat and chest. He fell to his knees and died.

The horses that followed were those of Orendyn and his knights who had learned that certain knights left the castle rather abruptly that morning. There was an uneasy feeling about the castle in recent days so Orendyn decided to investigate. Since the death of Zorren a dark veil had fallen over Peregren. To Orendyn's shock he saw Carlen and Zorren, both dead.

"He murdered Zorren," Morden declared.

"And who murdered Carlen?!" snapped back Orendyn.

All present were silent as Orendyn climbed off his horse and walked over to two people that he had loved. He could not believe that Carlen was responsible for Zorren's death. Orendyn's bodyguards formed a mounted guard around him. Orendyn could see that Carlen had just been killed.

"We wondered why Zorren did not return last night. We thought that he rode to Holmgren to see his fair maiden, but this morning the bishop told us to follow Carlen as he suspected that something was amiss," Morden blended some truth with his lies.

Orendyn ordered that the bodies of the two knights be taken back to Peregren Castle along with Zorren's armor. There arose in Orendyn's mind a few questions if Carlen was the supposed killer. Zorren's body received so many hacks. Was Carlen mad?

The armor looked as though it was trampled under horse. Why then would Carlen trample a dead man under the feet of his horse?

Why would Carlen remove Zorren's armor?

As Orendyn thought, Morden interjected, "It is hard to believe."

"If Carlen killed Zorren, then why and who killed Carlen?" Orendyn asked again.

"Some knights are very passionate about their oaths and cannot support those who are not," Morden stated.

"Who killed Carlen?" Orendyn stressed again, "On your oath as a knight, who killed Carlen?"

"I do not know," replied Morden.

There was silence for a moment until Morden suggested that the young maiden Jill be informed. Bishop Spehar revealed Carlen's dream to them and the part about taking Jill away. Morden and his party of knights were fully prepared to travel.

"May I suggest your majesty, that we ride to Holmgren to inform the young maiden Jill. She and her family should like to know about this news before hearing it from others. My knights can ride off there in the moment," Morden proposed.

"That will not be necessary. Your knights will take the two bodies back to Cardinal Wilkieson. I will go to inform Jill," Orendyn said.

Morden thought to himself, 'well, look who else is interested in that strawberry patch'. He collected himself with anger to lend authenticity to his devotion and belief that Carlen was guilty.

"Take them to the cardinal? You mean that traitor is going to get a Christian burial?" Morden objected.

"What happened here and when it happened remains unknown. Until that time that we learn what happened, these noble souls will get a Christian burial. If their souls are in agony over guilt, that I am sure that God Almighty will attend to," Orendyn professed.

It was done as Orendyn commanded. He sent a personal rider with a message to let his father and mother know that he rode to Holmgren. Then he rode for Holmgren with his party of knights to inform Jill about what happened to Zorren. Orendyn left for Holmgren immediately from the place that Zorren and Carlen's bodies were discovered. When he arrived at Holmgren it was late in the evening. They had made good time but they needed to locate where Jill's farm was. With the royal standard flying before them, getting that information was easy. The farm was formerly Zorren's but now belonged to Todd and Heather. They had worked the land for over seven years and Zorren had no heirs. No doubt Zorren would not object to their having it. Todd and Heather were his beloved Jill's parents. Orendyn brought the news to Jill who was heartbroken over Zorren.

Strangely enough, Orendyn did not detect sincere sympathy over Zorren's death from her parents. Orendyn humbly suggested to them that Jill come to the castle with him. She could be a lady in waiting for his mother, Queen Agate. To be a 'lady in waiting' for the queen meant that Jill would be the ward of the queen with all its responsibilities and privileges. Queen Agate was a good queen but firm with discipline. Jill would undoubtedly learn to read. Orendyn assured her parents that Jill should manage well under the queen's guidance. Orendyn explained that soon he would have his own castle at Braemar and Jill could live there if it pleased her.

The future king of Rothaynen knew that the heart of Jill belonged to Zorren, but he would do all he could to see to her safety and happiness. Todd and Heather could not be more pleased. In their mind, it was the prince who was asking for their daughter. Orendyn felt that Zorren would appreciate Jill being looked after properly and not being used as a commodity to barter. The impression that Orendyn got from her parents was that they saw her as a commodity to barter. At some not so distant point Todd and Heather saw their days of toiling on the land as a thing of the past. They assumed that they would live with their daughter in the castle. There would be servants no doubt to see to their well being.

Upon his return to Peregren Orendyn informed Cardinal Wilkieson about what happened with Carlen. Bishop Spehar was immediately summoned for questioning by the cardinal. After Spehar was questioned about Carlen, he stated that he came to look for Cardinal Wilkieson and was most insistent on speaking only to him. Spehar declared that Carlen told him nothing. Spehar added that Carlen seemed agitated and perplexed. In his experience Spehar concluded that Carlen was not quite himself and rather desperate. In this way Spehar sought to justify why Carlen would have killed Zorren, and why he himself was executed. Orendyn was tempted to ask Bishop Spehar why he let Carlen go out in that state. Cardinal Wilkieson thought the same thing. In their mind, Spehar was a bishop with skills to discern what was on the mind of his people. Both Orendyn and the cardinal thought that he could have spoken to Carlen about what was bothering him. Orendyn looked over to Cardinal Wilkieson, both were uneasy about what happened to these two fine knights of Rothaynen. Spehar was not giving up any information. They both believed that Bishop Spehar knew more.

Eternal Repose

A few years earlier, when Zorren returned at Holmgren with Tomett's body for burial, the castle staff and tenants recognized that Zorren was the heir to Tomett's property. The tenants knew that the future of Holmgren was secure under the guidance of Zorren. The priest was summoned anew for a burial rite at the cemetery that was on a hill at the back of the castle. It was a quiet place where the grass was green and thick. Stephanotis grew about the graves. The older grey head stones were beginning to flake. The stone markers could use straightening up. The shifting of the ground from many years of winter and summer caused them to move as if they sought a more comfortable position. The grave stones marked the previous lords and family members of Holmgren who were at rest.

Zorren would now be added to the cemetery of Tomett's family members. The sons who were knights had their shields laid over their gravestones. The shields had weathered time well, but then it had only been one generation. The older stones had flaked as time, water, heat and cold joined forces to reclaim the proud head stones back to the aerde. Zorren had excused the entire staff for the entire day to attend the burial of Tomett. It was about a year ago. Zorren had not counted on joining his 'father' and mentor so soon. Orendyn's party arrived with Zorren's body to plant the knight in the family cemetery.

Todd and Heather realized that their daughter was beautiful and would buy them position if she was mated with the right person. Prince Orendyn seemed to be interested in her. There was no doubt in their minds that their daughter would end up in the king's court. Jill was very beautiful and very young. Many established knights had made fun of Zorren to embarrass him. They made him the center of their jokes. They thought that by putting him down, Jill would fall into believing that Zorren was not so special. By that time one of them could court Jill away from Zorren, have their fun with her and move on. Zorren's intentions for Jill however were of the noble quality. He loved her voice, her face, her hair and her eyes. She was the only person who had been kind to him. He could not imagine what his life would be without her. Jill felt the same way about Zorren, but now he was dead. Orendyn knew all this and more. He grieved the loss of a knight that was ordained by the fire of the Holy Spirit. In everything Zorren did, good triumphed over evil. His heart was pure. Zorren's love for Jill and her love for him attested to purity and devotion. It was something that Jill's parents could not see.

Todd and Heather decided that their daughter should have a knight that came from the southern part of Rothaynen. They thought that just because Zorren got lucky with inheriting Holmgren, his castle was in ill repair and still in forsaken country. At Holmgren summers were cooler and shorter, and winters were colder and longer. They did not want their daughter to go to the solace of Holmgren. If the kingdom was attacked from the north, Holmgren would be the first castle to be attacked. It was no place for a young girl. With the death of Zorren, Todd and Heather were almost pleased with the news. Their daughter was above marrying a peasant boy. Now that Prince Orendyn offered Jill to be Queen Agate's lady in waiting, the parents could not be more thrilled with her prospects.

The selfish parents conceded in thought that Zorren was not that bad of a boy, but Jill should look to her future. Now that he was dead, they were thrilled to meet Prince Orendyn of Rothaynen. Of course they thought that their daughter was too young to make important decisions, but with the prospect of the prince they could not have hoped for more. Orendyn himself found Jill to be quite the beauty in look, spirit and kindness. She was Zorren's love. Orendyn respected that love when Zorren was alive and even now. Someday Jill would move on and he thought that she might be interested in him. For the moment came the task of burying Zorren.

Vanessa had leaked out rumors that were damaging to Carlen without stating anything publicly. Carlen was yet another lovesick suitor whom Vanessa had to turn from lest her lord learn of his desires for her. All the evidence pointed to Carlen murdering Zorren as well, but Orendyn did not believe it. Vanessa rejoiced in her scheme that turned two fine upright knights against each other. Now, Zorren would perform no more 'miracles'. Sadar could employ his politics and grow more powerful. As for Carlen, who was once revered by knights old and young, he would be buried but in disgrace. There would be questions, conjecture and controversy looming over his death. There was a certain peace that a good man who died was expected to find. It would take Carlen a little longer to realize that peace. The story that people were led to believe about him was not completely the truth.

Canonization of St. Zorren

Years earlier King Lyndorn commissioned a castle on the site where Thermanden Bay met the River Brae. The stone quarries were busy well ahead of time in anticipation of building material. Cardinal Wilkieson was thrilled with the plans for the new church that was to be built within the castle walls. It so happened that the church within the walls of the new Braemar Castle was erected before the south towers were completed. This was due of course to the dedicated work of the Bendire Brothers who assisted the stone masons and wood framers tirelessly. Although they were not skilled to begin with, their dedication and work ethic made them efficient. The church was completed in time for dedication on Pentecost Sunday. There was only one person that came to mind in connection with Pentecost Sunday.

Progress on the rest of the castle proceeded in accordance with quality. The stone masons had laid all the stone and brick work in place to form a solid structure. Even the south towers whose foundations lay on the water of Thermanden Bay were carefully erected on the stone dolomite floor. The waters of the bay were diverted during the foundation work. The carpenters and other craftsmen were called to adorn the interior walls of the king's hall and all the bedrooms and halls. Even the kitchen was to be ornate. For the roofs, slate was imported from the neighboring Galles. The fact that it was Pentecost again brought many memories back for the cardinal. He even remembered what happened a few years ago.

One of the last things that Cardinal Wilkieson did was to endorse the application for the canonization of Zorren. It was sure to be approved by the Council of Cardinals. Cardinal Wilkieson was very ill and could not attend the council meeting. In his stead he sent Bishop Walden. Bishop Spehar was infuriated over not being chosen to go. In truth Spehar was clearly the better prepared politically of the two. With Bishop Walden the cardinal sent numerous papers in a leather pouch that would provide the evidence that Zorren should be declared a saint. Wilkieson was so sure that the application would be approved, he sent

Walden who was not a politically savvy or disputative soul. Wilkieson thought that the gentle demeanor of Walden and the proofs set in the leather pouch would be enough to get approval. Cardinal Wilkieson's endorsement was affixed to the letters as well. Cardinal Wilkieson was most respected and his work and reputation attested to that respect.

Approved, the application would be as Bishop Walden's sincerity, humility and the facts would prove beyond any doubt the merit of Sir Zorren of Holmgren's sainthood. The approval of the application did not happen before Cardinal Wilkieson did something impetuous that was synonymous with youth. An old, ailing man now, he had often counseled against making hasty decisions without getting proper authority. Cardinal Wilkieson saw that Pentecost Sunday was an ideal time for the dedication of the church in Braemar Castle. He also knew the name of the saint. Wilkieson informed King Lyndorn and Queen Agate, Prince Orendyn and Prince Arlenden about his plan, on that particular day. There was no objection from the royal family. Before it was approved by the Council of Cardinals, the proper name of the new church in Braemar Castle was the 'Church of St. Zorren'.

The Punishment of Xemaya

To see Huynsten ships in the harbor was nothing new for the people and merchant traders in Xemaya. To learn that a large fleet of Huynsten ships arrived and had discharged a large armed force was. The armed force was sent to assist the tax collectors in their role. The collection of taxes was sloppy from Xemaya as merchants in the great city of Tirmiz had become complacent with paying their taxes. They assumed that if they did not claim all of their business, they could get away with paying fewer taxes. Some merchants hired mercenaries to murder the Huynsten authorities in the ancient trade city of Tirmiz. They believed if enough strife was created, it would leave the Huynsten authorities weary of governing there. After paying for mercenaries, the Xemayan merchants truly did not have the money for taxes. In his island kingdom of Merkor, Nodunn approved his councilors proposal to double taxes in all Xemaya, and collecting them.

Naturally there would be resistance, but with the armed force ready to take away credit, it was hopeless to resist. Some rich families that were established in Tirmiz used their money to hire mercenaries. It was a good idea but a hired fighter prizes his life over money. The mercenaries scattered when they heard of the force that arrived. They rode away east toward Beracka in the mountains. In Xemaya, the Huynstens were serious about collecting taxes. Managing a growing empire was costly. It was the citizens that benefitted from the construction of roads, aqueducts and public buildings. Engineers and architects, material and labor cost money. Even the slave labor needed to be fed and governed. The money raised from taxes was how these civic items were paid for. It was the citizens' duty to support the government in their endeavor.

There were a substantial amount of Xemayan leaders that were executed due to their stiff backed approach to paying the Huynsten taxes. These were prominent people with family titles that they traced back to the judges and kings of long ago. These prominent citizens aligned themselves with the thieves and brigands that once stole from them. They were ringed together against the common threat of the Huynsten invader. All the elements of the Xemayan society came together. They now shared the same fate. The average citizen applauded the Huynsten authorities who removed thieves and brigands from the city. However they were anxious when their prominent leaders were executed alongside them. The heads of these leaders and brigands who incited insurrection were displayed on long pikes over Tirmiz' city walls for all to see.

Assault on the Summit

The Huynsten force had no sooner crushed the resistance to the taxes in Xemaya when they had another task. The entire force that was sent to reinforce the policing force at Xemaya started up the mountains in the east. To the citizens of Xemaya it appeared like a military drill. Huynsten scouts were sent ahead to chart a route. On the other side of the mountain were the scattered Kirman tribes who for years sold their wheat and traded with the Huynsten ships on the coast. The Huynstens used their coastal city of Terris until they occupied it. These mountain inhabitants resented the occupation and now raided the Huynsten governance of Terris on the coast. The infamous raids were hard to anticipate and could happen at any time, night or day. Over time they were wearing down Huynsten patience and resolve. The raids also cost valuable trade commodities that often went up in smoke.

In a surprise campaign the Huynstens were going to do some raiding of their own. In the thick of winter, these raiders from Kirman tribes were confident that the Huynstens were worn down. After the constant raids and losses inflicted against them at Terris, the Huynsten soldiers were feeling demoralized. The soldiers waited in anticipation for their relief columns that were to arrive from other posts in their empire. The Kirmans would give the new soldiers a rest and then start their raids in spring. The soldiers counted the days as the relief was late in coming.

The Huynsten soldiers stationed at Terris could not protect the coastal town and search for raiders up in the mountains at the same time. Besides if a Huynsten patrol did come to the mountain passes, they would be ambushed. The Kirmans kept careful watch on the coastal city and the mountain paths that led to their villages. They noted the number of Huynsten ships that came and went, but there was never any significant build up of Huynsten soldiers that arrived in Terris. Instead the Huynstens landed the relief soldiers in Xemaya to assist with collecting taxes first.

The Kirmans never expected the resolve of the Huynstens to weather the attacks at Terris. All the while the Huynsten plans to quell the tax resistance in Xemaya had been an overwhelming success. Now they were going to execute the second part of their campaign. Regardless of the fearless battle worthy Kirmans, who scratched their living in the mountains, the extinction of these raiding men was next on the Huynsten plan. In the dead of winter with the snow to act as a backdrop, the Huynsten forces climbed up the mountains in East Xemaya. After a few days' travel the Huynsten army reached the summit, they came upon frozen waters and followed them to one of the Kirman villages.

The Kirmans were taken so unawares that they stood there for a moment in surprise. The Huynstens surrounded them. All that they could do was watch. They could not even dispatch a messenger to warn the other villages. The villagers watched as the mighty Huynstens were poised to attack them. Perhaps the Kirman leaders thought that they could negotiate for their lives. Surely these well furnished soldiers of war would not kill men, woman and children. It was no contest so they did not engage the Huynstens. In their surprise they realized that they would have to submit to the overwhelming force that came to their high grounds. The Kirmans believed that there were none more worthy, beautiful or hardworking than their own daughters. Their boys would someday make fine warriors and it did not matter at this point who they served or fought for, so long as they were alive.

The elder tribe leader dropped his sword and shield. The Huynstens had a different idea. Their directive had not changed. Ponty, the Huynsten commander did not utter a word. Instead Ponty looked at his centurions and they read his mind. The archers' arrows overwhelmed the Kirmans; men, women, boys and girls. Ponty watched from his horse as he saw his men extirpate the village to screams of horror that echoed in the mountains. The silence that followed, the smell of smoke from the fires and the smell of people's blood on the snow gave proof of their incontestable destruction. This was the price of opposition to Huynsten authority. The job had just begun.

Ponty followed the stream source. Water was the one commodity that no living creature could endure without. Parties of scouts were sent out ahead to locate every village as the army marched. One by one each Kirman village fell to the same fate. Ponty sent only one hundred men with a centurion to relieve the garrison at Terris. The governor of Terris was worried about so small a relief column. The centurion informed the governor of Terris that there would be no more threat from the mountain people ever. When Ponty sent word to Merkor, Nodunn would be pleased. They were the same men that were ordered to relieve the soldiers at Terris. The relief finally came but it took a longer, more scenic route. Ponty had eliminated the source of the raids.

The relief force had annihilated all opposition to the Huynsten presence in Kirma. Ponty had commandeered the relief forces' services while the Huynsten garrison at Terris waited. The news that the relief soldiers brought was good indeed. The bulk of the Huynsten force returned over the mountains to Xemaya just in case the remaining merchants in Tirmiz got confident about an uprising or cheating on taxes again in their absence. The real reason that the force returned to Tirmiz was to establish itself permanently. The Huynstens had designs for the lucrative trade routes in Tamerana. The cold, rocky shores of Wendover would have to wait.

The next step in conquering the great continent of Tamerana would be the land of the Berackites who resided on the trade route in the mountains. Ponty awaited word from Nodunn's council as ordered. If he had his way, he would have kept the reinforcements for Terris and ventured to the Berackite stronghold straight away. The element of surprise along with the number of men under his command could obliterate the Berackites, but orders were orders. The revolt in Tirmiz was rather brave and needed to be completely uprooted. Ponty knew that the continued presence of an unrelenting force could break the spirit of an uprising. As an experienced general, he understood that action should have been taken earlier to stop the purchasing of mercenaries. The merchants in Xemaya got confident. They were not taxed enough or taxes were not collected in time. How else would they have the money to purchase mercenaries?

As a concession to moving against the Berackites, Ponty had to set the record straight for citizens of Xemaya and in particular the merchants in Tirmiz with established names. The merchants of Tirmiz would pay him a new tax for protection in the same fashion that they paid for the services of the mercenaries. No doubt, he thought Nodunn would be pleased.

Pastoral Roysford

Ranton, Rheymand and Danther were banished to Roysford which was formerly Enyja's Duchy. The former Leemite councilors arrived there in the middle of winter. The master of the manor was Lord Gant who served Enyja and her father, Duke Cardem, with many years of loyalty. Lord Gant was informed of the uprising affected by these men. It was hard for him to believe that anyone could find better leadership than in that of Queen Enyja. Gant had lived in a time of growth and prosperity, it was hard for him to imagine politics and ambition. He thought that the Leemite councilors had made the mistakes of youth that go hand in hand with restlessness and worry. Gant was a careful man but he had always served under Duke Cardem who ruled with fairness and justice. It was hard for Gant to imagine dishonor in others when he himself was a man of honor.

Ranton was very clever to come to the aging man's aid where matters of accounting came into consideration. Rheymand and Danther were compelled to follow through with labor duties. In a short time, Ranton was able to make himself indispensable to Lord Gant. With his bookkeeping talents, Ranton was able to free Rheymand and Danther to assist him in the taking of Roysford's first census. Lord Gant was a wise old man but he was not set in his ways. He knew that in matters of routine that there was room for improvement. Plans were made to take a census now that matters had slowed down for winter.

Ranton thought of conducting this census at the church service as it would lend importance to it. When Bishop Andrews objected to the use of the church and using the day of rest to conduct matters of state, Ranton relented. Bishop Andrews did not feel comfortable with this census. Ranton reminded the Bishop that King David conducted a census among his people. Bishop Andrews reminded Ranton that the Lord did not approve of that census. It collected information to allow a handful of merchants the means to control the people. Ranton did not like Bishop Andrews. When the people gathered for worship the next Sunday though, Ranton used the assembly that gathered to inform them of the census. Ranton informed the people that it was their choice whether they would take a few moments after the church service to register or make another trip at midweek. Ranton had his census. With this census, the former Leemite councilor would gain valuable knowledge with the accountings and other numbers.

They say that knowledge is king, and it is true. A census was never done in Roysford. Every aspect of life ran smoothly with the good Duke Cardem and the good, dedicated, hardworking people. Ranton convinced Gant that a census would be an excellent way to determine matters as simple and as important as how many loaves of bread should be baked daily. The farm people baked their own bread based on their need. In Springton where all the trade people established their shops, the bakers baked bread for the community. In the past every baker in Springton, where Cardem's castle stood, baked bread for the people in the town. If there was a surplus of bread, those loaves would go to the needy. Being needy could happen to anyone. One year a family that had prospered comfortably for generations fell on bad times when the breadwinner became disabled under the wheel of a fully loaded ox cart.

The good bishop did not feel comfortable around those men from Leems. When he learned that they were banished to Roysford for opposing Enyja, his suspicions grew stronger. It was the assurance of Gant who laid the bishop's mind at ease a little. Somehow Gant felt that the men had learned their lesson and were working for the betterment of their community. Bishop Andrews could not deny anyone opportunity despite an ill feeling in pit of his stomach. He could not express exactly what it was but he did alert Gant to a profound fact.

"The Lord was not in favor of the census ordered by King David," started Bishop Andrews, "the Huynstens also take censuses. They count every grain of every blade of wheat and set themselves as gods before simple people distributing food as though to farm animals."

"I am sure that any information, yea anything could be used for good or bad. It depends on the person," suggested Gant.

"These were former councilors of a kingdom that fell. Our queen has already had to deal with their sneaky ways, now you entrust them with taking a census?" retorted the bishop.

"Tell me why the Lord did not approve of King David's census?" asked Gant.

"King David's councilors sought to control the people. What better way was there than to have knowledge over every aspect of their lives starting with how much bread to bake daily?

"When the people work in good faith to serve one another, all their efforts will be rewarded. From the surplus even the needy can have a portion.

"When every task is measured so finely it creates shortages, excesses and more needy people.

Gant did not fully understand what the bishop was trying to say as he had never witnessed a community torn apart because of the shortage of flour to make bread or shortage of greens or shortage of the flesh of lamb or goat. He was however happy to let Bishop Andrews clear the air about his feelings. Gant did not fully understand what the bishop was trying to say.

The First Truth

In spring there were many shades of green in Roysford and the rain kept them green well after the snows retreated. The grasses grew to provide a feast for a shepherd's flock. When the sun shone you could not believe the beauty and brightness of the open meadow cast against the tall forest trees. Evergreen trees were in bounty and made the scenery pretty year round. The budding of field flowers and those on the fruit trees were a majestic sight and the wild, bulb-flowers pushed into bloom. It was especially pretty when a gentle breeze whirled the flower blossoms off the fruit trees. It felt like a heavenly ordained ceremony all done for the children of God. There were new sheep, goats, pigs and calves to tend, wheat and other grains to plant along with the garden greens. The shepherds and farmers alike would get busy to assure that with the help of the Lord, the harvest would be bountiful.

Finding a Market

The farm people of Roysford were no match for the sophistication of the three former councilors of Leems. The pastureland of Roysford was totally undervalued in Ranton's calculation. They produced garden food and it was of the finest quality. There was a need for a new market, especially now that trade with Leems had terminated. The price of garden produce would fall if a new market was not established. What is more, the produce would rot and their ability to buy what they needed would be effected. With the help of the merchants in Roysford, Ranton learned about all their close neighbors. To the south of Roysford is Rothaynen. There is a castle at Holmgren, Sydor, Malchida, Torkow and numerous other castles in the north part of the kingdom. Their produce came from further south, they were informed. Although the northern castles, by virtue of their vicinity to Roysford, were a good place to sell their produce, they were amply supplied with garden greens from their own gardens of Marmora. Ranton was not aware nor was anyone else in Roysford aware that Marmora would not supply the northern castles.

There was a surplus of garden greens in Roysford from the previous harvest. The cold winter temperatures made the produce last longer in the storehouses and barns, but spring would come soon and what was not used would be buried for fertilizer. The cargo of greens that was normally shipped to Leems lay in the barns and storehouses of Roysford. It was certain that the greens would perish if not used or sold in good time. By virtue of their experience with the larger world around them, Ranton, Rheymand and Danther came to the rescue. They advised the elder statesmen in Roysford to appeal to Queen Enyja. She was to make arrangements with either the Irminians to the island in the west or the Arsgardian tribes across the Aggregian Sea to trade the excess greens to them. At the same time, Ranton suggested taking the produce to Holmgren to see if they could not sell it in their market for a better price than the produce that came from Marmora. In place of seeing it rot, they could certainly offer a good price. Certainly, he reasoned, that it would not hurt to ask.

At first the merchants of Roysford did not like having to sell their hard earned produce for less than they got in the past year. In the end though, farmers agreed that getting something was better than nothing. Danther was quick to point out that if they did not take action, the produce would break down and be returned to the ground. Danther pointed out that the farmers could not trade for what they wanted. It would be a lean winter this year and a long one. Rheymand encouraged the farmers that it would be better to get some value than none at all. The opposition to the idea was silenced.

Some of the merchants did not trust these new accountants, but Gant saw the common sense reasoning behind the idea and agreed with it. He noted that Ranton and his cohorts had a refined manner of approaching the farmers. The farmers liked the facts that their wishes were considered and acted upon this time. The merchants were convinced that the trip into Rothaynen would result in losing the produce anyway. There was no guarantee that the produce would sell, and if it did, it might not have been worth the trip. On the other hand, there were some merchants that felt that Queen Enyja might send the produce to Skarsgard in an attempt to buy their friendship. Ranton said nothing to appease their worries. With Gant watching him he wanted to show that what was decided was the will of the farmers and merchants.

Appropriating Portions

In Norsendan Queen Enyja was surprised to hear that the suggestion to sell the produce to Irminia or Skarsgard came from Ranton and his cohorts. The men were scoundrels but it did not make them stupid when it came to managing affairs. Shipping produce to Skarsgard without an agreement could be disastrous from the matter of collecting payment. Brento could say that he did not need it. Either way the produce would go bad if they did not take action. Enyja decided to ship the perishable greens in Norsendan's storehouses. It was a positive gesture to Skarsgard from her kingdom. Then the produce in Roysford would be purchased to replenish Norsendan's storehouses. The money to pay for the produce would come from her treasury. Enyja expressed the idea to her councilors and they agreed that it could be done this year if expenditures were cut elsewhere.

The council agreed that the money to pay for the produce would have to come from the navy. Since Brento was now an ally, they were sure to save money on naval expenditures for defense. The council agreed that if Enyja so wished, she could directly purchase the excess produce and trade it for some return. It might even prove profitable suggested one of the councilors. Arturus could not find fault in the argument to cut the naval budget to finance a worthy cause, but he did not like it. In his experience surpluses could quickly become deficits. In all his years he learned that the only true assurance of being respected by your neighbor was the strength of one's own armed forces. In the case of Craigroyston, it was the navy that needed to be kept strong. It would not do to prepare for battle after a war started.

Arguments to cut funding to the navy were always being made by those whom the navy provided the freedom to make the argument. Some people did not realize that the cost of freedom was not free at all. Freedom unfortunately came at the price of human sacrifice. If a nation did not stand against tyranny then it would fall for anything. To follow through and shrink the navy and not maintain the vessels or the mariners skill level would prove costly if they let it happen. In

Arturus' mind, Craigroyston might not have the chance to recover if a determined foe pressed their advantage. You cannot properly train a new mariner in the midst of battle. You cannot conjure up a ship when needed immediately if it does not already exist. You cannot tell your enemy to come back later because you are not ready.

In the wake of the Huynsten threat, Craigroyston needed to be on their guard, so did their allies. Just before winter there was the talk about building ships for an ally. In Roysford there is talk of selling excess produce. The Huynstens expanded their tentacles over the years and had recently attempted to spread their terror in their region. If the Huynstens had taken hold in Wendover, Craigroyston would this very instant be heavily involved with arming itself. Arturus believed in the need to expand the navy let alone its maintenance. The Huynstens failed in Wendover because three Craigroyston navy ships intervened. Their captain was nearly lambasted for it at home. With the report from Brento that Eisenholm in Hammarsgard was massacred, who knew what the Huynsten plans were for that summer?

A New Customer

To the surprise of everyone, the market to the south of them in Rothaynen was most interested in buying any and all foodstuffs from Roysford at a fair price. In fact with the vicinity of shipping it was more economical to sell produce from Roysford down the road to Rothaynen's northern castles, than to cross the winding roads through the rocky land of Craigton. Gant was impressed by the efforts of Ranton and his cohorts. He was not aware of the reason why the market in Rothaynen became available. Of course it was Lucio in Peregren Castle that created this opportunity for the northern castles to be supplied with foodstuffs from a friendly neighbor. This was the solution to the problem of food supplies for the northern kingdom that Lucio needed. The northern castles of Rothaynen would receive its produce from Roysford.

Of course Enyja would have to send the produce slated for Leems to Skarsgard but now there was no expenditure buying up Roysford's surplus. The money that was saved would be directed to Arturus for the navy. Word of the trade news from Roysford impressed Gant and even the skeptical farmers. Lord Gant wrote a favorable letter to Queen Enyja about the former Leemite councilors. He wanted to inform Queen Enyja of the development. Enyja for the moment was pleasantly surprised with the news. She did not know how the former Leemite councilors would get along in Roysford. They seemed to be doing well. There was no indication that Gant was worried about Ranton, Rheymand and Danther. Enyja had no cause to worry about them. The produce in Norsendan's storehouses that was to be exported to Leems was indeed sent to Skarsgard. It was indeed a good Christian gesture at Christmas time. The farmers in Roysford were overjoyed to hear that all their surplus produce, vegetables and fruits now had a market. The surplus barrels of apples and pears, sacks of flour and even livestock in Roysford would go south to Holmgren. Thanks to these Leemite account overseers, there was a market for their excess product and future product. The merchants were glad that with this added demand, they could get a fair price now that there was a market for their food in Holmgren.

Whatever effort the farmers had put into sowing and growing would not go to waste that year. They could also plant anew with confidence in spring. The popularity of Ranton and his cohorts was growing and in a positive manner. Enyja was pleased that the produce was destined for Rothaynen as they were allies. Unfortunately Enyja was not told all the facts nor did Gant gather them. Lord Gant was sincere and trustworthy. Craigroyston unknowingly took a hand in supplying Lucio's northern castles with foodstuffs and not Graedon's Rothaynen as was believed.

Ranton got permission from Gant to accompany the Roysford farmers to Holmgren to make the trade deal. Ranton left Rheymand behind in Roysford to watch matters and took Danther with him. When Ranton arrived at Holmgren, he was welcomed by Sir Khotryn who insisted that they travel to Peregren Castle to meet with Lucio and of course Vanessa. Ranton accepted. Gant sent Nicola, who was Selwyck's brother and a senior steward now in Roysford to keep an eye on the trade delegation. Ranton wanted to go ahead to Peregren with Danther but Nicola insisted on taking Danther's place. Noting that the escort was under Nicola's charge Ranton agreed. Somehow Ranton felt that this meeting with Lucio would be very lucrative.

When Vanessa and Lucio left Braemar Castle, they brought King Graedon's treasury with them to Peregren Castle. Vanessa had planned for such a contingency. When Vanessa learned that Ranton was from Leems, she was interested in learning everything about Leems and what transpired in that part of the aerde. Nicola was left with Danther to discuss matters with Lucio while Vanessa removed Ranton from the discussion. Ranton was captivated by the stunning beauty of this temptress. He was told that the amount of gold at Peregren was limited. Certainly it was not true, but Peregren had more arms than gold. Once spent, gold could not be reproduced, but Peregren could make weapons and weapons and more weapons. Instead Vanessa managed to talk Ranton into trading for arms in place of gold. The circumstances were perfect for both Vanessa and Ranton.

Peregren was neither in want of gold or food, but there was the future to think of. Lucio wanted to secure ample food for his side and this meant acting now and paying a fair price. To acquire the foodstuffs Lucio would have agreed to anything. Ranton could not be happier with the circumstances and the presence of such a beautiful young woman. The present arrangement to accept weapons was even better. Ranton would use the gold to purchase weapons anyway. In this arrangement the weapons were already for delivery. They weapons were ready to be used to take Roysford and rule from Enyja's former keep. Ranton could not let Nicola learn of this arrangement so he had to figure out where to horde the weapons until they were needed. Vanessa proposed storing them at Holmgren with Khotryn until Ranton was good and ready. In fact Vanessa pledged Khotryn's aid to him.

Ranton had to horde the weapons without Lord Gant's knowledge and Holmgren was the closest castle. What would he tell Gant when he returned with nothing?

Vanessa suggested a promissory note. To show that Ranton did receive something, he was given a promissory note signed by Lucio for a future payment in gold. If only he could convince Lucio to let him have some gold to return to Roysford with a good faith down payment. When he asked Vanessa for the 'down payment', she smiled and he knew that the deal was done. He had the gold to buy the merchants and farmers with. Ranton's design on overthrowing Enyja was not only rekindled but it appeared that it would take less time than anticipated. In Vanessa's presence his plan to divide Craigroyston made him proud and he gained confidence in its success.

Speaking to Vanessa was an inspiration. She listened to Ranton explain what happened in Leems. Vanessa was inspired too by what she heard. She was no stranger with the dark advisors at Nodunn's court and this information would be of great value to them. Vanessa was pleased with Ranton. She knew that where there was greed that was senselessly bent on destruction and conquest for self fulfillment no matter the cost, that her craft was welcome. There was ample opportunity to introduce pleasures unspeakable to Ranton. She would see to it that Ranton would feel that he alone could conquer the world.

If the Huynstens had been successful in their invasion at Wendover, Vanessa might be celebrating the new order in Rothaynen at this very moment. Instead for the safety of her son Lucio, they had retreated to Peregren from Braemar. Vanessa did not like to retreat. She did not like delays. At this point she had waited and waited for years to reestablish her order of Furminatae. Vanessa got closer and closer to her heart's desire. She had not planned on leaving Braemar at all but did not miss the castle. Braemar Castle was too bright, too inspiring and too awesome. Now with the information about Leems, she had a new plan. All the while that Vanessa seduced Ranton, she was scheming anew. It was easy for Vanessa to draw an unfeeling, cold, self-serving man into her spell.

Ranton had not counted on trading for weapons. He had not counted on being ready to move against Enyja, so soon. Ranton had not counted on finding such a charming and irresistible young woman. He was given the grand tour of Peregren Castle which of course meant visiting the 'pits of Peregren' where the fires of industry never die. Through the dark castle corridors Vanessa led Ranton. She seemed to contrast the dark and dingy corridors with her feminine shape that was draped in white, sheer fabric. When she turned to look at him her black hair had white streaks and her lips were so deep red they appeared black. Her perfume was maddening on the senses. It was not long before they arrived at an overlook of the black smiths' forges. The sound of the fiery blaze from beyond the open doors provided a background noise for the many pounding hammers on anvils. The metal crackled in its tinning red color. Every so often could be heard the hissing of the water on the hot metal as the sweat of the forger fell upon it.

When Ranton walked through the arched doorway and entered the underground smithy, it was like a world unto itself. He thought, 'how could anyone fail with the weapons that were created in this place'. All that was needed was an army of men worthy to wield the weapons and Ranton knew that he could move people to the point of action.

The craftsmen that worked there were dedicated and guarded their posts with jealousy. He looked up into the spacious natural ceiling of rock and then he looked down. He wondered whether the workers were human. The sight of these creatures did not bother him though. These miscreants were here to forge his future. Vanessa liked that about Ranton. The labor came in all sizes. There were lean bodies twisted to allow them to fit the task at hand. The miners were shorter and stout. If you saw only the ore diggers' hands they were easy to identify. Their hands had grown around the handle of picks and shovels. Their hands stayed that way whether they were wrapped around the handle of their tools or not. The blacksmiths were huge men each capable of holding the aerde on their shoulders. They looked like they did not have faces and their hammers were but a small toy in their hands. They pounded and pounded the metal like the wheel of a mill turns as the water runs by. The guilders who fashioned the swords and shields were smaller people. They had long thin noses and eyes that protruded from their sockets. It was as though the job qualification called on the ability to distinguish the finest detail and they were born for it. Each group of laborers was more than a team and practically looked identical to the next member.

The laborers wasted no time on grooming themselves and the condition of their clothes was insignificant to them. The hard leather clothing that they wore was softened by the heat and shaped in place with the sweat of their bodies. The blank looks on their faces and constant focus to their mission made it an eerie observation. It was chilling to observe. Where did these workers go to eat and rest and sleep?

Did they eat rest or sleep at all?

There was a part of Ranton that allowed him to observe such facts. Those notions were drowned by his ambition and the mere presence of Vanessa.

A cacophony of labor was at work in the 'pits of Peregren'. The laborers performed their duty in a well choreographed movement of purpose and efficiency. The workers were bent on one goal; to produce weapons of war. They were also bent over as they worked. Their shape was governed by their yearning to fit into the larger machine that made the instruments of death.

The fires in the pits consumed all of the trees in the forests surrounding Peregren years ago. It was worrisome when the forest got thinner and thinner. A forest of trees aging over 500 years could not be replaced unless the trees were replanted and then one waited 500 years. Then coal was discovered to burn hot once it caught fire. Gases that were once unstable within the aerde's bowels were also harnessed. It seemed that in the effort of building bigger and better weapons of destruction, there was no problem that science could not solve. How did they come about this knowledge?

In the large coal pile one of the men looked up only for a moment before resuming his shoveling. It was enough for Ranton to notice that he looked anemic. With an open mouth that revealed threatening teeth, the figure was gruesome. Ranton wondered if any of these workers had ever seen the light of day. Then by contrast was the feminine figure and beautiful face of Vanessa with her ruby-red lips. He did not want to disappoint her with trivial chat about his observations. She smiled pleasantly. Ranton was taken by her beauty and perfume which contrasted the sights and smell of the place. A cackling laugh could be heard from the pits as some creation thought that the picture of Vanessa and Ranton was amusing.

An agreement was reached in Peregren. Ranton and Vanessa agreed to the sale of Roysford's produce to Peregren for weapons, some gold and an alliance. Nicola was only shown the promissory note and a token payment of gold. This was the opportunity for Ranton and his cohorts to seize power once more. With the new alliance he had in Lucio and Vanessa, his strength could grow unchallenged in Roysford until it was too late for Gant to do anything to stop him. Then overthrowing Enyja in Norsendan would follow. Ranton thought that Craigroyston's 'almighty' navy would be useless on land. In fact if Queen Enyja herself was captured, the seafaring navy would not bombard its own city of Norsendan and the castle. Where could they get rearmed and supplied?

Since the stock in Roysford was sold to Peregren, Enyja could not send anymore stock to Skarsgard. Apparently Brento was very happy to receive the food supplies formerly slated for Leems and asked to trade for more. Since the raid on Eisenholm in Hammarsgard, the entire Arsgardian people prepared for the defense of Skarsgard and there was never too much food. The Arsgardian sea captain was aware that more stock existed in Roysford and that they would be happy to sell or trade it. Unfortunately Craigroyston and Queen Enyja would lose face with Brento now that there were no more stock to send to them. All that Calogerus had gained for Craigroyston with diplomacy in Skarsgard could very well be lost by what could be perceived as an about face.

The Problem in Rothaynen

As time passed, Lucio held Princess Elayne captive in Peregren Castle. She was the rightful heir to the kingdom of Rothaynen. The noble dukes that were loyal to King Graedon were literally left out in the cold. In the mean time Lucio had just solved Peregren's potential food problem and secured an ally of his liking in Roysford. Lord Barton was the only other legal heir, but that was after Elayne. Barton was also aging and feeling his years. He had hoped to see two things. One was the marriage of Princess Elayne to secure an heir for Rothaynen, the other the marriage of his own daughter Bethany. The old duke knew that she was interested in Marius, and the fine young knight was interested in her. This was the very reason that Lord Barton sent Marius with Brandyn to Craigroyston. The old duke was thinking of Marius and Brandyn's safety. The two fine young men would have tried the risky scheme to infiltrate Peregren Castle and gotten themselves killed. Barton thought back to simpler times, many Christmases ago when his Bethany and Elayne were young girls.

Meanwhile after the liberation of Braemar Castle, Barton and Welledon did not have a clue that the sale of produce from Roysford would supply the northern castles. The dukes of Rothaynen were not aware of the alliance with Ranton either. There was interference from Roysford to supply Peregren with food. In Barton and Welledon's mind, Peregren was expected to implode from dissension brought on by the lack of food after Peregren supplied the northern castles as well as itself. Lucio was holding out against the collected forces of Rothaynen loyal to Graedon's daughter Elayne. He had a design for her and it would be very soon. Lucio gained an ally in Ranton and the former Leemite councilors. These circumstances were not foreseen by the loyal dukes of Rothaynen. It was possible that a civil war would take root in Rothaynen and tear the kingdom apart.

Since Lucio solved the problem with the food supply for the northern castles of Rothaynen, he made assurance sure again. Lucio, Vanessa and Ranton now had the opportunity to advance their personal agendas at the expense of many, many people. It seemed that this time, unlike the past when the good dukes rallied to the rescue, it would be impossible to take Peregren Castle by force. If the forces of Rothaynen were to be successful, they would have to seek a new way. A daring plan would be needed to take Peregren Castle and rescue the Princess of Rothaynen. Marius and Brandyn thought of one but two other more experienced knights would be sent in their stead.

Escape From Periforia

As they were advised by Hannalora, Nivron and Daminar kept out of trouble. They played docile and eager to serve. They feigned that there was no pride in them except to serve the haughty and proud. In a short time they were seen as fixtures in the Periforian paradise. Paradise would be what the very rich would call the place. For in the time that the wicked shirah took over by deposing the former, rightful shirah there were only two kinds of people. There were the very rich who exercised their will, and the very poor dependent on providing servitude for their very existence. It was from sheer good fortune that the rightful shirah took back his throne. He could not have done it without the help of Nassered and foremost the intervention of Nivron and Daminar.

In his appreciation, Kamalkov handed Nivron and Daminar each a sword made of a new, special, light-weight metal that was deadly with an effortless swipe. The new metal was developed by alchemists of Periforia and forged in their great furnaces. It was lightweight, strong and durable. The new metal was named Tung stone after its father. Tung was a dedicated exacting craftsman: not happy with a sword until it was perfect. Tung had been making swords with Ting, his alchemist father, ever since he could remember. Ting was relentless in his quest to make the perfect sword. Tung's early efforts were put down. In fact one day Tung crafted a sword of great beauty but his father threw it back into the molten fire because it could be better. The early frustrations that came from pleasing his father made Tung uncompromising in his search for quality and perfection. Despite this Tung had great respect for his father's mastery of the craft. From his father Tung learned to refine his formula in the search for the perfect balance of elements that would create the perfect sword.

Every so often, Tung noted that the odd sword that was forged was more brittle than ones that came from the same mixture of raw ingredients. When a particular sword was brittle it was surer to crack when he tested it against his heavy hammer and anvil. Like his father Ting, Tung developed a quest for perfection. His father had introduced cooling a newly formed sword by thrusting the blade into the body of a condemned prisoner. There were properties in the carbon elements of the human body that sealed the strength into the sword. Tung carefully observed his father's methods. The purity of the metal was the key to purifying the mixture of elements; that and heat. As costly as it was to keep fires burning to remove the impurities, he spared no expense. One day by virtue of experimenting, he came across a raw material which added strength to the iron but reduced its weight. Later he discovered that when the blade was sharpened and fashioned, it was not only as strong as before and lighter, but could effortlessly cut and did not require sharpening.

Nivron observed as Kamalkov took one of the swords and swiped at some thick candles that were used to light up the throne room. At first it looked as though Kamalkov was clumsy with his swipe. It seemed that he had missed his target. After all the fighting that Kamalkov did to recapture his crown, had he missed his target?

He then turned and indicated his wish to a servant who reached over to one of the large candles. He grasped the candle wick within his thumb and index finger and proceeded to lift it. The sword did not even disturb the candle or leave it askew. These two swords were heart given gifts from a grateful man; a most grateful man. Nivron and Daminar would cherish the swords forever as a token of their friendship with the Shirah of Periforia.

With the help of Nassered whose ancestry served the Shirah's of Periforia, Kamalkov regained his throne. Kamalkov could have exacted revenge on his captain of the guard but showed mercy and spared him. It was true that Nassared had supported the usurper, but without his help Kamalkov's return to power would have been impossible. It was the only mercy that Kamalkov showed. He had taken back his title to rule Periforia and decided that only those who were worthy would be exalted to the greatest heights. The others would be made to feel what he so unjustly endured. You can imagine Kamalkov's pleasure with Nivron and Daminar. The two young boys were the instruments that released Kamalkov from the hell on earth of that prison.

Justice had its way with the rebellious councilors who died in their struggle to keep their false shirah and their fortunes. The rebelling people caught up with them. Kamalkov remembered back to his lot in life when he was chained to a wall slapped and spit on. In captivity he did not know if he could trust his food for fear of it being poisoned or someone having spit on it. In Kamalkov's wrath, all traitors were swiftly put to the sword. With the loss of Hannalora, Kamalkov showed no mercy. There was no more compassion in him. From now on everyone would have to work and earn their daily bread.

Kamalkov had previously treated all his subjects with respect and consideration. When he was the considerate, generous leader he lost his throne. Not even the masses that he defended against the rich nobles came to his defense. Instead the people came to the aid of those who deposed the shirah. The people thought that Kamalkov was too soft to be their leader unlike Careem, the usurper. They were more content to act like sheep for him. Now the true master had returned. The true master was now ready to shear his sheep. The people would pay dearly for their indifference and their betrayal. It would have been different if Hannalora had survived the ordeal. From that moment on, Kamalkov would rule Periforia with an iron hand. The people of Periforia finally bore arms and took back their great city. Nassered proclaimed to the grateful crowd of people that they had restored the true master to his glory. Kamalkov was never going to forget the cruelty and inhumanity he underwent at the hands of the cruel Careem, his brigand friends and the apathetic followers.

Biting Off Too Much

On the Island of Merkor, King Nodunn's disappointment with the failed invasion of Wendover brought him some unplanned opportunity. Due to the Kirman resistance, in Xemaya Nodunn's authority was being challenged by pockets of wealthy merchants. These merchants were happier with their profits and control over Xemaya before the Huynsten takeover. They resented the conqueror despite the fact that all the capable people were put to work building roads and buildings. Under the Huynstens the poor were actually fed better, but that did not matter.

The wealthy merchants united and purchased mercenary fighters to attack the Huynstens where and when they least expected it. Huynsten reinforcements were needed to crush the rebellions that occurred in this ancient trade region. The region was not fully stabilized after its defeat. The rebels gained confidence due to their successful raids against Huynsten authority. The scattered Xemayan tribes were unified by their nationalism; something that they never realized before with their own squabbles over gold, silver, land, water and anything else.

Even the least of the Xemayan merchants dared to claim less business profit in order to pay fewer taxes. Nodunn realized that it was because these nobles and merchants had too much money that they were opposing him by paying for mercenaries. Nodunn decided that an example would be made of them. The Huynsten advisor who recklessly orchestrated attacking both at Wendover and occupying Kirma in a boastful show of force was put to death. In the end the Huynstens were only human. They were only human but cunning and industrious in their organization. Nodunn also lashed out against his naval captains for the failure at Wendover and actually condemned the massacre at Hammarsgard. The Arsgardian people never entered the water east of their rocky mountain fortress. They never threatened Huynsten ships. The Arsgardian raiders interfered with commerce from Craigroyston. Without their threat of raids, it left the seas safer for Nodunn's enemies. Now Craigroyston's navy had less distraction on the open seas.

Nodunn realized that he should not have been so ambitious so quickly to sweep into Kirma and mount an invasion of the Wendover Lowlands at the same time. There would be no backlash from the Wendover Lowlands as they had no ships, but with the sea pirates from Hammarsgard killed off, it would make things easier for Craigroyston's navy. Regardless of the expansion to the west, Nodunn now wanted to settle the score with the Xemayan resistance; first and foremost. The two-faced swindling nobles and traders and merchants of Tirmiz, who swore oaths and made an agreement with Nodunn, would pay with their lives. Their successors would swear new oaths to Nodunn or die as well. Then that very army would climb the rocky mountain and surround the Kirman settlements in the high mountains.

When the Kirman rebels returned from the raids on Terris, they would get a surprise. There the Huynsten army would annihilate their resistance forever by killing every man, woman and child in their midst. Hezikan, an advisor of Nodunn informed his king that it was winter and it would be risky for their army to go where it had never been before. The transport of food and supplies would be more difficult in the harsh climb up the mountain and there was no telling what the weather would be like. The area was uncharted. Nodunn looked at him condescendingly. He was not amused. Nodunn did not raise his voice in anger. Instead he spoke calmly.

"These 'Kirms' should think that we will be happy to dig in, keep warm and make no major offensive. They think that they have us at their mercy between the rocks and valleys in land familiar to them. They think that it safe to strike out against our men.

"It pleases them to attack and kill our men. They raise fear in the other men who do not know when or where they will strike next.

"However, it is we who will surprise them. Village by village they will perish. The one's living on the plain will resist our will no more." Nodunn turned to Hezikan, "It is winter for them too; only it will be colder for them, dead colder."

A Royal Appointment

In Leems the people had anticipated the worst. It had not come, yet. Still both Leemites and Karpretians were cautious. Kilkenny Castle was a cacophony of trading activity before the Leemite Christmas holiday and the ongoing Festival of Fire that the Karpretians celebrated. Karpretians and Leemites alike were cautious at first, but other than the different dress, habits and customs, trade continued inspired and rather orderly as it had in the past. The popular commodity that was sought after by the Leemites this year was dates. The Karpretian tribes had amassed a great crop and they were in abundance. Prior to this, dates were not available in large commodity.

In contrast the Karpretians were attracted to the baked bread of the Leemite custom. On the steppes flour was not leavened and the flat cakes that were made were a staple commodity. The cakes turned hard and did not smell like the bread of the Leemites. The Leemite bread that rose so thick and was so soft was of particular interest for a change in diet. The two peoples found themselves trading what they had in surplus for what they did not have.

The shortest day of the year was chosen by Karnivron to marry his daughter off to Haaron. Each day after this one would have more illumination. The day was after the Karpretian Festival of Fire and before the Christian observance of Christmas. He was a learned man despite his inability to read. Karnivron made it a habit to listen to the learned. When one speaks he is not learning. As a child he remembered challenging the authority of his step father but little good did that do for him. It was not until he stopped talking and stopped being critical of others and started listening, that he truly began to learn and improve himself.

Immediately after the departure of Queen Ellen and her faithful from Leems, Karnivron put his plan into effect. First he secured the appointment of Cardinal Connor to stay. It was a symbolic gesture. With the cardinal firmly in his church, he could administer his council for the people of Leems. The Leemites were a significant minority in their own country. Karnivron knew that with their church securely present, the Leemites would feel that they were treated fairly and would remain industrious for Leems. Karnivron was fully aware that the Christian doctrine of 'love thy neighbor' could not hurt anyone if it was duly practiced. He hoped that fair trading would accomplish this end.

The next thing that Karnivron hoped for was for the marriage of his daughter to the first Knight of Leems. This part of the plan was more challenging because it involved how Mara and Haaron felt about each other. Karnivron could see that his daughter was intrigued with this foreign man. Haaron had won both the respect of Karnivron and Daminar. The concern was how would the foreign man who was set in the ways of his Christianity feel about marrying his daughter. She was a non-Christian. Karnivron was fully aware that you can silence a man, but you cannot change his heart. Karnivron knew that he would have to make some concessions with regards to the Christian ways. He knew that Cardinal Connor would not grant his wish of a marriage just because it was a good idea or that it pleased him. For starters the bride and groom would have to consent and Mara would have to convert to Christianity. If one wishes to wed a Christian in a Christian church it is not an unreasonable expectation. In Karnivron's assessment, the concession would be worth it.

Karnivron educated himself with the beliefs of his neighbors so he could understand them better. He knew that these Leemite people tied themselves to a single God whose plan for them was selflessness and the people serving one another. Their holy book was full of stories that taught valuable lessons for living. In fact the Christian holy book referred to many holy men and prophets known to the Karpretian tribes. Of course the Karpretians also had other gods that took their place on tried superstitions. For instance the anger of the god of the wind was not something to arouse. Windeo could mercilessly whip an entire tribe with the grains of sand. There were stories how Windeo buried an entire tribe under sand because his wrath was kindled against it.

One Christian story impressed Karnivron greatly. The story went through the caravans that God had sent his son among his people, but some of the people were jealous of the son's inheritance so they killed him. They were sure that they would get the inheritance. In the end though, it was this Son of God who defeated death itself by rising again. Both Karnivron and his wise Daminar were cynical about this story but as time passed, they thought on it. Incredible as is may have seemed to learned men, there was one point that was astounding. What amazed Karnivron and his grand vizier the most was that in their experience, after a leader dies, their movement ends. In the case of this Son of God however, the movement toward tolerance and peace and fairness and justice kept growing. The disciples of this man had no army and traveled ill prepared but managed to tell the message of life wherever they went. These Christians were not only able to survive against the mighty Huynstens, but increased in their number and acquired converts. Now that was amazing.

The Leemites believed in one God. He was the same one God of the people of Xemaya. Even the nomadic tribes referred to this one God and shared the same prophets and judges. Karnivron was familiar with the rule of Henrickard. The Leemite people were persistent, hardworking people who endured many challenges and hardships to preserve their kingdom. To Karnivron's understanding the Leemites believed that if one accepted the Son's sacrifice, that on the 'day of judgment' He would intercede before God himself on behalf of the imperfect man. This was the kingdom and people that Karnivron had acquired. He did not look at these Leemites as a conquered people. Karnivron had always treated the Leemites with respect from the days of Henrickard''s reign. Karnivron realized that if he could unite the people of Leems to his people, they would both benefit. On the Aerde, the threat of Huynsten swords was very real.

Cardinal Connor ascertained that there was a basis for the marriage of Mara to Haaron; foremost because they loved each other. He was fully aware of the short comings of Mattic III and his councilors that brought about the near ruin and annihilation of the people of Leems. In his wisdom, the cardinal, like Karnivron, knew that the proposed marriage would be good to keep order and stability in Leems. With a weakened Leems, the Huynsten threat would wash in like a tide and enslave them all. The Huynstens would loot and destroy the very church that he preached to. Connor was not referring to the church building as much as the well being of God's people; the church. The next step that Connor took to lead Mara and Haaron toward marriage was to call for the baptism of Mara. Cardinal Connor was a little reluctant to profess the need for Mara to be baptized. He did not know how Karnivron would react, but rules are rules. Connor was not surprised that Karnivron accepted, but that he understood and could explain the sacrament of baptism better than any Christian.

"Baptism is a rite that allows the individual to commit their soul to God. With it comes the Son of God who will defend you before all charges against you on the 'day of judgment'," Karnivron told him.

The barbaric warrior had communicated his understanding plainly to Connor as a matter of routine. It was a positive indicator. At that point Cardinal Connor knew that this marriage would have the approval of God, and that he could continue. Cardinal Connor was satisfied in the sincerity of Karnivron, Mara and Haaron as well. Connor was grateful to God for delivering the people of Leems, his church, from what everyone thought would be barbaric treatment at the hands of a conqueror. At the conclusion of the arrangement, Cardinal Connor asked for Karnivron to stay behind. After waiting for everyone to leave, Connor then apologized to Karnivron.

"They called you a barbarian, and I believed it too," Cardinal Connor confessed, "you are not a barbarian by any means. You are a learned man and worthy of honor and respect."

"Good man of the church, you cannot be a man and not be a barbarian. The two are one. We are all born barbarian and must learn how to harness our desires, and how to get along," Karnivron professed.

Connor made no reply as he considered the wise words of the revered, conquering warrior. It seemed that God had sent this man to do what no other man could do. Connor was pleased that Karnivron was a reasonable man and not an angry, frustrated dictator. Karnivron in turn was proud that Connor would one day teach his future grandsons to read and how to live. It still had not dawned on Karnivron that he might have granddaughters. He had not given Mara the recognition that she deserved until almost the very end, but then old habits are old habits.

Mara's Baptism

The baptism of Mara was performed outside on a cool day at the waters of Blau Tonner that thundered down from the mountain of Wallach where Leemite kings were baptized and later laid to rest in the mountain caves. The baptism was held outside and presented more visually the intent for a person to receive this baptism into the Christian family. The Karpretians followed their kar to witness this baptism for Mara. At one point Karnivron had entertained the idea of baptism himself, but that idea might be too much too soon for his tribes to absorb.

The ceremony was performed quickly in the bright sunlight and the cool, brisk air. Afterwards, Leemites and Karpretians alike were invited for a feast in the castle. Karnivron like the wise Cardinal Connor realized that if the people got used to breaking bread together, that would be a foundation for a lasting peace. The baptism of Mara went over well for all concerned. The Leemite and Karpretian people generally accepted that Haaron and Mara would soon be married. Leems would again have a king and queen. Provided that everyone observed the laws of respect and consideration for one another, Leems was home and welcomed Leemites and Karpretians. Haaron and Mara would soon be invested to govern the Kingdom of Leems.

New Order in Leems

It was an uneasy start at Kilkenny Castle in the former Kingdom of Leems. The old line of kings was severed. It was strange how all the castle gates were opened and the courtyard was crowded with vendors and buyers in the market. The White Brick Court was now accessible to Karpretians who were once the nomadic tribes of the steppes. The Karpretians had a wise leader though. Karnivron wished to invest Haaron, the pride of the Leemite forces, as the new king in Leems. It was rumored that a wedding would take place to unite Haaron to Mara, the great Karnivron's daughter. Karnivron placed a great deal of trust and respect in the wisdom of Haaron and Mara to govern the land of Leems.

Daminar the wise, the kar's former vizier, was also supportive of Haaron and Mara. For years he was the only advocate that encouraged Mara to rise and lead her tribe. Haaron had earned that respect over the years of service to King Henrickard. Karnivron intended for Leems to function as it did before Mattic was ousted. He meant for the sea port to continue its trade freely, and, the strong Leemite army to guard and support it from Port Comley to Strachan. Karnivron believed that Leems was for Leemites. He never had a design to conquer the Leemite people. The survival of his own people was his only concern. In Karnivron's mind, neighbors that were reasonable as the Leemites were under King Henrickard were no threat to Karpretian safety.

Karnivron wanted Kilkenny Castle able to stand strong and pose veritable resistance to the threat of the Huynsten forces that lay far to the east of Leems and his beloved steppes. What Karnivron could not control was how Leems' traditional trading partners would react to the new kingdom. It would be interesting to see how Craigroyston reacted to the new kingdom, given that the former queen was from Craigton and was deposed. For the new start, Karnivron ousted Mattic's entire court of councilors and that included Queen Ellen. Haaron managed to talk Arno into escorting Queen Ellen to assure that the truth would be told at the Karley when they arrived in Craigroyston. Haaron did not trust Ranton and his cohorts. Unknown to Haaron, Ranton knew where Arno's loyalty lay and he had Rheymand deal with him. The assassin followed Arno on the deck of the ship. He hit him on the head. When he was sure that nobody was looking Rheymand threw Arno overboard en route to Craigroyston.

Karnivron had faith when it came to trade. He knew that people needed what they did not have and needed to sell what they had in abundance. Fair trade was the key to tolerance and peace. He figured that in time all would return to how it was before in Leems. Time healed all wounds, but there were concerns. Would the rift over the deposed monarch of Leems heal in time?

Would trade resume any time soon?

Would Craigroyston help if the Huynsten navy threatened Port Comley?

Timing, Karnivron realized, was everything. At the very earliest, he would send an emissary to the lands that traded with Leems. In the past Karnivron had dealt with Arno, Henrickard's emissary, but he was nowhere to be found. When he asked Haaron as to Arno's whereabouts, Karnivron was impressed that Haaron had already dispatched him on the diplomatic mission. Arno was well known and respected in Craigroyston, so when he explained what happened in Leems, it would have credence. Karnivron thought that Haaron had been very wise to do as he did. Neither was aware about what happened to Arno though.

Karnivron's confidence in Haaron and his daughter Mara was a source of inspiration for both their peoples. There were reservations on both sides however. Efforts were made to build this new arrangement into a viable, working solution after the fall of Mattic's kingdom. The Leemites that remained in Leems surmised that it could have been worse. They lost the battle at Strachan and chose not to engage Karnivron at Kilkenny. The Leemites that left could have been ambushed. The Leemites that did not leave could have been taken captive to be sold into slavery. At least, with Haaron in a position of influence, the Leemites gained confidence and hope. At least they would be governed by their own Haaron and his judgments under the former Leemite Laws.

Although much wisdom and common sense laid the foundation of Karpretian justice, their tribes had no written law of their own. Under the new arrangement, the Leemite Christians could attend their place of worship free of reprisal and were encouraged to do so. Except for the former administrators of Leems that fled to Craigroyston with the queen, everything would be the same. The Leemite people held their breath as they hoped that things really would be as they were before.

There came a wedding announcement which was no surprise to anyone. To the surprise of everyone, the wedding between Haaron and Mara would take place in the Cathedral of St. Steffan according to Leemite custom. Karnivron insisted on a Christian ceremony so that his grandchildren were subjected to the one God and his written laws. The news was most encouraging for Cardinal Connor. He had thought that he had lost both his religious followers, and the cathedral. To Cardinal Connor, Mara seemed to be a wise woman, and although young, very capable. In his mind, Cardinal Connor thought that if Mara converted, she would be most influential in the conversion of many of her own people. Since there was no formal objection to the wedding, it would not be long before Haaron and Mara were married and crowned king and queen of Leems. Karnivron, the dutiful father, did not believe in long engagements.

Reena the royal dressmaker of Leems and her company was called upon to make the gown for the new bride. Only the finest raiment would do for the new queen. The design would be Leemite but take into account Karpretian tradition. For Mara it was most exciting. She was not able to enjoy the splendor that a young girl had about marriage. Her previous suitors were chosen for her. Her previous husband was chosen for her. Haaron was her choice for husband and not a duty. Under the circumstances Haaron tread softly where pomp and ceremony were concerned. He did not want to appear as lavishing opulent expense on himself, his bride and this royal wedding. He thought that this is where most leaders went wrong. On the other hand, Mara and he must appear regal.

Under the urging of Terence and other prominent captains of the soldiers, they paid the silversmiths to fashion Haaron a well ornate suit of armor 'fit for a king'. It was a heartfelt gesture of their esteem for Haaron. The people could not say that Haaron lavished the new suit of armor upon himself, but they realized the support that his knights gave him. Haaron was especially overwhelmed with the confidence that his knights still bestowed on him. The Leemite knights respected Haaron before, but after he was jailed for speaking the truth against all odds, they understood his selflessness. It was evident that King Mattic should have listened to his advice.

The Leemite knights realized that Leems might still be in Mattic's hands and bloodshed could have been avoided. If only King Mattic had listened to Haaron and not certain dominating court advisors. With present matters being what they were, the Leemite knights indeed supported Haaron becoming king. There was no one else in Leems that was more worthy of the position now that Mattic died in disgrace. It was quite a prize to be declared the monarch of a new Leems. The Leemite knights realized that Mara would have a say with how matters were conducted as well. As for Mara's tribe they were ever loyal to her for all the years that she ruled them.

To Haaron, Mara was the true prize. Haaron's father and mother could not be there. They died when he was young and could not be there for most of his life. Haaron's father was a champion for tolerance and peace who was familiar with Karnivron from the early days. Haaron was certain that his father and mother would approve of his marriage to Mara. He noted that his father and mother were not judgmental when it came to people. Haaron was certain that his mother and father would have loved Mara.

Despite the efforts that Haaron put into coming to Mattic's aid, he felt some guilt for not saving his king. It was especially hard for Haaron since Mattic's father, King Henrickard, had been like a father to him. Haaron felt bad on Henrickard's account. In the end Haaron did his best to prevent bloodshed and keep the pride of the Leemite army at a high. It was Mattic and more correctly his advisors that cost Leems its king, land and pride. Since Haaron was treated like a son by King Henrickard, it was not so wrong that he should assume the throne. The people came around to this way of thinking. Haaron's knights thought so too. Karnivron the great insisted.

A New King and Queen

The people of Leems had quite a turn of events in a short period of time. They learned that half their Leemite army was destroyed at Strachan at the hands of Karnivron's forces. They also learned of the reason. Many believed that this would never have happened if Haaron would have been in charge. Many families lost their sons to this event and had now observed the same enemy evicting their monarch and enforcing order in the land. There would be uneasiness among them. The people surmised that something had gone awry when it was rumored that Haaron returned from Strachan and was sent to prison. Now the very Haaron who was the hero knight of Leems was to marry the daughter of the mighty Karnivron. Karnivron endorsed him and his daughter as the new rulers of Leems. Some wondered if this was not a planned arrangement. Had Haaron betrayed Leems for his own interests?

For the good number of people, namely those who lost husbands or sons in the battle, it was not a happy time. For others, namely the peasant farmers, especially those who were from Strachan, they understood that Haaron was a hero worthy of praise for his efforts to bring order to Strachan. In their minds, Haaron deserved to be king.

On the other hand, the Karpretians who weathered the sneak attack late into the dark hours were suspicious of the Leemites. They too wondered what their Mara was doing marrying the very man that was revered by their enemy. As far as they were concerned, Haaron defeated Verganton and Manod and Pespitar. Karnivron's sons were the forerunners to take leadership of the Karpretian tribes. Despite the circumstances they were dead as a result of Haaron. There was a story that spread of how Mara actually rescued Haaron by killing Pespitar herself. The rest of the story that included Pespitar's conspiracy to murder Daminar was acknowledged but was almost irrelevant, with some. The Karpretians managed to accept the story of Pespitar's conspiracy however.

Karnivron was supportive of his daughter marrying Haaron and in the end, the Karpretians that were evicted from Strachan returned.

Some of them claimed vacant land on the north side of the river too that was formerly owned by Leemite landlords. Most of the absentee landlords that had claim on the land north of the river were on their way to Craigroyston with Queen Ellen. Although there were some Leemites that resented losing their land, they were the very ones that left the region in the first place. It seemed that some people just like to lament anything and everything.

A wedding is a happy time and it should be. Not only do two people celebrate their personal vows to each other by calling family and friends to witness their pledge to each other before God, but there is celebration; food, sweet breads and drink. The wedding of Mara to Haaron was meant to unite both peoples and manage Leems in the manner that it was managed before with respect for the Karpretian tribes in the south. Leems was to hold its own like it always had under good leadership now provided by Haaron and Mara and what was left of his knights and army.

Massoud Al Jazeer was a respected Saracen. He was not their oldest but their most effective when it came to braving out responsibility and security for Karnivron and his people. Perhaps he had the most trying time in the ordeal as he would be called to witness the marriage of the only woman that he had ever desired. He had fallen in love with Mara since she was an adolescent girl and he in his early twenties had won the right to be a Saracen like his father before him. So wise, so young, so strong, he was the dream of any woman of the Karpretian tribes. He was a fighting man committed to the protection of the kar's family and there were plenty of skirmishes and battles within their own tribes.

Massoud had met many women in his time. The younger women lacked the wisdom and experience that comes with age and their capriciousness could lead a man to ruin. The older women that were available were usually ones who had their heart already pledged, or were free by some disagreement or the loss of their betrothed to war.

To Massoud's thinking, Mara was young and yet not foolhardy. It was natural for a man to fall for Mara. She did not throw herself at anyone like a silly girl. Despite the frightening episode with her brother Pespitar, she decided to focus on the goodness in people. She was not blind to the desire in the eyes of men or the lies on their lips and betrayal in their hearts. She was totally aware of the potential for them to take what they pleased from a woman and then discard her like an unwanted garment. Thus she herself was able to lead one of Karnivron's tribes and did so more effectively than her former husband.

Massoud had come to grips with his infatuation. He could not say to himself, the princess Mara did not know of his feelings toward her. There were many occasions that she could witness how he felt about her. Mara was fond of him, but only as a loyal friend and protector of the family. Massoud thought that this was the final time that he would put himself through this torture. He realized that Mara did not want him for a husband and he could now come to grips with it. Massoud pledged to himself that he would make every effort to lead the way toward improved relations between his Karpretian people and the Leemites. Massoud was well aware that despite being a Leemite, Haaron was every bit the worthy man he was renowned to be. He could not come between the love that Mara and Haaron shared, so he would turn away from his desire. It was Karnivron's wish and Mara's too.

Everyone Loves a Winner

With the news that Haaron would take Mara as his wife, there could be nobody happier than Cardinal Connor. He was not about to marry them for convenience however. He took the sacrament of marriage very seriously. It was like a dream for him because he did not have to abandon his church, both the building and the people that it served, and this supposed conquering pagan warlord recognized their God. It was a lesson in humility as Karnivron could have deported or sold the Leemites into slavery. Mara had agreed to be baptized and after the dunking into the water of the cold river, Leemites and Karpretians alike walked in procession from Wallach and crowded the church of St. Steffan for the baptismal service. How many times had a conquering warlord respected the culture values of his conquered people? How many times had a conquering warlord assumed on behalf of his daughter the religious values of his conquered people? How many times had a conqueror not acted like he was a conqueror?

It was unbelievable for both the Leemites and Karpretians to observe this requirement of Mara's baptism before their marriage. Some Karpretians presented themselves for the breaking of the bread at communion as well. They observed that Leemites left their church benches and lined up to receive a portion of bread. They asked themselves, why should they not do the same?

Cardinal Connor was faced with insisting that religious doctrine be adhered to or making an allowance for all the newcomers into the church. Connor reasoned that to deny communion bread to the Karpretians who came to the altar was not Christian. They would feel discriminated against. This act of exclusion might drive them further away. On the other hand it was the teaching of the church to open its arms for all who hungered. Hunger was meant to be both symbolical and practical. All people were to come and be fed with the word of the Lord and then the bread of life. Cardinal Connor could not deny these newcomers to the church the communion bread. It was Mara's baptism and he believed that making this allowance to feed the people, all the people was the best course of action. The Son of God did not

344

discriminate when it came to feeding the people. In time, he thought, they might even come back for regular worship.

With Karnivron's example, the Karpretians observed the ways of the church as Cardinal Connor conducted them. Even Karnivron had considered this baptism. He thought about his grandsons. Some day they would be baptized. Karnivron thought that at this time he would not get himself baptized. To totally change everything and immerse himself into this Christian religion might not be wise or popular with all his people. So far though, more had been accomplished peacefully to promote respect and understanding between Leemites and Karpretians than was first imagined. When considering the religious beliefs of a people and clashing with another people's religious beliefs, people become territorial and ready to defend their beliefs and customs, even unto death.

Cardinal Connor could respect the vigor to defend one's beliefs, but he learned from experience that sometimes these beliefs were used to mask greed and the thirst for power. People who chose to worship God in their ways and wrote inspired books to guide those beliefs were no threat to each other. A committed person to the ways and teachings of these religions was no threat. It was the uncommitted people who did not feel shame or remorse for stealing and killing to get their way that were the ones to beware. Connor observed that mankind had suffered so much in the name of defending these beliefs under false pretenses. Perhaps it was possible to live side by side with a neighbor, sit and break bread together, and come to each other's aid.

Wedding Preparations

Some of the finest wines were gathered from the country side for the wedding feast. The wine that was made that fall was almost premature for the event. The grapes were gathered a little late and the sugar content made the wine stronger. It tasted a little rough. In fact when it was poured into a goblet, the alcohol lingered at the rim where the wine met the goblet. With the anticipated large number of thirsty guests, there would be no problem with its consumption, especially with all the food that accompanied wedding receptions in the castle. Generally the new wine would be ready by Christmas, but this year the harvest was late. Michelis, the vintner discriminated when it came to the quality of wine, but the demand for the wedding forced his hand. The new wine would probably taste more of spirit than grape he thought, but Michelis accepted that at worst it would lend itself to a good night's sleep. The fact was that the nature of that wine foretold the future of this upcoming kingdom.

Cardinal Connor would have liked more time but conceded that with the looming doom of the Huynsten hordes, it made it necessary to move things along and crown a king and queen. He was both satisfied and thankful that Haaron and Mara were sincere in their pledges of love for one another. Karnivron was the first to realize the impact of the Leemite land falling into Huynsten hands. Those power hungry conquerors only needed the scent that Leems was weaker to capitalize on the prize. In no time they would bottle up Port Comley with their ships and surround Kilkenny Castle. With no means to keep itself supplied and a diminished army, Kilkenny would succumb to the siege in no time. To make certainty sure, Huynsten land forces in Xemaya to the east would march into Leems through Strachan from the south.

Leems was fortunate for the moment that with the civil disobedience in Xemaya and the resistance in the next land corridor over the mountains, King Nodunn was bent on revenge against them. He was ready to fasten all his enemies to a stake along the roads that lead them to further conquest. Karnivron hoped that Leems would be spared until the new king and queen, Haaron and Mara could get established.

Only time would witness the outcome. The challenge was for their two diverse peoples to come together and preferably sooner than later. So the people of Leems and the Karpretian people of the steppes got into their roles to prepare for the wedding.

A Wedding Gift

On the wedding day, Mara was dressed in attire fitting a desert princess. Her face was veiled. The veil was adorned generously with majestically worked gold and silver jewelry with turquoise that the Karpretians acquired through eastern trade. She waited in her tent that was pitched not too far from her father's. Haaron was in his fine armor that was polished to a light-reflecting shine. The wedding couple was a little younger than usual to be crowned king and queen. It was certain however that the marriage party would look splendid together.

Before the ceremony, Karnivron sought Haaron to return to him Bastoque, the sword of Leemite succession that was captured from Mattic III. It was a most symbolic gesture that he made. The sword of Leemite succession would again be in the hands of a Leemite. It was Massoud Al Jazeer who took the sword from the former Leemite king on the night of the shameless attack on the Karpretians. Mattic was already dead but Massoud pried it from the dead monarch's hand and presented the sword to Karnivron. Massoud asked Karnivron if he could cut off the infidel king's head. Karnivron thought that it would be a better negotiation gesture to return the body of the king to his queen.

On that night when the Karpretian counter attack was in full flight, Massoud led his Saracen knights and they carved a path straight to King Mattic. The king and his body guards were in full retreat. When it was noted that the escape to the north was cut off, Mattic turned his horse around. The first person that Mattic's eyes beheld was Massoud Al Jazeer with his scimitar in hand. In defiance Mattic drew Bastoque, the sword of Leemite succession. Mattic would tell you that drawing his sword was the last thing he remembered doing before he was cut down. The captured sword was turned over to Karnivron who on the day of his daughter's wedding, returned it to another Leemite. This Leemite he knew would govern with more wisdom. The restoration of Bastoque into Leemite hands was an inspiration. The sword rightfully belonged to a Leemite king, and now it was Haaron's.

Reflections before a Wedding

Karnivron, the feared warlord, was the most accommodating when it came to taking instruction from Cardinal Connor on points of the wedding ceremony and church etiquette. Karnivron was proud to be father of the bride, and he would have his place in the wedding too. His role was not unlike the wedding role that took place in the steppes where the grains of sand stood equal and together for the length of time that anyone would have to observe them. The goal in the end was the same, but the scenery was a bit unusual to the Karpretian people of the steppes.

The confines of the church of St. Steffan proved to be humbling. There was order and ceremony, and the presence of God. Like young children who discovered church for the first time, they looked up at the carved roof and the art on the walls, and the tapestries all depicting Christianity in Leems. Karnivron had assessed the benefits of all this change. He too had made concessions not unlike Cardinal Connor. The warlord made alterations in the Karpretian tradition of his people to assure both people's futures, and that of his grandchildren. If these changes were approved by Karnivron, his people would follow. To the Karpretians, the Christian wedding was treated like a gathering of the tribes. To their way of thinking, there was always hospitality under a friendly tent.

The Leemites felt a little uneasy to be participating in this wedding since Karnivron had defeated the Leemite army and literally overthrown the monarchy of Leems. Leemite fathers and mothers lost sons in Strachan. Still there they were. No one had removed the Leemites from their homes and farms. The same farmers too could easily have been cut down when the Karpretian forces moved on Kilkenny Castle. Even the church was going on as before. It really was not as bad as the people imagined it would be. It would take some time for the wounds to heal. It was odd how the mighty Karnivron; the barbaric conquering warrior and his people were not that much different from them. Apart from clothing, regional language, custom and religion, the Karpretians got hungry too and hoped to feed their children so they could grow up in safety.

The Wedding Day

The wedding day had come. The sky that morning was red as the sun shone brightly through the sporadic cloud cover. In the midst of a fallen kingdom that braced itself for winter, the Cathedral of St. Steffan was decorated for the occasion. The colorful tapestries had competition in looking ornate with all the bows of evergreen garland and red ribbons. There were crocus and selected winter flowers everywhere. The scent of pine and the perfume that came from the flowers added warmth to the stone and wooden beams of the church. Haaron stood at the front of the church before the altar in his new suit of armor. The knights looked fine in their armor that was shined especially for the occasion. They stood up at the back of the church and waited to escort the bridesmaids before the altar. The knights formed a line from the senior knight to the most junior. They looked regal.

Both the Leemite people and the Karpretian people entered the church and filled the long benches at the front. Cardinal Connor left word to the boy servers that one side of the seats was to be reserved for members of Mara's family and friends. Connor did not want the entire front church benches to be occupied by Leemites alone. Other Karpretians entered the church cautiously and waited. They seemed spell bound at the ornate wood work that formed the roof and the artistic depictions on tapestries and those painted on the walls and windows of the church. They noticed the detailed carvings on the wood pews. They had to touch them as if doing so meant that they could be a part of these beautiful artisan works. A number of young altar servers escorted the Karpretians along to the seats on their side of the church. Despite their familiarity with the church, the Leemite people looked up at the wood works and artistry as well. Both peoples appreciated the awe of the craftsmanship and artistry.

All twelve rows on either side of the main aisle were filled. There was only standing room at the back and in the aisles and around the stone columns. Soon there was no room at all. There was a sense of joy and great gladness. Leemites and Karpretians had gathered together under the same roof. A sense of humility befell everyone in the beautiful church. A wedding was to take place and everything looked beautiful. The young children spied other children that they had not seen before. They exchanged looks of curiosity. Some exchanged smiles and could not wait for church to be over so they could meet in the courtyard. To the children it was just another wedding and there were other children to meet. It was not just any wedding however. Leems was to have a new king and queen anointed as well. In church, the tension was relieved and one could not help but smile like a child. On that account the children were well ahead of the others.

When the trumpets announced the arrival of the bride and her bridesmaids, it was easy to determine what was most beautiful. In the end the most beautiful of sights was the bride and her bridesmaids themselves. The bridesmaids were dressed in fine, long gowns that dragged behind them and clung to their legs revealing their shape. Their gowns covered their arms and hugged their necks. Reena and her seamstresses at Leems worked busily through late hours to make these gowns. Apart from Mara's elaborate gown, three were fitted for ladies of the court. There were three Karpretian acquaintances of Mara's that dressed in their own ceremonial garments who looked beautiful in layers of veils. They too were escorted to the altar.

In Karpretian custom the bride's escort of girls would dance for the couple to be married. The aisle was so crowded with people though, that these elegantly dressed girls just managed to pass. They were led to the altar at the front of the church. Before they went Mara instructed her friends not to perform their dance in church. Although they agreed they were too full of joy and lived to dance. So far there was no room for them to perform. When the dancers arrived at the altar they were taken with the awesome ornate woodwork of the table. The dancers bowed with reverence and decided not to dance until the reception in the castle.

Somehow everyone could tell that the altar at the Church of St. Steffan was a solemn place. The altar was a place to be taken seriously. The Karpretians believed that this place was holy. They believed that if this God was almighty and powerful, he would not be offended by their presence and offering of joy. Everyone took their place and showed respect for the affairs of the church. The Karpretian guests were very gracious when it came to tolerance. It was a new experience for them. A few Leemites felt territorial but remained silent. After all, they thought that it was their church. Some people forgot the teachings of the Savior who welcomed any and all people. For the most part the Leemites were quite tolerant too.

When the church doors opened everyone that was seated stood up. Karnivron entered through the large heavy doors at the front of St. Steffan's Church with Mara on his arm. They were followed by five large Saracen knights that guarded them. Massoud Al Jazeer and Naveed Al Bhutan were two of them. Providing this escort was especially hard on Massoud who loved Mara to the point of fanaticism practically the whole of his life. The bride and her father paused for a moment to look at all the people before them. All the faces in the great church turned and looked upon them. Karnivron wore a ceremonial dark blue tunic with a dark blue turban. The cummerbund and turban shimmered in the light. Mara was in the beautiful, white wedding gown sewn to Leemite tradition and standards. The sheer fabric, lace and jewelry were added to comply with Karpretian custom. The mere presence of Mara was breathtaking. Mara's piercing dark eyes looked over her veiled face and gold ornate jewelry. Her beautiful black, long, flowing hair left everyone awestruck and looking on in silence.

A path cleared for the bride and her father to proceed toward the altar at the front of the church. Trumpets from the gallery at the back of the church startled newcomers in the holy edifice. The trumpets heralded the bride and her father's entrance as they began to walk down the aisle. Mara's head gear, arms and slender hands were decorated with gold jewelry formerly worn by her own mother. The jewelry, by Leemite standards, was a little ornate and excessive but Mara was the bride and it was her day. Mara was truly beautiful and carried herself like a true queen. Karnivron was very proud to be escorting his daughter with his Saracen body guards following behind him.

Karnviron knew that the people of Leems would learn that Mara was as wise as she was beautiful. With all the people's eyes focused on them as they walked toward the altar, it was a breathtaking experience. As Mara approached the altar the awe of the church filled with people seemed to vanish. Haaron's presence became more apparent to her. He stood tall and proud, and yet humble. For his part, he could only see the bride. As Mara came closer, Haaron looked into his bride's eyes. Despite the sense of never being married, Haaron knew that this was the woman for him. The young ladies of Leems now had their answer as to who would get Haaron.

When Mara arrived at the altar, Karnivron stopped and turned to look at his daughter. He looked like a distinguished father. Mara looked back at her father and thought that she had finally been recognized as to her person. She wanted to say 'I love you father and thank you' but she could not utter a word. Her father could see what she wanted to say by her eyes. Karnivron was never nervous and performed his part flawlessly. Massoud had watched all of this. Massoud had managed to walk down the far right aisle of the church practically unnoticed. Naveed kept an eye on Massoud as he was positioned on the far left side of the church.

Karnivron stood proudly before the altar stairs with his three Saracen body guards standing behind him. Both Massoud and Naveed had made their way behind pillars on either side of the altar. They were well within range of protecting their kar. Haaron came forth and bowed his head slightly to the great conqueror. Karnivron stretched out his arm with Mara's hand on it and guided her to the bridegroom. Karnivron did not lift her veil nor did he kiss his daughter as they did in Leemite custom. Karnivron placed Mara's hand into Haaron's hand and let go. The bride and groom looked at each other. Then they turned and climbed the few stairs to kneel before the altar awaiting the cardinal's instruction.

Karnivron remained standing before the stairs of the altar with his Saracen body guards standing behind him. Cardinal Connor and his host of priests and altar servers took their places. With everyone standing, the cardinal welcomed everyone in the church over the joyous occasion. After the opening rites, Cardinal Connor asked those who had seats to take them. He noted that Karnivron remained on his feet, proudly before the stairs of the altar with his Saracen body guards standing behind him. In fact Karnivron stood proudly before the stairs of the altar with his Saracen body guards standing behind him through the entire service.

It was rather unusual to have a party to the bride or groom stand before the stairs of the altar as though they were of special importance. Under the circumstances, Cardinal Connor did not take issue with Karnivron standing before the altar. The cardinal realized that this man delivered his daughter to be married into the church. Although he was not baptized a Christian, his daughter was. In the end Karnivron was not just any man. Karnivron had defeated an unscrupulous King Mattic in battle and could have annihilated the rest of his army, but did not. Surely some allowance should be made for this man who gave his blessing to the Leemites staying and the church proceeding in its usual manner. Karnivron even agreed on Mara being baptized into Christianity so his grandchildren would someday take the religion of their father and not worship from a multitude of gods.

The Coronation

Many thoughts ran through the minds of the Leemite spectators as well as the Karpretian onlookers. Haaron and Mara both followed Cardinal Connor behind the altar of the church. There the cardinal spoke blessings and performed the ritual of anointing the new monarchs. It was a rather personal ritual as Cardinal Connor spoke in a soft voice to the couple. Then he christened the new king and queen with the holy charismatic oils. Haaron and Mara's foreheads were anointed as well as their hands.

The people in the church looked on as two bishops bearing Leemite crowns on a lush, red pillow of velvet walked over to the cardinal. Cardinal Connor sprinkled holy water over the crowns. Then he took the crowns, one by one, blessed them and placed them on Haaron and Mara's heads. The sign of the cross was made over them. Cardinal Connor raised his shepherd's staff and said a silent prayer. At the prayer's conclusion he directed them back to the altar. Haaron and Mara returned to their place before the altar stairs and waited to take their vows.

The Wedding Ceremony

The wedding was about to start and the cardinal nodded to one of his priests who was stationed at the inner doors of the church. The priest had two boy servers close the large thick doors at the entrance into St. Steffan's Church. The creaking noise of the tall doors closing made all the people turn back and look. The priest then climbed up the stairs and gave word to the choir to begin. Trumpets heralded the beginning of the ceremony and harps and mandolins started playing a hymn. The church choir situated on the overhang at the church entrance started singing and the angelic voices inspired awe. The Karpretians turned and looked back up at them. Again the presence of these voices gave the spectators in the benches something to feel the awe and majesty of being in a church. The singing voices were truly beautiful to listen to.

The cardinal waited at the altar with Haaron standing before him. On Haaron's right stood his ring bearer, Terence and the other knights were Carlen, Evald, Blakeney and Teodore. To Haaron's left stood the proud bridesmaids beginning with the veiled matron of honor Ishtar. Ishtar was Mara's half-sister, and Nicolette, Maya, Catharine and Tonia followed in line. However all eyes were focused on the ornate bride in shimmering silk and her knight in shiny armor. They were the bride and groom who were coronated and would now be married.

Cardinal Connor stood between his two bishops behind the altar. Connor was especially charismatic this day as he greeted all the people in the church. After the greeting everyone took their seats apart from Mara and Haaron who kneeled before the altar. The cardinal foresaw the saving of the church and a new hope for Leems and all its peoples to start anew. The traditional readings were given by his junior clergy members that came from the surrounding regions of Leems. It was poetic to the nomadic tribes to hear that God had given man dominion over the aerde and all living things. According to the story man was to name everything living or otherwise. Of course no suitable mate could be found for him. Then God waited for the man to fall asleep and took one of his ribs encased it in flesh and made woman. To the Karpretians it seemed noble how the man upon waking and discovering a true mate declared that he had found his mate. 'Flesh of my flesh' man described his mate. The story captivated them.

The next passage encompassed a means by which the man and women should act. After putting God first, the man and woman were to love one another. The woman was to submit herself to the man and the man was to love the woman as he loved himself. They were heartfelt messages encouraging selflessness in marriage. There were rights and responsibilities placed on each man and woman that entered into marriage. Some in attendance noted how strange it was that some people stress their rights but make little effort to honor their responsibilities.

To the Christians, it seemed that the Karpretian people treated their women as slaves and property. They were not allowed to show their faces in public and the workload for them seemed unending. In fact anything and everything that happened was a woman's responsibility. There was no need to thank a woman when things went right, it was their job. When something did not work out though, it was the woman's fault. In that respect ironically, the woman in either culture, Leemite or Karpretian bore the brunt of matters.

Oddly enough, the Karpretian men felt the same about how the Leemite men treated their women. Leemite girls were allowed to be put on display and tempt boys. It was for a girl's protection that they should veil themselves in modesty. That is why Karpretian girls were veiled and covered their faces at puberty. It was their beauty that was tempting and not necessarily the right man for them. So out of respect for girls and as a token of reverence for their beauty, Karpretian girls were veiled. A good girl did not go about tempting men with her femininity. The father and mother took a hand in arranging for a suitable mate. There was persuasion in varying degree by Leemite parents as to choosing the suitable mate as well. In both cultures once a girl had fallen from grace she did not receive attention and protection anymore. It was as if there were girls to revere and girls to put into servitude. In a roundabout way, the values of the two cultures were very much the same. There was certainly room for improvement when it came to justice let alone equality for all. Cardinal Connor was sensitive to this point and did not avoid it. Instead he drew attention to it in his deliberation.

"It is imperative for a young girl not to give herself to anyone until she finds the right man. For a girl to give herself out of wedlock is foolish. In this way Karpretian girls do not reveal their beauty but to the proper husband when he is found," Connor explained.

This Karpretian value was explained so simply and so well that he impressed Karnivron with his consideration and wisdom. The Karpretians were proud of this fact. Connor was welcoming the values of the new guests in the church. In the end, there was not that much difference if any.

"Wisdom allies itself with any worthy person regardless of culture, strength or wealth. Wisdom never allows itself to be compromised therefore will never be compromised. A wise girl should follow that example," concluded Connor.

Cardinal Connor continued to counsel everyone with regards to having respect for one another in marriage and having respect for everyone overall. The family was the most important means for people to survive. Love and mutual respect were imperative to individual relations, the family and the nation as a whole. Cardinal Connor made mention as to how Mara was an exemplary woman. Not only was she feminine in her beauty and demeanor but she was fully capable to reason and defend her thoughts and if need arose, she could defend herself in battle. Mara had led her own tribe capably. Connor spoke of a woman submitting herself to her husband's will. The idea bothered neither the Leemite nor the Karpretian men. Mara was a little perplexed until she heard the rest of the prescription that compelled a man to love and protect his wife as he would himself. If that were true, Mara thought, every marriage would be a success.

Connor also spoke of Haaron's duty to love Mara as dear as himself, putting her interests first and foremost.

"Remember Haaron, treat Mara as if God was your father-in-law," Connor added.

On top of having to worry about Karnivron as a father-in-law, now Haaron had to worry that God was also his father-in-law. It did make sense though if a man truly loved his wife. Mara smiled under her veil. Haaron said nothing, but his eyes were immersed in deep thought.

When those words were spoken there was total silence as Leemite men were used to hearing this, yea though it was not necessarily practiced. It was merely something holy that was said in church. Karpretian men thought it absurd to make such a profession. Of course a woman should be looked after, but no more than the sheep, goats and their horse or trusty camel. Naturally she would be loved more as the mother of her husband's children. There would be more deliberation on that subject that evening at Kilkenny Castle where the reception for the wedding was to be held. In fact there would be more deliberation on that subject in every household. Thus far it was a positive start to this, for lack of better description, mixed marriage that was taking place. This union was going to be a beacon for all to observe that true love transcended race, creed, color and beliefs. Love between different peoples was possible in this time and on this aerde.

Cardinal Connor looked out into the congregation and paused a moment until all eyes were on him. The time had come.

"King Haaron. Queen Mara. You have come of your own free will before God to profess your love and loyalty to one another.

"Is there anyone among you who with just cause, objects to the union of these two individuals? Let them speak now or forever hold their peace," Connor declared boldly.

There was no objection from anyone. Naveed turned his eyes toward Massoud to read his face. Besides Massoud, Naveed knew how heavy his master's heart was. Massoud did not speak out and object. It was of no consequence. Naveed wanted Massoud to object but he stood silently by. Naveed believed that if Massoud objected he could muster the support of the entire Karpretian tribes and rally them to his cause with ease. Instead of a wedding Naveed thought that there would be a blood bath and the end of Leemite knights. The Leemite army would be void of sound leadership.

Despite the self discipline of Massoud Al Jazeer, the hardened warrior stood bravely by the pillar, silent. He looked magnificent with his tall stature, bearded face and perfect posture that came from a lifetime of work and commitment to mind and body. However a light breeze could have knocked him down as a certain weakness took his power away from him. It was as if someone had thrust a dagger into his heart and he could feel his warm blood pouring out of him. An inexplicable heat came over his face. Despite all the reasoning and reconciliation that he did on the matter, he had loved Mara with full devotion. He had loved her with purpose all of his life. A true love never dies. It certainly was not an uncommon feeling for anyone whose genuine loving emotions were not returned genuinely. The rest of the ceremony was a blur for him as he struggled to keep his composure.

Naveed Al Bhutan was the only person who knew his master well enough to observe what the matter was. It sickened him. Surely his master could have been more direct, more forceful with Mara. He reasoned that she was Karpretian. She should have taken Massoud for a husband. In Naveed's mind, he calculated that they had conquered the Leemites only to restore them to power with a Karpretian princess. Naveed thought that his master, the great Massoud Al Jazeer was not so great anymore. Massoud looked like a rock from the outside, but inside he was weak and soft. He was as soft as the watered-down couscous that the women made for the children. A real Saracen knight would take what he wanted and justify his actions later, if at all. Naveed was somewhat angry with the great Saracen. He had held Massoud in awe as a man of legend. Naveed was disappointed.

Cardinal Connor continued with the wedding ceremony.

"Do you Haaron, newly anointed King of Leems, defender of the faith and servant of the Lord God Almighty, take Mara to be your spouse and queen, to have, honor and cherish, to comfort in sickness and in health, until death do you part?" asked Cardinal Connor.

"I do," replied Haaron.

"An do you, Mara, newly appointed Queen of Leems, defender of the faith and servant of the Lord God Almighty, take Haaron to be your husband and king, to have, honor and cherish, to comfort in sickness and in health, until death do you part?" the cardinal repeated.

"I do," Mara said softly.

Cardinal Connor asked for the wedding rings. Sir Terence produced the ring with the seal of Leems for her majesty the queen. Ishtar brought the ring with the seal of Leems for his majesty the king. Both rings were handed to Cardinal Connor who placed them on a pillow that the bishop held. The rings were sprinkled with holy water and a blessing was bestowed upon them. Then Cardinal Connor handed the bride and groom the ring that they would give to another. The entire church watched as they saw Haaron place his ring on Mara's slender ring finger. Then Mara placed her ring on Haaron and it was done.

Karnivron felt so proud that he had to fight back tears. With all the losses he incurred of late, here was something to rejoice about. He had achieved his goal of securing Leemite cooperation to the north of his tribes, and, his daughter was happy. He took a moment to think about what his former grand vizier told him. Daminar had always said that Mara would make him proud. After all the warrior sons he raised, in the end it was Mara who represented wisdom with her warrior spirit who was at the head of her people and now her husband's. Karnivron realized that this match was Mara's choice. Previously he had made the decisions affecting his daughter's life. He believed that he knew better. He truly did love Mara, but the pride in his sons kept him from appreciating her fairly but that was in the past.

Karnivron's presence in the church at the marriage of his daughter, now the Queen of Leems, was an indicator of his support. It was clear to everyone that Karnivron's design for Leems was in the interest of its people, all its people. Anyone who wanted justice and was willing to work for a living was welcome in Leems. Allied with Leems, the Karpretian tribes on the steppes could focus on watching out for the Huynstens. Their back was protected. Cardinal Connor was justified in thinking that the Lord had sent Karnivron to these ends.

"Then in the presence of God, your kinsmen and subjects, I join you king to queen, man to wife, Haaron to Mara," Connor paused, "what God has joined this day, let no man divide."

A great applause and cheering accompanied that declaration. The cardinal's final words rang out as a threat to Massoud as he came out of his trance. He understood what was said full well. Religious beliefs varied but when a proclamation was made in a holy place of worship by a holy man, the God of everyone heard it. Massoud would keep the peace and come to the aid of both Haaron and Mara, the king and queen of Leems. He swore an oath to himself to do so. Massoud looked at the married couple, amidst the cheering and pouring out of joy. Haaron removed the veil across Mara's face and took her into his arms. He knew it was the kiss of true love. To the Karpretians who witnessed the removal of the bridal veil at the altar of St. Steffan's Church, this act was shocking. It was violating the reverence for the purity and honor of the bride. The Karpretians believed that the revelation of the bride's face was but for the husband alone.

Mara had not even resisted the gesture. The two were in each other's arms at the altar. With the look of joy on the Leemite faces, the Karpretians made no scene but observed in silence. For the Karpretians such a display was excessive. Acts of affection were not permissible for others to observe among the Karpretians. For them the love between a man and a woman was a personal matter that was not put on display before the masses. When a woman revealed her face it was the summoning of temptation among the men.

The cardinal turned to his assistant who poured wax on an open scroll that was placed on the altar. He indicated for Mara and Haaron to come to the altar. After affixing the seals of state from their royal rings on the wax, the certificate of marriage was complete. The cardinal then declared that the service was over.

"The marriage ceremony has ended. As we leave this holy place, remember that out of diverse people you are now one in service of the truth. May you all leave in peace to love and serve God, your king and queen, and one another!" Cardinal Connor concluded.

Outside the Church

Haaron took Mara and marched her down the aisle and outside the church as the trumpets and horns played most admirably. They stopped at the landing on top of the stone stairs leading up to St. Steffan's church doors. They were followed by their escort party of knights and bridesmaids walking arm in arm. The bridal party stood lined up behind them to allow the procession of people to pass and to greet the newlyweds. Inside the church, the nobles and knights and the people now filed out in rank order. The nobles, gentry and the common people vacated the church. It was a happy day. Not familiar with the order of things, Karpretian traders, tribal leaders, and Karnivron's emirs joined the departure from the church in what appeared to be out of rank and disorderly. The fragile union of the two peoples faced it first challenge as some Leemite nobles still followed the stiff habits acquired under Mattic III's rule. These nobles paused and gave way. They also gave condescending looks at the Karpretians for breaking order.

As the people passed outside the church, a second challenge presented itself. The Karpretians were not too happy with the Leemite nobles that approached Mara. They even took her hand and kissed it. In nomadic custom the bride was only to be touched by her husband once arrangements and approval was given to the satisfaction of the girl's father. For their part the Karpretians merely walked by and bowed their heads at their new queen and king. The Leemite nobles received the very looks that they gave the Karpretian traders and tribal leaders earlier inside the church. Then a handful of members from both peoples on alert exchanged glares. Both peoples were proud and had a stake in the new monarchy. For a moment the atmosphere got a little thick. The rest of the church body began filing out. In contrast the common Karpretian shepherds and Leemite farmers were thrilled by the event. These common people were filled with joy and it saved the moment. They smiled at their lieges and cheered. It was a happy day for them.

When Karnivron came out the church door it had a calming effect on the stiff-backed few. He walked directly toward the married couple followed by Massoud and Naveed. The problem diffused itself as nobles and tribe leaders went their ways. Then the rest of the people came out of the church. Again they were the common Leemite farmers and the Karpretian shepherds who waited their turn to leave the church. The thing that they both shared in common was that they were in touch with working the land. They were honored and grateful to have been a part of the ceremony.

The last time the Leemite farmers were that excited was at Mattic III's coronation. The Karpretian shepherds were in awe of the new experience as well. Soon they would be fed at the banquet too. In the Karpretian shepherds view, they could coexist with the Leemite farmers. They looked forward to trading with the Leemite farmers as Velosp's tribe did in Strachan. The farmers looked forward to trading their surplus produce for Karpretian goods that were quality items but less expensive than those that came through Port Comley.

Reception at Kilkenny

The large hall in Kilkenny Castle had a series of large tables set up on the perimeter. Ale and wine were in abundance and a feast was prepared for the guests. In the kitchen spit were three entire roasts of pork. The ovens roasted mutton and foul of every availability. Vegetables were being cut up and used in dishes both raw and cooked. Potatoes from Galles were peeled and boiled and then mashed in a portion of their own water. It was a new method of preparation popular in Galles where they knew a thousand-and-one ways to prepare potatoes. What fruits were available at this time were dried or in the form of preserves and in pies due to the time of year.

The dogs that roamed within the castle hall were tied to chains. The chains were the only thing to prevent them from satiating their lust for the food. The aroma of cooking and fine food was in the air. The smell of that food proved to be cruel to the dogs or anyone else that was not at the wedding feast. If experience served the dogs well, they noted that whenever a feast of this size was prepared, there was much to feast on after the master ate. One thing was for sure, the dogs were alert.

The hall in Kilkenny Castle was decorated with branches of pine and spruce that kept their color and added a fresh aroma during the festivity. Red bows were fastened to the evergreen color of the branches adding a pleasant magic to the atmosphere. The castle walls that the garlands decorated were so cold that needles stayed fresh and would not fall from the off-cuts until well into January. This year the decorations would serve a dual purpose. There was the coronation and wedding of the new monarchs, and Christmas Festivities only days later. The hall walls were all covered in tapestries of brilliant colors. With the supply from of the Karpretian traders, red taffeta and much sought silk were used to decorate pillars, window sills and stair cases. Silk streamers were strung across the ceiling of the hall.

The fire places crackled and roared to create the heat that would make the bridal party and their guests feel cozy in its midst. By night's end, the hall would even get too hot. Some guests would be forced to go behind the drapery to the open windows to cool down. The two great hall doors were then opened to allow heat to escape. Many guests would exit the hall for a small period of time to get fresher air in the vestibule outside the hall doors. The consumption of ale and wines helped sustain the warmth. For the Karpretians however, the consumption of any beverage that included alcohol of any kind was not permissible in any of their faiths. On this point all factions were in agreement. There were many gods and superstitions worshiped by the different nomadic tribes of the Karpretians, but on this one point they all agreed on in principle. After produce from the earth was crushed, they could not consume it after it soured. Grain and grape that were used for ales and wines were not permissible for Karpretians to consume.

When the bridal party entered the hall they could hear minstrels playing. It was not evident when all the people had collected for the celebration but the hall was full and noisy. It was very warm in the hall. There were parties of people that were gathered and immersed in conversation. Cardinal Connor and Karnivron had entered the hall with their escorts and taken their place at the same table off to the side. For their places in the hierarchy of Leemite society, it was rather a humble corner of the hall. As the guards opened the large hall doors Terence stepped in and announced the arrival of the newly married king and queen of Leems. At seeing the doors open the music all chatter ceased. The people all rose to their feet if they were not already standing. The trumpeters readied themselves to herald in their lieges.

"I give you their majesties, King Haaron and Queen Mara, the new monarchs and defenders of Leems!" Terence declared.

Everyone cheered in happiness as the trumpets heralded the announcement. For the Karpretians who usually spared excessive emotion, it was a good sign to hear the Leemites cheering at their Mara too. Some Karpretians even joined in on the cheering quietly. The new king and queen entered the hall and walked arm in arm together to their respective places at the royal supper table. They were followed by the bridal party who also walked arm in arm. The men escorted their ladies to their chairs at the table. They were situated male and female straight across with of course the central place of honor reserved for the king and queen.

Before the meal could begin Cardinal Connor offered up a prayer of thanksgiving to God. He thought it wise to begin immediately now that the guests of honor arrived. Connor began to speak over the chatter that relented after he started.

"Lord almighty God, creator of Heaven and earth, all that is on it and everyone, hear our prayer.

"We thank you for the appointment of Haaron and Mara to serve you as our monarchs.

"May they reign with wisdom and be happy and compassionate.

"May their subjects be grateful and understanding and serve them willingly with their hearts.

"Let us truly be grateful for that which we have received from your bounty. May this food nourish our bodies and minds to make us into the children of peace that you so desire us to become.

"We ask this in the name of your son Jesus Christ," Connor professed.

"Amen!" the Leemites answered.

The Karpretians were not used to Leemite customs so they waited and sat down when the Leemites did. The prayer was received well by both Leemites and Karpretians alike.

Despite the lack of participation by the Karpretians when the Leemites made toasts, the meal was beginning to go over famously. Who needed to listen to toasts when such a fine meal was prepared and awaited eating?

Karpretians did not consume fermented drinks as an observance and a matter of custom. It was cold outside, the wedding ceremonies and the excitement of the day created a desire for a well-cooked, hot meal. All the subjects had their fill of flesh and vegetables, fruits and pastries, wine, ale and water. The Karpretians were content to consume cool water with their meal. In the summer water was for the most part warm. In the winter it was a special treat to drink the cool water. The Karpretian elders however insisted that water should be consumed at a moderate temperature, neither cold nor hot. The young disagreed preferring it as cold as it was possible to be. It was funny that by the time the young grew old, they too agreed that consuming water should be done at a moderate temperature. The Karpretians witnessed the merry making of the Leemites as both cultures were getting more comfortable with one another.

Love Unrequited

Massoud Al Jazeer represented the Saracen knight that every Karpretian boy aspired to be. He was wise and strong and of very few words. He acted with presence and a command of affairs. Like all the young boys, Naveed Al Bhutan worshiped this Saracen more than the kar himself. The image he and many others had of Massoud was so reverent that he could do no wrong. In matters of state and domestic affairs there was no one like Massoud. What Naveed witnessed outside Kilkenny Castle at Leems was the chink in the great man's armor. Naveed thought that Karnivron practically gave Mara away to his enemy. Mara never looked more willing or happier. Massoud's heart was broken. It was the last straw and he could endure no more. All of Massoud's illusions died. He could not even dream anymore. The incident also disillusioned Naveed toward Massoud. He could not understand how a woman could bring this weakness about in a man as great as Massoud.

Mara had been the woman of Massoud's dreams. Massoud had suffered through her being given in marriage to Fahd until he was killed. After that every noble suitor that courted her left him bouncing between his hopeless love and madness. Massoud never lost hope because that was all that he had. Massoud was delighted with the wisdom of this young widow who spurned suitors left and right. In Massoud's mind the only constant in Mara's life was his love for her. In truth after the death of Fahd, Karnivron had assigned his finest body guard to look over Mara's affairs in the tribe from the steppes of Ranamacora. He sent Massoud. Massoud protected Mara instinctively and fiercely. Mara for her part was fond of the tall, strong, handsome man despite his being nine years older. Massoud was younger than Fahd was, but there was nothing in Mara's heart that carried love for Massoud; not the kind of love that he wanted.

It was Massoud's duty to protect Mara and he did. Massoud thought that with the incident between Mara and her brother and the loss of her husband, it would be a matter of time before he was noticed. Time passed. Now it seemed that time stood still as Mara was given away to a Leemite knight; the enemy. The tall, proud, strong man was shattered. Although Massoud kept the heartache to himself, it was easy for Naveed to notice it. Naveed had studied him so closely followed him so closely and hung on his every thought and word so closely. The familiarity with his master allowed Massoud to judge him with contempt. Massoud could not function. Naveed's hero was drowning and there was nothing that anyone could do. Only Mara could save him but she gave herself to another.

Massoud's behavior angered Naveed. Naveed's life dedication became an illusion. Naveed did not see Mara in the same light as his master. Mara was the same age as Naveed. To Naveed, Mara was not only just another girl but one with an unchecked attitude. He believed that Mara was able to get away with anything because her father was the great Karnivron. Naveed believed that she acted more like a son than a daughter. As far as he was concerned, her brother Pespitar had the right idea when he tried to impose himself on her. He realized that Mara was a thinking girl that you would have to discuss matters with and give reasons and explain your thoughts. What pleasure was that?

Naveed thought that unless you were willing to follow Mara's lead, what fun was there to have with her?

Massoud Al Jazeer was a noble servant of Karnivron and there was no way that he would interfere with his kar's wishes and least of all Mara's wishes. Naveed suggested to his master that perhaps Karnivron did not know that he has been in love with his daughter. Perhaps Mara did not know. Massoud thought it was better that way, but he was sure that Mara knew how he felt. With all the opportunity that Massoud had to make his intentions toward Mara clear, she was fully aware of his intentions. She knew but was too polite to reject him outright, so she avoided the matter. Massoud could have any woman that he desired, but he could not have Mara. Mara looked up to Massoud and respected his advice when she asked. Mara trusted Massoud because her father trusted him. Massoud realized that at best, he and Mara were only friends. He realized that they could only be friends and no more.

The great Saracen was smitten by this love that he carried for Mara. Unfortunately, for Massoud, no one else would do. One could imagine the fortitude it took Massoud to go on with his duty when he learned that Karnivron announced that Mara was to be married to Haaron. Karnivron had even agreed and endorsed Cardinal Connor's insistence that Mara be baptized in the Christian tradition. The Cardinal knew that if Karnivron and Mara agreed to baptism into the Christian faith and understood the meaning of communion, he was confident that the marriage would be significant and not just ceremony. Karnivron's mind was already made up, he planned to have his future grandchildren raised in the Christian faith. That meant that Mara would receive all the sacraments pertaining to the faith so she could teach her own children about the one God. Massoud was aware of all these facts.

Massoud Al Jazeer could not for his own life get his mind around what was happening. It would take time for him to get over this conversion and marriage. By now he should have been used to it, but he was not. When Mara was first married and all the times that other suitors courted her attention, the anger within him came to a boil. He could execute death with the same ease of breathing air, only swifter. For some reason this enemy he could not fight. This enemy did not materialize but mocked him like an unclean spirit seeking company. Massoud did not like it, but in due time he tolerated it. In fact this time he convinced himself that he was much older than Mara. More importantly, Massoud realized that despite might, wealth, position or whatever else, you cannot make someone love you. What else could he be to the beautiful, intelligent Mara?

Massoud was a Saracen knight with nothing but Mara's well being on his mind. He loved her with all his existence. His mind, body and soul were given with all his heart to Mara. Not any other woman would do. Massoud was embarrassed somewhat because one of his most dedicated students had seen him drowning in the very air that he breathed. It was over what Naveed perceived as 'frailty over a female'. Massoud realized how Naveed thought. The boy had followed his every word, his every command with the dedication of a fanatic. Naveed was disappointed in his mentor. In fact Naveed became disillusioned with Massoud. It seemed that Massoud Al Jazeer was only human after all. Massoud would make every effort to get along with Mara's Leemite subjects starting with her husband the king. Massoud would come to the aid of Haaron and Mara.

In The Spirit of the Occasion

Most Bedouin tribes never drank wines and spirits or alcohol of any form. Living in the desert the tribe moved from oasis to oasis to find water. They were constantly in search of grassland. All the while they were tracking and being tracked by their enemies. Survival occupied all their time. Add wind, drought extreme heat by day and cold by night and there was no time for folly. Nomads had to keep their sobriety both day and night. If it was imperative to move and if you could not move, you perished. A Bedouin could not let his guard down, not even for a moment. It was a simple matter of life and death. Wines and spirits were akin to folly and loss of control. Since you could not control when the wind would whirl and whip the sands into your face, you did not want to give up control of something that you could control; your own faculties. Karnivron's tribes could not afford to sleep off a day. It could very well be the day that you were required to be at your best and could not be. It could end grimly for the person who was inebriated. So, consuming spirits was not done. It was a lesson passed down from the days of the great flood that covered the aerde.

On the other hand Leemite tradition did not forbid the drinking of wine and spirits, in moderation of course. Wines and spirits brought merriment and celebration in the case of special festivities. On cold winter nights it was not uncommon that the wealthy overlords would take a cup of wine and stick a red hot poker iron into it to warm up the wine. The fine drink was akin to many a good night's sleep. The farmers had very little wine if any but the apple cider that was not consumed by October turned into what was known as 'black-jack'. Depending on the sweetness of the apples, black-jack could be very powerful so very little was consumed by a level headed farmer. For other warmth the farm people turned to their work of keeping the farm animals, milking cows, distributing grain to the foul, making bread and chopping wood. The wedding reception would be a fine place for the two cultures to see firsthand the practices of each other and hopefully bring a tolerant understanding.

Turning a New Leaf

If the new Leems was to flourish it would depend on all people getting along; rich and poor, noble and farmer, Leemite and Karpretian alike. Haaron gave instructions to Terence to make efforts to win Massoud, the great Saracen knight, to their confidence. Only good could come from such a friendship. The Leemite bridegrooms agreed that it would be a good idea to include Massoud Al Jazeer in their celebrating. Massoud was ever watchful of his kar. He did not take anything for granted when it came to Karnivron's safety. Not far away from Massoud was Naveed who was ready to carry out any instruction his master commanded. Terence informed Evald and Blakeney who were close by of his plans to invite Massoud to their table. Terence asked them to inform Carlen and Teodore of the same.

After talking with the other bridegrooms Terence approached Massoud to invite him to the head table. Massoud looked over to Karnivron who was speaking with Cardinal Connor. Haaron and Mara finished their meal and were joining them to have a word. The Saracen never left Karnivron unattended unless he was dismissed. At night, Massoud even checked on the guards that he left around his lord's tent. Karnivron and Connor both overheard the invitation made to him to join the Leemite knights at the head table. Massoud turned to look at his master. Karnivron nodded, urging him to go. Massoud believed that he had set his mind straight over Mara. Yet as Massoud approached the head table he could still not shake off his true feelings for Mara. She was a part of his existence.

It was clear to Massoud that Karnivron wanted his trusted body guard to build a rapport with the Leemite knights. They would have to build a working rapport sooner or later and this was a good opportunity to start. Before Mara and Haaron got t0 the table, Massoud turned to Naveed. With a look Massoud communicated for him to take his place overseeing the kar's safety. Massoud did not doubt Leemite sincerity or Karpretian solidarity behind their kar, but it was his duty to assure Karnivron's safety. In such a cramped hall his kar was never more in danger if someone had wished to execute him. When Mara and Haaron arrived, Massoud bowed before them. On Terence's insistence Massoud followed him to the table of the Leemite knights.

In the meantime Blakeney, the 'boy knight' as they referred to him, was chosen to make the announcement about the bridal party's first dance. He walked before the center of the head table and climbed a few stairs and stood before the throne chairs of his monarchs. Haaron and Mara were of course visiting with Karnivron at the cardinal's table. At this time the minstrel troop were queued about the traditional married couple's first dance. The minstrel troop was made up of three smaller unrelated groups that traveled about Leems entertaining and passing on notices and messages. During the feast each group took turns performing music to enhance the dining experience. It was pleasant to have music provide a background for the noise that arose from the dinner conversation. For the dance celebration that followed after supper, the musicians gathered between the corner and the great fire place to the right of the head table. Together all their instruments would provide the music for the gala affair. Blakeney stood on the stairs behind the head table and appeared a little nervous.

"If I may have your attention," started Blakeney.

He caught the attention of some people. Blakeney turned to look over at Terence who mouthed the word, 'louder' at him.

Blakeney swallowed and started anew.

"May I have your attention! Your attention! Attention please!" exclaimed Blakeney.

The noise settled and then quit.

"At this time I call on their majesties King Haaron and Queen Mara of Leems to lead us in dance! Blakeney smiled as he spoke.

The people in Kilkenny's large hall turned to see where their monarchs were and cheered. Haaron looked on his bride and arose to his feet. He had danced many a dance in that very hall with some of the most beautiful and eligible maidens in the entire kingdom of Leems. Now here he was, no less the king, with his wife the warrior queen.

The queen looked beautiful in her dress and gold jewelry. The veil that lay affixed over her face could not hide the magic in her eyes. At that time Haaron could not help staring at Mara's veiled face. Haaron escorted his bride onto the floor of the great hall and looked into her eyes. The musicians began playing a 'volta' which called for the partners to hold hands and spin in time with the music in a smaller circular motion while moving in a larger circular motion in the opposite direction. The dance was still considered a scandal by many of the elderly Leemites as the dance partners held hands and seemed to be embracing on the dance floor. It may have been a scandal to the elderly Leemites but the Karpretian observers were not used to such public displays at all. On the steppes the bride even ate her dinner with the women while the bridegroom ate his dinner with the men. What came about between the groom and his bride was their affair. It did not need to be made public. In their minds, nature had a way of taking its course. Haaron swung Mara around till they were in their own world. He looked into her eyes and there he found the promise of tomorrow.

At the head table wine pitchers were never far from the goblets. The copper horns and clay steins full of ale were delivered as fast as they could be filled and refilled. The Leemite knights respected the fact that Massoud Al Jazeer's customs did not allow for him to consume fermented juices of grain or grape. As the celebrating and drinking continued two things happened: the atmosphere got friendlier and Massoud witnessed that his hosts were rather relaxed, trusting and of goodwill. Teodore was another young knight of Leems. He was fortunate to be left behind at Kilkenny Castle when Mattic attacked Strachan. He was upset with being left behind as a few other knights gloated. His father Duke Slaaman was entrusted with coming to Kilkenny Castle from the east to provide reinforcement. Naturally

Slamaan called his son to stay behind with him because he was too young to engage in real battle. Teodore thought that he was cheated as the other knights would be heroes and not him. If he had gone, Teodore would also have perished. In the spirit of friendship and in his innocence, Teodore boldly offered a drink of ale to Massoud.

"Massoud, will you join us in raising a toast to Haaron and Mara?" Teodore asked him.

There was a pause at the table and the conversation stopped there. Massoud briefly hesitated in his reply. On one hand consumption of that mug of ale was prohibited to him, yet it was offered in sincerity and naivety by a young knight who did not know of his customs. Massoud's eyes caught Mara looking at him. Terence was about to politely make an excuse for Massoud when to his surprise the Saracen accepted. Massoud was fully aware that his invitation to the table of Leemite knights meant that he was to get acquainted and build a working rapport with them. He knew that it was also Karnivron's wish. Besides, those who consumed the ale and wine around him were still capable of purpose. If anything he observed that those beverages made the men more friendly and willing to forget their woes and partake in the spirit of brotherhood.

As the evening continued Massoud raised many a mug of ale. Massoud could keep up with any of the old, well seasoned Leemite knights. Massoud was quite capable to join in the discussions that they had involving their respective customs. Massoud answered many questions about Karpretian ways and thoughts and he also asked questions about the Leemite ways. Both sides learned of the similarity in their cultures. They were aligned when they spoke of the Huynsten threat. In that they realized Karnivron's wisdom in making Leems and the people of the steppes allies. During the celebration Massoud became curious as to how the wine tasted too. The wine was a dark purple color that left light purple stains on the cloth that was draped over the table. At that time Terence and Evald were distracted and away from the table. Had they been present they would have advised Massoud not to mix ale and wine. It was not a good idea for a well seasoned drinker. Massoud on the other hand had never drunk neither ale nor wine before. During his time at the Leemite table he was never out of Naveed's observation. Naveed had never seen his master drink or talk as much. He even smiled, a lot.

Massoud's eyes caught Naveed as he turned his smile at him. Naveed did not understand his master's smile and he kept a solemn visage. For Massoud he was able to befriend the very people that were not a short time ago enemies. The Leemites with their former, ill-advised king, sought to wipe out their existence at Strachan. Massoud now rationalized that these very enemies were not so bad. However, he thought, they now lived as if they had been the conquerors. To top everything Mara was espoused to one. Espoused to one, he thought, she was the queen of this new Leems with her husband Haaron. Haaron, he remembered, was the revered knight of Leems that Daminar and Karnivron spoke of and admired as a son. Now Haaron was married to Mara and Karnivron's son-in-law. The bliss that he felt over the new friendship with the Leemite knights accompanied by the ale and wine he consumed, had made him forget his innermost conflict for a while. The look from Naveed though, made him sober enough to feel his heartache again.

Evald returned to the table and by this late hour Massoud decided that it was time to retire for the night. He noticed that Karnivron was gone. He left earlier and Naveed escorted him out. Of course, he reasoned, that was his job. Massoud had told him to take his place. Massoud had forgotten that Naveed was doing his job and left the wedding celebration a while ago. He remembered seeing him leave, but he should have been informed. Naveed was not happy that his Saracen hero had consorted with the Leemite knights. It changed everything. Now Massoud had drank fermented grains and fermented grape juice. At this point Naveed did not know what to think about his hero, but he was happy to leave when Karnivron retired. He thought that Massoud had made new friends now. Despite the new friendship Naveed declared to himself that if they were to fight against the Huynstens together, he did not want to depend on a Leemite. Even Naveed was beginning to accept that the Leemites were to be allies.

Among friends at the head table there was much fun making. Massoud actually laughed. It was not a well developed laugh as he did not have much practice. Soon he began to tell stories of his experiences too. Rest assuredly these stories were tales worth listening to. His company enjoyed them to say the least. Haaron had earlier come to the table with Mara to drink a toast to his knights. They also toasted the new king and queen. To show diplomacy Massoud joined in the toast but Mara did not. Her elders taught her literally not to put poison into her body. She was told never to put anything in her body that her organs had to extract in order to purify her. It was another reason that fermented drinks such as ale and wine were not permissible to be consumed by Karpretians. Water was known as the 'drink of the gods'. At some point that Massoud could not remember, Haaron and Mara were announced to be retiring for the evening. The celebration at the head table however was going on well into the night.

Massoud had consumed quite a bit of ale and wine. He seemed to consume the ale like water which was practically all that he knew how to drink. Apart from cacao beans that were crushed and cast into boiling water for a bitter drink that stimulated awareness, that was all that Massoud had ever drank. Nobody cautioned Massoud about the effects of the alcohol in the ale. He also drank wine. Besides he felt that he truly was among friends. The Leemite knights would agree with him. He was a great friend to have on your side. If Massoud drank too much they thought that one of the Leemite knights would see to his safe return. Massoud's tent was outside Kilkenny Castle on a hill next to Karnivron's. Since Karnivron insisted on staying in his tent despite the insistent invitation to stay in the castle, someone would have to take him out to the Karpretian camp. The nomadic kar did not like castle corridors and bolted doors. Naveed escorted Karnivron to his tent with the full confidence that Massoud would be alright with his new friends. Actually he was a little jealous.

The time came to leave so Massoud mustered all his strength and stood to his feet. The alcohol hit him. Massoud's head was spinning and he began to stumble. He managed to catch the table and the back of the chair that he sat on to prevent himself from falling. In the spirit of friendship, the Leemite knights let out a wholesome laugh. It was all in fun and they figured that in about two days from now Massoud would be back to feeling himself. In Massoud's mind, he thought that he had been tricked. In fact he thought that he had been poisoned. He thought that he had been betrayed as sweat fell down his brow. It was as if the whole aerde was off its course. His head was spinning. There were none of his Saracen knights around. There was only the sound of laughter and it mocked him. He had never been in this situation before and he did not understand the reason for this betrayal. In his inebriate state he could hear the distorted laughter of the Leemite knights around him. Massoud was afraid. Massoud was also Massoud.

Massoud was an experienced warrior skilled at killing. By chance Teodore was closest and his laughter stood out from among the others. Massoud turned into his direction and focused all his energy on the chosen target. None of the Leemite knights expected what happened next. None of the knights had any time to react until it was over. Massoud bent his knees a little and adjusted his feet to allow him to keep his balance. Then in the same movement Massoud drew his dagger, stepped toward Teodore and slit his throat. Terence reached for Massoud's arm. Because the Saracen was inebriated, Terence prevented him from slitting other throats. Evald and Blakeney were needed to disarm him and to hold him. Terence spoke to Massoud and his voice seemed to register. He calmed down and did not continue striking out to kill. With all that happened Massoud then vomited profusely before himself. The Saracen's body was dispelling the foreign drink from his person.

Terence sent Evald to summon Haaron. Wedding night or not he had to know. The moment was serious to the point that it was not clear what to do next. Terence could define the dilemma perfectly. A Karpretian Saracen killed a Leemite knight. It was not any Karpretian though he was Karnivron's chief Saracen. Since the death of Daminar,

Massoud shadowed his kar with the devotion of a son, a good son. With his extensive experience he offered any advice that he had to give when he was asked. Karnivron knew that Massoud's counsel was well founded and intended. Although he could kill, Massoud did not spill blood carelessly and without reason. He was respectful of all life as God was its author.

It was obvious that Massoud's judgment was affected by the drink, but it did not excuse the fact that Teodore was dead. The young knight came from the castle of Slaaman, a loyal Leemite duke. Old Slaaman was loyal to Haaron from previous military campaigns. He was one of the dukes whom King Mattic assigned to stay back at Kilkenny Castle. Mattic's decision as to who was going to Strachan that night was based on geography. He had sent word to Slaaman but there was no way that he could be ready to go in time for Mattic's departure. Now the untimely death was like a game of chess. One piece advanced and took an opponent, now the opponent would make his move. It was easier to resolve the matter in thought than to say anything for that matter.

Terence did a good job of getting Massoud to feel at ease. The drive to kill everyone in his vicinity was calmed. Massoud recognized that there was absence of malice toward him. Now Massoud was fighting to stay awake as his world turned about him. He was guided into a nearby chair and he sat on it leaning on the table. Massoud's head was spinning. Terence turned to Blakeney with a somber look.

"Blakeney get on a horse. Ride out to the Karpretian camp and summon Karnivron," Terence said.

"I could run there with the time it takes to bridle a horse," replied Blakeney.

"I am sure of that, however if you go on foot you may be mistaken as an assassin and come to harm, possibly death," Terence informed.

"I will get the horse," Blakeney replied.

Before Terence could say anymore, Blakeney ran off in a hurry.

"Blakeney!" Terence added, "Do not tell him what happened. Just tell him there was an incident in the hall and that he is needed urgently."

Terence continued the deliberation in his mind. If Massoud is pardoned, the Leemites would believe that there is a dual standard in Leems. They will no longer trust the new union. To put Massoud to death would enrage the Karpretian warriors. Massoud was their revered hero. All Terence could do was to await the arrival of Karnivron and Haaron.

The Wedding Night

Haaron and Mara were already in their matrimonial bed when a knock came to the thick chamber door. It was unbelievable. Haaron did not tell the guards that they should not be disturbed, but he thought that they would realize that it was their wedding night. Perhaps, Haaron imagined, if they ignored the knocking they would come to their senses and leave. What could not wait until morning?

The knocking continued and this time Haaron could make out Evald's voice calling his name. Mara smiled. As the knocking and name calling continued, she began to laugh. She was amused by how irritated her husband was. Haaron decided that he should answer the door if they were ever to have peace that night. Then and only then he could dispel the nuisance. He threw on his clothes in frustration and pulled on his boots. In Haaron's mind, it was their wedding night. They were the king and queen of Leems. He thought that the interruption had better be for a good reason and it better be brief.

Upon opening the door however, the look on Evald's face was discouraging. Evald did not know how to begin but briefly came to the point.

"Massoud has killed Teodore," he whispered to him.

Haaron wished that the news had been anything but what Evald told him. Haaron turned to Mara. He did not know what to say to her.

"Something," Haaron searched for a word, "something, important. I will return as quickly as possible."

The look on his face told Mara that there was something wrong.

"My father! Is there something wrong with my father?" asked Mara.

"No, no, just other news," Haaron said.

He did not say anymore. Mara would not be shut out of state affairs. She reached for her clothes and began to dress. She planned to be fully aware of what happened in this new kingdom. There was certainly something of great importance or her husband would not leave their bed on the wedding night. She wanted to find out what was so important. Haaron did not stop her, but he did not know how to tell her.

Sleep Interrupted

There was a mist outside Kilkenny castle as Blakeney set out to summon Karnivron. The moon was hidden behind the cloudy sky. Blakeney was intercepted well before he even got close to Karnivron's tent. Blakeney was not armed, but he was searched anyway. He was brought before Naveed. Blakeney told him that there was a matter of importance and Karnivron was needed back at the castle. Naveed's eyes smiled as he guessed that something went wrong between Haaron and Mara. It pleased him to consider that something irreconcilable between Haaron and Mara was the problem. He was ready to make a lecture to his peers regarding this mixed marriage. Inside him, he hoped that they were fighting. Naveed asked Blakeney to tell him.

"Tell me and I will assess whether it is important enough to disturb the kar at this late hour," Naveed told him.

"I cannot tell you. It is imperative that you let me speak to Karnivron," Blakeney said.

Naveed thought he might guess at the matter.

"Did something go amiss between Mara and Haaron?" Naveed smiled.

"No," Blakeney answered.

With that answer Naveed wondered what else it could be. Then he remembered that Massoud had not returned. It made his dark complexion darker and his veins filled with anger.

"Where is Massoud? What have you done with him?" Naveed questioned

"I must insist on speaking to Karnivron or I shall be forced to yell out his name," Blakeney threatened.

Naveed looked at him for a moment. For lack of a better course of action, he went to call Karnivron from his sleep. Karnivron, a light sleeper, was already disturbed by the voices outside his tent. When Naveed entered to wake Karnivron, he was instructed to show Blakeney into the kar's tent. Karnivron did not shirk away from news no matter what hour it arrived. He preferred bad news ahead of good so that there would be more time to deliberate a solution. Karnivron braced himself for the news but took comfort in the fact that both Haaron and Mara were married and crowned king and queen in Leems. Nothing, he thought, could change that fact.

When Blakeney entered Karnivron's tent, he told him that it was important for him to return to the castle. Karnivron was worried about Mara and Haaron.

"Has something happened to Mara or Haaron?" asked Karnivron.

"No my lord," Blakeney replied, "but something awful did happen and it needs your attention. Please my lord you will understand when we get there."

"Tell me," Karnivron said sofly.

"A Saracen has slain a young Christian knight," Blakeney whispered.

Karnivron was relieved to hear that his daughter and Haaron were not the cause for this late disruption, but now he wondered. Blakeney did not mean any disrespect by withholding the details of the gruesome story, but he did convey that something of great importance happened. Naveed did not hear what Blakeney said but he gathered that it had something to do with Massoud. Naveed swore an oath to himself that 'if something happened to Massoud, he would kill the man who hurt him and it did not matter who that was, not even Haaron himself!'

Naveed also thought that if this was an attempt on the life of Karnivron he would show no mercy to the infidels. Horses were quickly saddled in the early hour after midnight. Karnivron immediately returned to Kilkenny Castle with Blakeney and a large armed escort led by Naveed. They rode in all haste.

Back in the castle Haaron arrived at the great hall. The wedding reception was over and this was a time better allocated for sleep. There was Teodore who lay on the ground in a pool of blood. He was covered up by a thick blanket. Haaron saw a few of his Leemite knights standing about the table where Massoud sat in a chair with his head lying on the table. Terence looked over to him and said nothing. He waited for Haaron to observe the scene for himself. Haaron was in shock. He could not imagine how it happened and yet he figured it out. The situation was serious. One of his young knights lay dead and Massoud who drank ale and wine for the first time in his life lay draped over the table. There was the stench of vomit rising from the stone floor before him. Before he could walk over to any of them, Mara entered the hall. She quickly ran over to Massoud and called at him.

"Massoud," she waited, "Massoud! Massoud!"

Her voice was registered into the mind of Massoud so deep that despite his sorry state, he lifted his head. Massoud looked into Mara's eyes and she could read volumes. She saw the sorrow in his eyes, the regret. It was too late. He was sorry for what he did and what it meant to Karnivron. He realized that he put the kar's plan for a Leemite and Karpretian union in jeopardy.

Mara was his queen and must now deal with the facts. A Saracen knight killed a young Leemite knight. The culprit was immediately apprehended and awaited judgment. So the newly crowned king and queen of Leems must past judgment. It was the last challenge that a newlywed king and queen needed to face on their wedding night under these circumstances. If the facts were all of it, it would just be difficult. The Saracen knight was not just any Saracen knight he was Massoud

388

Al Jazeer, beloved of Karnivron. Massoud would never do anything to go against the kar's wishes. Massoud even swore that he would come to the aid of Haaron and Mara, the new king and queen of Leems. So why would someone so revered among his people who was loved of Karnivron, slit the throat of an unsuspecting young, Christian knight?

He did so because he was not used to alcohol.

Mara did love Massoud but for his loyalty and service to her family, not as a husband. Haaron approached Massoud and stood by Mara. He put his hand over Massoud's shoulder. Haaron looked at Massoud and then looked over to Terence. Massoud understood the predicament that he put Haaron and Mara in let alone himself.

"We have sent for Karnivron," Terence informed them.

From the outer doors of the hall could be heard the sound of horses approaching. The tower watchmen heralded a call. Karnivron arrived. Haaron thought, surely he will understand what must be done. Haaron did not like it but he must call for the death of Massoud Al Jazeer. Mara knew that she could not save Massoud from death, but that her father might.

The Trial of Massoud Al Jazeer

Karnivron entered the hall with his Saracen knights led by Naveed. After all that had happened before and the glimmer of hope for his people and the Leemites now some fool had ruined it all. Karnivron's heart was heavy for in the time it took to travel back to the Great Hall of Kilkenny Castle, he knew what had to be done. What he did not know was who the Saracen who slew the young Christian night was. When Karnivron approached the table where Massoud laid his head he realized how cruel the fates were. He knew that the spirits in the drink were responsible for Massoud's action. Not too far away lay the young boy knight. He thought that 'it was not decreed in their law for nothing'. Despite his disappointments of late in Massoud, Naveed was happy to see him alive. Naveed knew that no Leemite could befriend him more than he. They were not told anything by Blakeney and Naveed had imagined that harm had come to Massoud.

Karnivron walked directly before the table. He was followed by his Saracen knights. He looked up at Haaron and the Leemite knights on the other side of the table. Cardinal Connor was informed of the mishap and rushed back to the castle hall. The cardinal entered the hall in his simple sleeping vestments and was silent. He feared for everyone. Connor walked over to where the slain body lay. He looked down, crouched and pulled away the blanket. It was the young, flushed face of Teodore with the look of terror in his eyes. Connor shook his head in horror for he knew what this death meant.

Teodore was a good upstanding and faithful young man. A tear came to the cardinal's eye. He had taught Teodore in the way of the Christian faith since he was a child. Cardinal Connor realized what it meant for Teodore's family to bare the loss, and, what would happen if justice was not done in the eyes of the Leemites. Connor further realized that which Massoud Al Jazeer meant to the Karpretians. Matters in Leems seemed to be improving. Connor knew that it would take time but things were off to a good start. Now in a single moment the fragile trust was destroyed.

Since no one was speaking, Evald decided to start.

"Of course now, a life calls for a life," Evald said boldly.

Evald was thinking of Teodore's father. Slaaman had loyally served under Henrickard and was proud of his only son. Massoud's act was careless and senseless murder.

"It was you who poisoned Massoud. Look! Look what happens when you drink that poison!" Naveed interjected.

Among the nomadic Karpretian tribes, spirits, and alcohol were not used at all. Their lifestyle did not allow for them to develop the skill to make spirits as they were always on the move. In most Karpretian religious factions, spirits were forbidden and in some carried a death penalty. These spirits were seen as a device of evil. Spirits were known to cloud a man's judgment and bring out desires to the exclusion of civilized manners and consideration for others.

In contrast the use of spirits was a common practice among the Leemites who knew the skill of making wines, spirits and elixirs. They were used for medicinal purposes and celebrations but there was no intention for the drink to enfeeble a man. In fact one or two drinks seemed to invigorate a man. The abuse of the substance however rendered a man debilitated.

Blakeney declared, "We welcomed Massoud in the spirit of brotherhood. It was he that committed murder. Are there not laws amongst your tribesmen that forbid murder?"

Of course the Karpretians had a code that prohibited murder. Their code dealt with punishment too. For a murder the murderer was put to death. Murder as a result of consuming forbidden substances was certain to carry the penalty of death. Naveed did not make reply but his anger kindled. The two parties were getting agitated as they aligned themselves with their own kinsmen.

"Silence, everyone!" cried Connor, "You know that killing begets killing and more killing. We are tired, all of us are tired."

Cardinal Connor wanted the parties to go and get sleep. The next day they could discuss what was to be done with cooler more rested heads.

Massoud Al Jazeer was a loyal, trusted Saracen whose bloodline could be traced back to the service of every kar of the Karpretian tribes. With the murder of the young Leemite knight who introduced him to ale, it spelled death for the Saracen. By their own laws, the man who took a life needlessly forfeited their own. The fact that Massoud consumed the forbidden drink added to his guilt. Karnivron looked at Massoud. The mighty Saracen knight bowed his head as he understood the dilemma that he put his kar in. Massoud was supposed to build a working rapport with the Leemites, not slice that young knight's throat.

Karnivron had retired for the evening to leave the hall to the young. He was of the opinion that the youth was supposed to make a new, better world. He now saw that they were more likely to destroy it. Mara stood by Haaron and they both exchanged glances with Karnivron. The new king and queen said nothing. The great Karnivron said nothing. The discussion among the Leemite knights and the Saracens continued. Each side made a valid point but fell short of condemning the other. Naveed was proud and sure that no harm would come to Massoud. He reasoned that Karnivron was there and so was he. Naveed took comfort that no Leemite blade or knife would pierce his master.

The situation was tense as the bickering continued. Karnivron assessed what had to be done. He was aware that this new political kingdom of Leems was delicate. The decision as to what to do about Massoud would be the first order of business for Haaron and Mara. Karnivron further realized that a more divisive opportunity did not exist. No matter what was decided, it would not sit well with one side. Karnivron reasoned that if he supported Haaron to have Massoud executed, on top of the new changes that Karnivron had allowed, he might lose support among his tribes let alone confidence among the Leemites. If Massoud was pardoned due to his condition, then the pledge about fair and just treatment would mean nothing to the Leemites.

Karnivron had grown even older now that he had to contend with this dilemma despite his experience. He and Daminar had already handled their share of no win dilemmas. Karnivron did not want to rock the fragile union by having Haaron declare that Massoud be put to death. So in the same fashion that Massoud had used to slay Teodore, Karnivron walked over to Massoud with purpose. He drew his sword. Without hesitation or anger but determination he slit the throat of Massoud Al Jazeer. The mighty Saracen knight kept trying to swallow as the blood flowed from his throat. He looked directly at his kar but not in anger. If Karnivron had waited any longer he would never have been able to do it. It was Karnivron who slew Massoud Al Jazzeer. This was his wedding present to Mara and Haaron.

As difficult a task as it was, it was the only thing that Karnivron could do. He wondered what Daminar would have advised, and this was it. Karnivron had thought that he had lived too long after the deaths of his sons, Manod and Verganton; he loved them so. Daminar was murdered by his son Pespitar who was executed himself. The loss of his friend and advisor Daminar was costly. Finally, Mara was enthusiastic about a man, Haaron the Leemite knight. Mara's happiness was tied to this man and the fragile new Leems. Though he had done the right thing, Karnivron felt himself grow older and he felt weaker.

Moments earlier Karnivron had acted so quickly when he executed Massoud that he demonstrated the reflexes of the younger man he once was. Everyone stood speechless and frozen at what happened. Naveed was in total shock to see what happened to Massoud. The shock for Naveed came from seeing who slit the throat of his master. It was unbelievable. Naveed saw Massoud fall to the stone floor of the hall. As Massoud's blood pulsed out of his throat, he looked upon the man he loved as a father. Karnivron knelt before the slain warrior and placed his hands on Massoud's face. Karnivron drew the victim's head toward his breast and wept bitterly. He loved Massoud for his devotion to his family's security; for his love and respect. Karnivron knew Massoud's father and his father's father. What Karnivron did brought a pain to his own heart.

He saw Massoud grow up from a child. He was the son of a loyal Saracen and was like a son to him. If Mara had chosen Massoud to be her husband, Karnivron would have supported it with all his heart. He could not control his emotions. For Naveed it was the second time he saw a mighty Karpretian warrior lose control of his emotions. In his mind this would not do. The Karpretian people needed strong leadership that would not crumble as Massoud did over Mara and Karnivron did over Massoud. Karnivron did not stand tall and firm after he killed Massoud. It did not make sense for a warrior who meted justice to regret his actions. Naveed could not understand the dilemma.

The act left no doubt that justice had swiftly been carried out. Haaron sat on his throne and understood the sacrifice that Karnivron had made. When Haaron and Mara hesitated, it was not considered having a lack of purpose and confidence in their own judgment, but rather an act of respect. The king and queen sat on their throne where they belonged. Mara could not sit any longer. She went to Massoud as tears came to her eyes. Mara placed her hand on the back of the dying man's head. Massoud looked at Mara with a sense of peace as his heart was light. Mara had finally come to him and she would leave him no more. It was Massoud who was leaving her.

The act of killing Massoud put a mill stone weight on Karnivron's heart. Karnivron had incurred nothing but loss in the period of time marked by the routing of Velosp's tribe from Strachan. The loss of his beloved sons, his grand vizier and now another son by his own hand was maddening. It was the right thing to do but it came at quite a cost. He sensed his people's anger personified by the look that Naveed gave him. He knew that his grip on power was not that which it was. His authority was rattled and every move he made was being watched and judged by the very people that he once judged.

The slaying of Massoud Al Jazeer led some of the younger tribe leaders to challenge Karnivron's motivation and loyalty. The young could not see their kar's wisdom. The notion that arose from the young tribal leaders, who were blood related to Karnivron, was one sided. They felt that Karnivron favored his daughter Mara and this new foreign knight whom she obviously preferred to wed. At least these leaders voiced their opinion. There were those who merely listened and kept silent. They were silent but would use this judgment as a wedge against Haaron and Mara some day when it was convenient and served their purpose. Malcontents will be malcontents forever and always.

Naveed Al Bhutan was critical of his teacher Massoud Al Jazeer. He did not respect the fact that the brave Saracen legend had fallen apart due to his feelings for a woman. Naveed knew that there were countless girls, both more beautiful and younger than Mara who would gladly have served Massoud Al Jazeer. Mara had previously been married and by Naveed's standard, she was also an older woman. No one was shocked more by Karnivron's action than Naveed. He was sure that Karnivron would have spared Massoud's life from death. Instead his kar executed him. In his anger, Naveed contemplated drawing his own scimitar and running Karnivron through. He could have done it easily. He imagined that the Saracens would not act against him. However Haaron's knights would seize him and Mara would pass judgment of death upon him. Naveed stopped himself at the last instant. Instead he stood there brooding in his wrath.

What no one realized was the experience and wisdom and foresight of the great warrior. Karnivron looked into their future and felt helpless about leading his people. People were quick to forget bounty eager to recall failure and pettiness with their own neighbor. In his entire life Karnivron struggled to unite his people and survive. He was closer to the end now. Because of persistent pettiness, he foresaw the crumbling of his Karpretian union. There was always someone that was more content with killing and bringing hunger and pestilence, and seeing women and children destitute if it meant that life could be better for them alone. Greed, avarice and stupidity were the snares that worked with one another to accomplish these means. Karnivron's mind was made up. He had brought his people this far. The heart ache of having to execute one of Karpretia's favorite sons was the epitome of punishment for him. This was his reward, he thought.

Cardinal Connor whom Karnivron respected understood his predicament. Connor reminded him of King Solomon the wise. As King Solomon approached death he too became disillusioned with his people. From the moment that we are born we approach death. From the moment a man builds something it begins to crumble. So what a man builds needs to be maintained. In order to maintain what is built requires communication and understanding from man to man and generation to generation. In the struggle to build from generation to generation to generation, Karnivron noticed that what it took a lifetime to build could be destroyed in moments.

Distrust and misunderstanding were the keystones to failure. The frustration of King Solomon, the wisest of the wise, concluded that there is a time for everything and everything would have its time. Karnivron needed to be reminded that what he had accomplished took more courage and was more than most men dreamed of accomplishing. He also needed to be reminded that he was not alone, he had Mara and Haaron. There still lay the threat of the Huynstens. They were a threat to his people and their neighbors. The Saracen guards that witnessed the execution of Massoud Al Jazeer understood that a law was only a law if it applied to everyone. Karnivron had no choice but to mete justice.

Naveed was still standing there. He did not think that the law applied to the rights of Leemites over the life of a Karpretian. From the time Massoud was killed Naveed's emotions evolved from shock and fear to anger and vengeance. Once again it would take very little for him to draw his scimitar and begin hacking at Karnivron let alone anyone who got in his way. He looked over to Karnivron and caught his eyes. Karnivron addressed his escort.

"Let us go from here," Karnivron said, "it is done."

"How could you? How could you?!" Naveed challenged the great kar and warlord.

"My son slew an innocent man and was made to atone for it. It is in accordance with our own laws. It is done," Karnivron repeated.

"Our own laws!? How could you betray your own blood for…he loved you as one of your own sons," Naveed continued, "and Mara! You chose our enemy to husband you. Were you not aware of the love and reverence that Massoud had for you when any fine woman would have done anything to be his handmaiden?"

Mara was speechless as she listened to the observation of her tribesman. It was as if Massoud's feelings for Mara were transparent. At no time did she encourage the great Saracen but that was not a matter for others. Karnivron allowed Naveed to finish what he had to say. He wanted to hear that which he had to say. It needed to be said and he wanted to hear it. What Naveed said was the general consensus of what his people thought. Karnivron understood what he heard, but he did what had to be done. It was the balancing weight that had to be added onto the scale of justice. Karnivron had made the decision and executed justice. There was no turning back now. So, he reaffirmed his judgment.

"Enough!" Karnivron exclaimed.

It was of no consequence. Naveed left the great hall of Kilkenny Castle. The next time Naveed returned to Kilkenny, he vowed to be the enemy of this Haaron and Mara. Sayed, Omar and several other Saracens called out for Naveed to stop but Karnivron told them to let him go. Karnivron foresaw that Naveed would be the seed of trouble. He should have stopped him then and there, but he could not go through with it. He could not kill him for uttering threats then and there. There had been enough killing for one night. Karnivron knew that he would regret not detaining Naveed. He could not force Naveed to follow his wishes at the point of a sword so for his insolence he too would have been executed. Karnivron hoped that the other Saracens observed his leniency and understood that their kar was merciful as well as firm.

Adolescent Perception

Back in Craigroyston the promise of the shipment of more produce from Roysford that was made to Brento could not be honored. The merchants in Roysford by way of Ranton, Rheymand and Danther found a lucrative market for their excess produce goods as well as livestock. The former councilors of Mattic were able to negotiate an agreement for top prices for their agricultural products. The merchants were happy despite only partial payment. Along with the grains and greens, sheep and goats, pigs and foul were being purchased by Holmgren Castle for distribution to the castles in northern Rothaynen. Peregren and the northern castles were purchasing foodstuffs as though they expected a famine.

Enyja was not aware of the circumstances that took place in Rothaynen even though they affected Calogerus who was sent as an emissary. To save face with Brento, Enyja sent some of their own produce in Norsendan to Skarsgard. Of course the councilors of the Karley unanimously disagreed with her wish, but the queen did not want to lose the prospect of peace with Skarsgard. With winter already there it was easy to understand her councilors' concern. A kingdom did not want to run out of food over winter. Arturus pointed out the needs of the navy when it came to feeding the brave men that protected Craigroyston's commerce on the high seas. Fortunately there were the salted cod stocks in good supply. In the end a little belt tightening might occur if winter proved to be longer, but Arturus agreed that was gained by the gesture to send food to Skarsgard would win another round of peace.

With all the pertinent matters that occupy a monarch who is ruling her people, there was another matter that came up. Enyja was faced with Princess Concetta who was worried about her appearance. The younger sister of the two noted that the eligible boys seemed to flock to her older sister because of her beautiful face and defined features. She noted that her sister whom she had been so close with now preferred the company of boys to the exclusion of her. Concetta went to her mother and cut straight to the point.

"I am ugly. How come I am not as beautiful as Julia?" she asked.

"My dear child your sister is older than you. Naturally the boys are attracted to her. In time, you will also have admirers as well," encouraged Enyja.

"In time?" the princess grimaced, "How much time?"

"In time, you will see. It will help if you do not pout and act miserable. That tends to drive away everyone let alone the boys. Remember the phrase 'a happy bridesmaid makes a happy bride'?" Enyja asked.

"Sure I do," answered Concetta.

"Well if you can be happy for others when it is their time for love, this will not go unnoticed. Someday you will have a boy of your own who will look at you as though you are the only girl on the aerde," said her mother.

Concetta accepted what her mother said and it seemed to cheer her up for the moment. She had developed a longing for a certain visitor who was an unexpected guest at her parents' court not too long ago.

"Truly the person who recognizes your beauty apart from anything else before anyone else is usually that special person. You must however remember one thing, do not covet the happiness of others.

"Do feel genuinely happy for others who have found themselves in love. "As far as this 'I am ugly', remember we are all beautiful in the eyes of God. There is however one sure way in which we can truly become ugly, and it is by choice," Enyja paused.

"By choice, how and why would someone choose to be ugly?" asked the curious Concetta.

"What is truly in the heart will surface. Greed, envy, jealousy, sloth to name a few will prevent you from enjoying your own life. You must remember never to steal hope from anyone; it may be all that they have. "If you steal hope from others, it will only weigh down, hinder and burden your own path. That lack of compassion is an ugliness that comes from the heart and gets under the skin.

"If a person does not cultivate consideration for others that is born of the milk of human kindness, the milk sours. In some people it can turn into venom. The venom will surface through to the skin and it will make you ugly. There is no cure for it. It will make you ugly," professed Enyja.

Concetta seemed concerned about her mother's revelation and tried to remember when she had last been mean to anybody. Enyja could see right through the sincerity of her daughter.

"Do not worry your head my precious daughter. You forget to appreciate things sometimes, you are carefree, but you could not be cruel to anyone. For that your father and I have been most proud of you," reassured Enyja.

The mother's words comforted her daughter. Concetta reached for her mother. Enyja put her hands gently around Concetta's head and stroked her hair. She drew the young princess to herself and held her head to her breast. Given the definition of what made a person ugly, Concetta did not feel so bad. The idea of having to wait for her chance at true love would not be a bad alternative. Concetta was particularly taken by the visit of Rendan, the Arsgardian captain who was Brento's son. She had fallen for the young, gentle man. She was not going to share that thought with anyone just yet.

Insurrection

As word got out about what happened to Massoud Al Jazeer there was disbelief among Leemites and Karpretians alike. Teodore's family and friends were angered but could not dispute the decision made and carried out by Karnivron himself. Duke Slaaman believed that as a father he had lived too long. Despite Naveed's efforts to rally his own people against Karnivron, no Karpretian would oppose the great warlord who had been like a father to all his people. The Karpretians were not happy with what occurred in the great hall of Kilkenny Castle, but then neither were the Leemites.

What happened at the great hall reaffirmed Karpretian superstition about a closed in place. With the death of his mentor, Naveed thought of using Massoud's reputation and the people's admiration for him to unite Karpretians against Haaron. Naveed wanted to start this movement to oppose Haaron and Mara's rule. Naveed wanted to fight the Leemite forces mano a mano. There would be no hiding behind stone walls. Like Karnivron had done, Naveed promised his tribesmen half the spoils of all conquests. Half the plunder was the reward of any man willing to fight and take it. Although the Karpretian Saracens empathized with Naveed's cries for vengeance, they could not dispute the fact that justice was done.

Naveed went from tent to tent in the open Karpretian encampment professing a call to arms at the top of his lungs. He did not care if Karnivron executed him as he had done to Massoud. All listened, even Leemite ears were aware of his ramblings, but no one did anything but empathize in silence. Naveed appeared to have gone mad. Karnivron's people understood the dilemma that their great kar was under, so did the Leemites. They understood why Karnivron carried out his judgment against his beloved Massoud. Naveed's attempt to create an insurrection against Leems and Karnivron's leadership failed. Both Leemites and Karpretians saw that Naveed Al Bhutan's reasoning was the instrument to bring about their demise. They took pity on him because he was close to Massoud. It was evident to both peoples that they needed each other if they were going to survive the Huynsten threat that occupied Karnivron's thoughts.

Naveed was seen as a rabble rouser who would stop short of nothing to promote strife. He would even invoke terror to achieve his personal vendetta. The well-respected Sayed tried to calm him down and reason with him. Naveed responded by drawing his dagger and slashing at Sayed's arm. Omar stepped in between them and looked Naveed in the eyes. After receiving a cut to his arm, Sayed stood back in silence. A voice of reason does not stand a fair chance against a sharp, angry knife. Naveed's complexion turned the darkest it had ever been. The veins in his throat were prominent. He seemed to grow older. Naveed insulted his colleagues and countrymen calling them cowards as his mouth foamed. Like a madman he rambled on at the top of his voice. Before he lost his voice, Naveed blasphemed a curse upon them and vowed vengeance for the murder of Massoud Al Jazeer.

"By all the gods of our people I will swear vengeance for the death of Massoud Al Jazeer. I will not rest until the blasphemy of his murder at the hands of our own kar is avenged!" declared Naveed.

Karnivron stayed in his tent and heard all of it. Karnivron could have had Naveed's head for what he said. The disgruntled young Saracen mounted Animanera, his horse, and rode off. Cardinal Connor who was present with Karnivron was concerned for his friend. The cardinal approached Karnivron in order to support him. At this time Connor thought that Karnivron might need to talk to him. Connor knew that it was not easy to do what Karnivron had done. He was going to tell him about King David and Solomon the wise. Karnivron had administered justice in the preceding case and Connor wanted to let him know that he understood how hard that was. Connor believed that if Karnivron could talk things out, he would start his healing. Karnivron knew that Connor meant well but he did not want to see anyone at this time, nor discuss anything. Karnivron preferred to be alone.

Vindicator

Naveed Al Bhutan mounted Animanera, and rode off to disappear in the dust. He had gathered no provisions, no water, but rode like a madman. He traveled south to south Leems and crossed the Blanchette River at Strachan before he thought of resting. He planned to cross the steppes of Karpretia and make his way toward the mountains in the land of Beracka in the east. There he would seek Stoldar of the Berackites. Stoldar was a young sheikh who would soon succeed his aged father to become the Calyph of Beracka. It was once proposed many years earlier for him to be wed to Mara back when she was 6 years old. Naveed traveled with his father who was an envoy in service of Karnivron. He knew that Stoldar was familiar with Massoud Al Jazeer and that affiliation would allow him an audience with him. Naveed had a lot to tell him.

The trip across the steppes was even longer now that he crossed all alone. Eventually Massoud arrived in Beracka and was granted an audience with the prince. In truth Stoldar did not remember Naveed or Mara for that matter they were all about 6 years old. He knew that she was slender and had beautiful, long hair but he could not remember her face. Stoldar's interest in Mara was promoted purely as territorial. At that time Karnivron was seeking to secure a peaceful alliance with the Berackites. There had been skirmishes between their people and the right to trade with the caravans that came from the east. The Calyph of Beracka was eager for his son to wed this young girl of position and begin breeding. The Berackites dwelt in the south eastern mountains and would prove a formidable strategic alliance.

Karnivron planned to send his young daughter Mara to the Calyph of Beracka as a wife for the young prince Stoldar. The idea was that this marriage union would strengthen Karpretian ties with the Berackites of the south eastern mountains and bring peace to the tribal skirmishes. What Karnivron learned was that Bhutroc the Calyph of Beracka was a wise man. He was a man of reason who also wanted peace between his Berackites and the Karpretians. Neither man wished to go to war over small disagreements that their people had over trade. Skirmishes on the trade route were a natural part of conducting commerce. The trade caravans enjoyed the competition for their goods they did not enjoy being raided by thieves. Stoldar nearly forgot all about Mara except that she was young and beautiful. She was all but forgotten to him except when he learned that the ugly, old Fahd with yellow teeth that visited his father had married her. Later the ugly, old Fahd with yellow teeth died in a battle with a band of thieves that disturbed a caravan bound for Beracka. At that time, Calyph Bhutroc informed Stoldar that the worthy Mara was again available and would make a fine wife. Stoldar was still not in the market for a wife as he had his choice of fine women from among his people. There was no reason to be tied to a Bedouin princess when, at least 4 or 5 times a year the caravans from the east brought new, young girls with every trip.

Upon his arrival in Beracka, Naveed recognized a former advisor to the Karpretian tribe that was led by Pespitar. It was Petrofar, the former advisor to Karnivron's son Pespitar. Petrofar escaped Karnivron's judgment for his part in the murder of Daminar. However, Petrofar held Mara responsible for the murder of Pespitar. Naveed informed Petrofar of everything that he knew and they immediately built a rapport with each other. Petrofar saw that nothing had changed as far Karnivron was concerned. Now another great Karpretian, Massoud Al Jazeer, was dead at the hands of Karnivron's reckless judgments. Petrofar saw the same opportunity that Naveed saw to exact vengeance against Karnivron.

Petrofar believed that since Mara was wed to Haaron, the Leemite King, she would gain a new sense of importance for Stoldar. From his meek beginnings in the court of Beracka, Petrofar gained enormous influence over Stoldar. Bhutroc saw Petrofar as an older, wiser steadying voice of wisdom for his son. Petrofar always leaned toward the calyph's judgments and skillfully advised Stoldar to his father's point of view. With Naveed's information from afar, Petrofar would arouse in Stoldar a new interest for Mara. Now that Karnivron had defiled their customs and murdered his own Massoud, the case to intervene became stronger. Deposing Karnivron from ruling the Karpretians would serve as revenge for the death of Pespitar whom Petrofar loved and served with all his heart.

Naveed believed that Petrofar's voice could arouse emotion among the Berackite people that would move them to act against Karnivron and permit the different factions of the Karpretian tribes to join their cause. Massoud Al Jazeer was well renowned by the Berackites. It was respect for Massoud's reputation that kept the Berackites at bay on the Steppes of Ranamacora, but now he was dead. Naveed hoped that Stoldar would see this as an opportunity to expand his influence over the Karpretian tribes. Naveed thought that Stoldar could invest him as the new kar over the Karpretians. Stoldar could act as the protector of the steppes and leave the ruling of the Karpretians to him. Naveed would be the new sultan for a tidy tribute to Stoldar.

When Naveed Al Bhutan rode off from Karnivron he did not know what to expect. He did not know where his next meal would come from. Naveed did not know that there was an ally waiting for him in Beracka. It was Stoldar's new vizier Petrofar. Petrofar had served Pespitar, Karnivron's son, until his demise at Strachan. Pespitar was killed by his sister's hand. Petrofar saw the opportunity to avenge his master's death and the disgrace he bore before Karnivron caused by Mara. Petrofar knew exactly what to say to sway his master toward a 'just' war. He would first kindle the flame of desire until it boiled over into jealousy.

For Stoldar, everything had been given to him. He took what he wanted, when he wanted it, and from who he wanted it from, despite the right or hardship that he caused. With his upbringing and support, he thought that the whole world was his. As he grew older, he was better able to control this trait in him. The land of Beracka stretched far after you crossed over the eastern mountains. It was true that what Stoldar did not have, he did not want. He had enjoyed first choice of anything that came from the east on the caravans. Petrofar with the help of Naveed were about to give him something from the west; something to want. Something that was given to him long ago that was now in the possession of another man. This possession was in the hands of a renowned Leemite knight of legend whose army had been weakened and his kingdom occupied by nomadic people. Stoldar never liked anyone having what was his. He was like the dog in the manger. Now what does a dog need with a manger? The dog does not need a manger, but he will see to it that no one else will use it either.

"It is obvious that Karnivron, a great man in his day, has now grown old. He does not savor fighting anymore so he feels it should not be done. It is not unlike your situation, oh great one," Petrofar told him.

Upon the death of Bhutroc, his father, Stoldar would assume his birthright. Not that he was denied anything but, Stoldar was anxious to take control of the Berackite people. However he would never consider murder to achieve that end as it was his father. The Calyph of Beracka had been most generous and loving with his son.

Bhutroc had been very generous to his son. Although anxious to rule, Stoldar was content to dream and live carefree a little longer. Given his lifestyle one would think he was already the calyph. With the finest raiment and a striking figure, all he needed was the title. For his part Stoldar knew that he would be the calyph soon enough. Petrofar had an idea to make his lord's dream come true sooner. With Naveed now in league with Petrofar, it was a perfect union. Mhutak, the captain of Bhutroc's Saracen knights and head of the army, was loyal to the old calyph. Petrofar would test that loyalty with a scheme designed to eliminate both the calyph and his loyal servant. In Petrofar's opinion he much preferred to see Naveed Al Bhutan in the honorary role of captain of the guard. Naveed was much more cunning and hungrier than Mhutak. These were qualities that Petrofar held high. Above all, Naveed was unwavering and loyal to his purpose and direction. Petrofar himself was nothing if not unwavering and loyal to purpose and direction.

In important matters such as war that involved the Berackite people, Bhutroc would have to be consulted and would ultimately have the final word. Knowing this Petrofar counseled Stoldar to make his case before the calyph's council so that the battle lords and merchants could hear the lucrative proposal. If Bhutroc turned down the idea in private, that would be the end of it. With the words that Petrofar gave him, Stoldar would be irresistible. Petrofar knew that making the proposal before the council would catch the calyph by surprise. Anything could happen when someone was caught by surprise.

Stoldar had an easy time selling the idea to his conquest thirsty Berackite countrymen. To the council, the merchants and those who hungered for glory in battle, the proposal was music in their ears. Bhutroc was indeed impressed by the manner in which Stoldar addressed the council with confidence and conviction. He knew that his son had good qualities of leadership. Bhutroc knew that his son meant well and that he made a very good case in one way. Before the calyph's court, Petrofar was seen as the loyal servant humbly standing by his master. Bhutroc thought that Petrofar should have advised his son to present the idea to him first.

Although it was sound military practice, the idea called for an attack on Karnivron's nomadic tribes whom they had been at peace with for quite some time. Bhutroc did not like that part of the plan. In a conflict, people got hurt. When necessary, every effort to win a conflict should be made, but to attack a neighbor because of internal strife in their camp was not to the calyph's liking. The plan was unscrupulous. Bhutroc believed that as arrogant and spoiled his son was, he would never allow him to backstab an ally. The plan was supported by someone who was experienced and somehow gained pertinent information about Karnivron. Bhutroc did not like the idea but like a fair and just leader and father, he listened to his son nevertheless.

According to Naveed's report, Stoldar informed his father and the council that King Mattic evicted Velosp's tribe from its rightful home along the waters of the white river. Naveed had stressed that Karnivron betrayed his tribes by avoiding a full cleansing of the Leemites when the opportunity was given to him. Stoldar did not need to remind the war lords that were present about opportunity. Stoldar continued to tell them that Mattic, the Leemite king, led his forces to Strachan to meet with Karnivron. When the Leemite forces arrived at night, Mattic saw it as an opportunity to murder the Karpretian forces in a surprise attack. Karnivron turned the table on them. Then he spared the Leemite knight in charge there. Further, Karnivron had even converted to their Christian religion. Mara was plunged into cold water and then married Haaron in their holy place.

Petrofar had well advised Stoldar who stressed the ridiculousness of it all. Imagine Karnivron installing his daughter Mara as queen to King Haaron the Leemite. Petrofar questioned why Karnivron would bestow his beautiful, warrior daughter to Haaron. Stoldar was fully aware of whom Haaron was and he did not like the fact that he was awarded Mara. Mara had been intended for him years earlier. A new interest in the desert cousin was kindled in Stoldar. The new interest was like a seed that was planted and nurtured. Stoldar's desire for Mara kept growing.

When Stoldar presented the news to the counsel as Petrofar suggested, despite the eloquence, Bhutroc was upset that his son did not go to him in private first. Stoldar instead continued to attack the sanity of Karnivron's actions. Stoldar used phrases and words that questioned Karnivron's judgments in relation to his age. The criticism that Stoldar directed to Karnivron even made Bhutroc wonder if he was not also referring to him. Bhutroc fit the descriptions of an aging leader, but he gave his son the benefit of the doubt. After all Stoldar had never challenged his father before and despite his arrogance and self-centeredness, he did love his father. The calyph continued to listen, but he did not question the wisdom of his old friend, Karnivron.

"The great Karnivron lost three sons at Strachan and then he relented when the capture of Leems' castle was at hand. He then gave his daughter to them in return for peace. I cannot understand it except that it is time for our desert brothers to seek a new kar that has not gone mad with age," Stoldar professed.

There was a pause in the counsel as Stoldar's words sank in. Stoldar turned to look at his father. The prince favored the idea of taking over the Karpretians and then installing Naveed as their leader who would pay tribute to Beracka. Bhutroc's eyes were firmly planted on his son as he continued to listen.

"Do you think those infidels would have relented against the Karpretians if they had won at Strachan?" Naveed challenged.

Petrofar raised his hand at Naveed to calm and silence his outburst. In truth Petrofar thought that Naveed's emotional appeal was perfectly timed. He had liked Naveed from the beginning. He arrived at a most opportune time. Now Petrofar quickly hatched a scheme that would reveal to him where Naveed's loyalty was placed. He had no doubt that he could trust Naveed and with this deed their fates would be sealed and bonded together forever.

"When my lord is done he may wish to let you speak and we will listen," Petrofar directed at Naveed.

Naveed knew full well that Petrofar was playing to the calyph's court.

"I have said all that I am going to. Let this brother of the steppes speak," Stoldar said.

"What more disaster lies for my brothers on the steppes if this outrage is not avenged?" Naveed appealed full of emotion.

"We here are honored that you have come to inform us of this madness. For ages we have lived with our desert brothers in peace. You were once so proud, you, our Karpretian cousins. Karnivron united your people and gave them sons to keep them strong. Manod, Verganton and Pespitar were testaments to Karpretian strength.

"Now they are all dead. There remains one question. What designs does Haaron have for the other Karpretian tribes? Is he feigning love for Mara to betray her and her people by turning them against each other?" asked Petrofar boldly.

Petrofar spoke as though he were a natural Berackite despite his having joined them not so long ago. He had never been so bold and it concerned Bhutroc. Petrofar's questions were not about getting information as much as making insinuations and leading the council and the people. Petrofar's reference to Mara stirred up emotions in Stoldar. Stoldar now saw himself as the only one who could save the Karpretian tribes and Mara from a fate worse than death. He thought that the former tribes that bowed to Karnivron would now bow to him. He could expand his father's dominion by more than three times and have access to the sea. Then in time Stoldar could get ships too and he would have a trading empire free of Xemaya under the Huynsten heel. His trading empire would be secured by all the Saracens of Beracka and Karpretia so the riches from beyond the east could circumvent going through Xemaya.

Stoldar stood proudly before the calyph's counsel and the assembly of tribe leaders. He had the support of the distinguished Petrofar who gained respect and looked the part of a wise advisor. With him stood the plight driven Naveed from the Karpretian steppes to lend authenticity to his argument. The sheer presence of Petrofar made everyone take note and listen. Naveed's story was also close to home. The three had made quite an impression on the calyph, his counsel, the war lords and the rich Berackite merchants that were present. The proposal of war was most attractive when considering what could be gained. The merchants would gain whether there was immediate success or the war was long and drawn out. The cost in misery brought on by hunger, disease, injury and loss of life were the furthest items on their minds. These items were not even considered.

Calyph Bhutroc, the aged leader, was the only one in power that was not caught up in greed and the dreams of conquest. He was also the last word when it came to deciding whether or not to go to war. Bhutroc was fully aware of what conquest meant. He had ruled his people. Right or wrong, he had ruled his people. Bhutroc was not impressed with the proposed expansion. It seemed too large an endeavor, too quick a time table, and then there was the task of administering the territory that could crumble as easily and as quickly as it came together. Bhutroc's ability to assess the future was not something a father could easily transfer to his son. Knowledge could be transferred but not necessarily experience. Bhutroc knew that an unhappy people with just cause would eventually resist, drag their feet and rebel when you were not looking. It would be another challenge to convince those with lust in their eyes for conquest to believe these hardships. There are challenges in conflicts even when things go to plan. There was never a thought given to the possibility of failure. No party akin to starting a war thinks that they will lose.

Before the council, saracens, merchants and observers, Bhutroc voiced his objection to go running in. Those assembled might not have understood that Karnivron survived Mattic's cunning attack on him at Strachan and it was not due to luck. Bhutroc proposed speaking with Karnivron himself. That is how a neighbor treated a neighbor. Not even the avid aggressors in the council could deny that. It had been too long since Bhutroc and Karnivron last spoke. His people and those of Karnivron had lived in relative peace since the reign of Kartiputh. Bhutroc remembered when the noble Kartiputh gave his daughter and his kingdom to the young Nivron.

All listened as the calyph spoke about the past, his acquaintance with leaders in other lands and what he learned. Unfortunately Bhutroc's wisdom fell on deaf ears. To his rich merchants and advisors, Bhutroc seemed to be reminiscing about old times. Those who favored the conflict listened politely but it was Stoldar's idea that they supported. Peace was a dead deal as the lure of conquest and riches blinded and deafened those in the assembly. There was no respect for the wisdom of years and the many lessons that Bhutroc had amassed in governing his people. When a lesson is forgotten, that lesson is destined to be repeated.

During the calyph's speech, Petrofar came up with a means to assure that there would be a problem. His plan would test the mettle and loyalty of Naveed. Petrofar was certain that Naveed would not disappoint him. The plan was to prevent the great Karnivron from ever meeting with the calyph at all. Petrofar turned his eyes toward Naveed. They seemed to be thinking the same thing. By the end of the council meeting the two met and the plan was confirmed. The plan was to assassinate Karnivron. With the death of Karnivron preceded by his great warrior sons, the former union of Karpretian people would be in disarray. They would be in disarray until his Stoldar united them again. The Karpretians were ripe for the taking as a date laden tree in late, late summer.

In the court of the calyph's palace, Karnivron was portrayed as a feeble old man who lost the lust for conquest. He failed to secure the integrity and safety of his people by not following through on a complete victory over his enemy. They thought that his judgments divided his once loyal tribes. Without the presence of someone to defend Karnivron, the members of the court were apt to believe what was said about him. First on Petrofar's list of course was the death of his master Pespitar. There was no consideration for Pespitar's death, the would-be vizier noted. There was no mourning nor did the murderer get punished. Petrofar however knew the truth.

He also knew that Karnivron was no fool. The installation of Mara as the queen of Leems with Haaron as king had its merit if you were fortifying Leems. Petrofar knew full well that Mara would not give herself to any man, not for a piece of dirt. He knew that she must truly be in love with that Leemite, Haaron. By all accounts Haaron must be in love with the nomadic princess as well. It was of no consequence because Petrofar would not reveal these facts to anyone. The truth did not serve his plans.

In the end Petrofar knew that the Berackite soldiers would do Stoldar's bidding. Stoldar was their proven leader as he kept order and safety in the ranks for his army. Stoldar did not get involved with petty arguments regarding the distribution of goods. When his generals won something there was only one concern for Stoldar. Provided that his father got half tribute, the rest was for his generals to divide amongst themselves. The custom of 'half tribute' was initiated by Karnivron although Stoldar did not know this. The notion that Stoldar did not take a share seemed noble, but he was fully aware that his share would come from his father's portion. Stoldar stepped into his robes of state with ease and commanded the same respect that his father had. Stoldar had earned that respect standing by his wise father to that point.

It was different now however. The path came to a fork in the road. Bhutroc was old and Stoldar made no attempt to stand behind his father's wish. He would not even consider talking to Karnivron. Somehow Stoldar knew that talking to the great warrior would conclude in peace. Besides, Stoldar realized that Bhutroc would one day be dead. There might not ever be a more opportune time to move on his plan. Stoldar was not about to pass up the opportunity to gather the Karpretians to him and take Leems. It was clear to Stoldar that their paths parted but he had no intention of killing his father.

For his part, Naveed did not waste any time. Petrofar sent him on his way back to Leems to carry out an assassination. Karnivron was the target. Petrofar was confident in Naveed and he made him a gift of a special sword to carry out his mission. The sword was truly a special one that was very light and would be of significance to Karnivron. It was the same sword that was given to Daminar by the Shirah of Periforia. Karnivron was in possession of the other identical sword. Petrofar acquired the sword when he killed Daminar and it pleased Naveed that he should be given that sword of significance.

It was understood that the other identical sword be taken from Karnivron upon his demise. Petrofar and Naveed had built an immediate working relationship. Petrofar realized that no one else carried the respect among Karnivron's own saracens like Naveed did. Under the stewardship of Massoud Al Jazeer, Naveed was placed so close to Karnivron that he could not fail. With the death of Karnivron, the Saracens would turn to Naveed's leadership toward Stoldar and in the end, Petrofar's will. Petrofar knew that Naveed was one man that he could count on. It might be risky now that Naveed had left on bad terms but that did not bother him. He would gladly return to execute their plan.

Naveed was a true Saracen of the steppes who could not be motivated by the fear of the yoke, the lash or the sword. Naveed was no serf or shepherd. No means of pain could turn his mind's conviction and he was skilled with the knife, spear and the sword. He had trained and developed under Massoud Al Jazeer. There was only honor to his sworn duty as a Saracen, or death for him. Massoud's reputation was known and revered even in Beracka. He was the mentor and Naveed was his student. All that Naveed needed was a deed worthy enough to give him a reputation and establish his name. Petrofar counted on the assassination of the great Karnivron to do just that.

Uneasy Rest

Back in Leems the news of what happened on the wedding feast of Haaron and Mara got out. It was tragic. Both Leemites and Karpretians alike were sickened by the occurrence, but they could not complain about how the matter was handled. Justice was meted out by Karnivron. The unfortunate loss of Teodore was felt by his colleagues and especially his father Slaaman, but they could ask for nothing more. The man who affected the young knight's death was himself put to death. The Karpretian Saracens who loved Massoud could not argue with what happened. It was their kar who killed Massoud. They knew that Karnivron loved Massoud like a son, but justice was justice. This was one of the bravest and hardest things that Karnivron had to do. Perhaps it was the bravest and hardest thing that he had ever done. It was justice, but it was still hard to swallow. It was taking a toll on the old, wise warrior.

For some reason Karnivron felt uneasy. It was not only with the killing of Massoud. The slaying had proved hard enough but there was something else that he sensed. Somehow he felt a sense of urgency to do all that he could to assure the safety of Mara, Haaron, Leems and his Karpretian people. He realized that fate was working against his wishes. Time was passing faster and faster. He and Daminar had averted threats to his leadership and the governing of the Karpretians before. The earlier challenges were relentless and seemed to continue and compound, but they were child's play now that he looked back. After summoning Mara and Haaron he called Sayed to come forth. He asked Haaron to summon Terence too. Karnivron had the idea to call on a favor bestowed upon him by the Shirah of Periforia.

When all the parties were present Karnivron did not waste any time. He called for Sayed and Terence to travel south through Leems, across the Karpretian steppes and over the mountains to find the paradise of Periforia. The Shirah of Periforia would recognize the fancy sword that Karnivron handed over to Terence. It was one of the swords that Kamalkov gave Nivron and Daminar when they were boys. The swords were a gift for the help that they gave to return Kamalkov to power. The other sword that was given to Daminar was not found after his assassination. It was assumed to be stolen by the killer. Karnivron could easily identify that sword even in the dark. He believed that it would appear in some market, some day. The killer and thief would then be tracked and was sure to be caught and executed when the sword arose one day. It had not yet happened and with everything else that happened, that fact made him uneasy. He had promised himself that he would learn the identity of Daminar's murderer before he died. Compared to what he faced in keeping his people united, solving the murder of Daminar was not the foremost priority but seemed to occupy his thought. Karnivron did want Daminar's sword returned to him. The sword belonged to the man that stuck closer than a brother.

Since Sayed and Terence were being sent to Periforia, Karnivron prepared them especially for the hardships that they would encounter on their journey to Periforia. Karnivron remembered the mountain cats and the Osarkane Desert. Karnivron planned to send an escort to protect the two knights as they faced the perils climbing the mountain. The escort would see them to the crest of the mountain. Then this time they would be given camels and plenty of water to cross the desert. The two knights that Karnivron was sending would not have to repeat the foolish mistakes that Daminar and he had made many years ago. The sword that they possessed would be their admission into the Shirah's Court. The members of the shirah's guard would recognize that the sword was forged there in the secret furnaces of Periforia.

Haaron turned to Mara and told her that they should send a messenger to Brandyn at Wendover and Karnivron agreed. Haaron would send Blakeney across the sea to Rothaynen. There he would find Brandyn at Wendover. He could check on the Leemites that fled Leems and welcome them back to the new order there. With the help of Brandyn Blakeney would get an introduction to King Graedon. With Brandyn's help they could speak to Graedon about the imminent threat of the Huynstens. Rothaynen remembered the near invasion on their soil. It should be clear now that Graedon should send help abroad to thwart Huynsten success there. With the experience on the battlefield provided by knights, archers and an army from Rothaynen, the Leemites could hold the Huynsten advance on the plains of Leems. Haaron was sure that King Graedon understood that a decisive set back to the Huynsten advance in Leems could very well prevent them from attacking him at Wendover again. Of course if Leems fell, then Graedon could count the days when Huynsten ships, their knights, archers and army would again threaten Rothaynen.

With any luck, Haaron thought that the Huynstens would not attack before spring. Brandyn had told him about the Huynsten attack at Wendover when he was in Leems. Rothaynen was a possible target but it was more likely that the threat would come to Leems first. By spring the Huynstens could prepare their army for a full assault against Leems and catch the farmers busy with seeding. With the condition of the sea in spring the Huynstens would put their navy in the offensive. Haaron was certain that the Huynstens would wait for spring. He was also sure that the news of what happened at Strachan would spread by caravan traders and encourage the Huynstens to make Leems their next target. Haaron believed that if he were a Huynsten general he would attack Leems by land and use the navy to bottle up Port Comley. By landing more and more new troops he would surround the prize. That was exactly what he would do. There was still hope however if he could rally the help of friends. Haaron counted on his friendship with Brandyn to convince King Graedon to act.

After meeting with Graedon in Rothaynen, Blakeney would then travel on with Brandyn to Craigroyston. There they would join Arno to support his effort to inform them of the peril that Leems faced. If successful, Arno, Brandyn and Terence would be escorted back to Leems via a warship. On that day Haaron would know that he had a reliable ally with a navy. The navy of Craigroyston was the only way to keep the sea friendly. Without Craigroyston's navy the Huynstens could land men and weapons at will from the north shore and continue their offensive from the vulnerable south. It would be a matter of time before Kilkenny Castle was stormed with an overwhelming offensive.

There was not a moment to lose. Blakeney was swiftly sent on his way with two young knights to accompany him. Crossing over the rough waters to get to Mead would be difficult in winter. It was even more perilous in a small ship. Apart from the dangers on the high sea, the cold weather and wind could team up to make a man weary and put him to sleep. Then he would freeze to death. Although the trip was riskier in winter out in the cold, it was not impossible. The crossing would however be pleasant for Terence and his cohorts compared to the challenge that awaited him at Rothaynen. They were not aware of the events that took place at Braemar Castle.

Karnivron Meets His End

With Karnivron's plan in motion for Sayed and Terence to secure help from the Shirah of Periforia and with Blakeney and Willem sent to Rothaynen and Craigroyston, there remained a glimmer of hope for the survival of Leems and the Karpretian Steppes. It dawned on Karnivron that he should send word to Bhutroc the Calyph of Beracka with regards to the impending Huynsten threat and what had transpired in Leems. Karnivron was sure that Bhutroc already knew about it. He was calyph in Beracka for a long, long time. Bhutroc was aware of the Huynstens and would have made preparations for any threat. There was great respect among the two leaders. Regardless of who approached whom first, Karnivron sent the young Ahmed ahead with a small escort party to reach out to the Berackite leader. These were the acts of a wise and considerate neighbor.

Karnivron believed that it was time to initiate an official alliance with the Berackites against the Huynsten threat. If they remained divided, the Huynstens could pick them off like figs on a tree. Together they would be more formidable against the enemy. Karnivron also planned to travel to Beracka to talk to his old desert cousin in person. Not too long ago the two peoples could have been linked by the marriage of Mara to Stoldar. The espousal parties were not enthusiastic and there was no imminent threat from other neighbors so it passed and was almost forgotten. The mere meeting of Karnivron and Bhutroc was enough to assure each other that wisdom prevailed. Presently Karnivron reasoned that it was better to have an alliance in place before hostilities started.

With an established alliance, all parties concerned would know their duty and could respond accordingly. A plan of attack or defense in this case could be drawn up to avoid confusion. The preliminary meeting could be done and out of the way. Karpretians, Leemites and Berackites needed to come together now to stand up against tyranny. Karnivron saw the larger picture above the petty squabbles of ethnic tribes. Even among his people there were differences over a barley loaf. Once you drew a line in the dirt, the person on the other side was a competitor.

It was so childish in Karnivron's opinion. Many good men were lost due to these disagreements that were a matter of honor over a trifle.

Just when it seemed that everything that could be done had been done, Naveed Al Bhutan returned. Fellow Saracen knights called his name as others looked to see if it was true. It was true. Naveed had returned. He was calm and appeared penitent. He received the welcome of a brother who went astray but gained the sense to return home to his father. The Saracen knight rode to the great tent. He jumped down off Animanera, his horse and was greeted by his colleagues. Karnivron was aware that he returned. He grabbed a sword in its scabbard and went out to see him. Naveed got down on his knees before him and remained silent. It pleased and lifted Karnivron's spirit to see him return. Naveed was a son of the steppes.

Karnivron did not know where Naveed had wandered as a week passed since the fateful wedding night. After he greeted him he did not ask him. The assumption was that Naveed rode back to the steppes and took some time to think and get over the grief of losing Massoud. When Naveed left Karnivron in anger, he had no provisions so he must have spent his time in thought and scrounging for food and water. In fact Naveed rode back with his former clothing that weathered the trip to and from Beracka. Along the way on the return trip Naveed did not wash so he would look dusty and dirty.

After Naveed washed up his face, feet and hands, he was offered food in the tent of Karnivron. The Saracen guards were happy and smiled when they saw Naveed enter the kar's tent. They assumed that the rift between them over the execution of Massoud was reconciled. Foremost, Naveed's behavior was understandable and quickly pardoned. Naveed entered the tent and he did partake in the hospitality of his kar. Karnivron was interested with Naveed's thoughts. With all the distance that Naveed had covered, he was much too tired from his journey. Instead Naveed asked if he could be excused to get some sleep. Looking at his tired visage it was understandable and he was excused to go sleep. Naveed bided his time however as he waited for the night. With no one suspicious of him, Naveed would carry out his plan that very day at nightfall. The sooner he killed Karnivron the better. Then in full flight he would ride off to join his newly placed allegiance in Petrofar and serving Stoldar.

Naveed did not have to feign fatigue. He was tired and let alone to sleep in his own tent that was nearby. Before he retired for rest he went to draw some water from the large jars outside the guards' tent. He managed to put some fine powder into all the water jugs without being noticed. Then he entered his tent and slept the rest of the evening as the sun fell. His fellow Saracens thought that he would sleep well into noon the next day. By nightfall though Naveed awoke and was ready to kill the lord of his people. The night had come. Naveed knew that it would not be easy. Karnivron was a wise leader. Sometimes he did not sleep easily. Being leader of the Karpretian tribes was not as easy as it looked on the surface. You were given great power to have your will carried out, but only if you were successful with the decisions that you made. The people needed to agree and more importantly your army and warriors needed to agree. Sometimes the concern over this was enough to interrupt your sleep.

Karnivron had nothing but stress since the loss of Daminar, the loss of his beloved sons and his entry into Leems. He was struggling to keep his people united and free. The effect of King Mattic's ruling against Velosp's tribe had repercussions that forced him to take action. There were some Karpretians that still thought that they should remove the Leemites entirely. Recently though the incident that took place at the wedding reception of his daughter to Haaron was the most serious setback to unity. Between Haaron and Karnivron they had sent out emissaries to Rothaynen, Craigroyston, Periforia and Beracka. All that could be done was done. All that there was left to do was sleep and get rest. Tonight with the return of Naveed to the fold, a lost son in Karnivron's eyes, the kar could finally get some measure of restful sleep.

It was not long after dark when most of the encampment was at rest apart from the watchmen, when Naveed struck. There was a strange orange haze around the moon that night. During the day the Saracen guard had drank of the water in the jugs that Naveed tampered with.

These Saracens fell into a deep sleep. The watchmen drank of the water in the jugs as well. They were unusually drowsy. They were not prepared for what sleek execution that Naveed had planned. Naveed went out to saddle the well-rested Animanera with some water skins and provisions for a quick escape.

After his restful sleep he bathed in oil and perfumes and dressed into his best black ceremonial robes. Under his robes he carried the special sword that was given to him by Petrofar. Naveed then walked out of his tent with confidence. He made his way back Karnivron's tent and made his way into the inner chamber wherein lay the kar. Naveed was swift and silent. A few of Karnivron's concubines who slept alongside him were fast asleep. Ever so gentle and light-footed did Naveed move gracefully toward the kar. The ground was ready to scream if he trod heavy. The assassin made his way onto the large mattress and was careful not to disturb it or those who dwelt on it. Everyone seemed to be in a deep, innocent sleep. Naveed moved closer and closer to his intended victim.

When Naveed got close enough he crouched down before the sleeping Karnivron and looked at him. Naveed's angry countenance gave way for a cynical smile. He looked mad. Naveed retrieved his dagger from its brass housing. Then Naveed drew the special sword that Petrofar gave him from its scabbard for this purpose. He had wanted Karnivron's eyes opened so that he could see who it was, but nothing must compromise a sure and safe escape. Naveed held onto the dagger with all his might. If Karnivron resisted while he slit his throat, Naveed would cover his mouth and repeatedly thrust it through his heart.

Naveed then slit Karnivron's throat. The wounded man could not move as he gasped and swallowed. This was the sensation of drowning that Karnivron experienced in his dreams. Only this was not a dream. Naveed then sprung to his feet and to assure his success in the mission, he thrust the special ornate sword into Karnivron's chest. The effort he put on the sword was more than he needed to run through the great man. With one gash the sleek sword penetrated through the ribs and scraped the man's spine. With one gash, Naveed accomplished the task that would make way for him to assume leadership of Karpretia. With one gash he had avenged his mentor and attained satisfaction for himself.

Karnivron opened his eyes. He could not speak due to the gash in his throat but he recognized the sword that was impaled in him. It was the same as the sword he handed to Sayed and Terence. But surely, he thought, it was not that same sword. Finally, he realized that he would learn who assassinated Daminar. Karnivron saw a dark figure as blood flowed from his throat. He tried to swallow but it was no use. He needed a little more time to collect himself. However, time waits for no one. He began to rationalize. Naveed had returned and this was the reason that he returned. Where had he been and who did he speak to?

How did he get that sword?

The warning signs were there and Karnivron had read them. He had foreseen this moment and had been uneasy about it. All those years of suddenly awakening because he felt like he was drowning in the night. Now blood flowed from his throat and it felt like he was drowning. Many times he had such a dream and awoke in a sweat. He had recounted the dream to Daminar who comforted him. Daminar told him that 'under his watch he should fear nothing'. Daminar had kept his word to him. Daminar however was dead, he himself was the victim of an assassin in the night. In the dark Karnivron could not make out who it was for sure. He would have fought despite the loss of blood but he could not move. He lay there and imagined who it might be. He knew that he was mistaken about Naveed when he returned to them. In his mind he could not imagine anyone else. It became easier for him to slip back into a weary sleep. Then the assassin spoke softly and Karnivron learned the identity of his killer for sure. He was right about Naveed, but failed to act when he could.

"It is your time to die now," Naveed professed, "Petrofar wanted me to give you this sword, but since you will not need it anymore, I will take it."

Naveed withdrew the sword from the fatally wounded man. Karnivron had finally learned the true identity of Daminar's murderer. It was Petrofar. Now he lay dying himself. The sword that was used was the same one that killed Daminar. He thought about the two swords that were received as gracious gifts from a noble friend. One of the swords had spilled both Daminar and his own blood. Under the circumstances it was a pointless observation.

In an escape that rivaled Petrofar's escape from the slaying of Daminar, Naveed was able to walk out of the tent virtually undetected. He marched with confidence and purpose to his black steed that awaited him. Of Naveed's departure it could be said that he disappeared. All that could be heard was the sound of his horse's hooves that blended with the sleepy heartbeats of those at rest in their tents. Animanera pounded the ground swiftly and faded out into the night. The watchmen were in a weary trance. They assumed that the sound that they heard was one of their own messengers going on an errand.

The Young Emissary

Due to Naveed's desire to be well away and return to Beracka as soon as possible, he traveled with haste through to the dawn. In the early morning, he caught up to Ahmed at Strachan. It was the small escort that was sent for an audience with Calyph Bhutroc in Beracka. Naveed was finely dressed and took advantage of this opportunity. He took special care not to make his newly acquired sword noticeable. Naveed knew that Petrofar would wish him to spy on them. He also needed more water and food supplies for the remainder of the trip. The rest of Ahmed's diplomatic party would soon awake to resume their travel to Beracka. Naveed told Ahmed that there was a personal message that Karnivron wanted to add for the calyph. He told them that Karnivron insisted that he dress in his finest and join the delegation. Since it was Naveed who came and he was highly revered, there was little suspicion in the mind of the Karpretian emissary or his escorts. In fact they were all happy to see that Naveed had returned to them. Ahmed was happy that Karnivron forgave Naveed and that he still had confidence in him.

Naveed knew that he would be safer the farther that he got away. Though he could not ask them to pull stakes and ride any quicker without arousing suspicion, he got a little rest. Animanera appreciated the rest. A few hours later in the early sunrise, Naveed was the first to wake everyone for the journey ahead. Thus far no riders and news came from Leems. Karnivron's encampment must have been a cacophony of confusion as the kar's dead body was discovered. The Saracen guards were all influenced by Naveed's concoction that left them groggy. No doubt, one of Karnivron's concubines would be first to discover him lying in a pool of his own blood. Haaron and Mara would be notified by now and who knows what they would do. After their questioning, there would be no doubt in their mind as to who killed Karnivron.

Naveed was sure that Petrofar did not want this meeting between the calyph and Karnivron's emissary to take place. It was clear in his mind what he would do. They were about to leave Leems and enter the steppes. Naveed would use the ruse of the diplomatic mission until he figured out what to do. Even now if someone came to inform them of Karnivron's murder, Naveed could feign grief. Then he could claim that Karnivron sent him along with a 'personal message' for Bhutroc. With regards to this personal message, Naveed would have to make something up and he did. He would declare that the special sword he carried was to be a gift for Bhutroc. If worse came to worse Naveed would hack at them and ride away on Animanera.

Naveed decided that once they left the land of Leems and entered the Karpretian Steppes, it would be safer for him. It would be a matter of time before Haaron and Mara would call for the apprehension of Naveed. His luck would have to hold up until they got closer to Beracka. Before the diplomatic party got to Beracka though, Naveed would kill them all and hide their bodies. Then Ahmed and his escort party could not deliver Karnivron's message. In fact they would be heard from no more. He was sure that Petrofar would approve.

As the diplomatic party pressed on, opportunities to kill them did not present themselves. Killing Karnivron's emissary and escort was easier proposed than done. For one there were five persons to kill. Ahmed was a careful man who kept two people awake and on watch for the night. On top of that Ahmed hardly ever slept himself. He was that last line of defense in case someone else faltered at their post. Naveed discovered that Ahmed did not need to sleep much in that regard he was like Massoud Al Jazeer. It was too bad Naveed used all the sleep powder to assure his success in Karnivron's tent. He might have put Ahmed's sleepless ways to the test. On the second night of camp as the party was well out of the land of Leems, Naveed awoke and scouted the two watchmen. Out of nowhere, Ahmed approached Naveed to ask him whether he had trouble falling asleep. Naveed was surprised by Ahmed. He realized it would be extremely risky to affect the murder of Karnivron's diplomatic party. It would be better for now to secure his own credibility and be a part of the company. At least Naveed could put his head down to sleep with confidence. So he did.

The Approach to Beracka

Naveed had not yet succeeded in his plan to kill Karnivron's diplomatic party. The steppes of Ranamacora were nearly crossed. Soon they would enter the foothills of Beracka and no opportunity worth the risk presented itself. Naveed was daring and had not in the least lost his nerve, but to ambush Ahmed and his men would be madness. As the diplomatic party approached the lowlands at the foot of the mountain leading to Beracka, they were spotted by the keen watchmen of Beracka. A party of riders came out to meet the strangers that approached their lands. At once Naveed was recognized but he made no effort to greet the riders. Mammoud the head rider made no effort to acknowledge Naveed either. Naveed merely communicated using his eyes. The careful Saracen thought that there must be some reason that Naveed did not greet him.

After Ahmed explained their purpose, Mammoud asked him to follow his lead up the mountain trail. Mammoud rode ahead with Ahmed at his side followed by a few Berackite Saracens. Naveed and the Karpretian escort followed them and at following them were the rest of the Berackite Saracens. Naveed thought that if he could get word to Mammoud about the opportunity at hand, they could do away with the party of diplomats from Karnivron and no one would ever know about them. As they rode upward toward the summit of the mountain, Naveed rode on to speak to Mammoud. He caught up to him as Ahmed was concentrating on the ascent up the mountain. Mammoud rode ahead slightly and Naveed followed. Naveed started talking as though what he had to say was for public record.

"My lord Karnivron has sent me with a personal message for Stoldar," Naveed started.

Naveed pulled ahead and continued to ride with purpose. Mammoud followed. When Naveed was sure not to be overheard, he told him.

"Listen carefully," Naveed said quietly, "it is the wish of Stoldar that this party of men does not speak with Bhutroc."

"Then they shall not speak to anyone," assured Mammoud.

Mammoud was loyal to Stoldar and answered to Petrofar. He had been fully made aware of Naveed. Mammoud was ready to do what had to be done. It was an excellent place to silence the diplomatic party of riders. Each could be chased off the mountainside and meet their doom crashing against the mountain side and the firm rock waiting below. The carrion that flew in the sky would clean up the rest. At that moment there came the sound of horses approaching from the mountain top. Mammoud noted that they were led by Ayden, a young captain who was fiercely loyal to Bhutroc. Mammoud felt that it was not a good time to dispense with the diplomats.

"Hold your horse. It is not a good time," whispered Mammoud.

"If not now, when?" wondered Naveed?

Naveed fell back into the ranks with Ahmed. Ahmed was not sure that he felt safe among Mammoud's men. He had an uneasy feeling.

"We must be careful Naveed. I do not trust this escort party. Something is not right," warned Ahmed.

"You are so right," replied Naveed.

At that instance Naveed rode his horse into Ahmed's toward the cliff. Naveed drew the sword that he used to assassinate Karnivron and swung it at Ahmed's face. As Ahmed's horse bucked, the full sword hack just managed to scratch his face. The Karpretian escort drew their swords to come to Ahmed's aid. Naveed forced Animanera against Ahmed's horse. Ahmed was thrown with his horse over the cliff as the animal struggled to establish a firm footing. Ahmed's scream could be heard descending until it was heard no more. With the attack on Ahmed, the Karpretian escort attacked Naveed. Before they could bring harm to Naveed they were cut down from behind by Mammoud's palace guards. From the mountain it clearly looked like a case of self defense. Naveed was grateful to the Berackite Saracens for saving his life. At that instant the palace guards that were on maneuver arrived to investigate what had happened. Ayden, their captain, observed the attack and wondered how it came about.

Since Mammoud was in charge of his patrol, he was quick to report.

"When we saw the travelers approach the road. We descended as a matter of routine. When the foreign riders approached closer on the mountain path, they turned on Naveed Al Bhutan and tried to ride him off the cliff.

"Without warning they turned on Naveed Al Bhutan so we intervened on his behalf, since he is in favor with our lord Stoldar," concluded Mammoud.

With the drawn swords, the slain Karpretian escorts and Mammoud's explanation, Ayden still wondered what had happened. It was a choppy story.

Naveed interjected, "I owe you my life, Mammoud. If it were not for your swift action and that of your men, it should be my body that lay at the bottom of the mountain."

"You knew these men?" inquired Ayden.

Naveed explained, "I was familiar with Ahmed, the one who tried to kill me. The others I never saw before.

"I had returned to speak to Karnivron as Bhutroc had willed. Shortly after leaving Karnivron's tent, I was joined by Ahmed and these other men en route to Beracka.

"Ahmed claimed that Karnivron sent them to escort me. It is clear to me now that these escorts were sent to assassinate me to prevent the meeting with the calyph.

"There is much unrest among my people and leaders as this incident clearly attests, but the calyph should hear Karnivron's message of brotherhood!"

Ayden thought that the situation was ironic. A message of brotherhood and his own people tried to kill the messenger. Still things did not seem right in Ayden's mind. There was plenty of opportunity for five men to murder one man. Why would they wait until they were on Berackite lands to murder the messenger?

Ayden ordered members of his palace guard to escort Naveed directly to the palace. Before Naveed left with the palace guard, he looked at Mammoud who understood that he was to report what happened and all details to Petrofar, immediately. Mammoud did not waste any time. Ayden however waited until they all left and then sent other men down the mountain to investigate the man that was forced off the mountain. This Ahmed might have something on his person that could shed light on the situation.

Preparing for the Calyph's Court

With Mammoud reporting the return of Naveed, Petrofar was certain that Karnivron was dead. Petrofar went to see Stoldar. The priority now was to intercede on Naveed's behalf if matters did not go well with the calyph after he learned what happened. It would not take long for the calyph to put the pieces together. Petrofar now felt that Stoldar would have to push for a war on the Leemite Kingdom despite his father's objection. Petrofar recapped the facts for Stoldar. He told him that Leems had a weakened army under Haaron and Mara's rule. The Leemites were no longer the strategic threat that they once were and depended on Karpretian riders. Despite the Leemites skill at war, their numbers were cut down significantly. As far as the Karpretian tribes that were in Leems, Petrofar was sure that they would turn to follow the leadership of Naveed Al Bhutan if Stoldar backed him. The Karpretians would not go against a strong Berackite army on behalf of a Leemite king. Petrofar also told him to stress the attempt that was made on Naveed's life after the demise of Massoud Al Jazeer. Stoldar was to stress that the Karpretians were breaking up into warring factions.

With the authenticity of Naveed's report, Petrofar believed that attacking Leems did not pose a risk to the Berackite forces. He knew that the Leemites were not invincible, not now anyway. If Stoldar committed all his resources into the conquest of Leems, he thought that the matter would be over quickly with little bloodshed. Petrofar convinced Stoldar to take Leems and to take into his bosom the Karpretian tribes. United they would become stronger and could expand their influence. Petrofar advised Stoldar to invade across the Karpretian Steppes into Leems. If they acted now, they could crush any resistance one tribe at a time. With the people they acquired from such a conquest, it would increase the Berackite numbers. The experienced horsemanship of the Karpretian tribes, their swift mobility and accurate archers on horseback would only add to the Berackite arsenal.

The acquisition of such good warriors would strengthen Berackite might should the Huynstens have designs on them. The Huynsten army would be frustrated when they moved their army across the steppes from place to place with no result. The steppes would force long supply lines for the Huynstens. Meanwhile the Berackites, with the help of the Karpretian riders, could move their army about at will and administer offensive lightening strikes at will. These strikes would frustrate and demoralize the enemy.

"My lord, do you not want your lands to touch the sea? If you let the Huynstens take Leems, you will never be able to expand your trade influence toward the sea. They will hem you in and then eventually they will come after you.

"Look at what the Huynstens did to the Xemayan traders who resisted them? Solman, Ayaar, Dagmir: all established sheiks of business that traded with our Berackite merchants. Where are they now? Holding Leems is the key to our survival," Petrofar fueled with rhetoric.

A Juggernaut Rests

While Haaron sent a message for Brandyn at Galles via his young knights Blakeney and Willem. Time was passing and there was no way to find out whether their mission to get help from King Graedon was successful. It was urgent that Leems received help. The Huynsten penetration into the Great Continent halted after the scourging of the Xemayan merchants and annihilation of the tribe at Kirma Superior. The mountain brothers had resisted the Huynstens and came to the aid of their fellow tribe at Kirma Inferior. Inferior and superior referred to where they lived: the Kirmans that lived in the fertile valley were 'inferior', and the Kirmans that lived in the higher lands and mountains were 'superior'. The nomination referred to the elevation of land that they inhabited. Regardless, the Kirmans in Kirma Superior were no more as they were either killed in battle or impaled on stakes. Originally the act of impaling on stakes was a Kirman method of warfare designed to take away the desire of their enemies to make war on them. It was a gory display heightened by the human anguish it brought to the victims. The method was effectively used by the Kirmans for many, many years. The Huynstens collected these methods from the cultures they conquered and absorbed and made them their own.

In fact the only Kirmans left were those in the fertile valley of Kirma Inferior but they were sold into slavery. The Huynstens were aware that people were proud of their culture and even after a while they would resist their captors and turn to nationalistic notions. However when slaves were separated from their families and distributed to other regions far from their home, then the matter of culture was a distant second to survival. The only people who knew what it was like to be taken from their family and sold into slavery were those who experienced the ordeal.

In the early campaign against the Kirmans, the Huynstens were not successful. Where the Huynstens marched in with great numbers they were invincible, but when and where they least expected, the Kirmans would ambush a selected few and leave them impaled alive. Ponty, the Huynsten general ordered his impaled men put to death if not already

433

dead. He wanted to end their suffering and keep their abominable condition from wreaking issues with the fighting warriors. In Ponty's mind, a wounded man that was not killed by the enemy was a constant reminder of what could happen. The dead man, he reasoned, called for vengeance, so he much preferred his warriors victorious or dead. Ponty had been an astute student of Nodunn himself.

In the mean time Nodunn had been a quick study. This time he listened to his advisor who agreed with his generals. In the previous year, the generals were against invading Wendover and the Great Continent past the city of Xemaya at the same time. The act spread the forces too thin with a narrow supply line and competition for the supplies. It gave the Xemayan merchants the confidence to oppose Huynsten rule and they did.

With the failed attack on Wendover, the Huynstens redoubled their efforts on the Great Continent and reestablished their rule. Their savage strategy against the Xemayan merchants was very effective. Nodunn could have sailed his forces up the river to Xemaya, but instead decided to procure a show of power. The new Huynsten army marched from the coast into Xemaya and seized delinquent merchants and burned property along the way. They left a path of destruction from the coast all the way to Tirmiz, Xemaya's trade city. For days the citizens of Xemaya could see them coming and do nothing. Reports of their advent struck terror into the people of Xemaya. Those who resisted along the way were put to death. The influential merchants who bought mercenaries to do battle against the Huynstens perished like their money. So did the mercenaries who escaped by riding out of Xemaya.

The Huynstens had a good sense for commerce. The former servants of these Xemayan merchants were made the new masters. The Huynsten army was sure that the fear of what they saw would keep them honest about the payment of taxes and tribute to Nodunn. The same army was sent to reinforce the ailing Huynsten army in Kirma. However instead of marching or sailing back to the coast and joining their comrades from the sea coast, they climbed over from the mountains. The Kirman Superiors were surprised in the middle of winter when no enemy had ever before tread on their soil in winter or summer. It ended in savagery. The snow covered mountain was stained red with the blood of the mountain brothers. They would never conduct anymore raids on the Huynsten plans for the fertile Kirma Inferior ever again.

The Huynstens had the Great Continent of Tamerana by the throat with numerous points of entry. With division and unrest among the inhabitants of the Great Continent, penetrating deeper to acquire the Berackite city of trade was the next logical step. The Karpretians were of no consequence as they kept to the steppes and moved about freely. The Huynsten influence encompassed the fresh-water ways that every person needed to survive. Anyone needing water would have to come to them sooner or later. When they did, they would be subject to Huynsten law and taxes. The Berackites however were situated at the source of the water stream. They did not need to come down off their mountain for fresh water. As a matter of fact the Berackites could divert the water and dry up the hopes of an enemy bent on conquest who relied on the water from their stream. Ponty was fully aware that the conquest of Beracka would not be as easy as the slaughter of the Kirmans of the mountain. The Berackite numbers were greater, they were prepared and had water. So Ponty sent word back to Nodunn of his accomplishments and plenty of tribute and the taxes.

The great Huynsten general planned to use the rest of the winter to prepare his men for a spring assault on Beracka. The assault would come from two places. The Huynsten host would assemble at the foot of the mountains, as expected, and from the mountain passes where the former mountain Kirmans resided. From there it would not be expected. Ponty would take Beracka first. After establishing himself in Beracka, he would strike out at Leems. To attack Leems, Ponty stressed to Nodunn that he would need the Huynsten Navy to bottle up Port Comley. From there they could land men to attack Kilkenny Castle from the sea to the north. It would be tempting to go after the many tribes of the steppes but that would be a costly error. Ponty had a strategy about the Bedouin tribes. He would avoid the Karpretian tribes unless they attacked him to fight on his terms.

Ponty figured that when he marched his columns across the steppes to Strachan, the tribes of the steppes would not dare attack him. There was no reason for the Karpretians to attack him. Furthermore if history held true there was no way that the Karpretian strength on horseback could be harnessed by their neighbors. The Nomadic tribes fought each other like savages often killing for the sake of killing. Ponty believed that when he arrives at Strachan in south Leems, the Leemite forces would be divided between defending Kilkenny Castle and Strachan. It would be a short matter of time before fatigue would make the Leemite forces collapse. Nodunn had full confidence in his general and could see Ponty's design. It was ambitious, careful and could not possibly fail. It was approved immediately by Nodunn's councilors as well. In Merkor the council agreed that Ponty certainly seemed to be the warrior to watch. King Nodunn was reminded of his own rise to power.

Leems Calls

Haaron had sent Blakeney and Willem with an urgent message to Rothaynen. He had hoped to secure Brandyn's intercession with King Graedon. He had hoped that Brandyn would impress the importance for Rothaynen's knights and army to come to the aid of Leems. Haaron gave word to Blakeney that Martov and Cambryn, the Leemite knights sent to look after Leemite settlers in Rothaynen, should return immediately to Leems with as many volunteers as possible. Leems would need all the experienced knights that it could muster together.

The Leemites that settled in north Wendover however were not willing to return to Leems to fight. They had gone through quite enough with reestablishing themselves in this new land. The idea of returning to fight and die was not appealing to them at all. Those in Rothaynen whose hunting grounds the Leemites disturbed would not have minded them leaving, but now they were a part of the scenery. Woodcroftston was almost a formal village. Soon it would be recognized by the king himself. The efforts of Brandyn, Martov and Cambryn would also be recognized.

Soon the tenants of Woodcroftston would pay taxes to their landlord and that was alright with them provided they had peace and enough food so they could raise their families in safety. The two brothers of Bendire were aware that the Leemites did not have to pay taxes to Graedon. Woodcroftston was built on church land. The decisions about taxing the new Leemite community would be at the discretion of the Cardinal. The two monks were not yet aware that Cardinal Spehar was killed in the attack on Braemar Castle, let alone the death of King Graedon. With humble backgrounds the two religious leaders felt that they would answer for the accounting on the taxes when the request was made. For the time being they told no one of their plan for the taxes.

Polito and Carluce did not mention the ownership of the land to anyone. It was church land and it was used to provide food and shelter for the children of God. It did not matter that they were from another part of the Aerde. In the mean time the two brothers of Bendire Monastery collected a tithe from the new residents. The tithe was not sent to the

Cardinal's treasury. Instead the tithes collected were redistributed to the needy people in the same community. The two Bendire monks kept precise record of the collection and disbursement of the funds. Polito and Carluce had a great deal of faith in people. The farmers of New Leems trusted them because of the service they provided in caring for their children and them when they first arrived. Polito and Carluce had earned their respect and place in Wendover and Woodcroftston.

Haaron needed the help of Craigroyston's navy to keep the Huynsten navy at bay. In his mind, if Huynsten forces were denied landing at Port Comley, then the combined Leemite, Karpretian and Berackite land forces would stand the best chance possible in resisting the Huynsten land force. It was up to Ahmed to convince Bhutroc to fight with Leems and Karpretia. It would be up to Blakeney, Willem and Brandyn to convince King Graedon to send his forces. Then they would have to turn to Craigroyston to convince the monarchs there to help. Haaron did not know that King Jonquis had died. He knew that his sister Queen Ellen of Leems and her advisors would not have kind things to say about him at their court. It would be up to Arno to speak the truth. If Brandyn, a party to Rothaynen, accompanied Blakeney and Willem to make his case it would lend credibility to their side of the story. Haaron believed that telling the truth would be enough. Since the Huynstens were a threat to Craigroyston's commerce ships, it was a good reason to intervene on the Aggregian Sea.

An Early Challenge

With the advent of Naveed Al Bhutan in Beracka and the rabble rousing of Petrofar, the passive Stoldar was stirred to a serious point of ownership. In his argument Petrofar portrayed Mara as Stoldar's property that ended up in an infidel's hands. Petrofar reminded Stoldar that Mara was the daughter of the great Karnivron. Her blood was royal blood. Mara was a descendant of the kar's of Karpretia even before Karnivron himself. Karnivron had only outnumbered Mara's grandfather who gave his daughter, her mother, to the warlord. To add to the blasphemy, Naveed told Stoldar that it was Haaron who killed Massoud Al Jazeer, not Karnivron. Naveed told Petrofar the truth earlier and neither of them batted an eyelash at the lie. Stoldar knew who the great Saracen was. He distinctly remembered the look that he and Massoud exchanged when Mara was brought to the desert oasis on Berackite land. Mara was brought to meet her intended husband. Stoldar remembered what respect Karnivron and his vizier Daminar commanded. He also remembered what a big shadow the great Massoud Al Jazeer cast. Massoud frowned seriously, but that day the look in his angry eyes was directed toward Stoldar. Now he knew the reason. It was because of his love for Mara.

At that time Stoldar was not excited about the idea of marriage to Mara. Stoldar had for himself a harem of his own with the youngest, most beautiful girls in all Beracka. He further enjoyed the finest women that could be bought from the eastern merchants who traded with his father. Mara was desirable but in the end only 'one' girl. Stoldar would have to go to the trouble of marrying her. She had already been married to the ugly Fahd whose reputation for being loud and boisterous preceded him. Mara was not Stoldar's idea of a dream girl at 12 years old, but now she was an attractive commodity. Now that she was in the hands of the Leemite knight of legend, she became more valuable and desirable. Stoldar had not seen the young girl mature into the woman that she became.

The most skilled tribe leaders of Karnivron's Union were dead. It was hard to believe that the great Manod was defeated. By Manod's sheer size, let alone resolve, he could outlast any man in battle. Verganton with the inherent skills of his grandfather Benbarte was a skilled warrior. Verganton carried out lightening strikes with his riders, the 'thunder of the plains', but he perished as well. Pespitar, despite his guile, cunning and sinister self-absorption, had good qualities of leadership. According to the beliefs of Petrofar, he was betrayed by one of his own brethren. Petrofar, though he knew the truth, never told the Calyph of Beracka all the circumstances behind the death of Pespitar. If he told Bhutroc that Mara killed him, he would naturally ask more questions. Petrofar merely professed to the calyph that Pespitar was betrayed by a member of his own brethren. Petrofar told the court of the calyph that after Pespitar's death, he feared for his life due to his loyalty to his slain master. That was why Petrofar fled the Karpretian tribes and made his way to the calyph's court in Beracka.

The finest Karpretian leaders met their death at the hands of the Leemite knight named Haaron. If Stoldar swept in and defeated the Leemites, killed Haaron and married Mara, he could be calyph over a territory four times greater than his father could leave him. This was an opportunity worth the risk. His kingdom would stretch from Beracka in the mountains, across the steppes of Ranamacora through Karpretia, and extend all the way through Leems to the sea. Trade with Xemaya could be circumvented altogether. He thought of the increased population that he would rule. Stoldar would take a lesson from Karnivron and allow the different people to keep their customs and their gods so long as he came first in their minds.

The Calyphs' Court

No one could have imagined the events that were about to take place in the court of the Calyph of Beracka. Bhutroc had always commanded respect and obedience from all his countrymen. Stoldar entered the chamber with Petrofar and Naveed who followed like advisors. Patient and wise, Bhutroc allowed his son to speak and address the assembly in the throne room. Stoldar for his part repeated the story and facts and made an excellent case. His proposal was to save the Karpretians and expand their territory while they were at it. Bhutroc may have been old but he was wise. He trusted his son implicitly but he could see that he was being influenced by other forces. The other forces were present and relishing the conquest of the moment while looking humble and dutiful. When Stoldar was finished, the calyph asked for Naveed to come before him. There was a silence and Naveed stood still for a moment. Bhutroc waited patiently as Naveed rose and approached the landing before the throne. Bhutroc looked at him. Petrofar was concerned.

"Are you aware that the great Karnivron is dead?" Bhutroc announced.

Naveed's eyes opened wide as he feigned being surprised by the news. In a moment it would be much easier for him to be surprised.

"I sent an emissary to him after our last gathering. He returned only moments before I came to the throne room," informed Bhutroc.

There was silence in the court.

"Now a few days ago you stood here before us and announced that Karnivron was infirm. You were at odds with him over the slaying of Massoud Al Jazeer. The Karpretian tribes were unhappy with him. There was disarray. Today you return as his emissary. You must have traveled back to him if you were made emissary and given a message for me. Did you?" Bhutroc asked.

"Yes," Naveed answered.

"If then you are doing the will of the great Karnivron, why would your escort, presumably highly placed in Karnivron's tent, want to kill you?" Bhutroc questioned.

Naveed paused as he knew exactly what he was going to say. It would make sense and there was nobody that could refute his testimony. The look of confidence came over him as Petrofar was happy to see things turn in his way. The unfortunate thing for Naveed was that the battered body of Ahmed with the slash across his face was discovered at the bottom of the mountain. Although he was badly broken up, Ahmed was still alive. He had survived the fall and was alive. Bhutroc's surgeons did the rest. Ahmed was laying on a bed in one of the palace suites. Lying in the bed, Ahmed was carried into the Berackite court. Bhutroc the great, Calyph of Beracka had spoken to Ahmed in person earlier. When Naveed's eyes met with those of Ahmed, this time he was truly surprised and in shock. It was all over. Naveed said nothing. The Calyph then spoke.

"Seize him!" Bhutroc commanded.

The palace guard seized Naveed. He neither begged nor made a plea for himself, but stood tall and defiant. Bhutroc was distressed more with the fact that his beloved son Stoldar was in league with these serpents. They had infiltrated his son's confidence and goodwill. They were respected advisors of his son. Bhutroc had been aware and suspect of Petrofar's actions for quite some time. Stoldar did not know what to say as he looked to Petrofar. Petrofar said nothing as though the surprise of it all put him in disbelief. The calyph continued with his case.

"You see it was Ahmed who was sent to speak to me. You Naveed Al Bhutan joined them like a thief in the night and rode with them to find a means to prevent their meeting with me.

"But there is more. It is my guess that you are the murderer in the night. Who else could gain entry to Karnivron's tent like a son and then betray him in the most callous way?

"Who could murder Karnivron in his sleep, but a cut throat assassin? Take him away!" affirmed Bhutroc.

As the palace guard removed Naveed to palace prison, Bhutroc looked at his son Stoldar. He was a fine son and a great warrior. He was loved of his people but he was still young. He did not see hatred in men's eyes masked by a smile. He could not yet fully discern the lies on their lips or the evil in their hearts. Before the entire assembly of his court, his son was exposed and naked to this basic requirement of leadership. A leader must have vision to discern who is trustworthy. Nobody had to tell Stoldar that he had been a fool. What could he do now?

If he did nothing it would be admitting to being deceived by his advisor. Stoldar would lose the confidence of his people. They could forever laugh at him and hold that point against him. If however he pressed on, he would have to oppose his father forthright and perhaps even use force.

In the eyes of the Berackite people, Bhutroc had won. The people were reminded of the wisdom of their calyph. Bhutroc would never send their sons to die needlessly. They also learned of the treachery that brought down a great leader and their neighbor, Karnivron. However there were others who had much to lose if they did not go to war that did not agree. The palace guard had the assassin in custody. Although Bhutroc was disappointed, the fault did not lie entirely with his son but rather with the treacherous Petrofar. Bhutroc glared at the indifference of him. Petrofar neither spoke nor looked away. Bhutroc wondered how his son could befriend such a man as advisor.

"Petrofar, you are no friend of peace and justice. You advise on your own twisted behalf. Away with him!" Bhutroc declared.

Petrofar made no effort to escape though there were means for him to do so. He looked solemnly toward Stoldar as he was apprehended and escorted to the palace prison. Stoldar was infuriated. He felt that he should be the one to deal with Petrofar; as if he could not punish ill advisors. Stoldar became rather sore at his father. Stoldar felt that his father could have left that task of ordering Petrofar's arrest to him. It should have been his decision as to what to do about Petrofar. Stoldar was upset because he thought that his father could have done this in private. Since Stoldar's proposal for war was done in open court and he had captured certain people's imagination. Bhutroc was forced to follow suit in open court to alert his people to the treachery within.

After the arrests, Bhutroc dismissed court as there was no immediate need to prepare for war. He reasoned that the less pressing issues could be heard when matters settled down more after all the excitement. For now the people could think about what just happened. Perhaps they might appreciate that when a war was not necessary they should be grateful. He was rest assured that the Berackite people were aware of matters. Those in court observed that the evil doers were in custody and matters would return to normal.

"There will be no further discussion this evening as I shall retire for prayer. I advise you one and all to retire for prayer and thanksgiving for being delivered from treachery. Indeed, pray for wisdom that we may be delivered from future strife," Bhutroc advised.

Everyone arose and bowed their heads. Some did so grudgingly. The merchants who would gain from a war were gravely disappointed. Those who had conquest on their minds were unhappy about the result of that session of court. Despite all the disappointment, the council, merchants and subjects of Beracka were once again reminded of their calyph's wisdom. The calyph arose and was being escorted by his palace guard to his private chamber.

As Bhutroc walked down the corridor, Stoldar came in pursuit of his father. They conversed en route to the calyph's chamber. The palace guard escorted the father and son.

"My father, you jail my friend and advisor for encouraging our expansion at the most opportune time," Stoldar lit.

"When the truth was exposed I thought you might be more appreciative of matters. Leading people into war is necessary when it is necessary," replied Bhutroc.

"The truth is that we have never had a better opportunity to expand across the steppes and through Leems to the sea," Stoldar summed up.

"In truth, you could have had the steppes by marriage long ago without shedding any blood," Bhutroc reminded, "ally yourself with the Karpretians and the Leemites and you will have the same expansion from here to the sea without spilling blood. All that we need they will trade for. We can all exist, side by side. Though there are differences, people are not so different. That is the truth."

"What is this 'truth'? You always speak of truth. Truth is what we decide truth should be!" Stoldar affirmed, "The people do not know what or how to think, we must do it for them."

Bhutroc stopped in his steps. He was disappointed to hear that his son had turned from serving his people to using them. He turned to look at his son eye to eye. Stoldar understood the look that his father gave him. He had seen this look when he was younger. It meant that the great man did not approve. Somehow he had fallen short of his expectations, again.

"Why do you befriend and listen to cut throats?" Bhutroc paused, "Listen to them and it will impend your doom. Your people will follow the man who can lead them to plenitude and a long life."

"I suppose all your conquests were won fairly," Stoldar needled.

445

With that said, Bhutroc turned and slapped his son's face. After all that Bhutroc had tolerated, this was a point that he was not prepared to tolerate. Leading people and assuring their survival was not a matter of making simple and equal decisions. Leadership included making mistakes and the use of larceny along the way. Bhutroc was aware of what it took to govern around the treachery of councilors and fickleness of the masses. He was getting judged by the son who would inherit all that he had built and governed for him. Bhutroc did for his son what his father and forefathers did for him.

Stoldar was startled by the slap. It was a physical slap that smarted hot across his face. He saw the uncompromising look on his father's face as he swallowed and caught his breath. It was the moral slap in the face that hurt. Stoldar felt it push him away from his inheritance. It kindled anger in him. The palace guards observed this non confidence as eyebrows raised and they came to even more sober attention. Stoldar saw them assess the situation and form their conclusions. He did not like what they saw. The calyph's body guards knew how much Bhutroc loved his son and how well loved his son was of the warriors, merchants and all the Berackite people alike.

The slap however was demeaning to Stoldar. He knew that without his father's approval that the people's confidence would turn from him. He looked across and saw his father standing boldly before him. This time his father was not as tall as when he was a young boy. Still Stoldar noted that Bhutroc was looking down on him in a condescending fashion. It was the same stance, the same look and the same attitude that the calyph had imposed over him his entire life. Only now, in Stoldar's mind, he was old and not as imposing. Bhutroc would not last forever. There he was standing before him and a unique opportunity for conquest lay in the balance. It was Bhutroc that was standing between Stoldar and his fame.

Stoldar now felt that Bhutroc was old and it was time for him to step down. He imagined that Bhutroc could have transferred his power to him with honor and dignity. There could have been a fitting ceremony to make the announcement official. Stoldar had imagined his acquiring the title of calyph under more pleasant circumstances. Stoldar felt a heat coming over him as he ground his teeth behind a firm face. Before anyone could move it happened. In the heat of anger Stoldar drew his dagger and stuck it into his father's heart. It happened so fast that even Stoldar could not believe what he had done. It happened so fast that the palace guards were in shock. They could not seize the calyph's son and yet he had attacked his father. Stoldar stood his ground with pride as though what he did had to be done.

Bhutroc for his part would have fought his attacker to the death, but it was his own son whom he loved. He was powerless to raise a hand against his own son. In fact as he fell he grabbed the palace guard's sleeve. Bhutroc fell between the palace guard and his son. Stoldar stood proudly before all present. He was the heir. Some of Stoldar's body guards stepped in to secure their own master's safety. The palace guards were held at bay as their master wished. They now awaited the outcome of the attack on their master the calyph. Stoldar stood his ground boldly as though what he had done was on behalf of the people of Beracka.

"I will make you proud of me, my father," Stoldar told him.

"My son," gasped Bhutroc, "I was already proud of you."

They were the last words that Bhutroc spoke. The calyph died from the knife wound. It penetrated through to his heart. More truthfully, Bhutroc's death occurred from the heart break of realizing that his son's hatred won. Either way, Bhutroc died of a broken heart.

Back in the court the assembly of sheiks and merchants could sense that something had occurred where the calyph was en route to his bed chamber. Most of the assembly had not yet left the large court when the word came that Bhutroc was dead. They were not aware how Bhutroc died, but they were patiently awaiting details. All that the merchants could think was that their hope for war was still alive. Petrofar and Naveed who were freshly jailed would find their incarceration a minor inconvenience. Stoldar sent for their release immediately. The palace guards that were loyal to Bhutroc remained silent. They gathered that a civil conflict within the Calyph's court could easily break out. The fact was that the calyph was dead and his son was the new Calyph of Beracka. Bhutroc's guards knew that their lives lay in the balance and a divisive uprising could be long and costly in blood. Herac, the chief palace guard for Bhutroc came forth and made a proclamation that he hoped would prevent bloodshed.

"The calyph is dead, long live the calyph!" Herac declared.

The court responded by declaring, 'long live the calyph'. Stoldar walked back to the throne room and appeared before them. He addressed the people of Beracka for the first time as their new calyph.

"Let us have our time of mourning. After the last rites of my noble and worthy father, prepare for war," Stoldar informed them.

The people who thought that the discussion before Calyph Bhutroc's court had been settled against having a war stood in silence. They could not move or utter a word. All around them was thunderous applause. There were happy, elated and ecstatic faces. The enthusiasm could only be compared to a hungry pack of wolves that spied a lagging antelope. The solemnity of the moment over the death of Bhutroc was lost. It was no time to think about the dead. The living were hungry and they craved war.

Would you like to see your manuscript become a book?

If you are interested in becoming a PublishAmerica author, please submit your manuscript for possible publication to us at:

acquisitions@publishamerica.com

You may also mail in your manuscript to:

**PublishAmerica
PO Box 151
Frederick, MD 21705**

www.publishamerica.com